There was someone there—
A MAN!

Garnet caught her breath and stood frozen for an instant. Gone were all thoughts of bathing in the cool forest pool. She had unlaced her dress and pulled it off. She stood now in her half-petticoat with bodice unbuttoned. A few seconds more and she would have been quite naked with that stranger lying half-hidden in the grass—watching her! Furiously she began putting her clothes on again at top speed, her back to him.

"Pray, don't hurry on my account, my dear," she heard him say. "I've all the time in the world."

His voice was mocking—as mocking as the smile she had glimpsed in his hazel eyes in her first quick view of him. His voice was polished, too. It matched the clothes he wore. He was a gentleman, but obviously he did not realize that she was a lady—the daughter of Sir George Mallory on whose property he was trespassing.

> *Before their encounter had ended,*
> *he would discover more intimate*
> *facts about Garnet, and she would*
> *learn enough to decide that he*
> *was the man she loved. . .*

Garnet

PETRA LEIGH

WARNER BOOKS

A Warner Communications Company

WARNER BOOKS EDITION

Copyright © 1978 by Peter Ling

ISBN 0–446–82788–6

Cover art by David Group

Warner Books, Inc., 75 Rockefeller Plaza, New York, N.Y. 10019

W A Warner Communications Company

Printed in the United States of America

Not associated with Warner Press, Inc., of Anderson, Indiana

First Printing: December, 1978

10 9 8 7 6 5 4 3 2 1

CONTENTS

Part One: At Home

Part Two: Abroad

Part Three: America . . . .

PART ONE

At Home

1

A Stranger at Markwick

There was someone there—a man . . !

Garnet caught her breath, and stood frozen for an instant, her hands suddenly powerless as she stopped in the act of unbuttoning her bodice.

There was a man, lying half hidden in the grass, watching her.

In this single instant, thoughts raced through her mind. It wasn't anyone she knew, it wasn't her brother Gerard—or young Jem from the stables, or any of the gardeners. It wasn't one of the men from the home farm, and it wasn't one of the dozen indoor servants, from Pip the kitchenboy to Charles the butler. And it certainly wasn't father; Sir George Mallory was not in the habit of lying sprawled in the long grass at the side of the fishpond. Quite apart from his dignity, his rheumaticky leg would never have permitted such a thing.

No, this was someone completely unknown; a total

stranger . . . In the first second that she saw him, she took in all the details of his appearance—the riding-habit in russet-brown broadcloth, and the high white cravat under his chin . . . the broad shoulders, and the cut of his strong firm jaw; the mocking smile in his hazel eyes . . . mocking *her!*

Garnet remembered where she was and how he must have seen her—and she turned away, fumbling with buttons, feeling a hot flood of shame rising into her cheeks. Bad enough to be seen by any man, half-undressed, when she had thought herself alone, but to be spied on by a trespasser—a man who was an unknown quantity, a man with a teasing, insolent look . . . This was too humiliating. Quickly she adjusted her bodice and pulled on her loose summer dress of cheap flowered muslin, tugging it over her head, smoothing the material down and making sure that her breasts were well-hidden. As she touched them, she noticed that her nipples were standing out, proud and firm, under her shaking fingers . . . just as they were that day two summers ago . . . at this same place by the fish-pond—when she and Jem . . .

She pushed the thought from her mind angrily. She must stop these stupid memories of Jem, and the day she went swimming.

Of course, that was what had started it all, really.

Only half an hour ago, young Garnet Mallory, age seventeen—daughter of Sir George Mallory, Bar., of Mark-wick Hall in the County of Surrey—had walked out of the big house for a breath of air. She had spent the afternoon in the schoolroom, not that she had lessons any more nowadays, but she was passing the time by making a watercolor painting of some apples on a plate. If the picture turned out well she might finish it off with a velvet ribbon and a calendar for the coming year—1812—and make a present of it to Papa for Christmas.

Of course, Sir George wouldn't show the slightest interest; he never cared whether she presented him with a gift or not. Last year she had embroidered a handkerchief; he had accepted it with a grunt, stuffed it into his pocket, and never referred to it. No doubt the calendar would meet with the same reception. This thought, as she dutifully struggled to keep the outline of the apples smooth, round and firm, discouraged her, and she lost interest in her picture.

She had thrown aside the paintbrush then, and walked swiftly out of the schoolroom, which smelt of dust, and old paper, and dried orris-root. Sir George had decided that it was unpatriotic to employ a French Mademoiselle as a governess for his two children while England was at war with Bonaparte, and so packed her off, bag and baggage, and Garnet and her brother Gerard had received no further education. Sir George looked forward to the day when Gerard would go into the army, to follow in his father's footsteps; he felt sure the boy would acquire a lasting education there—"In the school of life, sir!" as he insisted, thumping the floor with his silverheaded Malacca cane.

As for Garnet—well, she was a girl, and therefore not worth her father's attention. What should she need with reading, writing and figuring? Doubtless one of these days she would catch some young fool for a husband, and leave home once and for all. He washed his hands of Garnet, and couldn't wait to be rid of her.

Once outside the big house, walking down the flight of curving stone steps that led from the classical pillared portico to the sweep of carriage drive below, Garnet had been taken by surprise when the full warmth of the afternoon sun hit her. Here it was September, the best of the summer long over, but still a hot day. In the coolness of the shadowy rooms of Markwick Hall she had hardly noticed the change in the weather; the morning had been chilly and overcast with cloud, but out here it was high summer again.

Her spirits rose, and she set off for a walk across the home park, not even considering where she was going.

And yet . . . It was strange how often her footsteps

seemed to lead her to the same place, down past the summer-house, through the shrubbery, and under the little grove of trees where she and Gerard used to play hide-and-seek, so many years ago. Under the trees it was very still; she could hear a gnat singing, and the crack of a twig—and the sound of her own heart beating.

Why did her pulses race so fast? What was this strange sense of excitement that made her almost breathless, as she kept on, farther and farther from the house, drawn with each step nearer and nearer to the hayfield . . . And the pollarded willows, and the alder tree—where the blue sky was reflected in the smooth surface of the fishpond.

What was she looking for? Why did she come back here, time after time? What could she hope to find—two years later?

Brought up short by these questions, she tried to be honest with herself. She *wanted* it to happen all over again. That was the truth of it.

When she was very small, a kind visitor had given her a magical toy on one of her early birthdays. It was a kaleidoscope, and when you put it to your eye and rotated it gently, various fragments and slivers of colored glass and tiny bright beads swam together, clung, then fell apart, making and remaking an endless series of glowing patterns. They never lasted, never stayed for you to admire them—they swam past your gaze and were gone, just as Garnet now seemed to see a hundred vivid pictures of that afternoon at the fishpond when she was fifteen years old . . .

A kaleidoscope of words and images tumbled through her mind . . . Herself, hidden in the alder tree, stretched out along a branch that hung above the water. And the boys didn't know she was there, watching and listening.

The boys—Gerard, only thirteen then, and very young for his age, standing up to his thighs in the water, half-laughing, half-nervous, naked except for his thin drawers. And Jem from the stables; Jemmy Bolt—three years older, and with the physique of a grown man already. Jem—

his shirt open to the waist, showing the curling blond hair that matted his chest—his head thrown back, roaring with laughter at Gerard's shyness.

"Go on, Master Gerard—don't be afright—plunge in! It's rare sport once you've ducked your head under!"

"I—I daren't . . . I'll get my drawers wet—and then I'll be in trouble at home."

Jem laughed again. "Little jack-rabbit—use your head, boy! Take 'em off and leave 'em on the bank—like I'm a-doing . . ."

And as Gerard hesitated and blushed, turning his head away, Jem stood up and began to strip, flinging his shirt onto the grass, kicking off his heavy boots, and unbuttoning his breeches, still laughing.

"We're as God made us, I reckon—and that en't nothing to be ashamed of. Come on, Master Gerard, you're not a little shy missy—get undressed, and I'll teach you how to swim!"

Gerard was unprepared for the amazing sight of the male body standing before him, proud and completely shameless in its nakedness, and wouldn't look; but Garnet looked—and looked again—inching forward along the branch to see more clearly, peering down at the splendid, muscular torso, with its surprising fleece of tangled blond hair—in such unlikely places, too—

That was her undoing. *Crack* went the branch and *splash* went Garnet as she fell, gasping, into the water.

The kaleidoscope shook and settled again—fragments of the scenes that followed scattered past her mind's eye . . . Gerard, shamed and terrified, running for cover, disappearing into the hayfield . . . Jem plunging into the deep water to rescue her—Jem's muscular arms like steel bands as he dragged her to the shallows . . . Her own wet clothes, spread out to dry—her own voice, sounding husky and quite unlike herself, saying, "Jem . . . Please . . . Will you teach *me* to swim—instead?"

And Jem's heavy-set face breaking into laughter again as he looked down at her, saying "There's plenty as I could teach you, Miss Garnet . . . If you're a-willing to learn."

And the feel of those strong arms about her once again —and his firm rough hands still cool and wet with pond water, slipping round her waist, and up higher, cupping her breasts . . .

She stood dazed, confused by her daydreams, and gave herself a shake. She wouldn't let herself remember any more. Not now, not here. Perhaps later on tonight, alone in her bed, she would permit herself to recall the rest of that incredible, far-off afternoon, but not now.

All the same . . . She found she was trembling, and when she brushed a hand across her forehead she felt a damp dew of sweat. And instantly remembered the precept Mademoiselle had tried to instill in her: *"Horses* sweat, *ma petite* . . . And *gentlemen* perspire . . . But ladies—ah, *mon Dieu*—young ladies only *glow."*

She wouldn't think any more. Thinking was silliness— and of course it was only the warm weather that made her so restless and uncomfortable. That was when she eyed the cool, deep water of the pond longingly, and said to herself: Why not? Who is to know? There's no one about; I can take a swim by myself, surely; nobody need ever find out, this time.

So she had unlaced her dress and pulled it off, standing in her half petticoat with the bodice unbuttoned, eager to be free of her hot, uncomfortable clothes altogether. One moment more, and she would be quite naked—as she had been, that day with Jem—

And that was when she saw the stranger.

He smiled his mocking smile, lying there half hidden in the long grass, in the shade of the alder.

Furious, appalled to think what she would have displayed to his appraising glance in just a few seconds more, she had begun to put her clothes on again at top speed, her back to him.

"Pray, don't hurry on my account, my dear," she heard him say. "I've all the time in the world."

His voice was mocking too; musical and polished—as a fine violin is polished. Yet, just as the fiddlestrings have a deeper buzz that echoes under the pure beauty of each note, so there was an undertone in the stranger's voice too . . . Something far more human and more physical . . . Something that stirred and unsettled her still further.

"Well?" the voice continued behind her. "Aren't you going to say good day?"

"Why should I?" She spoke at last, defiantly, over her shoulder, half expecting him to leap up and cross the stretch of grass in two or three long strides—and take her by the shoulders and turn her to face him.

But he seemed content to stay where he was, in the shadow of the leafy branches, and his voice was still lightly amused as he continued. "Oh, it's the custom, so they tell me, when two people meet for the first time. Aren't you going to introduce yourself, so we can get acquainted?"

"No, I'm not!" She fastened the last button, and now felt brave enough to swing around, facing him defiantly. "You've no business to be here at all—go away this minute!"

"But I want to know more about you." His lips twitched as he added, running his eye up and down the length of her slim figure. "After all, I know quite a lot about you, already . . ."

This was too mortifying to be borne, and she bit her lip angrily. "Sir, you are impertinent!"

"So I've been told—frequently." He shrugged. "But there—it seems to be my besetting sin, and I can't cure myself of the habit. Don't look so fierce, my dear. Who can tell? In time you might grow to like it."

She took a deep breath, and lifted her chin, gazing far above his head at a flock of birds wheeling in the late afternoon sky. "I think it's highly unlikely, sir, since I am quite sure we shall not meet a second time. I suppose you realize that you are on private property?"

"I felt sure I must be. Thank you for the information."

15

"This is part of Sir George Mallory's estate, and there is no right of way across this land—so you'd best be gone as soon as possible, before they set the dogs on you."

"Ah, I'd go willingly, if only I could. But that's the devil of it, you see . . . I can't."

She clenched her fists, not knowing which annoyed her the most: his idle, unconcerned banter, or the way he threw in a casual blasphemy, swearing in her presence as if she were a common drab. Glancing down, she realized that, in her cheap gown, over a plain shift and bodice, she must indeed present a spectacle quite unlike the young lady of Markwick Hall. All the same, he had no right to speak so coarsely in her hearing, and she reproved him for it. "I'd be pleased if you would remember your manners, sir. And as for leaving—I advise you to be off at once, before I call one of the grooms."

"I told you, my dearest girl . . . I can't go. I'm your prisoner."

"What?"

She stared at him now. What did he mean? Was this some new joke at her expense?

He raised himself on one elbow, awkwardly, and tried to explain. "My own fault, too, which makes it all the harder to bear. Riding home across the common land, I was covering the distance at a fair canter, when a bird flew up out of a furzebush right beneath my horse's hooves. The poor brute got the fright of its life, and reared up before I knew what had happened."

"You were thrown—?" Despite herself, Garnet found she was smiling a little. The idea of this superior stranger being tossed from his horse appealed to her.

"As I say—my own stupid fault. If I'd been thinking what I was doing—but there, my thoughts were far away . . . I was dreaming of you, instead."

"Of *me?*" The smile disappeared instantly, and she glared an accusation. "You never even saw me till this moment—"

"Well, perhaps not you exactly, but I was picturing

16

some dear sweet girl very much like you, I swear to that. And wishing with all my heart that I could meet such a one. So you see how strangely our wishes are answered sometimes, for here I am, and there you are . . ."

She lowered her eyes. He was fooling again, and his silky, caressing tone made her uncomfortable. She pursed her lips, and tried to ignore the pleasantry, as he rambled on. "But the problem is—how am I to get back to barracks?"

"The barracks? You're with the militia—in Guildford?" she asked.

"I am . . . Captain Edmund Challoner, Third Dragoon Guards, at your service, dearest young lady. I'd stand to attention and click my heels for you—if I were able."

"I see." She stole another look at him. Of course—he was an army officer; how silly of her not to guess it before! He had the bearing, the form and physique of those gallant young gentlemen she sometimes spied swaggering past her in Guildford High Street when she went shopping, or riding home after Church Parade on a Sunday morning. There was no mistaking that arrogant bearing, now she had been told. "Your horse has run off, has it?"

"Halfway back to the stables by now, I dare say. And here I am—a poor lame hobbledehoy, who can't even walk on two feet. I don't know if I've cracked my ankle or what, but it's damn painful, I assure you."

She gasped; another vulgar oath. But then the young man was in pain—one had to make allowances for that. She moved closer to him, and saw that he had started to pull one riding boot off, but now it was stuck, half on and half off his left foot.

He explained, "I was making some slow progress at first, limping along with an ashplant from the hedgerow as my walking-stick. I hoped if I found my way across these fields I might be able to take a shortcut to the high road, and knock a mile or two off my journey. But the pain got worse and worse, as my ankle swelled up; then I saw this pond, and I had the idea of bathing my

17

foot in the cool water . . . But as you see, I couldn't get
the infernal boot off!"

"Can I, perhaps——?" She dropped to her knees, and
began to tug at the polished leather.

Captain Challoner gave a sharp yelp of pain, and
begged her to stop. "It's like a corkscrew twisting through
the bone! If you go on like that, you'll have me laid out
in a swoon before you, and that would never do." He
pulled a small, shining knife from his pocket. "Here——
use this——cut the leather, and get me out of it as best you
can."

"Cut those boots? Oh, no——they're too good——"

"Don't be a goose——I've plenty more pairs like this. Go
on, do as I say."

Under his instructions, Garnet pushed the point of the
blade into the seam at the top of the high boot, up under
the young man's knee, and ripped——and tugged——and at
last the whole boot opened up like a giant oystershell, and
she was able to prize it loose without causing the gallant
captain too much discomfort.

"Good girl . . . Now my stocking——roll it down and
slide it off, there's a dear . . . Don't be shy——think of yourself as an angel of mercy."

Obeying him, she felt the warm, firm flesh of his calf
under her fingers, and——for a second——she remembered
Jem again; she couldn't help it——the smell of a man's
sweat, and the warm roughness of a man's skin touching
hers . . . She shut her eyes, shutting her mind to the past,
and removed the captain's stocking.

"Shall I douse the ankle with cold water and tie the
stocking on as a compress?"

"You're a jewel among women——clever as you are
pretty!" he approved, and patted her hand gently.

Flustered, she stood up and hurried down to the water's
edge. Two minutes later, the cold compress was in place,
and she tied the last knot firmly, asking: "Is that any
better?"

"It's a good deal easier . . . let's see if I can stand on it.

Be a good soul and help me up . . . what's your name? Molly? Polly? What do I call you?"

"My name's Garnet," she replied, breathing rather fast as she tried to help him onto his feet, feeling the weight of his body tense against her own, and the strong muscles of his thighs as he stumbled and pressed even closer.

"*Garnet?* There's an outlandish name for a simple girl —Miss Garnet, is it? Or would it be Missus Garnet?"

"I—I'm not married . . ."

She felt his arm slip easily round her waist, and she opened her mouth to protest at the familiarity, but—

"Ssh! Don't scold a poor invalid, my dear. I have to hold you very tight, for fear I might fall. Come, let me try to put my weight on this damn foot . . ."

They took a cautious, experimental step together, then another; he winced with pain, and clutched her to him so hard that she could scarcely breathe.

"Every step is a torment to me, Miss Garnet—don't let go of me, for pity's sake—let me hang on to you—so—"

She felt both arms about her now; and then he pulled her roughly around so that her face was only an inch away from his own . . . He was smiling again. One hand held her in an iron grip, and the other seemed to wander down—down to the small of her back, and farther still; she felt the firm touch of his fingers through the flimsy material of her dress and petticoat, and she tried to tell him to stop, but . . .

His mouth was upon hers, and his lips were hot against her lips. She felt as if she must faint—or cry out—or expire with the strangeness and the excitement of the rough embrace, but the tip of his tongue met hers, and she couldn't speak, or sigh, or put up any resistance. The leaves of the alder tree above them swirled around, like the fleecy clouds in the blue sky beyond, and the whole wide world revolved dizzily.

"*Miss Garnet—!*"

Her heart leapt, and she felt as if her blood had turned

19

to ice at the sound of an unexpected voice. At once Captain Challoner let her go, and she swayed and might have fallen had he not caught her by the arm and steadied her.

"We are not alone, it seems," said the captain, easily.

There, standing a few yards away, in a gap among the pollarded willows, stood Jem Bolt, his thick-set body braced, his fists clenched, and his square face dark with anger. How long had he been there?

"I did come for to find you, Miss Garnet . . . To tell you as it's time for tea."

She tried to speak calmly, but the trembling of her voice betrayed her. "Thank you, Jem . . . I—I'm obliged to you. But we have something more important to attend to. This gentleman is an officer of the Dragoons, and he has met with an accident. We shall need to get him back to the house. Fetch some of the other men from the stables—oh, and bring a shutter, to carry him . . . I have been trying to help him to walk, but—I couldn't manage it alone . . ."

She saw the look on Jem's face as he stared directly back at her; she saw the burning hunger in his eyes, and knew he had watched their embrace. He began to speak, thought better of it, then turned and started to make his way back across the water meadow.

So he knows . . . And I don't care, she thought. I don't care two pins what Jemmy Bolt may think—because—

She turned and looked at the captain, and he smiled at her; and with that smile, her heart turned over.

Because I am in love, she told herself. In love—at last.

2

To Our Next Meeting

It was a strange-looking procession that made its way back to the house, some twenty minutes later.

Whatever he may have been thinking, Jem Bolt had obediently rounded up three more helpers from the stable-yard, and between them the young men made short work of lifting Captain Challoner onto an old wooden shutter, which served as a makeshift stretcher.

With one strong pair of arms to lift each corner, the captain was soon hoisted up, and the little party set off at a swift pace—so swift, in fact, were the long steps of the stretcher bearers, that Garnet found she had almost to break into a run in order to keep pace with them. Her clinging ankle-length skirt was not made for such hurried movements, and it was with some difficulty that she trailed after the others, stumbling through tufts of saw-edged grasses or tripping on hidden tree roots. By the time they approached the tall archway into the yard which divided the stable block from the main body of the house, she was lagging some way behind, and more than a little breathless.

She might, perhaps, have found the going easier if she had looked down at the track she walked on; but all the while she had her eyes fixed on Edmund Challoner's face —his mouth shut tight, and his features drawn, as he tried to conceal the suffering that his ankle caused him. Once or twice, as he looked across to Garnet and saw her watching him, he forced a gallant smile, and she felt a glow of love at these proofs of his courage and endurance. Once, she even thought she saw his eyelid droop in a wink; the sign of a fond conspiracy, as they remembered their interrupted embrace.

Jem seemed to sense the silent communication that passed between them; he glanced back angrily over his shoulder with a sullen look at Garnet—and in doing so, he fumbled his grasp on the shutter and almost tipped his ailing passenger onto the flagstones of the yard.

Edmund winced and bit his lip, as he was rolled roughly onto his side, twisting his swollen ankle yet again.

Garnet heard herself cry out involuntarily: "Take care, Jem—for pity's sake, look what you're doing—the captain's injured!"

"Injured? What's that? Who's injured? What's amiss?"

Garnet stopped short at the familiar sound of her father's voice, knowing instinctively that her presence here would not be welcome. The stretcher party moved on into the stable yard, and Garnet followed more slowly, sidling through the stone pillars of the arch, but hanging back under its shadows.

There was a clatter of hooves and an exultant whinny, as one of the Markwick hunters reared up, tossing its magnificent chestnut head and glossy mane.

Old Sir George Mallory, leaning on his stick, had been in consultation with the head groom, discussing whether Achilles might be relied upon for the first meet of the season, but at the sight of the new arrivals, he pushed this problem aside, and demanded to know what was wrong—and who the young stranger might be?

The stable lads all began to talk at once, though Jem remained silent, and Sir George banged his cane on the mounting-block.

"One at a time, one at a time . . . Will none of you present me to the gentleman?"

"Sir, his name's Edmund Challoner, and he's a captain in the militia—" Garnet blurted out. Ever since she could remember, she had been brought up to address her father as "Sir," and it had never seemed odd to her. Indeed, any more intimate form of address would have been unthinkable. "And he's been injured, sir—his ankle—"

"Yes, yes, yes—be off with you, girl—I'm sure the captain is able to speak for himself—heh?"

He turned his back on Garnet, dismissing her contribution entirely, and thrust out his hand to the young officer. "I am pleased to make your acquaintance, Captain Challoner. My name is Mallory . . . You are very welcome here; I'm an old soldier myself, and any officer serving under His Majesty's flag is always welcome at Markwick Hall."

"How do you do, Sir George?" Edmund clasped the outstretched hand as formally as possible from his recumbent position. "I am sorry to make myself a burden upon your household, but I seem to have damaged my ankle, and I cannot walk upon it."

"What? What? Broken, is it?" Sir George prodded Edmund's foot with lively curiosity, and Garnet saw the handsome face contort with pain. She would have cried out and begged her father to be more careful—but what was the use? He would not listen to her; he never did.

"I—I cannot say, Sir George—" Edmund managed to reply. "I think it may be . . ."

"Allow me to differ, sir . . . I think not. You wouldn't be able to jerk your foot away like that if there were bones broken. It's a sprain, I dare say—but a confounded nuisance all the same. You'll need bandages and salve—and hot water and towels . . . One of you lads, go and fetch Mrs. Bolt . . . Ah, Jemmy, so it's you, is it? Good—run and find your mother . . . No, no—lower the captain to the ground first, you booby—*gently, blockhead—gently* . . ."

Without overmuch ceremony, the shutter was deposited on the flagstones, and Jem slipped away to the servants' hall. Sir George went on to explain: "The boy's mother is my housekeeper. She always knows what's best to be done in these matters. She'll soon have you to rights . . . No doubt she'll bathe your foot, and then strap it up afterwards—we'll need towels and bandages. Which of you lads can go and find them for me? No, no—I'll send my son, he's been doing nothing all day except skulk about with his nose in a book . . . Gerard, Gerard, do you hear? Come when you're called, you young scoundrel!"

A moment later there was a scuffle and the rattle of feet upon the rungs of a ladder, and Gerard appeared in the open doorway below the hayloft: a book in his hand and wisps of straw clinging to his untidy clothes.

"Did you call, Father?"

"Of course I called, boy—what, are you deaf as well as moonstruck? What have you been doing with yourself, heh?"

"I was reading, Father . . ."

"In heaven's name what sort of answer is that for a lively youngster? Throw that book away this minute, do you hear me? I've work for you to do."

Fifteen-year-old Gerard, still blinking in the late afternoon sunlight which now threw level shafts of gold across the yard, put his book down carefully—making a note of the page he had reached, Garnet noticed, so he could return to it as soon as possible—then stepped forward to answer his father's summons.

"What is it you want, sir?" he asked.

"There's been an accident, boy! Look alive, we need

assistance for our visitor . . . Stop daydreaming, and make yourself useful!"

Sir George moved away, scolding his son in his accustomed manner, and the stable lads withdrew to a corner, whispering together.

For a moment, Edmund lay alone and unwatched, and Garnet grasped her opportunity. She stole forward and dropped to her knees beside the shutter, whispering: "Does it hurt you very much?"

He smiled at her faintly. "Not when you look at me like that . . . Give me your hand . . ."

He took her hand in his own, and a tiny shock ran through her; his index finger was gently caressing her palm, teasing and titillating. It was as if her skin—her hand—her whole body was alive with a thousand little tingling thrills . . .

Perhaps he read her thoughts, for he looked up at her and smiled again, as if they shared a secret. "This isn't an auspicious moment, Miss Garnet, but—I look forward to our next meeting, my dear," he murmured under his breath, so quietly that no one else could possibly overhear.

At the same moment she felt a sudden pressure upon her thigh, as he slipped his other hand around her knee and caressed her leg with a movement that slid ever upward—farther and farther still—

Her limbs felt as if they were on fire and she would have pulled free of him, or cried out—but she dared not draw attention to herself with so many onlookers by. Breathlessly, she gasped: "Captain Challoner—you forget yourself—"

"I shall not soon forget you, Miss Garnet—that I'll swear to!" he retorted, and the exploring hand climbed higher yet . . .

But there was a sudden interruption that put an end to any further intimacy, as Sir George lost patience with his son.

"*How* did he come here? Confound the boy—how

should *I* know how the deuce the captain came here? Stop asking tomfool questions, and do as you are told!"

Sir George swung round, leaning heavily on his stick, in time to see Garnet scrambling to her feet. His scowl deepened: "And you, girl—plague take it, run off and leave us alone! Get back to the schoolroom—you're not needed here."

He waved her away brusquely, and Garnet bowed her head and did as he commanded. Not needed here? she thought, as she hurried toward the house. In my father's opinion, I'm not needed anywhere . . .

Escaping into the shadow of the archway, she heard Sir George continue in a far more affable tone: "But tell me, Captain—how is it we have the honor of your company at Markwick this afternoon? I mean, how do you come to be here, may I ask?"

Once inside the big house, Garnet felt a chill as she entered the cool corridors, and shivered a little.

Sir George might bark at Gerard and order him about, but at least in his heart she was sure he had a grudging fondness for his son . . . Just because he *was* his son, the one and only heir to the family estate. But as for me, he doesn't even trouble to lose his temper with me. I'm not worth that much consideration, because I'm only a girl, and therefore of no interest whatever.

How did she know that it had always been so, ever since the day she was born? Had a featherbrained nursery-maid chattered in her hearing, and had the words sunk into her baby consciousness? It was as if she had always known that when the midwife presented Sir George with his firstborn, and said the fatal words, "It's a girl . . ."

—At that moment, the old soldier's smile had faded, and he had turned his face away. He had set his heart upon a son, and he was bitterly disappointed. He had not troubled himself in the least about his daughter from that moment on; he did not even concern himself to choose a name for her. "Garnet" had been her mother's choice, for this was her favorite jewel, and the dark-haired child with

26

her unexpectedly warm smile reminded her of those glow-ing, wine-rich stones.

And then, two years later, Gerard was born, and that moment—which should have been all happiness for his father—was turned instantly to black despair, for Lady Mallory died in childbirth, and the tiny boy was not ex-pected to survive her by much longer.

As it happened, he took the doctors by surprise, and rallied bravely. Soon he grew up into a wiry, intelligent boy, with the soul of a dreamer and an enquiring mind—but Sir George never completely forgave him for having stolen his wife away. When, over the ensuing years, it be-came clear that Gerard was not destined to take after his father or share his interests, the old man retreated from both his children, and took refuge in his horses, his brandy, and his rheumatism.

Not that Garnet had ever had a moment of cruelty from her father; he had seen to it that she was adequately clothed and fed and educated. But neither had she had a single moment of his attention, or his affection, in all her seventeen years.

Walking along the draughty passage that led to the ser-vant's hall, Garnet shivered again, and quickened her step as she heard Mrs. Bolt approaching with Gerard, her voice echoing from the bare walls. "An army officer, d'you say? Dearie me—what a thing to happen—never fear, we'll see what we can do to make the poor young gentle-man comfortable. You've got the clean towels, haven't you, Master Gerard? And I've sent my Jem to draw hot water for his bath."

Cosy, comfortable Mrs. Bolt was almost trotting along on her tiny feet—surprisingly tiny, for the good lady was of very ample proportions; Garnet sometimes thought she resembled nothing so much as a cottage loaf with a cur-rant bun on top of it. But she didn't wish to get caught up in conversation with the housekeeper at this moment, and so made her escape up a side staircase, as Mrs. Bolt and Gerard proceeded on their way to the stable yard.

Garnet caught Gerard's eye briefly as he slipped by, and she fancied he gave her a rather odd, considering look. She wondered what he was thinking about.

She would have been very much surprised, if she could have known. For Gerard's thoughts were on Garnet herself—and the injured army captain out there in the yard.

Gerard was a dreamer, sure enough, but he had a sharp, observant eye for all that, and while his father was lecturing him upon the error of his ways, he had noticed—over Sir George's shoulder—the little moment of contact between his sister and the young officer. He had seen the firm, inquisitive hand on her thigh, as it slid upward to her rounded hip—and he had begun instantly to speculate on what might—no, *must*—have passed between these two, to allow such dalliance . . .

Now, as he joined the others in the stables, trying ineffectually to make himself useful, but being jostled first by the other lads, then swept aside by Sir George—his mind ran on the question . . . What had Garnet been up to with the stranger?

One thing he knew for sure. Whatever had happened, it would not have been the first time that Garnet had misbehaved; of that he was quite certain. On that fateful afternoon at the fishpond, when Gerard was only thirteen years old, and his first swimming lesson had been so unexpectedly interrupted, he had run for cover and hidden himself in the hayfield. As he crouched below a hedge, still dripping wet, naked but for thin drawers that clung to him uncomfortably, he tried to decide what he should do. He could hear muffled exclamations and shouts of laughter from the pond—and at last he made up his mind to creep back and try to retrieve his scattered clothes. Cautiously, stooping low, he made his way down through the tall grasses, and then stopped—his heart pounding—not daring to go any closer.

Garnet's wet clothes were now spread out in the sun to dry, and Garnet herself was quite naked. Jem Bolt, nude as a Greek statue, and glorying in his virility, stretched out

28

close beside her, his arm around her waist. And while Gerard held his breath, he saw Jem turn the girl toward him—and he saw his sister's body for the first time in his life, in all its loveliness. Her young, swelling breasts, each with its rose-pink nipple, and her tender thighs spread apart, with a mysterious valley between, veiled in a haze of downy hair . . . And he knew for certain in that instant what was taking place; knew as he had never quite known from all the lewd talk of the lads in the stables, or from the shockingly frank revelations of certain passages he had come across in Shakespeare's plays and sonnets . . .

Excited, terrified, hot with the arousal of his own desires, but also trembling with shyness and frustration, he had crept away again, and hid himself in the broken-down old hen-house at the end of the kitchen garden, until the sun went down. Then, in the dusk, he managed to make his way into the house, scrambling on top of the waterbutt and up a drainpipe, and so at last onto the flat leads that roofed the servants' hall—and with a perilous scramble, up yet one more floor to the open window of his own little bedroom—and safety.

There he had lain awake for most of the night, recalling every detail of what he had seen: Jem's bronzed, muscular torso and his proud manhood—Garnet's soft, inviting curves . . . He explored his own aching loins, and lay on his bed, panting with desire, and impatience, and envy.

That was the first time, but it was by no means the last.

And then—perhaps a month later—something else happened which gave Gerard another lesson in his haphazard education in human biology.

It was a moonlit night this time, and he had been standing in his nightshirt by the open bedroom window, seeking for any breath of air—for it was midsummer, and the nights were almost as stifling as noontime. He stood there, watching the dark shapes of trees and bushes outlined against the paler sky—shapes that sometimes seemed to

29

transform themselves in his fantasies into a woman's bos-om—a woman's beckoning arm—the curl of a woman's hair falling unpinned across her bare shoulders . . . And as he watched, he heard girlish voices, and wondered for a second if these too sprang from his feverish imagination.

No . . . He listened carefully, and picked out scraps of words and phrases . . .

"—Pale blue taffeta . . . Miss Garnet never wears it . . . Make over her old bonnet if she'd give it me . . . Why, Lucy, I declare—you're putting on weight, girl! What's that? Our Lucy in the pudden' club?"

And then a peal of knowing laughter.

He realized now what he was hearing. In the room one floor below and to the left, there was a light burning—he could see shadows upon the flat roof beneath. It was the big bedroom that served as a dormitory for some of the serving maids, and now they must be getting ready for bed.

As this thought crossed his mind, he pictured the scene—and at once he knew that he could not resist the temptation to go down and investigate.

He did not hesitate, but clambered swiftly over the window-sill, and began his descent—rather like a mountain-climber, using each rough edge of brick or projecting coping-stone, as hand-hold or foot-hold—until he could slither down onto the leads below, still faintly warm after the heat of the day.

The window of the girls' bedroom was uncurtained, and he crept closer. There was the scene—almost as he had imagined it, and yet a thousand times more exciting in its reality . . . Lucy, half-annoyed and half-laughing at the teasing of her companions, was trying to put on the plain white shift which all the girls wore by way of night-gowns—while her three friends held it up out of her reach and pointed accusingly at her uncovered figure.

"Lucy's getting heavy—Lucy's got a bun in the oven! Who was it, then, girl? Jemmy Bolt? Or Peter from the stables? Or was it little Tim the bootboy? Eh?"

Laughing and mocking, they circled round her, themselves only half-dressed, and unknowingly revealing their most intimate charms to Gerard, who watched in the moonlight outside, his heart in his mouth, almost suffocating with excitement.

Almost—and then, as he swallowed to clear his throat—he choked himself, coughed and spluttered aloud.

The four girls spun round instantly—and froze—then recognized the solitary figure at the window.

"Master Gerard—! He's spying on us—!"

Gerard was too petrified to move—and before he could make up his mind to beat a retreat, the girls advanced upon him.

"So that's your little game, Master Gerard! Playing at Peeping Tom, are you? Well, what's sauce for the goose is sauce for the gander!"

And simultaneously Gerard found himself grabbed by many hands—his arms and legs were tugged roughly, and he could not put up any resistance as they swept him off his feet and dragged him over the wide window-sill, and into the dormitory.

"Let's pay him out for being so bold. If he comes spying on us, we'll teach him a lesson—come on, Lucy—hold him down on the bed—"

They bundled him onto his back on one of the four narrow cots; his nightshirt was already riding up his legs, and though he kicked and fought, it was the work of a moment for the four girls to haul it right up and pull it off over his head. Helpless, he struggled in vain, his feelings in a turmoil, as shame and laughter and overwhelming physical excitement were all mixed together, sweeping him away on a rising tide that he could no longer resist.

One girl held his shoulders down on the rough straw palliasse, while two more grasped his legs, each sitting astride one of his knees, so he could not move or turn aside; and Lucy—pretty, pert, undressed Lucy—began to tickle his ribs and his waist and explore his thighs, teasing

31

and tormenting him with every touch of her relentless fingers until he giggled uncontrollably, threshing from side to side and begging for release . . . A release that came all too soon.

From that night on, there was a new awareness between Gerard and these four girls in the servants' hall. Sometimes one would take him off to the shrubbery, or up into the hayloft, whenever there might be half an hour to spare, and each one taught him some new, unimaginable tricks in the game of love.

But not as often as he would have wished; for after all, he was only a boy still, and there were many strapping young men in and around Markwick Hall who were far more appealing to the four serving maids. Gradually they lost interest in the young master of the house, and although he would sometimes try to put his arm round a slender waist, or pinch a rosy cheek, they would more often than not slap his hand away irritably, protesting: "Oh, Master Gerard—give over, do . . . Go and get on with your studying and your bookwork, there's a good boy!"

So, at fifteen, young Gerard Mallory was still a very frustrated and unsatisfied young man; and when he saw what seemed to be clear proof of intimacy between his sister and Captain Challoner, he felt envious indeed. Yes, Garnet would certainly have been very much surprised, if she could have known what her brother was thinking.

At this very moment, her own mind was on the self-same subject—as she paced her bedroom and let her thoughts wander back to Captain Edmund Challoner. She had been recalling what she heard Mrs. Bolt saying a little while ago—

"—To fetch hot water for the bath . . ."

A bath—for Edmund . . . The idea made her almost giddy. She imagined his tall frame, his broad shoulders unclothed, as he lay back in the metal hip-bath—his strong, muscular legs with one knee bent, the other lolling carelessly out of the water, his foot resting on the rim of the bath . . .

And who would look after him in his present sorry state? Who would help him to undress—to bathe him—to dry his firm body in a warm fleecy towel? Not Mrs. Bolt, surely? That would be quite improper. Garnet had sighed, and yearned with all her heart to minister to the invalid . . . If only she could!

As she mused on the situation, she realized that she must make herself ready for their next encounter, and decided suddenly that she too must be soaped and rinsed and newly-clean for the occasion, wearing her best gown, and looking in every respect what she was . . . The young lady of Markwick Hall.

It was a simple matter to call one of the passing maids and give her instructions, and then Garnet tore off her workaday dress, her bodice, shift and undergarments, and stood waiting impatiently for the ewers of hot water to be sent up to her.

She paused by the long mirror, an elegant cheval-glass that had once belonged to her mother—a little dulled now, and with a creeping contagion of brown freckles behind its silver surface—but it was high enough to throw back a full-length reflection.

She looked at her body thoughtfully, and tried to imagine what *he* would think of it, if he could see her as she was now: her ripening breasts, fuller than the budding pomegranates she had possessed two years ago, the rounded invitation of her velvet thighs, and the softly-curling tendrils of silken hair that crowned her mount of Venus. All at once, she knew with absolute certainty what Edmund would think if he could see her now . . . And her cheeks reddened at the very idea.

He should not have touched her as he did, nor fondled her in such a bold way—and yet . . . At the mere thought she could feel again the insistent pressure of his hand, and she glanced down at her thigh almost expecting to see the mark of his fingers still upon her.

She loved him, and she forgave him his over-eager advances. After all, he was a man, with all a man's natural

passions, and she would not change him even if she could
. . . Her own true love.

A sudden knocking at the bedroom door startled her,
and she seized up her flimsy *robe-de-chambre* and slipped
it on; this too had belonged originally to Lady Mallory,
and the fine silk was threadbare in places. Tying the
girdle about her waist, she called: "You may come in,
Lucy!"

The door opened—but it wasn't Lucy; it was Jem Bolt
who entered.

She stared at him, and lifted her chin indignantly.
"What are you doing here? Where are the maids?"

"Ma says as the girls is all too busy below stairs . . .
So I've brought you such hot water as is left over. Only a
bucketful—Ma says she can't spare you no more, till
after the captain's had his bath."

Garnet frowned as he set the bucket down with a thump
by the wash-stand.

"Oh . . . Very well—that will have to do, I suppose.
Thank you, Jem, you may go now."

But instead of retreating, Jem stepped forward and
came closer. "I'm in no hurry, Miss Garnet . . . And I do
want to talk with you."

She moved away, knotting the girdle at her waist, con-
scious of his hungry eyes upon her. "I cannot talk now,
Jem—please go at once. And stop looking at me like
that."

"Why shouldn't I look? I reckon as I've seen enough
of you before now . . ."

She gasped. "Mind your manners, sir! Or I shall—I
shall—"

He grinned wickedly. "You'll do what? What will you
do, Miss Garnet?"

She stepped away, taking refuge behind a chair, and
tried to make her voice clear and commanding, as she
said: "I shall report your insolent behavior to my father."

"Oh, aye—and tell him while you're at it how you and me went swimming in the fishpond that day—and what happened after . . . Yes, you tell him that, little missy!"

She clenched her fists. "It's cruel and wicked of you to remind me of that, Jem. You know very well I was only a young, thoughtless girl—not much more than a child . . . Surely we both agreed to pretend it never happened—you promised me you'd forget about it."

"I did try to forget, Miss Garnet—but it ain't no good . . . I reckon as how I won't never forget—and no more will you, I'll wager."

He made a sudden lunge and grasped her by the waist. "I want you, my girl—I've wanted you ever since that day—and I can't help my feelings. Why should you give yourself to a jumped-up toy soldier like him downstairs —and why do you turn from me?"

"I don't know what you mean—I haven't given myself to anyone—"

"I saw you, yes I did—you and him, kissing and a-cuddling when you thought no one was by . . . Why *him*, Miss Garnet? Why not *me?*"

His hand tightened, and she exclaimed: "Let go— you're hurting me—"

Out in the passage, Mrs. Bolt's voice called shrilly: "Jem! Bless the boy—where's he got to? Jem! Come you here this minute!"

Cursing under his breath, he let Garnet go and moved to the door, as his mother's voice continued: "You're wanted to help the captain into his bath! Come at once— do you hear?"

"Help him? I'd sooner drown him in it!" Jem turned back for one more plea.

"Miss Garnet—listen to me—I do love you, with all my heart . . ."

Feeling more certain of herself now, Garnet could afford to be a little gentler, as she responded: "I'm sorry, Jem . . . You must put me out of your mind . . . What happened that day is over and done with; we were too young to know what we did. But we're grown-up now, and I am a young lady."

As she said this, a tiny voice deep inside her said: But I would do it again . . . I *will* do it again . . .

"Jem Bolt! Answer me, can't you? Have you got bees-wax in your ears?" came an angry cry from the staircase.

"Coming, Ma!" Jemmy threw Garnet a last, imploring look—and was gone.

She shut and bolted the door after him, then leaned back against it to recover her breath. It was true—she hadn't forgotten that afternoon, any more than he had. It was all there in her memory, as clear and vivid as if it had happened yesterday.

She even recalled the last moments, as they began to scramble into their clothes—but of course, after only half an hour in the sunshine, her own garments were still sodden with pond water, and it was impossible for her to put them on. But then she had had a bright idea. Gerard had vanished—heaven alone knew where—and there were his shirt and breeches, flung in a heap on the grassy bank.

Laughing, she had made Jem help her on with them, asking for his assistance as her fingers fumbled with un-accustomed buttons and laces.

"If I take care and hurry in by the side door, no one will see me—and if they do, they'll only think I'm Gerard!"

She crammed his broad-brimmed straw hat down over her curling locks, and set off with Jem arm-in-arm, like two jolly plowboys coming back from the fields together at sundown.

She still remembered the extraordinary feel of Gerard's breeches upon her thighs; the heaviness of his belt buckled at her waist, the coarse wool of his stockings on her legs, and the sweaty male tang of his rough linen shirt. It was a sensation she would never forget—and she felt in some inexplicable way that it was a turning point in her life, never to be forgotten.

But now, as Jem's footsteps clattered away down the stairs, she banished these strange fancies from her mind and prepared to wash and dress and make herself ready to see her love again.

"To our next meeting," Edmund had whispered, and the intensity of his tone still echoed in her heart.

She would put on her best silk gown, and make herself look as beautiful as she could—so that when she and Edmund came face to face the next time, he would see what sort of girl she really was . . . She smiled to herself . . .

What a surprise it was going to be!

3

An Uninvited Guest

Surprises sometimes misfire, Garnet soon discovered,
and her plan did not work out quite as she had expected.

Half an hour later, duly scrubbed and toweled, dressed
in her best merino with some becoming cherry-silk em-
broidery at the low neckline, and a long silken stole (another legacy from the late Lady Mallory) draped from
her elbows, Garnet made her way downstairs. Not by way
of the back stairs this time, but the wide, imposing flight
of stone steps that led into the lofty entrance hall. She
crossed the marble floor and hesitated, guessing that their
uninvited guest would now be in the main drawing-room
beyond.

Quickly, she checked her reflection in a wall mirror
with an ornate gilded frame, and saw her anxious face
peering back at her. She adjusted the folds of her dress
as they hung straight down from her high waist, and
adjusted her countenance as well, assuming a cordial ex-

pression of greeting. Then she turned the handles of the double doors, and pushed them open.

Across what seemed to be an acre of rich Persian carpet she saw Edmund seated in a wing armchair drawn up close to the hearth. She guessed that Mrs. Bolt had given orders to light the fire especially in his honor, for the autumn had not really taken hold yet, and the evenings had not been cold enough to warrant fires in the drawing-room. Edmund had not heard her come in. He seemed lost in thought with his back to the door and his injured leg propped up on a low stool.

She took a deep breath, and walked toward him. "Good evening, Captain Challoner."

He recognized her voice immediately, and swung round to face her, a smile on his lips. "Why, Miss Garnet—my pretty rescuer—"

Then he noticed her transformation; quite evidently the young lady of Markwick Hall, come to greet her guest— and the smile faded from his eyes. For an instant, he was at a loss for words. "Miss Garnet—forgive me—I mean—"

She laughed gently at his confusion, and held out her hand. "Perhaps I should enlighten you, Captain. My name is Garnet Mallory—Sir George is my father . . . And you are very welcome to our house."

He took her hand politely. "You will excuse my rudeness in not getting to my feet, I am sure, Miss Mallory. And I hope you will also try to overlook my unforgivable stupidity. When you told me your name was Garnet, I thought you referred to your surname—as a Christian name, Garnet is unfamiliar to me."

"Of course. I owe it to my mother; the name was her own coining. I agree it is unusual."

"But very charming, nonetheless. In my ignorance, however, I never guessed you were the daughter of the house. How could I have been so blind?"

"It was very understandable, Captain. I was wearing

my oldest gown, and you took me for one of the household servants no doubt."

He withdrew his hand in a gesture of abject apology. "What can I say? Please try to forget I ever was so churlish, Miss Mallory."

"Oh—but you must continue to call me Garnet, Captain—please! Since we are already quite well acquainted . . ."

Saying this, she looked directly at him, with a glint of mischief. But there was no answering amusement in his glance, and when his hand pressed hers in automatic courtesy, there was no longer any tingle of excitement between them. At the moment when he realized who she really was, she had felt the warmth in his smile grow cold, and the light that danced in his eyes was extinguished.

But why? *Why?*

Formally, he bowed his head. "I am honored indeed, Miss Garnet . . . And perhaps you will be kind enough to call me Edmund."

"With very great pleasure." She lowered her gaze to his muscular leg, stretched out upon the footstool, and added: "I hope your ankle is not causing you too much discomfort now?"

"No, no—thanks to the ministrations of your good housekeeper, the pain is easing up wonderfully."

"But you must not try to walk too soon," Garnet said quickly. "I'm sure that would be unwise—you must stay here and let it heal completely—however long that takes."

"What, what? Of course he must stay—what stuff is this?"

Sir George's thunderous roar rolled across the high-ceilinged room as he advanced upon them, leaning on his cane, attended a few paces behind by young Gerard.

"You'll stay and give us the pleasure of your company for a day or two, surely? We have rooms and to spare for your accommodation, and I can tell you it will be a great treat for me to have an intelligent military man like your-self to talk to . . . We don't have many such interesting visitors at Markwick."

"Alas, Sir George—I would accept your invitation glad-ly, but I must return to barracks tonight, for fear that I may be posted as an absentee . . . However, perhaps I might be allowed to trespass upon your hospitality again, at some later date? It would be a great privilege, I do assure you." He glanced at Garnet with an appraising smile, adding: "And it would be doubly delightful to re-new my acquaintance with your lovely daughter . . . The all-male company that a barracks provides can prove wearisome after a time!"

"Hey? Oh—no doubt, no doubt!" Sir George sniffed, and dismissed this topic of conversation, continuing heart-ily: "But you'll stay and dine with us tonight at least, Captain? Do not disappoint me in that, I beg you. We dine early—we keep country hours here, you see—and afterwards I'll give orders to have my coach brought round to drive you back into Guildford. Come, sir—you shall not deny me!"

Edmund accepted the invitation gracefully.

At the dinner table, he sat at Sir George's right hand, and the two men monopolized the conversation. Garnet was ignored entirely by her father, and after one or two sallies by Edmund to draw her in, he was forced to give up the attempt, and contented himself with an occasional nod or smile in her direction. Each time he looked across at her her heart leaped, and she fell into a happy rev-erie . . .

Why had he seemed so shocked at first? What made the light in his eyes go out, in that first moment?

Gerard was treated with a little more consideration by his father, and included in the table talk—although he soon had cause to wish that he too could have been in-visible and inaudible, like his sister.

"Take my boy here—young Gerard . . . Now there's a

milksop for you—forever wasting his time with books and poetry and such nonsense, when he should be out riding or shooting or building his strength—"

"Father, I do go riding, often—" Gerard dared to protest.

"Hold your tongue, boy, and speak when you're spoken to. Yes—riding alone—ambling along with a volume of verse in your pocket and God knows what airy nonsense in your head . . . You'd do better to ride to hounds, sir—take an interest in some manly sport!"

He appealed to Edmund for corroboration. "Ain't that so, Captain? My dearest wish is to send the lad off into the army, and follow your good example."

Gerard bit his lip and raged inwardly, but dared say nothing.

"That's what he needs—toughening up. Boxing, now—he should learn to defend himself, but I'm too old to teach him. Tell me, Captain—do you practice the noble art of fisticuffs?"

Edmund admitted that he had learned to box at school.

"There! What did I say? A splendid pastime . . . I wonder, sir, if you might ever feel inclined to give my boy a few lessons, heh? When next you come to visit us—for I am determined that you shall visit us again, now we have made your acquaintance."

"If Master Gerard wishes it, I should be most happy to teach him as much as I am able." Edmund looked at Gerard inquiringly. "What do you say, Gerard?"

Gerard swallowed and mumbled, "Very obliging of you, sir, I'm sure . . ." with bitter resentment in his heart.

"That's settled, then. I shall look forward to our next meeting—and I look forward to seeing Miss Garnet also."

Garnet could hardly believe her ears as Edmund turned to her father once more, saying: "In fact, Sir George, I shall be more than happy to become better acquainted with your daughter. I hope we may continue our newfound friendship . . . And by your leave, I should be

43

honored if you will grant me permission to escort her to the Ball at the Assembly Rooms next month."

Garnet held her breath, feeling sure that the world must stop revolving or the stars drop from the heavens at such an overwhelming, inconceivable proposition. To be invited to a ball—for the first time in her life—and by the man to whom she had so recently lost her heart! . . . She felt quite dizzy, and gripped the edge of the dining-table until her knuckles showed white.

Sir George was equally taken aback, and gave Captain Challoner a long searching look—then turned and stared at his daughter as if he had never seen her before. At last he grunted: "Very well . . . If that's what you wish . . . I've no objection."

Garnet almost wept with delight and gratitude—and a sense of some deeper emotion, such as she had never known before. She looked into Edmund's eyes, and he smiled back at her encouragingly. So it was going to be all right, after all . . . How silly of her to have had any doubts . . . She loved him, and evidently he loved her; it was as simple as that.

The evening passed all too soon, and when Sir George saw the young officer into the coach at last, Garnet too went out to the carriage drive, and listened to the sound of the wheels as they bowled away into the night—and felt a part of her heart and soul going with them. When she could hear no more she turned back to the house, but Sir George had clearly forgotten her existence again already, for he had gone inside and shut the front doors behind him. Locked out, she made her way around the front of the building to the side entrance and the servants' quarters. She turned the corner of the house in the darkness, and then—

She stifled the scream that rose in her throat as a pair of strong hands closed about her shoulders and a shape loomed up before her, a blacker patch in the blackness of the night.

"It's me, Miss Garnet."

"Jem—you startled me!" She tried to control her voice. "What are you doing here?"

"I was a-hoping as how I'd find you. I had to harness the carriage horses—and then I waited to see the toy soldier off on his way. Good riddance to him, and all . . ."

"How dare you speak so of our visitor? You don't know what you're saying—"

"Oh, but I do, Miss Garnet. I know as he's setting his cap at you, and now he's planning for to take you to the ball—en't that right?"

"How do you know that? Who told you?"

"Charles was listening while he served dinner, he told us later, in the hall."

Of course—she had forgotten how the servants gossiped below stairs.

"Well, that's as may be, Jem—but it's certainly none of your business."

"But it *is* my business, Miss Garnet, because he's not the man for you, not never . . . He don't love you like as how I do."

He released his hold upon her, then grasped one of her hands in both his own.

"Don't be a fool, Jem—let go of me—"

"Put your hand here, and you'll know how strong the love is I do have for you . . . Just feel—and see what it is you do to me—"

He dragged her hand down below his waist, and pressed it against the coarse cloth of his breeches. Ignoring her protests, he forced her to yield, and she became aware of the strength of his manhood, ramrod-stiff, as if it had a life of its own. Excited despite herself, but also horrified at the brutal intimacy, she managed to snatch her hand away, and with all the force she could muster gave him a ringing slap across the face.

"Don't ever—do that—again—!" She spat the words out, in a fury.

Taken by surprise, he staggered back, off-balance, and

she took the opportunity to dodge past him before he could recover his wits; then she ran for the side door, and safety.

Cursing himself for having let her go, Jem trudged off slowly to his bed above the stables. So he had lost her this time; but there would be other nights . . . He was not going to give her up without a struggle.

And while he lay on his back, his body aching for her, Garnet herself tossed and twisted in her own bed, and tried to forget Jem—but how could she forget the feel of his hard masculinity under her hand?—and thought of Edmund instead. She fell asleep at last, drowsily weaving all these turbulent thoughts and feelings into one disturbing dream . . .

During the weeks that followed Captain Challoner returned to Markwick Hall on several occasions, to give his thanks for Sir George's generous assistance, and to continue the formal process of his steady addresses to Garnet. One day they strolled in the garden; another time, when it rained, they sat in the drawing-room and made polite conversation across a plate of ratafia biscuits and two glasses of Madeira wine.

And on each of these occasions, Gerard contrived in some strange way to be missing, so the threatened boxing lessons were never translated into action. Sir George grumbled at this waste of opportunity, and scolded the boy soundly when he put in an appearance at supper time—wide-eyed with innocent amazement, when he heard how the captain had come to call, and he had so unfortunately missed him.

Sir George also noted the ritual progress of Edmund's courtship, but made no comment. The idea did not displease him—the captain seemed an estimable young man, and was clearly of good breeding—and indeed he would not be averse to the thought of a new generation of Mallory children . . . All boys, of course, and all destined to follow in the footsteps of their father *and* their grandfather. But he kept his own counsel on that subject, neither approving nor disapproving; only biding his time.

However, when Edmund and Gerard had accidentally missed one another for the third time, Sir George's short temper exploded in an outburst of irritation, and he suggested to Edmund that he should come and stay at Markwick Hall for a weekend.

"—An opportunity for us to get to know you better, sir, and a diversion for you, after your round of barrack-room duties . . . And damme! I'll make sure that *this* time Gerard shall not sneak away from you; he shall have his first lesson in self-defense, even if I have to drag him out of the library myself!"

Garnet, of course, was equally delighted with the plan, and looked forward to Edmund's arrival on Friday evening with lively anticipation. They would have the whole weekend together; surely this time there must be a chance for them to be alone and at ease with one another. Their recent meetings had been all very well, but stiflingly polite and hedged about by a thousand conventions. She longed for a return to their very first encounter—the wild passion that had swept her away when he took her in his arms . . . She was impatient for him to behave with that old impudent freedom, and to abandon herself once more in the reckless pleasure of his embrace . . . Surely this could—*would*—all happen again—and soon?

When Friday evening arrived, Garnet was out on the front steps to welcome her love; she had spent most of the afternoon picking a huge bunch of late roses and early chrysanthemums from the gardens, and as he dismounted from his horse, she stepped forward and held the flowers out to him. A groom stood by to take the reins and led the captain's skewbald stallion round to the stables; Garnet noticed fleetingly that it was one of the other lads, not Jem—and was glad of it. Then Edmund kissed her fingertips, and smiled at the bouquet she offered.

"What's this? Some secret message in the language of flowers?"

Garnet colored slightly, aware that he was laughing at

her a little. "No . . . They are to go in your room. We have made the best bedroom in the East wing all ready especially for you, but I thought that you might like a *beau-pot* to welcome you."

He bowed from the waist, and offered his arm. "You are more than kind, Miss Garnet. Come, you shall lead the way and conduct me to my quarters!"

"What about your bags—your luggage—?"

"Oh, my man takes care of all that. He will have gone directly to the servants' hall—he knows what's to be done."

Garnet escorted Edmund into the main hall and up the stone staircase, along the double gallery that branched left and right, and there they turned right into the East wing. These rooms were maintained for guests, but rarely used, and since early morning a battery of maids and footmen had been hard at work to receive the visitor.

Garnet walked slightly ahead as they trod the carpeted corridor and wondered if at any moment she might feel the touch she longed for; the pressure of his hand on her arm—or even a more intimate contact, a caress on her back or her rounded hips—

But no . . . He kept at a respectful distance, two paces behind her. Yes, "respectful," that was the word. She identified his attitude with some relief. Why hadn't she realized it sooner? Now he was paying court to her, with a serious intent; his attitude was bound to change; of course, he *respected* her . . .

She turned the handle of the bedroom door, and flung it wide, saying: "You must make yourself entirely at home here, Edmund."

Then she stopped as if struck by lightning, and stared in amazement. Edmund, following into the room a split second later, was equally dumbfounded.

There, standing by the foot of the bed, stood a young lady, brushing her long blond hair, who turned to greet the intruders with mild surprise. "At home with me? But how companionable!"

The stranger was not one whit disconcerted by their arrival at such an intimate moment—intimate indeed, for she had apparently divested herself of her outer attire very recently, and was now clothed in nothing more than the flimsiest of silken petticoats and a wisp of some outrageous undergarment . . . The evening light from the window beyond shone so brightly through these insubstantial coverings that her trim figure was outlined in all its boldness, and for a fleeting moment Garnet had the impression that the pretty interloper was quite naked.

Now she continued, with a ripple of laughter in her voice—a voice which betrayed the hint of a Celtic accent: "Don't you remember me, lovey? Your very own cousin Bella? You must be Garnet, I feel sure . . . My, how you've grown!"

Then she turned to the captain, her hand outstretched, saying: "My name's Bella Delaney—of the County Cork Delaneys, you know . . . I do hope someone will introduce us soon, for I'm very happy to make your acquaintance, whoever you are!"

Flushing with vexation, Garnet picked up a lacy negligée that lay across the bed, along with a dozen other items that had obviously come from the newcomer's luggage, and quickly draped it around her bare shoulders, stammering in some discomfiture: "Of course—Bella—may I present Captain Challoner—a good friend of the family—"

With an ironic lift of an eyebrow Edmund bowed over the lady's hand, as she rattled on.

"Then you must be my friend also, for I'm one of the family, am I not, Garnet?"

"Oh—yes—I'm sorry, I should have explained—Miss Delaney is my cousin from Ireland, Edmund . . . I'm so sorry for this confusion, but we were not expecting you, Bella."

"Were you not? Now isn't that the strangest thing, for I sent your father a long letter only the other day, to warn him of my arrival. I'm on my way home from London, you see—after a heavenly three weeks with the Bullivants, at Hyde Park Gate . . . I went up for the Season, and I must say I enjoyed every minute of it."

Still chattering, Bella perched herself nonchalantly on the edge of the bed, and continued her toilet, brushing her long corn-colored hair without the least sign of embarrassment.

"But it's such a plaguey long drive back to Bristol by coach—so I decided 'twould be much pleasanter to break my journey here on the way—and much more fun, as well . . ."

She glanced up at Edmund under her long, curling lashes, and two dimples appeared at the corners of her mouth. "So I wrote and informed Uncle George of my intention—and now you tell me he never got my letter? Isn't that provoking—I do hope I'm not putting you out, Garnet dear?"

"Well—no—we have plenty of space and you are very welcome to stay, cousin—but how did you get into this bedchamber?"

"I must confess I was the least little bit cross when I found no one waiting to meet me . . . But I met one of the footmen in the hall, and he made himself vastly obliging, I'm glad to say. I told him I was come to visit, and he said yes, you were expecting a guest—and so led me up to this room . . ."

"I see . . . Well, Edmund, it makes no matter—we can easily find you some other accommodation. Perhaps you would accompany me? Bella, I will come back and talk to you later!"

So it was arranged; orders were given, maids were dispatched, and yet another guest room was made ready as speedily as possible. Then, when Edmund was safely established in his own territory, Garnet returned to her pretty cousin.

She found her still busy with her coiffure, now putting up her curls in ringlets on either side of her heart-shaped face.

"What a commotion I seem to have caused, to be sure! And what a fine figure of a man your captain is—for I presume he *is* your captain? Your latest conquest, no doubt?"

"Oh, what nonsense you do talk, Bella. Edmund is a good friend to us all—as I told you. It is my father who invites him to stay with us."

"But you have more than a passing interest in the young man—I could tell that at a single glance . . . Let me look at you, lovey—indeed, you've grown into a beautiful creature; I declare I'd hardly have known you."

"That isn't surprising, when you consider that we were both children when you last came to visit . . . How long ago was it?"

"Ten long years, alas—isn't that shameful? And here I am nineteen, and you are—what? Seventeen?"

"Yes—we have both changed a great deal." Garnet sat beside her cousin, and noticed that the negligée she had thrown over Bella's shoulders in an attempt to preserve some measure of propriety before the captain, was in fact of such fine lace that it was well-nigh transparent, and frowned at the realization.

"I am sorry we walked in upon you so rudely—it must have been quite mortifying for you, since you were so very decolletée at the time . . . "

"Oh, la—*I* didn't mind, I assure you! I dare say the gallant captain has seen a lady's undergarments before now . . . Yours, perhaps?"

Garnet drew herself up as haughtily as she could, and retorted: "Certainly not! . . ." But she remembered as she said it that this was not true, and felt her cheeks redden. "And in any case—even if he did—my garments would never have revealed so much of—of—"

She broke off in confusion; unable to put her thought into words.

Bella threw back her head and laughed. "Why—what do you wear under that severely cut dress? Let me see—"

And before Garnet realized what was happening, Bella

had tumbled her backwards on to the bed, and tipped her legs up in the air, pulling aside her skirts and fumbling under them.

"Lord-a-mercy—what old-fashioned drawers you wear, my dear! I thought none but old maids and vicars' wives still used such antiques! Compare them with *mine,* lovey—sheer silk, and they feel like the merest caress when you put them on! I shall lend you a pair to try, and you shall discover for yourself—"

Garnet, flustered as much by Bella's inquiring fingers as by the boldness of her words, rolled aside and made her escape, quickly rearranging her garments as she scrambled to her feet.

"Bella—you should not say such—*do* such things—"

"Oh, fie—who's to know? And it's not for the first time, anyway—remember when I was here before, how we all played at doctors? You and I and little Gerard . . . which reminds me—how *is* Gerard now? I haven't set eyes on him yet. He must be grown into a young man by now!"

They all met in the drawing-room before dinner. Bella greeted her youngest cousin with a swift, calculating glance, spoke half a dozen kind words to him and then dismissed him, concentrating instead on being especially agreeable to the two older gentlemen. Her uncle George Mallory, whom she made much of, seemed delighted by her surprise visit—and she was even more charming to Captain Challoner.

The weekend was a great success, except, perhaps, from Garnet's point of view, for she hardly seemed to have one moment of Edmund's company to herself. When they drove into Guildford on Saturday morning to do a little shopping, the captain was obliged to squire both young ladies and carry their little packages to the waiting carriage. When Bella heard of the plans for the Ball next week, she insisted on joining the party, and the captain was forced to include her in his invitation. And when they alighted at the front entrance to Markwick Hall,

Bella contrived to hang back so that Garnet stepped down to the gravel drive first, and went on ahead with her purchases . . . while Bella made a great fuss over climbing down from the carriage, and had to be assisted by the courteous captain, clinging on to his arm and squeezing his hand in the process.

Garnet, halfway into the house, saw nothing of this; but they were not unobserved, for a groom was present to unharness the horses. Jem Bolt watched what was happening and made a mental note of it. More than ever, he nursed his secret grudge against the "toy soldier," and with even more jealousy he plotted his revenge.

Saturday afternoon was bright and sunny, a last nostalgic reminder of the dear departed summer. The air was warm and golden, and Edmund suggested that the young ladies might care to go riding with him.

Garnet accepted with alacrity, and was secretly delighted to see Bella pout and hear her protest. "Oh—must you? I *nauseate* horses—perhaps it's because at home my family never seems to talk of anything else! It seems to me there are so many more pleasant ways of taking exercise . . . However, if you two choose to go, I will stay here and play solitaire until you return and deliver me!"

Garnet and Edmund went to the stables and picked two suitable mounts; as he was about to swing into the saddle, Edmund glanced up at the blue sky, and observed: "This is too fair a day to be weighed down with a coat—will you forgive me, Miss Garnet, if I divest myself?"

With her permission—which she gave eagerly enough —he stripped off his coat and tossed it carelessly over the half-door of the loosebox. Then, in plum-colored waistcoat, fine linen shirt and tight-fitting breeches, he vaulted onto his horse's back and the two riders set forth.

They cantered across the home park and down through the long meadow; Garnet glanced at the fishpond—glittering in the sunlight—as they passed it, and remembered, and wondered if he too were remembering . . . For although they were alone together at last, the ride was hardly companionable, as he kept up a brisk pace, always half a dozen yards ahead. When they had left the grounds of Markwick and were galloping across open common land—scrub, furzebushes, and a rusty fringe of dying bracken—Garnet called out:

"Can't we slow down a little? It's not so easy for me as it is for you!"

When she was a child and first climbed on a horse, she had always ridden astride, like a boy, with her sturdy knees pressed into the horse's flanks; but now she was a young lady, this was no longer possible. In her long skirt, she was forced to perch sidesaddle, keeping her balance as best she could. Secretly, she felt that half the joy had gone out of riding under these limitations.

Edmund apologized, slowed to a walk, and at last she was able to keep up alongside and talk to him . . . But his conversation was still impersonal and formal—he was very agreeable, but still seemed to keep his distance. They discussed the weather, the news of the war (the British army was fighting Bonaparte on the Iberian Peninsula now, and the troops were hammering the enemy across the length and breadth of Spain and Portugal), and the unexpected arrival of cousin Bella. Edmund expressed no very definite opinion on the young lady, Garnet noticed, but merely said that she seemed "very lively."

At length they returned to Markwick, and clattered in across the flagstoned yard. Edmund dismounted, and helped Garnet down, calling for a groom.

There was no reply; the place seemed momentarily deserted. Garnet said: "I dare say they're all in the servants' hall—they often go in for a mug of small beer and a hunk of cheese about this time."

"Then we shall see to the horses ourselves."

The captain knew what had to be done, and the two animals were soon returned to their stalls, the harness and tack hanging up in its accustomed place on the stable walls.

"The sun's gone down . . . And it looks as if there's a storm gathering." He glanced up at the sky, where a bank of purple cloud massed on the horizon. Certainly there was a heaviness in the air that had not been there before, and Garnet felt a slight headache coming on. There was thunder about.

"If you wait one moment, I'll put on my coat—now, where did I leave it? Ah, there it is—it must have fallen down . . ."

He picked up his topcoat from the cobbled floor of the loosebox where it lay, and slipped it on.

At that point, everything seemed to happen at once. Garnet heard a quick slithering sound inside the garment, and saw Edmund's face shocked with a sudden stab of pain; at the same moment a flash of lightning broke the sky, making the scene blindingly clear. In its livid glare, Edmund flung the coat off again, and as it fell to the ground Garnet saw the shining green length of an adder wriggle from inside one of the sleeves; with incredible speed the creature took refuge in a pile of straw and dung that stood in the corner of the yard.

Recoiling instinctively, her first thought was for the captain.

"Are you all right? Edmund, for heaven's sake—"

He was twisted in agony, his right hand gripping his upper arm.

"The brute got its fangs in me before I knew what was happening—" he gasped. "I can feel the venom working already . . ."

"What shall I do? Run for help?"

"No—there's no time—we must act at once . . . and you must assist me." He pulled his cravat undone with his free hand, then gave it to her, saying: "Tie this round my arm above the wound—as tight as ever you can, to stop the poison from spreading."

With trembling fingers she obeyed as best she could, pulling the knot so hard that the rough tourniquet bit into Edmund's strong biceps.

"Now—get my knife—it's in my right-hand breeches pocket—you must pull it out for me . . ."

He turned his right side toward her, and she slipped her hand into his deep pocket; it felt very warm, and her hand was aware of his firm thigh, pressing under the thin material—even at such a desperate moment she felt a thrill at the contact and despised herself for it. Fumbling nervously, her fingers closed upon the pocket knife; she remembered it at once—had she not used it before, when she freed him from his riding-boot?

"Good girl. Open it up—yes, quickly, quickly—and now cut my shirt so you can see where the skin is punctured."

Hesitating only for the fraction of a second, she slid the knife blade into the fine linen below his shoulder, and ripped. A long jagged slit appeared, and she tore it wider, revealing his sinewy, powerful muscle. There was the mark of the snakebite: a pair of tiny needle-pricks in his bronze skin.

"Now—cut into my arm with the knife—two or three quick slashes; I promise you I shall not feel anything . . . But do it—before it is too late!"

She had to steel herself for this command, but she knew it was necessary, and the extremity of his suffering showed her there was no time to be lost. With an extraordinary feeling of excitement, she pressed the sharp blade deep into his flesh, again and again, and watched the lines of blood well up instantly, beginning to dribble down his arm in long rivulets of crimson. She could hardly breathe, for the pounding of her heart in her breast . . .

"And now you must suck the wounds clean. There will be no danger to you, I promise. The poison is only fatal in the bloodstream, it will do no harm in your mouth. But it is the only remedy to save me."

Almost faint with shock, she obeyed him blindly; she

opened her lips as she put her mouth to his wounded shoulder and sucked the poison from him in what seemed to be the ghastly parody of a lover's kiss.

Minutes later, it was all over; he leaned back against the wall, panting a little. "There . . . All is well. I can feel the life coming back into my arm . . . There is nothing more to fear."

Giddy with relief, she almost laughed for joy, then broke off as a dark shadow fell across the cobbles. Jem had returned from the servants' hall, and stood watching them at the half-door.

Quickly, Garnet explained what had happened—an adder had found its way into the captain's sleeve somehow, and attacked him—

"And now it's hiding in that heap of straw—you'd best dispatch it as soon as you can for fear it should strike again."

Then she took Edmund into the house to bathe and bandage him, and Jem heard the young officer say as they disappeared. "That is twice now you have come to my rescue . . . What would I do without you, my dearest Garnet?"

A sudden clap of thunder exploded above the stables, and the horses whinnied in terror.

Jem stood unmoving, his face a mask of hatred—and black disappointment. Then he set to work to find the missing snake. When he had run it to earth he did not kill it, but instead picked it up in a cleft stick he had by him, and dropped it into a wooden box that was all ready to hand. Perhaps—soon—he would have another chance. And the next time, he hoped with all his heart he would not fail.

4

First Lessons

By evening it was quite clear that Edmund was going to come to no harm, and he enjoyed a good dinner and several glasses of port with Sir George afterward.

Garnet and Bella sat in the drawing-room, waiting for the gentlemen to join them, and passing the time by inspecting a series of watercolors of local scenes, which Garnet had executed since the departure of her governess.

"Vastly picturesque, dearest cousin," said Bella, smothering a yawn. "But how provoking of Uncle George to detain your gallant captain for so long at the dinner table . . . "

"You persist in calling him my captain—but I do assure you, you assume too much! We are simply friends, and nothing more."

"Really?" Bella's dimples appeared again. "Well, if he's not yours, I wonder who does lay claim to him—for such a handsome man cannot be unattached for long, I feel sure . . . I protest, I quite made up my mind he was your beau."

"Oh, he is very attentive to me, I confess—and he pays me pretty tributes every time he comes to call . . . But—there is something I cannot quite describe—a sort of *distance* between us."

"Tell me more," said Bella, with more signs of interest than she had shown all the evening. "You mean—the dashing captain betrays a coolness toward you, my dear?"

"I think it is his way of expressing a proper respect," Garnet tried to explain. "He is so very nice about the rules of conduct toward a young lady; he would not dream of—of taking too much for granted; of trespassing beyond the bounds of propriety—of any misbehavior—"

"La! You mean to say he don't even kiss you when no one's looking?" Bella set up a vigorous breeze with her little ivory fan, and eyed Garnet curiously. "How very singular . . . What sort of a man *is* he, I wonder?"

"A high-principled man—I'm certain of that." Garnet bit her lip, and added: "Though I must admit—between ourselves—I sometimes wish he would display just a *little* more warmth in his manner toward me . . . "

"To be sure you do, lovey—'tis only natural, after all. But never fear, your confidence is safe with me—I won't breathe a word."

At that moment, the double doors opened, and the gentlemen of the party came in, rather red of face and heavy of step—and the conversation changed to the burning topic of Bonaparte and the Portuguese war.

Much later, when the party broke up and everyone retired to bed, Garnet stood undecided in her room, wanting very much to have a word with Edmund in private before she slept.

At last she made up her mind to venture forth, and wrapping her *robe-de-chambre* around her, she crept as quietly as possible along the corridor and made her way to the guest wing.

Timidly, she knocked on Edmund's door, and a moment afterward he opened it—standing back in some surprise on seeing his midnight visitor.

"Garnet, my dear—what is it? What's wrong?"

"Nothing . . . But I would like to speak to you—may I come in?"

He hesitated only for a second, looking down at himself, for he was clearly unprepared for company, dressed only in a flowing nightgown with a front of ruffles unbuttoned to the waist.

"Forgive my appearance—I was about to go to bed—"

He picked up a velvet dressing-gown that lay across the pillows of his four-poster, and quickly put it on, tying the belt in a loose knot.

She came into the room and closed the door.

"I only wanted to be sure that you were not suffering any ill-effect from that dreadful accident this afternoon. You really are quite well now, I hope?"

"I am indeed. It's kind of you to be anxious."

"Of course I am anxious—you know that. Anything that concerns you, concerns me also."

His face softened into a smile, as he said: "You are very sweet. I hope one day I may deserve such care and affection."

"You do more than deserve it: it is yours, come what may—for surely by now you must be aware that I love you, Edmund, so very much."

He took her hand, and raised it to his lips.

"Oh, my dear . . . And you must know the feelings that I have for you . . . From the moment I first set eyes upon you—"

"But then you did not even know who I was . . . And that made a difference, did it not?"

"When I discovered the identity of my fair benefactress, I was overjoyed—you helped me when I was lame, and now this afternoon you saved my life . . . What more can I say to you in love and gratitude?"

She was emboldened by the sincerity of his tone, and dared to reply: "The first time you repaid me with a kiss ... Don't I deserve any such reward today?"

In reply, he opened his arms to her, and enfolded her in a generous embrace; his body pressed against her, and his hands clasped her tightly. She looked into his face as his curving lips bent to her own, and waited for the moment when she would be swept away by the warmth of his passion ... But even as his mouth closed upon hers, she knew that something had changed. His lips did not part, to permit his thrusting tongue to meet hers, and his eyes were grave and cautious.

Yes, it was still wonderful—the feel of his arms around her, and the male, musky scent of his skin—and yet ... It was not the overwhelming excitement she longed for.

At last he loosed his hold and said: "My dearest girl— you must go back to your own room. If you stay here another minute, I shall become quite reckless, and disgrace myself ... Sleep well, dear Garnet, and let us dream of one another."

He moved to the door and opened it cautiously.

"Good night, my love ... I will see you tomorrow."

She took one last look at him. There he stood, the very picture of masculine beauty, with his finely modeled features, and his broad, powerful chest partly revealed in the careless disarray of his half-opened shirt—the skin bronzed and gleaming in the light of the bedside candle ... She longed to throw herself once more in his arms, and forget propriety and convention—to live for this very moment, and enjoy it to the full ... But of course that was out of the question.

"Good night, Edmund," she repeated quietly. "Until tomorrow."

She slipped out into the corridor, and heard his door click shut behind her. With a sigh, she set off to retrace her steps—then stopped short, amazed.

Bella, dressed in a nightgown and her frothy lace negligée, stood flattened against the wall of the passage, trying to make herself invisible.

"Oh—so it's you, Garnet!" she blurted out feebly. "What a relief—I was quite worried . . . "

"What are you doing here?" Garnet asked in bewilderment.

"I—I heard voices, you see, lovey—and knowing that there was nobody in the East wing except for me and the captain, I thought I'd better investigate . . . For fear of intruders in the house."

"Oh—I see . . . No—there's no cause for alarm—"

"I had no notion it was *you* I heard in the captain's room . . . I declare, you have quite taken me by surprise, little cousin!" Bella smiled.

Garnet held her head high.

"As the captain's hostess, I thought I should make sure that he was quite comfortable, and that he had all he wanted for the night."

"And I am quite certain he did . . . It seems we are two of a kind, Garnet dear, both putting ourselves out for the sake of others . . . "

Garnet escorted Bella back to her own room, and left her there, then went to bed at last with a great deal to think about.

On the following day, Sir George insisted that Gerard's education in the noble art of self-defense should begin with no further delay or excuse, and so the luckless youth was forced to take himself off to the gun-room with Captain Challoner, for his first lesson.

They pushed the furniture back to make a rough space the size of a boxing ring, and then stripped off their upper clothes and flung them over the back of two chairs, until they were both naked to the waist. The two young men presented an uneven match, for Edmund's body was well-developed and muscular, while Gerard in comparison seemed—as Jem Bolt had once said of him, long ago by the fishpond—like a skinned rabbit.

Nevertheless, Edmund apologized in advance.

"I shall not be in my best form today, I warn you—for my shoulder is still a trifle stiff after my encounter with that infernal reptile . . . However, I will do my best."

He explained the principles of boxing to Gerard—bare-fisted, as all the pugilists fought, from the young bloods in their sporting clubs and fashionable coffee-houses, to the least of the gypsies who traveled the countryside, taking on all comers in a fairgrounds booth.

Gradually, Edmund expounded the mysteries of the lunge, the feint, the upper cut and the right hook. With sinking heart, Gerard prepared to put these instructions into practice.

They squared up to one another at last, in the middle of the room, and Gerard presented his fists in a crude imitation of Edmund's practiced stance.

"Come now—begin!"

At first they played at pat-a-cake—with Gerard making little dabs in Edmund's direction, and the older man parrying each half-hearted blow with ridiculous ease.

"No, no—go at me as if you meant it, lad—try to hit me hard! Don't worry, I can defend myself!"

Spurred on, Gerard redoubled his efforts, but soon found that, try as he might, he could not get past the other's guard. Each time he struck out, a powerful forearm deflected the blow, and he began to flail at empty air.

"Not so wild, Gerard!" Maddeningly cool, Edmund corrected him. "If you start windmilling your arms like that you make it too easy for me to retaliate and land a punch—so—!"

He deftly directed a straight left under the boy's defense, and connected smartly with the end of his nose. Taken completely unaware, Gerard rocked on his heels, and tripped backward over one of the chairs, ending up in a sitting position on the floor, clasping his injured nose in both hands.

Just as Edmund went to his assistance, saying, "I'm sorry, youngster—I didn't mean to hurt you—"

—the gun-room door swung open, and Bella walked in, followed by Garnet.

"I hope you don't object to spectators, Captain? Garnet felt we should be intruding, but I was quite sure you would forgive us . . . ."

She broke off, as Garnet exclaimed, "Gerard—are you all right? You're bleeding!"

Feeling very foolish—and very sore—Gerard mumbled: "It's nothing—only a nosebleed—go away, do!"

"But if you're injured you need some water, and a sponge, surely—"

"Oh, do stop fussing, Garnet, for pity's sake! It's nothing, I tell you—just get out and leave me alone!"

"Come, Garnet—let us go and fetch a basin of water," said Edmund, quickly tugging his shirt over his head.

Bella gave him an appraising glance as he dressed himself, secretly regretting that he had chosen to cover up his physique quite so soon.

"Shall I come with you, Captain Challoner? I would be happy to make myself useful in any way—" she began.

"No, don't trouble yourself, Miss Delaney, Garnet and I will manage perfectly. Why don't you stay here and keep the young warrior company till we return?"

Shrugging into his jacket, he made for the door, and offered Garnet his arm, saying: "We shall not be long, Gerard . . . Put your head back, and perhaps the bleeding will stop of its own accord."

Bella watched them go, frowning, then turned her attention to the boy on the floor, who now stretched out on his back, following Edmund's advice.

"Well, well, cousin—you have been in the wars, and no mistake," she said ironically, and produced a small handkerchief from the reticule that she carried. "Here—you may try to stanch the wound with this!"

She knelt beside him, and gave him the square of cambric.

He accepted it gratefully, and pressed it to his nose; a stain of crimson slowly spread across the fabric.

"Poor Gerard . . . " Bella allowed her eye to roam over his uncovered torso, and noted that his recent exertions had brought out a gentle sweat, so that his skin shone as if it had been oiled.

With one delicate finger, she traced a line from his shoulder down to his chest, where a few fine hairs clustered together, promising manhood.

"I see I have misjudged you, cousin," she said at last. "I thought you were still a boy—but now I notice that you are grown into a young man already."

Gerard looked up at her, and read a mischievous message in her eyes.

"Quite the fallen hero—and handsome, even in defeat!" she continued, teasing him lightly.

"Oh—Bella—" he stammered, and fumbled for her hand, squeezing it. "I know you're only making game of me—but—you are so beautiful . . . So very beautiful."

"And you are very gallant to tell me so, I declare," said Bella, disengaging herself and rising to her feet. "But alas! You are still too young for me, my dear; heaven forbid that I should ever be accused of cradle-snatching."

Half-struggling to sit up, he tried to detain her, and put out a hand, clasping one slim ankle as she stepped back.

"Don't go—stay and talk to me—I've no one else to keep me company—there's no one at Markwick who has any time for me, Bella."

"Then you must find some new friends of your own age . . . Now remove your hand, sir, if you please! We may be kissing-cousins, but that does not give you the right to any greater familiarity."

Before he realized what was happening, Bella stooped and gave him a swift, mocking kiss on the lips, then sailed out of the room, laughing.

After that one informal encounter, she never spared her youngest cousin a single thought during the entire week that followed: for Saturday next was to be the night of the Ball at the Assembly Rooms, and all Bella's attention was concentrated upon this splendid event.

So, in a less sophisticated way, was Garnet's; she looked forward to the evening of dance and revelry with anticipation so acute that she could hardly bear it. The idea of so many hours spent in Edmund's company, whirled around the floor in his arms, made her almost dizzy . . . Surely, after a whole night of such proximity, he would be tempted to abandon his high moral standards—just a little?

To achieve this end, she even enlisted Bella's help in persuading her father to spend a small sum of money on a new dress for the occasion. The scheme succeeded, for although Sir George might well have dismissed a direct request from his daughter out of hand, Bella managed to flatter and cajole the old soldier into a good humor, and he eventually dispensed a purse of guineas without a single objection.

The girls went shopping in Guildford the next morning, and called at the establishment of Madame Hoskins—the local modiste—where Garnet was soon fitted with a gown of deep emerald silk that showed off her dark hair and rose-pink coloring to perfection.

Bella looked her up and down judiciously, and expressed herself as undecided—she had some reservations.

"Oh, it becomes you excellently well—I'll not deny that. But I rather wish you had chosen some other color . . . To be sure, they do say that emerald green is an unlucky shade . . . "

But Garnet refused to listen to such an old wives' tale; she had fallen in love with the silk dress the minute she had tried it on, and as she admired her reflection in Mme. Hoskins' cramped little boudoir, with Bella at her shoulder pulling and tugging at a seam here or a pleat there, or running her restless fingers over the low-cut bodice, accidentally brushing the soft roundness of her bosom— Garnet made up her mind.

She declared that she wasn't in the least superstitious, she had taken a fancy to this particular gown, and would have no other. And since she might never have been able to buy it at all without her cousin's good offices, she insisted that with the money that was left over, Bella herself must have a brand new stole of glittering gold net, which would contrast brilliantly with her elegant cream-colored satin.

So it happened that by late afternoon on Saturday, both girls were in a state of high impatience, willing the slow hours to hurry by until it should be nightfall and time for the festivities to begin.

Of course, they had to spend some of the waiting time in preparations; they must be bathed, powdered, their hair ringletted and coiffed in the very latest style, like two figures from a Paris fashion plate.

"I have some exquisite bath essence, lovey," Bella told Garnet as they walked up the stairs to make themselves ready. "So why don't you come to my room when the pitchers of hot water are provided? Then we may help each other to become beauties!"

Half an hour later, Garnet presented herself in Bella's room, with her new dress over one arm, and her soap and towel over the other.

"Come in, come in, you little darling!" cried Bella, beckoning gleefully. "Quick, quick—get your clothes off and join me while the water is still warm!"

Hastily, Garnet shut the door, and averted her gaze. "Bella, for shame—! Suppose any of the servants had happened to pass while the door was open? Suppose one of the footmen had chosen to walk by?"

For Bella was sitting in the hipbath, in front of a blazing fire, the orange flames illuminating her glowing nudity. Bella threw back her head and laughed easily, as devoid of embarrassment, Garnet thought, as any heathen savage.

"There's no one to see me but you, sweet Garnet—and no one to see *your* charms but *me* . . . So waste no more time, and unveil those beauties you have been hiding for so long."

Flushed—not only from the warmth of the fire—Garnet slowly obeyed, feeling a little self-conscious, and aware of Bella's inquisitive regard. In her turn, she found her own glance sliding over her cousin's glorious nakedness, shining and shameless.

"Surely there's not room for two in that small tub," she said at last, as she stepped out of her petticoat and began to unlace her chemise.

"Well—no, perhaps you're right . . . Heigh-ho!"

With a small splash of soapy water, Bella stood up and emerged from the bath in all her loveliness.

There was a wide mirror on the wall beside them, and Garnet found herself face to face with a startling picture— a study of the female form such as a great painter might have envied . . . Herself, now half-undressed, in nothing but a pair of drawers and the unfastened chemise with her ripely-curving breasts completely exposed; and at her side, Bella's wanton display of physical perfection, with two pert nipples that seemed almost brown compared to Garnet's own coral-pink aureoles.

"Let me help you, my dearest," said Bella softly, her breath stirring the curls over Garnet's ear—and then she slid her hands into the top of her cousin's one remaining garment, pushed down and down—revealing the most private secrets of her femininity.

Garnet wanted to tear her glance away, but stood as if mesmerized by the spectacle in the mirror, at the sight of Bella's fingertips relentlessly exposing her whole body, inch by inch.

When she was quite bare, she turned away, her cheeks flaming, and said: "Now I shall bathe . . . Excuse me—"

She took Bella's place in the warm water, trying to shield herself as best she could from her cousin's unwavering gaze.

When she had lathered her breasts and rinsed them again, she knew she would have to raise herself up from the tub to complete her toilet, and contrived to turn away as she did so, presenting her back toward Bella.

"That's right, lovey," cooed Bella, suddenly close behind her. "Stay just like that—and let me soap your pretty shoulders for you."

And although Garnet protested that she could manage perfectly well by herself, she felt Bella's hands on her shoulder-blades, slippery and smooth as silk—and then the hands crept in slow circles even lower down, and down, to her trim waist . . . and below, to the swelling softness of her hips . . .

"No, Bella—don't—pray give me the soap, and let me—" Her voice faltered; she could not speak.

"Let you do what, dearest?" Bella's voice was barely a whisper now, and so close that Garnet could feel her warm breath upon her back. "No—do but allow me to perform this service for you . . . For we are almost like two sisters, are we not? And I am sure we share the same feelings— the same pleasures . . . The same satisfaction . . . "

Garnet knew she should have broken loose, or cried out, or forced her cousin to stop—but somehow she felt powerless under the hypnotic stroking of those skillful, tantalizing fingers . . . She felt a hand slip gently in between her thighs and begin a steady, insistent caress that took her breath away. She could feel a pulse beating in her head, and the regular lapping of the perfumed water and the insidious rhythm of flesh against flesh; and she felt a hot spasm of joy sweeping through her like a floodtide . . .

Then, suddenly, the spell was broken as something reminded her all in a moment of the noise of the adder just before it struck, slithering in Edmund's jacket . . . And the vision in her mind's eye of the green snake somehow recalled her to herself.

"Stop! Please, Bella . . . We must stop!"

As she spoke she lifted herself higher still, and in one movement stepped out of the tub, sending yet another little wave of soapsuds over the rim of the bath. But the voluptuous mood was shattered, and she was herself again.

She could not look at her cousin, but toweled herself dry, and scrambled into her clothes as quickly as possible.

Bella also seemed to recognize that she had trespassed too far on their sisterly familiarity, and did not refer to the incident again as they proceeded to make themselves ready for the Ball.

Only when at last their preparations were complete, and they stood once more side by side at the mirror, patting a stray curl into place or delicately rearranging the line of a necklace—their glances met in the looking glass, and an unspoken thought passed between them like a conspiracy. Bella smiled faintly and Garnet looked away.

"It's getting late. It's time for us to go . . ."

She wanted to put the whole episode from her mind, and pretend it had never happened, but all the same, as they went downstairs and walked out to the coach—as Captain Challoner cantered up the drive, preparing to escort them into town like an outrider on his skewbald stallion—as they arrived at last at the doors of the Assembly Room in Guildford's steeply-rising cobbled High Street— and as Garnet finally stepped into the dazzling fairytale world of the Ball, which seemed to be lit by a thousand flickering tapers, and stirred by the merry music of two score fiddlers—she could still feel the restless fever in her loins and the fire in her blood.

The whole evening was intoxicating enough in itself, but with the added excitement of that strangely enticing folly so fresh in her mind, she felt light-headed and completely carefree.

Edmund led her onto the floor for the first quadrille, and soon she was whirling rapturously to the music, held up by two strong arms, gazing into the face she loved so well.

As they revolved together in the patterns of the dance, she remembered their first kiss, and how the whole world had seemed then to spin crazily around, with their shared passion as its turning-point.

He looked deeply into her eyes at that moment, and she felt sure he was recalling the same occasion. "My dearest love," he murmured under his breath—for if any of their fellow dancers were to hear his words, she would be disgracefully compromised.

"My king of men—!" She responded in a louder tone, almost defiantly.

So the evening wore on; dance followed dance, and Edmund was forced by etiquette to share his attentions with Bella also, inviting her to venture onto the floor with him—an invitation which she accepted with alacrity.

Garnet watched them circle the room together, with a stab of envy in her heart. But she was certain that Edmund loved her truly, and therefore it would be foolish to give way to such petty jealousy.

As she watched, she saw a young officer in full-dress uniform come in the main door. He whipped off his shako and tucked it correctly under his arm as he looked around the busy throng, searching for someone. Garnet felt sure he was looking for Edmund, and sure enough, a moment later the young stranger stepped forward and intercepted the dancers, apologizing to Bella and drawing Edmund aside for a confidential word.

After that, everything happened very quickly; Edmund dismissed the messenger and came back with Bella on his arm, to find Garnet.

"Bad news, I fear," he began at once. "I have been recalled to barracks, and must leave you immediately."

"Oh, no—surely not—the evening is only half over—" Garnet protested.

"Duty calls, my dearest girl, and I must obey." Edmund explained as briefly as possible: "I'm told that half the regiment are being dispatched to Southampton at dawn, and there they will embark for Lisbon."

"Oh, Edmund—! You are being sent into battle?" Garnet put a hand to her heart.

"Not yet. My task is to make all the arrangements for their transportation; I shall stay behind with the remaining troops for some time longer. All the same, reinforcements are needed in Portugal, it seems, and if Lord Wellington calls us all into active service, I shall have to go and play my part in this confounded war."

He clicked his heels, and bowed to both ladies, expressing his deep regret at the unforgivable way he was deserting them.

"I trust you will find other companions to entertain you —and indeed, if my duties are completed in a reasonably short time, I hope to make amends by riding over to Markwick so that I may pay my respects to you, and assure myself you are both returned home safely, before the evening is done."

"We shall look forward to seeing you, Captain," smiled Bella, giving him her hand.

He raised it to his lips, then repeated the formal gesture with Garnet—but she felt sure with an additional, meaningful pressure in his touch, and an extra warmth in his level gaze as he said goodbye.

The rest of the evening was inevitably a disappointment. Garnet managed to find several neighbors to converse with, and Bella even captured an unattached young squire from Godalming, who bred hunters as a hobby and took a great interest in horseflesh . . . And, indeed, flesh of every sort, as she discovered when he took her into the green-bowered arbor adjacent to the main hall, which was used as a refreshment room.

When she finally returned to Garnet, Bella's hair was ever so slightly disarranged, and her eyes were shining.

But at last it was time to go home. As the two girls set off in the coach, Garnet sighed: "How unlucky that Edmund should have been recalled to duty tonight of all nights . . . I had been hoping for some conversation with him . . ."

"Conversation?" Bella threw her a teasing glance. "Time alone in the refreshment-room—that's what you had set your heart upon!"

"Well—perhaps . . . It would have been an opportunity for us to get to know one another a little better."

"Cheer up, lovey! After all, the captain *did* say he would try to rejoin us for one last nightcap before bedtime. And your father will have retired long ago, I'm sure. So we shall not be disturbed."

As they alighted from the coach at Markwick and made their way up the steps into the big house, Bella threw out a further suggestion.

"Garnet, my dear—I have had an inspiration! When the captain arrives, why don't I tell him that he is to go to the summer-house in the garden, and you will make sure that you are there already, to meet him—so you will be certain of a little time alone together, and the evening will not have been quite lost, after all."

Garnet held her breath. "Do you mean it? Will he come and find me, do you think? Or will he perhaps disapprove of the plan? He may feel it is not quite proper, to keep a tryst with a young lady, alone, at night, in such a secluded spot?"

Bella laughed softly. "If he's half the man I take him for, he'll jump at the chance! Be off with you, and wait for him, dearest . . . And I wish you joy of your meeting."

Garnet needed no further persuasion, and sped off into the darkness, making for the old summer-house which stood alone at the very farthest corner of the gardens.

Once she was safely out of the way, Bella turned to Charles the butler, who had come out by the main double doors at the top of the steps, to greet their return.

"Charles . . . I am going up to my room to refresh myself—and then I shall repair to the drawing-room." Clipped and businesslike, she gave him his instructions. "When Captain Challoner arrives, you may tell him that Miss Garnet and I both await him there . . . Do you understand?"

"Very good, miss."

The butler bowed and stood aside to let her enter the house, and the coach was dismissed to the stables. The groom who had been standing patiently, holding the horses' heads, watched it go—and stood lost in thought, his mind in turmoil.

Jem Bolt had heard every word of Bella's double plan, and understood her deception. So this was how the toy soldier treated Miss Garnet, conniving behind her back with that other shameless hussy . . . He was determined that Garnet should know, once and for all, how she was being deceived. Forgetting all about his duties in the stables—where the horses required to be unharnessed, fed and watered, and bedded down for the night—he made his way off in the opposite direction.

It had taken Garnet longer than she thought to reach the haven of the old summer-house. The path, which seemed so straightforward by day, became tortuous and troublesome by night, and she stumbled over loose stone copings, and blundered into an ornamental urn that suddenly loomed up like a ghost from the gloom.

The grass of the lawns was wet, and she could feel damp striking through the thin silk of her dancing pumps; a careless tangle of rambling rose hooked at her dress as she passed by, and a hanging cobweb brushed against her face, making her gasp. She wrapped her velvet cloak more closely about her, and hurried on.

At last she reached her sanctuary, and pushed open the summer-house door. It was pitch dark inside, and she made her way cautiously, feeling for the two cane garden chairs that she knew she would find there. She pulled one round to face the open door, and sat down to wait.

She did not have to wait very long. At the first sound of a footfall outside she tensed expectantly, and then smiled with joy as the figure of a man, silhouetted against the night sky, filled the doorway.

"Edmund—you found me! How quick you have been."

There was no reply, but the man stepped inside the summer-house, and then with a creak of rusty hinges, the door swung shut.

Now they were in pitch darkness—together.

"Edmund, my darling . . . " she began.

Outstretched hands touched and then gripped her by the shoulders; and instantly she knew something was wrong—she smelled a man's odor, but it was not the pomade and toilet water she associated with Edmund—it was a mixture of sweat and straw and horses.

"Jem!" The cry broke from her as she felt a chill of fear.

"Aye, Miss Garnet—'tis me . . . I'm come for to tell you some news."

"Take your hands from me at once—go away—"

"Not till you've heard what I do have to say!" His hands tightened on her, and she struggled to be free.

"How dare you! The captain will be here any moment If he finds you with me, you'll be thrashed for such insolence—"

"The captain en't a-going to find me, 'cos he won't be here . . . That's what I've got for to tell you, Miss Garnet . . . He en't a-coming here—he's off with that Miss Delaney, in the drawing-room—kissing and carrying on behind your back!"

"What?" Her heart stood still. "No—no, it's not true—you're lying—"

"I'm no liar! 'Tis God's truth I'm telling you—you see now, all I've said is true, from the very beginning—you mustn't trust him—he's not the one for you . . . Forget him, Miss Garnet, and come back to Jem—I may not be a fine gentleman, but I do love you so . . . "

Anger and humiliation fought within Garnet, and she hardly knew what she was saying. From the depths of her misery, she gasped: "You're mad! I won't listen to you—I want nothing to do with you—leave me alone!"

And with that, their struggle turned into a desperate trial of strength. Her scorn only served to rouse his passion still further, and he was determined to master her. She realized too late that she had no hope of fending him off by her own efforts, and tried to plead with him.

"No—Jem—don't—please let go—don't do that, I beg of you—"

But he would not—*could* not—listen to her; his violent longing for her made him deaf to her entreaties, and as she tried to back away, he grabbed her to him, his hands clawing at her body, tearing at her clothes . . .

She fought to keep her balance, but the chair behind her was knocked sideways and she fell back, half onto the wooden floor, half pressed against the rough wall of planks.

And then, in the thick blackness that enveloped them, as Jem panted and grunted like a wild animal, she felt him catch hold of her beautiful ball-gown, tearing it from top to bottom with a rending sound that rang in her ears like a scream—

So Garnet lay there, half-naked, and completely helpless—exposed to his assault.

5

Looking to the Future

When Edmund walked into the main hall a little later, Charles the butler helped him to remove his top-coat.

"I am come to pay my respects to the young ladies," Edmund explained. "Where may I find them?"

Charles paused for the fraction of a second, then replied carefully: "Miss Delaney told me to *say* that when you arrived, they would both be waiting for you in the drawing-room, sir."

He stressed the word "say" ever so slightly, and Edmund wondered at it briefly, then brushed the thought aside and let the butler lead the way.

"Captain Challoner, miss," Charles announced him, and departed, shutting the drawing-room door discreetly.

Bella rose to her feet and stood by the fireplace with one hand outstretched—looking more radiant than ever in her cream satin ball-gown.

"Captain, dear—come and warm yourself. I declare you must be perished, 'tis a bitter chilly night outside, I'm sure."

He advanced and took her hand politely, then glanced round the room. "Is Garnet not with you, then?" he inquired.

"No—isn't it a shame? She asked me to make her apologies—she was feeling a little tired."

"Oh—I'm sorry to hear that."

"Do sit down by me, Captain—this is the most comfortable spot, I think." Bella patted a space close beside her on the elegant sofa, and Edmund took his place obediently.

"Garnet isn't at all unwell, I hope? There's nothing wrong?" he asked.

As he spoke he thought for an instant that he heard a cry—a muffled sound, from somewhere very far off . . . But it was so indistinct, he could not be sure, and decided it was some night bird outside in the trees.

A little impatiently, Bella reassured him: "No, no—not in the least—Garnet's perfectly well—don't worry about *her* . . . " She drew slightly closer on the sofa, adding: "I want to talk about *you,* Captain."

"Me?" He raised an eyebrow and noted that she was brushing her dainty fingertips ever so lightly against the gold braid on his cuff.

"But of course. Do you realize that although we've been friends for several days now, I still know so little about you . . . And I'm determined to find out more—so much more . . . "

And now her fingers accidentally touched the back of his hand, like a butterfly alighting on a leaf.

"I thought this would be an admirable opportunity for us to get to know one another rather better, Edmund . . . Oh, dear—do you mind if I call you Edmund? But it's how I always think of you—"

"You are too kind, Miss Delaney," said Edmund, with a perfunctory bow. "Tell me—when you say that this is an admirable opportunity—do you mean because we are alone and unaccompanied by Garnet for the first time?"

"Exactly! I knew you would understand me!" She gazed up into his face, dimpling prettily—and then her smile faltered as she saw the steely irony in his gaze. "Why, Edmund, what is wrong?"

"That is the very question I have been asking myself, ever since I walked into this room," he replied evenly. "You see, I find it hard to believe that Garnet would have chosen to go to bed—unless she were either ill or totally exhausted—without wishing to say goodnight to me first."

Bella tossed her head. "You must have a very high opinion of your own charms, my dear man!"

"I have a very high regard for Garnet—and I believe she has an equal regard for me. That is why I am quite sure that she could not have gone to bed without leaving me some kind of message, at least."

And as he said this, he remembered the equivocal remark that the butler had made: "Miss Delaney told me to *say* . . . they would both be in the drawing-room."

"Come, let us be quite frank—I am sure you know where she is, and I am determined to see her before I leave," he concluded.

Bella looked at him and realized she was wasting her time. To avoid any further disagreeable complications, she abandoned her little ruse, and said crossly: "Oh—well— I think she said something about going for a walk in the garden."

"In the *garden?* At this time of night?"

"Perhaps she felt like a little fresh air—she may have had a slight headache—"

"And you told me a moment ago it was bitterly cold out there . . . Miss Delaney, I insist on the truth . . . *What has happened to her?*"

The answer to this question—had they but known it— would have appalled them both; even Bella could not have wished such a fate for her young rival.

Inside the summer-house, in total blackness, Garnet fought like a wild cat to defend herself against Jem's attack—but she knew all the time that she could not hope to outmatch his brutal strength. Her beautiful new gown was ripped completely open, and as she struggled desperately, pinned down by the weight of his body, she could feel him clawing at her chemise and petticoat, and heard the sound of fabric being torn apart. She felt his coarse woollen breeches against her own naked thighs, and—as they wrestled together in a horrifying intimacy, she was aware of those breeches being pushed roughly down, and the feel of his hot, sweating thighs—hairy and powerfully muscled, like the flanks of a stallion—pressed against her own flesh—pushing and pounding, and forcing her legs apart.

She had tried to scream for help once, and had been rewarded by the flat of a heavy hand upon her mouth, almost stifling her. Now they threshed about on the hard wooden floor, in darkness and silence—a silence broken only by Jem's lustful panting and the animal noises of his passion. It was at this moment, when all seemed lost and Garnet felt she could defend herself no longer, that she made one final attempt at retaliation.

She brought her teeth together sharply, biting as deeply as she could into the hand on her mouth, and was immediately grateful to feel him whip his hand back with a smothered exclamation of pain.

"Why—you little bitch—!" he snarled.

He would have struck her across the face, but she didn't give him the chance. Instead, she pulled one arm free and attacked again, the heel of her hand under his jaw pushing upward and backward with every ounce of force left in her. At the same time, quite instinctively, she brought up her knee sharply into his groin, and as he staggered back, groaning, she reinforced the assault with a well-placed kick, digging the toe of her shoe into the most exposed position of his anatomy.

With a cry that blended both anguish and betrayal, he

sank to his knees, clutching himself and gulping for breath.

"Just you wait—" he blurted out between spasms. "I'll kill you for that—kill you—"

She scrambled to her feet, preparing to fight for her life, wondering how to get past him to the door, with not a glimmer of light to guide her.

And then they both heard, from a little way off, a man's voice.

"Garnet! . . . Garnet, my dear—where are you?"

As Jem froze in alarm, Garnet took a deep breath. "Here, Edmund!" she shouted, as loudly as she could, her voice sounding overpowering in the little summer-house.

That was the end as far as Jem was concerned. He stumbled across to the door, seized it and flung it wide —then escaped into the night and was gone.

"Where, my dear? I can't see you—" Edmund was nearer now.

"In the summer-house," she called back.

Swiftly she took stock of the situation, and tried to think what she should do. To tell the truth would mean endless trouble and embarrassment. Jem would be caught and punished—she knew that her father would insist upon his being sent before a magistrate and sentenced with all the rigor of the law; life imprisonment—or deportation to the criminal colony of Australia—or perhaps—she was uncertain of the exact penalty—this would be a hanging matter . . . Although she had no desire to excuse or protect Jem, her whole being still recoiled from this thought; she was determined to avoid such a course of action at all costs.

So when Edmund at last walked into the summer-house, she fell into his arms in a storm of tears, and in answer to his questions, only replied, sobbing, "I got lost —in the dark . . . I fell down some steps—I'm hurt and bruised—and—oh, Edmund, my new dress is badly torn —I tumbled into some briars . . . You must not look at me . . ."

He soothed her as if she were a hurt infant, putting his arms around her, telling her not to cry, everything would be all right now . . . He helped her to wrap herself up tightly in her cloak, which covered her almost completely from neck to toe, then smoothed back her tangled hair from her brow and dried her tears with his own handkerchief.

"Poor love . . . what a woebegone little face—what a sorry sight indeed . . . "

"I beg you—don't look at me—I cannot bear for you to see me so," she pleaded, but he reassured her.

"My dearest girl—you still look bewitching to me, no matter how disheveled you may be . . . In fact—I love you all the more when you are like this!"

His consoling caresses turned into a more ardent embrace, as if to prove the point. His brotherly kisses on her tear-stained cheeks were replaced by a very different salutation, and he pressed his mouth to hers impulsively. She felt his body suddenly strain against her, and his lips open upon her mouth; once again, the tip of his tongue was honey-sweet and she clung to him eagerly, trying to drown her nightmare fears in the glorious ecstasy of the moment. It was like victory after battle; like sunshine after storm . . . Her own true love at last.

When her tears subsided, he said he would take her back to the house. Again she begged him not to let anyone look at her in her present plight, and they made their way round by the outbuildings at the back, then in through a side door, up the servants' stairs.

No one was about, and she led him to her bedroom, then said: "Edmund . . . Give me a few moments to make myself presentable, and then come in and say goodnight to me . . . And thank you—with all my heart."

"Thank me? For what? For nothing!" he protested.

"For being there—when I needed you," she said with a tiny ghost of a smile, and disappeared.

He waited patiently in the corridor for several minutes,

and at last she opened the door again and said: "You may come in now."

She was in her nightdress, demurely covered by the *robe-de-chambre* that he had seen before; her face and hands were spotless—he caught the perfume of her scented soap as she passed him—and her hair was neat and tidy. She was the young Lady of Markwick Hall again.

But, as she turned to him, she caught his hands and said: "Oh, Edmund—what would I have done without you?"

She let herself slip into his comfortable embrace, and he could feel her heart still beating wildly against his chest. Restored to herself to all outward appearances, underneath her composure he could sense that she was still a frightened, and frenzied, child—and he felt a deep compassion for her.

"My dear Garnet . . . It is high time that I should come to your aid at last—for you have rescued me twice already!" He smiled gently.

She looked up into his face, her eyes dark and lustrous with love, and said: "You really *are*—my king of men . . . "

"And you are my little princess . . . Who will one day become my queen," he responded, carrying on this pretty conceit.

"Your queen? Edmund—do you mean it?"

He looked at her and remembered the first time he had kissed her—by the side of the pond, beneath the alder tree . . . And he remembered what had just passed between them, in the darkened summer-house—and he made up his mind.

"Yes . . . I mean it, my love . . . I mean you to become my wife . . . If you will have me?"

"Oh, yes, Edmund—yes, *yes!*" She hugged him and kissed him in sudden rapture. It was like the happy ending to a fairytale.

But kissing and caressing soon gave way to plans and discussions; they sat side by side on the edge of the bed, and—as before—Edmund behaved with complete propriety, like the perfect gentleman he so evidently was. He told her that they must do everything in accordance with the strictest traditions of etiquette, and promised that he would announce his intention to Sir George as soon as possible the following morning, and ask him formally for his daughter's hand in marriage.

The interview duly took place at noon in the library, on Sunday morning after church; and over a fine glass of very dry sherry, Edmund put his proposal before the squire of Markwick Hall.

Sir George, of course, had seen this coming, and was not unprepared. He asked a good many pertinent questions about Edmund's family situation and his expectations, and explained that, although he would naturally make a very fair dowry over to Garnet upon her marriage, she would not benefit from the Markwick estate at Sir George's death, since the entire property was entailed upon her brother, as the sole male heir.

Whether Edmund had been expecting this disclosure or not, he gave no sign of being discomfited by it, but inclined his head civilly, and merely said: "Quite so . . . In any case, sir, I should think poorly of myself if I did not intend to support my wife through my own abilities."

"As a serving officer in the Dragoons?" Sir George cocked an eye at the young man. "Unless things have changed greatly since my day you won't get very rich on a captaincy, I suspect, heh?"

"I have ambitions, sir, to rise to a higher degree than captain before long," said Edmund, confidently. "And also—if the Third Dragoons are all to be posted to the Peninsula, as I foresee—I shall hope to distinguish myself in action, and perhaps bring off some prize money as a consequence."

Sir George's expression grew more serious, and he said, "That's another matter . . . If you are sent into battle, there's no escaping the fact that you will be running some risk of danger to life and limb. I would be sorry for

Garnet to become both wife and widow within a short time—as I am sure you will understand."

Edmund's lips curved slightly. "I should indeed be more than sorry for such an eventuality, sir . . . And I shall take all possible care that it should not take place!"

"Hey, what? Oh yes, yes, indeed, I follow your drift, sir," Sir George sniffed and humphed with slight embarrassment. "But what I mean to say is this: For the girl's sake I feel you would do well to settle for a long engagement. It would be a mistake to try and rush into marriage too precipitately . . . You must look to the future."

And so it was at last agreed. Looking to the future, Edmund and Garnet would be prudent, and wait patiently for their wedding date at such time as the war should be over, or at least Edmund might be safely returned to England and his affianced bride.

The announcement was made to the rest of the family over lunch, and was received with something a little less than rapturous acclaim. Gerard mumbled his congratulations to Edmund, shook hands with his brother-in-law-to-be, and kissed his sister on the forehead.

Bella smiled widely but unconvincingly, expressed herself as completely delighted with the news, embraced her cousin briefly, gave the captain her hand to kiss, and then declared that she had a touch of the vapors and would not be able to eat another mouthful. She retired from the room in search of a restful couch and some spirits of camphor.

When lunch was over, the little party dispersed; Sir George for his afternoon nap, and Gerard to wander off with a book, to amuse himself in his accustomed solitude. Edmund and Garnet went walking in the garden, admiring the leaves of the trees in the spinney that were now turning to gold as autumn crept upon them, and making plans for their future life together.

"It is tedious for us to have to wait, I agree," Edmund was saying, "but I have no doubt your father is very wise. I shall feel more secure if I know that I can present myself to you as a dutiful husband, safe home from battle, with a full complement of arms and legs!"

"Oh, don't say such things, dearest!" Garnet put her hand to her heart. "You make my blood run cold—I won't listen to you—"

Then she broke off, hearing hurried footsteps pursuing them along the graveled path. They turned to find the stout figure of the housekeeper, Mrs. Bolt, coming after them. Instantly, Garnet thought of Jem and was on guard, sensing some new catastrophe.

"What is it, Mrs. Bolt? Did you want me?"

"Yes, miss—please, miss . . . Could I have a word with you—in private?" The good lady was a little out of breath, and glanced sideways at Edmund, her cheeks suffused with color. "Begging your pardon, Captain Challoner, sir . . . "

"Of course—you have household matters to discuss, I'm sure." Edmund clicked his heels and stepped back smartly. "I will see you later, Garnet, when it is convenient to you . . . At your service, ma'am."

He sketched a bow to Mrs. Bolt, and strode off. The housekeeper watched him go, then asked Garnet: "Is it true, miss—what Charles is saying? That you and the captain are engaged to be wed?"

"Yes, it is true . . . And we are both very happy, Mrs. Bolt."

"I'm glad to hear it, I'm sure . . . " She folded her hands, then continued: "But 'tis not about the captain I came to ask you . . . It's my Jem."

Garnet hesitated a split second too long, before asking, "Your son—? What about him?"

"He's gone, miss. And I'm at my wit's end, as God's my judge . . . I don't know what to do, or where to turn."

"Gone? What do you mean—gone where?"

"I wish I knew. He en't been seen nowhere, not since last night. After you and the young lady came home from the Ball, he was supposed to see to the coach horses—but he didn't . . . He left them to the other stable lads, and

88

he took himself off—nobody knows where . . . That's the last any of us have seen of him, and I'm that worried . . . "

"I see. I'm sorry to hear it, of course, but—why do you come to me?"

"I thought as how you might be able to tell me some news of him, miss. 'Cos I'm quite sure he wouldn't never go off without seeing you first. He didn't say goodbye to me—his own mother—but I feel certain he'd want to take his leave of *you*, miss . . . He do think the world of you, I know that."

Garnet bit her lip, then said, as steadily as she could: "Yes, of course, I—we have known each other since we were children . . . Though our lives have taken different directions since those days."

Mrs. Bolt was not to be put off. She clutched at Garnet's hand, and said, "For pity's sake, miss—tell me true —have you seen him since last night? Do you know where he is?"

Garnet replied carefully, "I'm sorry . . . I haven't seen your son since last night . . . And I don't know where he might be now . . . Have you looked in his room, above the stables?"

"No, not myself, I haven't. But the other lads took a look up there—they say there's no sign of him."

"Let us go together, and make sure. He might have left a note, or some other clue to give you an idea of his whereabouts."

They hurried together to the stable-yard, and Garnet followed the housekeeper up the ladder to the loft which served as Jem's sleeping quarters. Portly Mrs. Bolt made her way from rung to rung with some difficulty, and Garnet realized why she had not searched her son's room until now.

However, she achieved the upper floor at last, with Garnet's assistance, and sank, panting heavily, onto his rough wooden bed with its straw mattress.

Garnet looked around for signs of the runaway, but there was nothing to be found; his spare suit of breeches and jacket hung from a peg on the wall, and a work shirt lay across a three-legged stool, where he had left it. A small wooden chest contained his few possessions: a knife, a piece of twine, a kerchief, and a small stone jar that had once held strong liquor . . . But there was nothing to hint at any reason for his sudden departure.

"Seemingly he just decided to go—all in a moment, without a word," sighed Mrs. Bolt. "Heaven preserve him, wherever he may be . . ."

She looked at Garnet consideringly, then added: "Excuse me asking again, miss—but are you certain sure you don't know nothing about why he's took to his heels in this way?"

Garnet felt herself flushing and averted her face, answering one question with another: "What makes you ask such a thing?"

"Nothing . . . Except that you must have been one of the very last as ever set eyes on him, yesterday night."

Garnet tried to frame some kind of reply, but at that moment she spied something half hidden under the rough pillow at the head of the bed—the edge of a small wooden box.

"Wait—perhaps this might hold some answer—" she exclaimed, and pulled the box out, throwing open the lid.

Both women recoiled instantaneously, and Mrs. Bolt choked back a little scream. There in the box, coiled up and torpid at the start of its long winter hibernation, lay an adder, lifting its evil head lazily.

Garnet slammed the lid shut, and said quietly, "Mrs. Bolt . . . I believe that is the same snake which attacked the captain last week. At the time we all supposed it to be an accident." Their eyes met, and the older woman turned pale.

"You wouldn't tell—"

"I shall say nothing of this . . . But for your own peace of mind, I suggest you order one of the grooms to take this creature out of here, and have it destroyed."

"You really think my Jem meant harm to the captain?"

"I believe he contrived the attack—and when that failed . . . " Garnet broke off, and ended simply: "He must have been afraid of what he had done—what he tried to do . . . And so ran away. I do not think he will come back here."

Mrs. Bolt began to cry, quietly, and made her way down the ladder. They both knew that the incident was closed, and would not be referred to again.

On this same Sunday afternoon, two other small events took place, both of which were to have an indirect bearing upon Garnet's future.

After lunch, Gerard had taken himself off to the old schoolroom with his book, fairly sure that here he could spend a quiet hour or two undisturbed. But in this he was mistaken.

Not long after he had settled down with the volume of verse open in his lap, sprawled back in a wooden chair that tilted dangerously on its two back legs, and with his feet propped up on the top of a plain school desk, the door opened, and Bella walked in.

It was hard to say which of them was the more surprised. Gerard started violently, and almost overturned the chair he sat in; but Bella recovered her composure at once, and laughed: "La, Gerard, do not look so alarmed! I am not come to give you a boxing lesson!"

He stood up with grudging politeness, asking, "Did my father send you to find me?"

"No, indeed—and even if he had, I should not have known you were here . . . No, I came in by chance. I cannot settle to anything this afternoon—I don't know why . . . I have been roaming round the house, going from room to room, looking for something to amuse me . . . "

She came farther into the room, and shut the door behind her, as she continued: "And now I have found *you* . . . Shall you amuse me, cousin?"

He shrugged and mumbled something inaudible.

"What do you say? Speak up, Gerard dear, for I can't hear you when you mutter so. What is that you are reading?"

He held the book out to her, and she glanced at the title.

"The Sonnets of William Shakespeare . . . love poetry, would that be?" And as he nodded and scowled under her quizzical glance, she returned it to him, saying, "Recite some of it to me, for I demand to be entertained—and I can't abide reading myself when there's anyone else to do it for me."

She perched herself on the edge of the desk, and looked around, sniffing the dusty air.

"Pah—the room smells of chalk still, after all these years . . . I remember when you and I and Garnet had our lessons together, at these very same desks . . . How long ago it seems now! We have said goodbye to our schooldays long since!"

She swung her pretty ankles, and pulled her skirt an inch higher, as she said, "Do read to me, Gerard. Read me the most romantic verses you can find, for I feel in a susceptible mood today."

He sat on the chair again, drawing it up a little closer to the desk, then cleared his throat and began:

> Shall I compare thee to a summer's day?
> Thou art more lovely and more temperate.
> Rough winds do shake the darling buds of May,
> And—

She interrupted him gaily: "Darling buds? You must tell me, Gerard—I'm so absurdly ignorant—what are 'darling buds?' . . . Have I got any?"

She leaned forward, until her bosom was only a few inches away from his face. He gulped, and could not answer; she laughed, and said, "I believe you're as ignorant as I am . . . Well, we shall be two little innocents together, you and I. Forgive me for interrupting—begin again at the beginning."

In a husky voice, he recommenced the sonnet:

"Shall I compare thee to a summer's day?"

But that was as far as he got, for she took hold of the book and whisked it away with a playful smile.

"Now that's a question I do understand . . . But what's the answer? Shall *you* compare *me* to a summer's day, dearest Gerard?"

He reached for the book, and found himself touching her soft skin instead: the curve of her breasts springing up from the restraining seam of her bodice as if they would burst free. She did not try to deflect his hand, or draw away—but continued to smile, invitingly.

"Well, Gerard?" she whispered.

Emboldened, he heard himself replying hoarsely: "You smell like a summer's day, Bella . . . You smell like sunshine—and June roses . . . "

"Come to me, then, darling . . . " Her voice was now so soft that it was scarcely more than a breath. "Come and gather my roses—while you may . . . "

And as he stood up and moved closer, her practiced fingers set to work, unbuttoning his shirt.

An hour or two afterward, several miles away in the town of Guildford, another tête-à-tête took place, and this too began with a shirt being carefully unbuttoned.

The officer in command of the Third Dragoons—Lieutenant-Colonel, Lord Hugo Deverell—was in his quarters, in the suite of rooms adjoining the barracks. Now he stood in his bedchamber, impassive as a wooden idol, while his body-servant prepared to dress him in his regimentals for dinner in the Mess.

Lord Hugo Deverell was an extremely handsome man in middle age, with a carefully cultivated and pomaded black moustache, and two very urbane eyebrows, one of which he habitually kept lowered, to secure in place a glittering monocle. For Lord Hugo's otherwise classic features were only marred by the fact that he had a very slight cast in one eye—not pronounced enough to be called a squint, even by his enemies, of whom there were many. His eye-glass corrected and disguised this small irregularity, and in consequence the lieutenant-colonel was hardly ever to be seen without it—even when, as now, he was engaged upon his toilet.

It was his manservant, Pilling, who did all the work; undressing Lord Hugo neatly, garment by garment, then clothing him again in a frilled dress shirt, fitting in sapphire studs and links, and tying his neckcloth in one single fold, unspoiled by any crease.

Meanwhile, Lord Hugo stood totally unconcerned in his shirt-tails, and gave an audience to the young officer who had recently asked for five minutes of his valuable time . . . Captain Edmund Challoner.

"Well, Ned—what's the news? You got your troops safely off to Southampton this morning, I trust?"

"Yes, sir." Edmund stood at attention, his helmet under his arm. "All present and correct, sir."

"Good boy, good boy . . . I wonder how long it will be before Arthur sends for the rest of us to support him."

"Arthur—?" Edmund queried uncertainly.

"Arthur Wellesley . . . The Duke of Wellington, my dear Ned—surely you've heard of our gallant commander-in-chief?" Lord Hugo put a hand to his cravat, and tweaked it to a better shape.

"No, no, Pilling—an inch higher—like so . . . My God, the man's a barbarian . . . "

Now the servant produced a pair of exquisitely tailored breeches, and knelt before his master, holding the garment out like a high priest offering up a ritual sacrifice. Lord Hugo stepped into the two legs, and drew in his stomach until it was as flat as a board, as Edmund continued.

"That was really why I came to see you now, sir . . . About the matter of the rest of the regiment being sent overseas."

"Oh, yes? What about it? . . . *Heave,* Pilling—tug as

hard as you can—what's the matter with you, you numb-skull? These breeches must fit me like a second skin—without a single wrinkle!"

"Well, sir . . . " Edmund struggled on, aware that he was hardly capturing his commanding officer's full attention. "If it's agreeable to you, sir, I think—I mean I'm sure —I would like to apply for a transfer before the regiment is shipped out."

"Transfer? Deuce take it, what's the dear boy trying to tell us—eh, Pilling?" Lord Hugo eyed his reflection in the pier glass critically. "It's still not tight enough—higher, Pilling—higher!"

"I want to transfer to service in London, sir . . . With the Household Cavalry."

"Really?" Lord Hugo smiled thinly. "What's the matter, Neddy? Taking fright at the imminent prospect of shot and shell—is that your trouble? Feeling a little windy, dear boy?"

Edmund clenched his fists and squared his shoulders.

"I think you know me well enough by now, sir, not to believe that. I would be happy to risk any danger for my king and country—but at this particular time, I have personal reasons for wishing to remain in England."

"Personal reasons, indeed? And what might those be, pray?"

Lord Hugo lifted his arms and let Pilling fasten a scarlet sash about his waist, as Edmund replied: "I propose to take a certain young lady as my wife, sir . . . I desire to be married."

Now he had Lord Hugo's undivided attention indeed. The officer spun round on his heel, his monocle dropping from his eye and swinging on its ribbon of watered silk.

"The devil you do!" He screwed the glass back into his eye socket hastily. "Married, you say? When? Where? . . . *Who?*"

Garnet lay in her bed, and watched the candle beside her burning low. She reflected on the events of the past two days, and stretched out under the sheets like a drowsy kitten finishing a saucer of cream, almost purring with satisfaction.

The Ball . . . The dancing and the music, the intoxicating rhythm that carried her away in Edmund's arms . . . And afterward—the summer-house—Jem Bolt—*No* . . . She reprimanded herself silently. She would not think about Jem—or the snake. Only think of the good things that had happened . . . Edmund's care and kindness, and the real warmth in his embrace last night . . . His proposal, and her father's agreement to the match . . . And now Edmund was trying to speed things along by obtaining a transfer to another regiment, so he might not be sent abroad, and they could be married all the sooner. She wriggled with happiness at the thought, and burrowed deeper into her pillow.

The nightlight nodded and danced, then spurted once or twice, and fizzed out into a little pool of wax, leaving the room in a deep shadow. But Garnet did not notice, for she was already asleep, and far, far away.

She dreamed of Edmund—inevitably, for he figured large in all her thoughts now, waking or sleeping.

She seemed to be by his side, in the stables . . . As they were on that day when they came back from their ride together—the day when the snake—when Jem—

But she must not think about that.

She tried to soothe herself with the presence of Edmund, his consoling arms, his tender embrace . . . She reached out for him—but where was he? And what was happening to the stables?

Suddenly the building she was in seemed much larger: a vast hall, stretching away into darkness, like some ancient castle, full of lofty space and echoes. And there were sounds she could not understand—a thunderous clangor of metal striking against metal—and a hissing . . . A hissing sound, like a snake, but ten times louder—and more violent . . .

Suddenly she was frightened of what she was about to see.

She turned to run away, and found herself almost blinded by a brilliant glow of light—a curtain of fire, leaping flames that seemed to reach up to the farthest corners of the roof high above . . . And as the noise increased, she saw with a shock of terror a monstrous shape silhouetted against the flames—

It was a centaur, rearing up: two hooves on the ground and two forelegs pounding the air—and from the horse-like body rose the torso of a man, his naked shoulders glistening in the dazzle and heat of the fire . . . Half-man, half-beast. And then he turned, and saw her. And she saw his face.

It was the face of someone she had never seen before, she was certain of that. The face of a god—or of a devil—with a scar above his left temple, and piercing eyes that seemed to look straight through her . . . Palest blue eyes, like crystals of ice.

Then the stranger spoke, and asked her one question. "Do you know who I am?"

She tried to answer, she struggled, and gasped for breath, the dream vanished, and she found herself lying in the darkness again, in her own little bed—her body shaking all over.

His voice still rang in her ears:

"Do you know who I am?"

She knew nothing . . . Except that she would never forget him—whoever it might be.

She would know him for the rest of her life.

6

A Runaway Match

Lord Hugo Deverell closed one eye, squinted through his shining monocle along the sights of the pistol, and took careful aim. He squeezed the trigger, so gently that the barrel never wavered by a hair's breadth, and—*Bang!*

The report of the shot rang deafeningly in Edmund's ears.

"Well, Ned? What did I score that time?" asked His Lordship.

"I think it's a bull's-eye again, sir. It's hard to be sure from this distance."

"I hope your judgment in marksmanship is more ac-curate than your judgment in matrimony," replied Lord Hugo, with silky courtesy. "Pilling, send a body to fetch back the target, so we may examine it."

His manservant stood by to reload. He was in charge of ammunition, and guarded an open case of pistols; one, the twin of that which Lord Hugo was now holding, lay in a velvet rest, awaiting its trial. Now Pilling jerked his head at a private soldier who waited nearby, in attendance on the Lieutenant-Colonel.

"Go on, you heard what His Lordship said—double!"

"And bring the target back inside one minute, dear lad —or the next bullet will be in the seat of your breeches," added Lord Hugo, with a winning smile.

The wretched orderly broke into a run and set off at top speed.

Pistol practice—with the best pair of dueling pistols that money could buy—was one of Lord Hugo's favorite pastimes; another was the gentle sport of striking terror into the hearts of all those unfortunate enough to serve under him. Upon this golden October morning, His Lordship was enjoying himself mightily, in exercising both these diversions at once.

Lord Hugo, with Pilling on one side of him, and Edmund at the other, stood and surveyed the shooting-range which had been set up for this especial purpose within the barracks' enclosure. He sniffed the crisp autumn air appreciatively, and examined his watch, keeping one eye on the scurrying figure in the distance.

"Half a minute to go," he said, raising his voice just sufficiently for the orderly to hear him. "I wonder—will he manage it in time?"

"Sir—I must speak to you in private," Edmund burst out. He had been awaiting the opportunity of this interview for some time, and was getting tired of the continual interruptions.

"You can speak freely in front of Pilling, you know that surely, my dear? He is the soul of discretion, and we may trust him with any little secret, eh, Pilling?"

Pilling blinked by way of response, but otherwise gave no sign of having heard, gazing stonily ahead of him, his lugubrious moustache drooping in its usual manner.

"Of course we may. Do continue, dear Ned. What is

troubling you?" Lord Hugo glanced at his watch again. "Three seconds left . . ."

"You referred to my judgment in matrimony just now—" Edmund was unable to finish the sentence.

Bang!

As the unfortunate orderly returned, panting and clutching the target-card, Lord Hugo Deverell fired a shot directly towards him. Certainly, he aimed deliberately high, and the bullet passed over the man's head without doing any damage, but the soldier's face was white and there were beads of sweat along his brow and upper lip as he halted, and stood to attention.

"*Next* time, my lad, it will be a different sort of bull's-eye—in that round little cherry-bum of yours. Very well, return to your post."

The lieutenant-colonel dismissed the terrified soldier, and as the man turned about, tapped him lightly on the rear with the muzzle of the pistol.

Edmund took a deep breath, and muttered, half-audibly, "Sometimes I think you take pleasure in tormenting others."

"Quite so, it's good for 'em, keeps the bodies on the alert!" Lord Hugo smiled modestly, as if he had just been paid a great compliment. "Why, I declare you were right. There is the bullet hole—smack through the very center of the target. You may congratulate me, Ned!"

"Yes, sir. As I was saying, about my forthcoming marriage, I would be glad to know the date of my transfer to London, so that I may make all the necessary arrangements—"

"Why in God's name do you want to rush into wedlock in this way?" asked the senior officer, replacing the pistol he had fired in its case, and taking up the other. "You are more precipitate than the Gadarene swine, intent on self-destruction."

"Surely, sir, you understand my feelings—I love Miss Mallory and I wish to marry her at the earliest possible moment. That's not unreasonable, I think?"

"Unreasonable? Indeed it is—I'd call it the height of insanity myself. Here, dear Ned, take this pistol and try your skill upon the new target. Let us see if you can match me as a marksman."

Pilling loaded the weapon, and at the far end of the range, a fresh target was set up, as Edmund tried to concentrate on the topic under discussion.

"We all know you're a dedicated bachelor, sir, but those of us with a different ambition—"

"Careful, Neddy." Lord Hugo screwed his eyeglass more firmly into place, and the gaze which he fixed upon Edmund was very chilly indeed. "Do not presume upon my good nature too far. As it happens, I have your own best interests at heart. For your dear sake, I have even put myself to the trouble of making a few discreet inquiries about this young woman whom you propose to pleasure."

"Sir—"

Edmund would have protested, but Lord Hugo continued: "Perhaps you don't know it, but the girl has no prospects. The family's wealthy enough, but there's a younger son, I hear, who is to be the sole heir. When old Mallory snuffs it, she won't get a brass farthing. Surely that must give you pause for reflection?"

"No, indeed!" Edmund accepted the pistol Pilling offered him, and squared his shoulders. "Miss Mallory's fortune—or the lack of one—is a matter of complete indifference to me."

He took aim, getting both fore and back sights in line with the target.

"Then you're a bigger fool than I took you for. Take the girl if you've a mind to, and then ride away. Fornicate—and forget! That's the Army motto!"

Forget her? Forget Garnet?

Edmund's hand trembled as he pulled the trigger, and the pistol kicked. The bullet clipped the top corner of the card—far from the concentric rings of the target.

Lord Hugo chuckled. "You see, my dear? Your aim is faulty—very faulty indeed."

As Edmund thought of Garnet, and tried to control his anger and humiliation, so Garnet thought of him, and made plans for their future.

She was alone this morning for Sir George had complained at breakfast of a recurrence of his rheumatism.

"This sudden change in the weather brings it on, you know—there's frost about at night, and I always get the first signs of it in my leg," the old gentleman grumbled, pushing aside his teacup. "No, I'll take no more tay. Where's the housekeeper? Where's Mrs. Bolt? She's the only one who can relieve the pain. Send her up to my room, Gerard. Tell her my bad leg is troubling me—ask her to bring the special salve."

He hobbled from the breakfast table, leaning heavily upon his stick.

Garnet, Gerard and Bella exchanged glances.

"Poor Uncle George, he is a martyr to the rheumaticks," said Bella. "We must all feel grateful to the Almighty that he has spared us an awful affliction. Just think, Gerard, how disagreeable it would be, if we were not able to use our arms and legs . . ."

Gerard bit his lip, and looked down at his lap, making a great business of folding his table napkin.

"And out of doors it looks to be such a sweet day!" Bella chattered on gaily. "Well, I shall make use of *my* limbs, anyway, and take a turn in the garden. Will you accompany me, dearest Garnet?"

"I would do so gladly, Bella," Garnet replied, "but I have some letters to write—and—other tasks to occupy me in my room."

"Then I must not try to distract you from your duties. Gerard, *you* shall be my companion. We will take a walk together, and make the best of the sunshine while we can, for I fear there will not be much more of it. What was it the poet said? 'Gather ye rosebuds while ye may'?"

Gerard pushed back his chair and stood up, trying not to blush. "Yes, Cousin Bella; it is from a verse by Robert Herrick."

"There now! I declare you must be a most excellent pupil, because you seem to remember every little thing that you have been taught. Come with me, Gerard, and keep me entertained."

So they went out into the October sunlight, and Garnet made her way to her room. She had a letter to write indeed—for scarcely a day passed when she did not dash off a few fervent lines to Edmund, sending them to be delivered at the barracks by any of the servants who had errands in Guildford. True, on most days Edmund himself rode out to Rosewood to visit her, but that made no difference. Even if they were only apart for a few hours, Garnet found she longed to be with her love, and the act of writing to him was in some way a tiny link to bind them closer. She thought of their wedding-day—however near or far that might be—and the unimaginable delight of sharing her whole life with him thereafter, of falling asleep at night in his arms and waking each morning to find him still there, beside her.

She had another task today, of a more practical nature: going through her meager wardrobe and deciding what clothes she possessed that were good enough to take with her when she set up her new life in London as Mrs. Edmund Challoner. There were pitifully few, and she realized that most of her gowns had better be handed down to the maids: she would need to buy some new dresses, fine enough for a captain's wife.

But Edmund was not over-wealthy; where was the money to come from?

She remembered the one real heirloom she possessed, and smiled again. Opening her dressing-table drawer, she took out the jewel-case that had once belonged to Lady Mallory, and lifted the lid.

Meanwhile, Bella and Gerard were enjoying their promenade in the garden.

"Do you think it will be warm enough for us to sit down and admire the view?" Bella asked. "For although the sun is bright, there is a wicked little breeze, I fear."

"We have the carriage-rug," Gerard reminded her; he carried it folded across his arm, secretly wondering why she had asked him to bring it with him. Did she plan to sit upon the rug on a rustic bench? Or even, he hoped, to recline upon it, on a grassy bank, safely out of the way of any prying eyes?

Since their one-and-only encounter in the schoolroom, which had taken him very much by surprise, they had never had an opportunity to be alone together again, and he was very excited now by her proximity as they strolled along the narrow garden paths, side by side. She had crooked her arm through his, and now he contrived to give her hand a gentle squeeze—but she did not respond in any way, and merely continued talking.

"Yes, yes, if it grows too bleak, we shall be glad of the rug, I'm sure. But I am so delighted we braved the climate and came out here—what a really beautiful morning it has turned out to be, cousin. Ah, we have reached the end of the yew hedge; which way shall we go now?"

At the bottom of the formal garden, the gravel path stopped at an archway cut in the tall hedge, and in the arch was a wooden gate.

"Why don't we go through into the orchard?" Bella continued, and she stood back, to let him open the gate.

"Of course, if you wish it," he replied, and put his hand on the latch.

At once she put her hand out also, and her fingers closed over his. "You are a dear boy," she said softly, and now there was no mistaking the pressure that answered his own.

His heart leaped, and his loins tensed immediately.

She smiled into his eyes, and moved on, through the hedge and into the orchard. He followed eagerly.

"Oh, how sad, the summer is really over now. Just look at the fruit trees." Bella surveyed the prospect before them.

Certainly the autumn winds had lain waste the rows of trim apples, pears and plums. Most of the leaves had fallen already, and such as were still clinging bravely to the branches were yellow or russet-red. The plums were long since finished, and the few remaining pears looked hard and uninviting, left to drop and rot away in the long grass. One or two apples remained, up high where the farm boys had not been able to reach, or had not bothered to climb.

"Why, there's one apple they overlooked—a beauty!" exclaimed Bella, pointing.

Sure enough, there it was: round, ripe and luscious—with a wine-red skin that tempted you to sink your teeth into the firm, sweet flesh.

Eve, in the person of Bella, turned to Gerard-Adam, and asked, "Well? Shall we?"

The problem was how to get the apple from the tree, for it was too far up to reach from the ground. Gerard looked about and spied a ladder, half hidden under the hedge, and dragged it out. He rather enjoyed displaying his strength to his pretty cousin as he swung the ladder up into position, erect against a tree.

"I'll fetch it for you—" he began.

"No, let me. I want to try," said Bella. "You shall stay at the bottom and hold the ladder steady."

He did as he was told, and standing below the ladder he looked up as she climbed, rung by rung, up into the tree. His head swam dizzily as she ascended; for once she was half way up, he found he was immediately below her, with a clear, uninterrupted view of her legs, as they vanished into the mysterious shadowy depths of her long skirt.

Greatly daring, he let one hand leave the side of the ladder, and slid it up, gently, but determinedly, onto her calf, and still further up to her knee . . . And above her knee . . . Would she stop him, or reprimand him?

Somewhere high up in the tree, Bella's voice floated down as if she were a million miles away: "I've almost got there now. I think if I try a little harder, if I go just a little bit higher, I shall manage it."

She sounded calm and unruffled, as if totally unaware of Gerard's exploring hand beneath her dress.

He touched lace—a lace frill round the edge of her drawers—and beneath the frill, her warm, satin-smooth skin. He probed further, and—

"There! *That's* got it!" she said triumphantly, and moved swiftly, so that he was taken off guard, and fumbled helplessly, closing his fingers upon a handful of silk, and nothing else.

"Now be a good boy, and behave yourself, there's a love," she said, and extricated herself deftly from his clumsy grasp as she stepped down the ladder.

"Here, Gerard, you shall have first bite, though heaven knows you don't deserve it."

She softened the reproof with a smile, and tossed the rosy red apple into his hands, as she jumped to the ground.

"Oh, Bella, I do love you," he blurted out.

"Love? What nonsense—you don't understand what love is, you're far too young," she laughed. "Now, let us find somewhere to sit comfortably and eat the delicious apple, both of us taking it in turns, bite for bite."

At the other side of the apple trees was a wooden bench, left behind when the apple-pickers had completed their harvest, still stacked with empty fruit boxes. Obediently, Gerard cleared the boxes from the bench, dusted the top of it with his kerchief, and made a space for her.

She beckoned him. "Come, sit beside me, and we'd best wrap the carriage rug about our legs, for fear we should catch cold—for the sun is going in behind those nasty clouds."

So it was arranged; they sat side by side—Gerard could feel the warmth of her body against him, her thigh pressed close to his—and Bella carefully tucked the rug around so they were cocooned together, as if they shared a double bed.

They did not talk much as they passed the apple back and forth, each one taking a bite until at last they got down to the core. Then Bella looked at the last spindly remainder of the apple and sighed, "All gone, there's no more left." She tossed the apple core over her shoulder, and leaned against Gerard. "You know, I really should be very cross with you, by rights."

"What for? Having the last bite of the apple?"

"You *know* what for. For your dreadful impudence in taking advantage of my position when I was climbing the ladder. You deserve to be scolded for such rude behavior!"

He hung his head. "I thought—I hoped—you would not mind. You let me, the other day—"

"Oh, the other day! Oh, yes, I felt sure we would hear about the 'other day' before long! And I declare it's unkind of you to remind me of what happened in the schoolroom. I was lonely and unhappy, and I let you take outrageous liberties, which a real gentleman would never have referred to again."

"You didn't *seem* so very unhappy, at the time," Gerard tried to defend himself.

She shivered as if she were suddenly cold, and plunged her hands deep under the rug for extra warmth.

"If only you knew. I needed comfort and sympathy—for my heart was breaking . . . And as to what happened between us—I must ask you to put it out of your mind entirely; pretend it never took place at all."

Gerard was bewildered. "Your heart—breaking? I don't understand."

"Then I must tell you, I suppose." She made a little sound that might have been a sob and pressed still closer to him. It was getting very warm indeed now, beneath the carriage rug.

"The reason that I came on a visit to England at all, was to try and recover from a tragic experience I had recently suffered, at home in County Cork. I won't go into details, but there's a certain Mr. O'Brian—with the looks of a saint and the black heart of a devil. I trusted him and he—he betrayed me . . . Need I say more?"

"Please do." Gerard felt even more bewildered, for now he was very aware of Bella's soft hands upon his thigh, gently stroking him as she continued:

"I cannot bear to recount the whole dreadful history; suffice it to say, when Mr. O'Brian rode out of my life, I had only two choices open to me: to bury my shame by going on a long visit to distant friends and relations, or to enter a nunnery and take the veil. Can you picture me, dear Gerard, in a nunnery?"

Since, at that moment, her hand had slid on to the front of his breeches, and was now intent upon unfastening them, Gerard replied with truth that he could not quite imagine Bella within the walls of a convent.

"But it was true, love, you understand; that is why I let him deceive me so; I gave myself to him completely in my girlish innocence. I loved him with a pure and perfect love, plague take this wretched button, I can't undo it, you'll have to help me . . . What was I saying? Oh, yes—a pure and perfect love—oh, Gerard. Oh, *Gerard*," she gave a little moan. "I had no idea you were so *passionate* . . . "

She put her arms round him, and turned him to face her. As they clung together, the rug threatened to break loose and slip away—

And it was at this slightly unfortunate moment that Garnet came through the archway of the yew hedge, in search of them. "I've been looking everywhere in the gardens, but—oh, I beg your pardon!"

She stood transfixed as Bella and Gerard both clutched desperately at the carriage rug and pulled it up to their chins.

"Please—don't be embarrassed," Bella contrived to smile. "We were just—playing a rather childish game. Take no notice."

Garnet hesitated, and said uncertainly, "I had not realized. I did not mean to intrude—"

"No intrusion at all, my dear," Bella assured her, still

rather out of breath. "We are glad of your company, aren't we, Gerard? I'm delighted that you have finished your morning's work so quickly."

"It didn't take as long as I thought. Then I remembered what you said, about making the best of the sunshine while it lasts; so here I am."

She would not look at them; aware, from the corner of her eye, that her brother was still engaged in Herculean struggles beneath the cover of the rug.

"Yes, what a good idea. You must come here and sit with us. Gerard, stand up and let your sister—" Bella broke off, correcting herself quickly. "No, on second thoughts, perhaps not . . . Now I come to think of it, the sun has gone in, and it looks as if we may have rain before long."

"Oh dear, I fear you may be right. Perhaps we had all better go indoors after all. Gerard?"

Gerard, who had still not succeeded in adjusting his garments completely, turned brick red, and mumbled, "You go on without me, I'll stay here—for a while. I'm enjoying the fresh air."

"In the *rain*?" Garnet began, but then, guessing something of the cause of his confusion, she too began to blush, and turned away, saying, "Whatever you wish, of course. I won't interrupt you any longer—excuse me . . . "

She beat a hasty retreat from the orchard and as she fled, she heard the unmistakable note of Bella's teasing laughter following her.

As she made her way down the gravel path towards the house, almost running in her vexation, her thoughts were in a ferment.

Bella and Gerard, together, playing and—and fondling . . . Bella's throaty laugh still echoed in her head, and the vision of her mischievous face, flushed and bright eyed, swam before her. To romp in such a way—and with a boy of Gerard's age—it was shameless, abandoned. Almost like two young animals.

Hardly able to see where she was going, she turned the

corner of the rose-walk, and ran full tilt into a tall, stalwart figure in uniform.

"Oh, Edmund!" She found herself in his arms, trembling with mortification and shock; and perhaps some more complex emotion that she could not identify.

"Did I startle you, my dearest love?" He held her tightly and smiled down at her. "I'm sorry, I had hoped to surprise you, indeed—but not so violently as this!"

"No—no, it's nothing." She recovered her self-possession as quickly as possible, and smiled back at him. "It is a wonderful surprise. I was not expecting to see you today."

"Nor I you, but I made up my mind; I had to talk to you. After the things that scoundrel Deverell said this morning . . . His face darkened. "Unforgivable things . . . "

"Lord Hugo Deverell? Your commanding officer? But I thought he was a good friend to you, Edmund?"

"So did I, till now . . . But don't ask me questions on that subject, for I'll not tell you, my love. Only that the villain has helped me to make up my mind. I'm going to London at the very first opportunity—and I want to take you with me. Deuce take long engagements—how quickly can we be wed?"

She stared at him, incredulously. "You're not joking? You want to marry me—very soon?"

"Today, if we could find a parson to do the job!" Now Edmund had steeled himself to take this step, there was no holding him. "We must tell your papa that there's been a change of plan. I mean to haste to the wedding!"

"Oh, my darling, it won't be easy." She hugged him fondly, but her smile was rueful. "My father is very strict, you know; he is a great one for rules and regulations. He might think there was something not quite decent about such an impetuous union!"

"Surely we can explain—I'll go to him—and make him understand."

"No. I think it would be better if *I* were to go to him.

111

This will need a very diplomatic approach, my love. Leave me to sound him out; I know he's in his room—do you wait for me in the library, and—wish me luck, Edmund!"

They entered the house together; he kissed her once—very sweetly, upon the lips—and she left him at the library door, then proceeded to the principal bedchamber upon the first floor, a spacious apartment with a magnificent four-poster bed, a huge mirror that covered almost one entire wall above the fireplace, and a window that gave on to the long vista of the home park, and the rolling Surrey hills beyond.

Garnet, intent on her mission, knocked quickly at the heavy door, and entered without waiting for any invitation. There was a folding Chinese screen between the doorway and the four-poster, and she heard a heavy movement, and the rustle of sheets.

Too late, she remembered her father's instruction—"Where's the housekeeper? Send her up to my room"—and thought that this might not be the most opportune of moments to come and ask a favor. And in the same instant, her eye was drawn to a sudden flurry of light, at the overmantel.

She thought for a brief second that there was a bird outside the window—two large white birds, like gulls, or swans even, white and curved, fluttering and swooping—but then she realized that the mirror over the fireplace was not reflecting the view from the window; the view that lay open to her gaze displayed the four-poster, at the other side of the Chinese screen.

Her eyes met her father's apoplectic stare in the glass, and at once she took in the entire situation: Sir George, clad only in a white shirt, half sitting and half lying, propped up against pillows. And the incredible bulk of Mrs. Bolt, kneeling on all fours across the old gentleman, stripped down to her white shift, her hair tumbling in disarray around her pink face, and her huge bosoms swinging low across his heavy flanks, as she gave him the relief he sought.

"Damn you, girl, get out, leave me alone, d'ye hear? *Get out of my sight.*"

She needed no second bidding. Taking to her heels, leaving the thunderous bellow of her outraged father behind her, she ran for dear life, as fast as her legs could carry her, and the door of the bedchamber slammed like a cannon-shot.

Moments later she was in the library, trying to recover her composure.

Edmund seemed ready to smile as she found him twice within the space of ten minutes, breathless and in a state of shock, and he began: "My dearest girl, what's wrong? Is the house on fire?"

"Yes—no—it is the people who are on fire . . . All of them—burning up with the fires of hell!"

"What are you saying? Dear heart, what is it?" He held her hands, and searched her face, his smile fading as he realized her distress.

"Nothing. Take no notice, I'm being very silly. I have been childish and stupid—but I'm a child no longer."

"I don't follow what you are saying. Did you see your father?"

"Oh, yes, I saw him." She frowned and turned her head aside as if to blot out the memory. "But there's no use asking him for his approval—he will never approve of me—nor I of him."

"Garnet, what's happened? Tell me!"

"There is nothing to tell. And I don't care. I don't care any more, Edmund. We don't need his approval, or his consent—it will be a runaway match. I'll run away to London with you, now, tonight!"

"*What?* But you must have his consent—you are under age, we cannot be married without that—"

"Then I will live with you outside marriage; for I love you, and nothing else matters. As for my dowry—I have a box of jewelry that belonged to my mother; we will sell that, and set up house together in London."

She flung her arms about him and clung to him, as if she were drowning and he was her only hope of rescue.

"Take me with you, Edmund, as soon as you can . . . But take me whenever you will—for I am yours."

7

One Last Kiss

From this moment on, everything seemed to speed up, and when she looked back afterwards, Garnet could scarcely remember all that had happened; incidents flashed past in a rapid sequence, as if she were flicking over the pages of a picture-book.

She remembered Edmund holding her in his arms, and swearing undying love and loyalty; she remembered his voice, deep and passionate, as he said, "You're prepared to give yourself to me—come what may? In spite of what your father may say, or whatever the world will think of us? You'd really risk so much for my sake?"

"For you, Edmund, always and evermore!" she had breathed, feeling warm and secure in the cradle of his embrace. "How soon can we go to London? How soon can I leave this hateful place?"

Another picture replaced it: Edmund making plans, looking at dates in a pocket calendar, working out sums on a scrap of paper . . . How much money they would need to hire a coach to take them to London—and how much more to provide lodgings and food when they arrived there, until such time as his transfer to the Household Cavalry should be approved, and he would be on full pay again.

She told him she wanted to contribute her share to their joint finances, and ran up to her room to fetch her mother's jewel-case: she recalled how she flew down again, with the shagreen-leather box in her arms, and how he stood below in the hall, looking up at her, his eyes fond with love.

This picture in turn was superseded by another: the interior of a little, low-ceilinged shop in Guildford, dark and cramped—loud with the ticking of clocks and watches, and the occasional chime of bells striking the hour or ringing the quarters. This was the establishment of old Mr. Grundy, clockmaker and jeweler, and Edmund and Garnet waited impatiently as he tipped the contents of Lady Mallory's case out on to a black velvet cloth spread upon the counter, and examined each item painstakingly through a magnifying glass.

"Yes—hmm, hmm—well enough . . . A good piece, that . . . And this—mighty pretty, in its way. What have we here? Ah, yes, indeed—hmm, hmm . . . "

He muttered and sniffed as he worked through the collection, talking, Garnet felt sure, more to himself than to them. Finally he lowered his glass, and looked up at them, through red-rimmed eyes set in a spider's web of wrinkles. "So, so . . . Tell me, if you please, Miss Mallory—does your father know you are here today?"

"Why, no, Mr. Grundy, I believe not." Garnet glanced at Edmund quickly for reassurance.

"Indeed? And if he did know, would he approve of your selling all your mother's trinkets in this way?"

Edmund spoke up: "All Lady Mallory's jewels were left to her daughter, upon her death. She does not require her father's permission to dispose of them."

"Hmm, hmm, very well, sir—if you tell me so, I must take your word, of course . . . but I do not want any unpleasantness later, you understand . . . I have the reputation of the establishment to think about."

"I promise you, Mr. Grundy, my father will not care what becomes of the jewels." She pressed Edmund's hand, as she added in a lower tone, "Or of me, either."

"What can you offer Miss Mallory for the entire list?" Edmund asked.

The old man relapsed into sniffing and mumbling again, and made some scribbled marks on a scratch-pad with a blunt pencil end. At last he peered up at Garnet and said, "I'll give you two hundred pounds on the nail—not a penny more, not a penny less. Take it or leave it!"

Edmund frowned. "You are not over generous, sir. I am no expert, but I dare swear those jewels are worth far more—"

"As you say, sir—begging your pardon—you are no expert. But I am—and that's my last word on the subject. Two hundred pounds. Well, miss, what d'ye say, hmm, hmm?"

Garnet clutched at Edmund's sleeve, and said urgently, "We could manage very well on two hundred pounds, dearest—surely it will be better to accept Mr. Grundy's offer and waste no more time? The sooner we can proceed with our plans the happier I shall be."

"Very well . . . We'll accept, and I hope for your sake you are not double-dealing with the young lady—"

"Watch your language, sir! Josiah Grundy is a man of honor, and I'll have the law of slander upon anyone who dares say otherwise. For two pins I'd refuse to do business with you at all—"

"Oh, Edmund, don't say another word, I'm sure Captain Challoner didn't mean to imply any slur on your character, Mr. Grundy—please, please give me the money and let us be gone, for I have a great deal to do . . ."

So the transaction was effected, and Garnet left the little shop the richer by two hundred pounds, which she stuffed, crisp and crackling, into her reticule. As she strolled along Guildford High Street, on Edmund's arm, they continued with their plans and preparations for the elopement: a post-chaise had been hired for the following Wednesday, only the day after tomorrow. Garnet could hardly believe that happiness lay so close at hand—a mere forty-eight hours away. The coachman was carefully instructed to be at the park gates, just beyond the lodge, at six o'clock in the evening. It would be dark by then, and Garnet would not easily be observed as she made her way out of the grounds of Rosewood to meet Edmund where he waited for her in the closed carriage. Meanwhile, she would bribe one of the manservants to carry her luggage down—a wooden trunk and a couple of hand-bags, which were all she would need—and hide it among the shrubs by the lodge, and then she would escape to freedom, to start a new life with the man she loved.

"It's too good to be true," she sighed, in a happy fervor of anticipation.

And so, all too soon, it proved to be . . . Too much like a sweet dream that fades at the moment of waking, never to come true.

But she was still blissfully unaware of this, as Edmund squired her back to Rosewood Hall for the last time, and kissed her hand in farewell.

"Adieu, my dearest girl—no, au revoir . . . For two whole days, until we meet again and you can bid goodbye to these stone walls forever!"

She watched him ride away, on his way back to the barracks, then hurried into the house, her head held high and her heart as light as air.

When Edmund arrived at the barracks, he found the entire place in a state of confusion; bugles were blowing and the rank and file, some in uniform, some half-dressed in shirtsleeves and breeches, were hurrying to and fro, all in a great hurry and turmoil.

"What's going on here?" Edmund demanded. "Ensign Blades, what the devil has got into everyone?"

The Ensign, a fresh-faced lad not long out of the schoolroom, paused only long enough to gasp: "Regiment's moving out, sailing from Southampton tomorrow, bound for Portugal!"

And then he too rushed off at the double, shouldering a heavy knapsack.

"Dear God, it seems I put in my transfer just in time," Edmund said to himself. "What a stroke of luck."

He decided he had better acquaint himself with whatever orders had been received, and so made his way up to the lieutenant-colonel's suite of rooms, overlooking the barrack square.

Here too there was a scene of hustle and bustle, as the worthy Pilling endeavored to pack all his master's dress uniforms into a series of trunks, and relays of perspiring orderlies dragged each piece of luggage out as soon as it was locked and strapped, to slide it down the staircase.

Lord Hugo Deverell sat on a wooden chest, his left leg negligently crossed over his right, supervising the scene calmly.

"Devil take you, lad, don't drop that box, it contains my best china tea service. Call another body to help you if you can't carry it alone, for I tell you plainly, if you so much as crack one single cup, I'll have you flogged, as an example to the others!"

He glanced across at Edmund, and smiled, "Don't stand in the doorway, dear boy, you might get your toes trodden upon in the mêlée. God's nightgown, how I dislike all this inconvenience; but there, we can't countermand the orders of our beloved leaders."

"Orders, sir?" Edmund queried, dodging aside as yet another trunk was lugged from the room.

"Orders to sail for Lisbon, hadn't you heard? It seems Wellington can't do without us after all; he needs our support, my dear . . . Pilling, do be very careful with that

119

jacket, if you pack it like that it might become creased, and I would never forgive you. Just because a gentleman is posted into active service, it does not mean that he must abandon all civilized behavior, or an elegant appearance. We are not brute beasts, Pilling."

Edmund moved closer, and broke in when the other paused for breath. "Excuse me, sir, but I was anxious to know, are there any orders yet, with regard to me? When am I to leave here?"

"Why, together with all the rest of the bodies, my dear, either at midnight tonight, or the crack of dawn tomorrow. Are you not packed and ready? Then you must make haste, Ned; it would never do to keep the regiment waiting. Punctuality is the politeness of princes, so I'm told."

"But—but—I'm not going to Lisbon, surely, sir? My transfer, my application to move to London and join the Household troops—"

"Oh, that," Lord Hugo smiled very sweetly. "Didn't I tell you? I've been so plaguey busy just lately, what with one thing and another, I never had a moment to authorize your application, or to send it through . . . And now of course it's too late—in fact, I used your charming letter of request to light a cheroot half an hour ago, didn't I, Pilling?"

"*What?* No—surely—you can't mean it—" Edmund stammered, with rising fury. "I told you—I can't be posted abroad—I have promised Miss Mallory—"

"The poor, pretty dear, she will be quite inconsolable when she hears of her loss, I am sure . . . But no doubt she will survive the disappointment, and I tell you, Neddy, you will be a thousand times better off without her. Far better, out in the Peninsula, covering yourself with glory. Far, far better off with me . . . for I swear, I cannot let you go, my dear." And he let one manicured hand fall very lightly upon Edmund's muscular forearm.

Edmund realized that any appeal was useless, and his cause was lost entirely.

"You devil," he said, when he could control his voice. "You clever, clever devil."

Then he took one pace back, saluted, with his expression full of loathing and contempt, turned on his heel, and marched out.

Lord Hugo laughed gently. "You see, Pilling? As I've often told you, everything comes to him who waits."

At this moment, Garnet of course knew nothing of these new developments, and was still happily contemplating her future happiness; she longed to tell Bella and Gerard, but dared not trust them with her wonderful secret. They would know all about it soon enough, after she had gone; she intended to leave a letter for them, in explanation. But not a word to her father; she refused to have any sort of communication with him.

Absorbed in her own thoughts, when she entered the library and found Bella and Gerard together, seated on a bench at the long table and turning the pages of some old books of poems, she made her apologies. "Forgive me, I did not know there was anyone here."

"Please, Garnet dear, do not run away!" Bella exclaimed. "I declare, we hardly see anything of you, nowadays. You keep yourself so very much to yourself, or is it that you are forever slipping off for a sly assignation with the gallant Captain?"

Garnet smiled; if only Bella knew the truth . . .

"Well, I will leave you both in peace, if you'll excuse me—for I have so many things upon my mind, I would be very poor company."

She left the library, and Gerard sighed with relief. "Thank goodness she's gone. We don't need *her* around. Two's company, Bella, I want you all to myself this afternoon."

"Why, Gerard, whatever can you mean?" Bella fluttered her eyelashes and dimpled provocatively. "We are only going to read some poetry, are we not? I'm sure that is what you told me when we came in here."

"Yes, poems of love; I want to show you what other men have felt for their mistresses, in years gone by."

"Mistresses? Pray, cousin, do not speak so crudely!"

"There's nothing crude about it. It is the most glorious subject in the world—the exchange of love between man and woman. Let me find you some verses of Andrew Marvell. No, better still, listen to what old John Donne had to say."

He turned the pages clumsily, his hands trembling with growing excitement, as he continued: 'And after the poetry, let us go to your bedroom, dearest Bella, and let us replace words with deeds . . . "

"Fie, sir, for shame! You presume too much. I see that I made a very great mistake in permitting your advances, for now you try to force your attentions upon me."

"Force my attentions?" Gerard was caught off guard by the accusation, partly anxious to disclaim any such intention, but also more than a little flattered by the implication. "Do I really do that? I don't, do I?"

"You've such an insatiable passion, dear Gerard, and you're so strong—look how you have me in your power, even now. Here in this very room, with nobody by to defend me. You could have your way with me, and I'd not be able to do anything to prevent it. Why, you only have to unfasten these laces, and my bosom would be totally revealed to your shameless appetites." She leant back against the table, her arms stretched wide.

Laughing a little, and breathing fast and hard, Gerard bent over her. "You mean, like this?" he asked, making a lunge at her.

The laces were quickly dispatched by his eager fingers and the bodice of her dress gaped wide, spilling its precious cargo before his delighted gaze: her perfect breasts, as luscious and ripe as two June peaches, were laid bare, their nipples erect and quivering.

"Oh, Bella, my beauty," he panted, and buried his face in her warm bosom, covering her with kisses.

They were both transported with delight, and so did

not at first hear the door opening, or remark the entrance of Sir George Mallory into the library.

Seeking to check some question of boundary enclosures and grazing rights, Sir George had come in search of a plan of the estate, and now stood dumbfounded at the sight that greeted him.

"Why—you young scoundrel!" he roared, when he could recover his breath.

Gerard shot up as if he had been struck by lightning, and being already in a precarious position, poised over Bella's wide-spread charms, he lost his balance, slipped and fell off the bench. Bella, equally disconcerted, sat up straight and grabbed at her bodice, struggling to cover herself as best she might.

"And you, miss, have you no shame?"

Sir George, having recently been surprised under similar circumstances, was suffering from an unwonted attack of high moral rectitude, and vented his outraged feelings upon the luckless pair.

"So this is the sort of game you get up to behind my back, heh? This is the way you take advantage of my good nature. Lewd and lascivious antics on the sly! I welcomed you to this house as a good friend and kinswoman, miss, but I shall pack you off home to your family without any regrets. I have been sadly disappointed in you, young woman."

"Pack me away? Oh, Uncle George," Bella protested, but he swept on thunderously.

"And as for *you,* you insufferable whelp, this is what comes of giving you liberty to moon about the place, doing nothing but read improper verses, with your head full of lewd daydreams . . . I said it before, and I say it again, you need a firm hand, sir, you need discipline, sir—you need to be taught a stern lesson!"

His eye was drawn to the window by the sight of a visitor arriving, the lithe, athletic figure of Captain Challoner, as he cantered up the carriage-drive on his skewbald stallion.

"Ha! That's the very thing, the Army. I shall have some words with Captain Challoner, and ask him to use his good offices to enlist you in the Dragoons, you young dog. I'll have you sent away to be a soldier!"

He hobbled angrily from the room, and as the clatter of his malacca cane died away, the young people turned to each other in wild dismay, and Bella burst into tears, falling into Gerard's arms, and whimpering, "Oh, dear, oh, lord, what is to become of us, cousin?"

Ten minutes later, and two floors higher in the house, Garnet too collapsed in tears, as Edmund broke the awful news of his posting overseas.

"Edmund—I can't—I cannot bear to think of it . . . How could anyone be so cruel?" she sobbed. "How can they send you away, when you had already asked to be transferred?"

Edmund soothed and caressed her, and lent her his best silk handkerchief to dry her tears.

"Such things happen in time of war, dear heart," he said. "The Duke of Wellington needs reinforcements in the field, and we must obey orders. It is hard for all those who have to be torn away from sweethearts and wives; try to remember that we are not the only two lovers to be parted in this way."

"Yes, but it *need not* have happened! That is what is so especially agonizing. To think, but two days later and we would have been safely away in London, and you out of all danger. Oh, Edmund, I feel as if my heart is bursting with grief . . . "

"There, there, dearest, try to see the bright side," he urged her. "We are not being separated forever—why, I've heard it said that this war will be over by Christmas, and then I shall come riding home again in triumph, to claim you as my rightful bride! I am sure your papa can never oppose our marriage then; think of that, and take comfort, my love."

"Christmas is still two months away." She shook her

head, refusing to be mollified. "Two whole months without seeing you? I shall die, Edmund, indeed I shall."

"What nonsense is this? You must be well and cheerful for my sake—so I shall have some joy every day in thinking of you, and remembering your smiling face. Come now, smile for me, Garnet."

He put his hand under her chin and lifted her face to his own.

"One last kiss, and then, farewell." He held her tightly against his breast, as if he could mold their two bodies into one by the sheer effort of will. "Then I must go. I should not be here at all, for there is much to be done before I leave at midnight. But I could not go without seeing you once again, and telling you what has happened—and kissing you for the last time . . . "

He brought his lips down upon hers, and she shut her eyes, striving to pour her heart and soul into the embrace, to give herself to him as never before.

But it was no good. His mouth was closed; his caress was, as so often, polite and respectful—and cool.

She opened her eyes and found he was gazing at her with an expression that held something of regret, and longing, and—could it be?—a touch of fear . . .

"Garnet," he stammered. "I love you so much—you know I love you—and I want—I mean, I wish—"

He hesitated, at a loss for words, then gently released her, saying, "But I can't explain now. It's late, and there is no time . . . I have to pay my respects to your father before I leave, and say good-bye to your brother, and Miss Delaney. And tip the butler, and—oh, yes, I remember now, I have to collect a parcel of linen, too; the last time I stayed here, I left behind a pair of shirts to be laundered and ironed. It's as well I had not forgotten them . . . Oh, my dear love—"

He caught her hands and stood back, holding her at arm's length, and gazing at her earnestly. "Good-bye, dearest Garnet. There is so much I wish I could say to you, but—that must wait till another occasion. And so—once more, good-bye."

He raised her hands to his lips, and kissed them tenderly, then made a swift departure, quite overcome by his unspoken feelings.

Garnet sank onto her bed, staring at the handkerchief she was still twisting between her hands, with his monogram worked into the corner. She felt quite drained by emotion; totally numb and lifeless . . . It was as if her own life had ended when he walked out of the room, as if he had taken her life with him, and left her with nothing. And nothing seemed to matter, any more.

When Edmund met Sir George in the hall, and explained the circumstances of this his farewell visit, the old man bade him godspeed, and wished him well.

"Write to us, if you have the time or the inclination, sir—send us a dispatch from the field, and tell us how many of the enemies you have accounted for, heh? We shall miss your visits to Rosewood—myself, and—and—"

At the thought of his two troublesome offspring, Sir George's color heightened, and a pulse beat dangerously in his temple. "There's one thing you could do for me, before you depart," he continued, gripping the young officer's shoulder and drawing him closer. "I've a mind to send my boy into the Army, to make a man of him. Could you arrange to take him with you, d'ye think? Enlist him as an Ensign in the Dragoons? I'd be much obliged to ye —very much obliged."

Edmund sighed. "These things take time, sir, and we are now in such a fluster to be off and away, I doubt that anyone could make the necessary arrangements. However, if you care to write a letter, applying for the boy to be listed, I will see that the Recruiting Officer gets it tonight, and then the matter will be in his hands. Possibly Gerard could be sent on to follow us to Southampton in a day or two? But rely on me, sir, I will do my best for you, and for the lad."

"Thank'ee, Captain, thank'ee kindly. I won't forget you for this."

So Sir George slapped him on the back cordially, and sent him about his business.

Garnet, too, was quite certain that she would never forget Edmund, never for one single moment, waking or sleeping.

(Sleeping . . . She shivered at a sudden recollection—the dream she had had, the other night. The terror and excitement of that strange, cavernous hall, full of shadows and clanging echoes, with its curtain of fire, and its heroic figure of a centaur; that face with two eyes of blue ice that had pierced her very soul . . . She shook herself, and tried to wipe the image from her mind. Why should she think of that dream now, of all times, when her heart was breaking? Why recall the face of a stranger, when Edmund had walked out of her life?)

Unable to rest, or think, or settle to anything, she went out of the house, and walked in the autumn garden, as dusk fell; trying to lose her grief in the growing darkness, pacing among fallen leaves, listening to the wind in the bare branches of the trees.

Without knowing how she came to be there, she found herself at last in the stable-block, and saw a light burning beyond an open half-door. She walked into the barn, where the hay was piled high, in reserve for the winter. There was a small lantern hanging from a rafter, casting a yellow glow—and there was the ladder that led up to the room above . . . Jem's room.

She never knew what made her climb the ladder, but something drew her to that little upper room again. It was almost dark in there, lit only by a faint glimmer from the open trapdoor and the single lantern below.

There was no sign of Jem's occupation now; his few belongings had all been taken away. Only the simple straw mattress remained; and now Garnet lay down upon it, hiding her face against the rough cotton ticking, and abandoned herself to a silent, shuddering ecstasy of tears.

The sobs racked her body until she could cry no more, and she lay there exhausted, thinking of Edmund, and her despair—but also thinking (for the ways of the human heart are very strange) more than a little of Jem Bolt as well.

Both gone away—both gone, perhaps forever . . . Never—forever—forever—never . . . The words rolled over and over in her brain like waves breaking endlessly upon a shore, until she almost fell asleep.

But not quite.

Suddenly, a sound cut through her unhappy reverie. It was the sound of a girl's voice—whispering, and giggling. A girl—no, two girls—she thought she recognized their shrill tones. It sounded like Lucy and Rosie, two of the maids. They must have slipped out of the servants' hall and crept into the barn for—

For what? Garnet wondered. Listening again, she thought she detected an unusual note in their excited, clandestine laughter. They appeared to be breathless, as if—

She found herself uncomfortably remembering the occasion when she and Bella had shared the bath-tub, and Bella had begun to soap her back . . . what could the two maids be doing?

As quietly as possible, she moved across to the open trapdoor, and looked cautiously down—and felt her heart almost stop beating at the scene below her.

Lucy and Rosie were there, sure enough, lying tumbled in the hay—stuffing their fists in their mouths, in an attempt not to make too much noise or attract attention. Both girls were nearly naked; Lucy wore only a pair of woolen stockings, and lay with her legs apart, and all the secrets of her body wantonly exposed in the soft lantern light; while Rosie, a year younger and more bashful, still clung onto her one remaining garment, a simple petticoat that had slipped down below her pretty, bouncing breasts; she struggled to pull it up again, but in vain . . .

For the two girls were not alone. There was a man with them. A man stripped to shirt and breeches—his shirt unbuttoned, flapping out above his belt and exposing his bronzed, handsome chest. A man whose regular features and whose charming smile were imprinted forever upon Garnet's heart—Edmund Challoner.

She stared down at him—she would have cried out with the shock of the discovery, but her throat was dry, and she could not utter a sound. So these were the two maids who had done his laundering for him, and this was how he chose to repay them for their service.

The greatest shock, perhaps, was her recognition of the impudent, reckless expression on his face, as he sprawled in the hay, laughing and carefree. This was Edmund as she had only seen him once, the very first time they met, beside the fishpond—and had never encountered again since then . . .

"Come, Lucy, help me teach this silly goose not to be so bashful," he was saying, and Lucy hastened to assist him.

Between them, they pinned the protesting Rose down on her back, and Lucy's devilish fingers tickled her ribs until she squealed and shook and flung up her hands to ward off the merciless attack—whereupon Edmund swiftly took advantage of her helplessness and pulled down her petticoat, tossing it aside, and leaving her entirely uncovered.

"A great improvement!" he chuckled, breathlessly. "Now I have the two of you as you should be, naked as nature intended!"

Rosie, giggling but still shy in front of Edmund's appraising stare, tried to hide her triangle of downy brown hair with both hands—but Lucy tugged at her arm.

"Don't be daft, girl, never mind how *you* look, what about *him?*" She launched herself without any further ado at the captain, pushing him backwards into the hay, and tugging at his belt. "Here, do you come help me, you ninny, let's get these clothes off him!"

Rosie needed no second bidding, and in a moment the three figures were entangled in a wild flurry of arms and legs, as the two unclad girls did their best to divest Edmund of his shirt and breeches; and although he swore, and wrestled, and threatened terrible vengeance, he was laughing so heartily that he did not put up very much of a struggle.

Garnet took one last look at him, as his body was finally exposed in all its virility—stretched out between the two girls, brown and thrusting between their soft pink limbs—before they closed over him, smothering him in their dual embrace, and she turned away.

Somehow, she crawled back to the rough mattress and flung herself upon it once more, covering her ears with her hands to blot out the sounds from below. But she could not blot out the memory of Edmund's face, exulting in his lusty pleasure—an Edmund who was almost a stranger to her.

How long she lay there, she never knew, but at some point she must have fallen asleep, vanquished by exhaustion and distress.

When she awoke at last, the lantern below had almost burnt out, and she only managed to make her way down the ladder with some difficulty, as the flame leaped and flickered, and huge shadows seemed to engulf the barn.

The hay lay tossed and turbulent, but the three figures who had romped upon it had long since departed. She shivered, and sat on the bottom rung of the ladder to think.

At last she understood the mystery that had always puzzled her; at last she understood what sort of man Edmund really was. With a woman of his own station in life, he would feel uneasy and inhibited—unable to unleash his innermost feelings, and reveal the true depth of his passion. That was why he had responded to her so immediately when they first met, when he believed her to be one of the household servants—and, perhaps, why she had felt a new warmth in his embrace on that other occasion, when Jem had left her sadly disheveled, her gown torn and her face dirtied . . . Edmund had not been in awe of her that night.

She clenched her fists. If only she had known—if she had guessed sooner, she could surely have done something to help him overcome this shy, gentlemanly reticence. She could have made him realize that she too was a woman, under all the trappings of gentility, a woman who wanted nothing better than to love and be loved by him . . . And now it was too late, for he had gone off to war— and when would she ever see him again?

She took a deep breath, and rose to her feet, with a new light in her eye.

"It's *not* too late. It can't be too late—for I will find him, and then I will make him understand, as I understand now . . . I shall go after him, I shall follow him to the ends of the earth if necessary, but we will be together again at last, and then I shall love him and he will love me—with our hearts and our minds, and our bodies, too . . ."

She opened the lantern, blew out the guttering candle, and let the darkness enfold her, as she walked out into the night.

8

Tomorrow — the Wide World

Tuesday morning dawned grim and bleak, and the atmosphere over the breakfast table at Rosewood Hall matched the weather outside.

Sir George still chose to ignore Garnet altogether, and concentrated his stern disapproval upon Gerard and Bella. He was implacable in his decision; they had betrayed his trust, and broken the code of good conduct—so they must suffer the consequences.

Charles, the butler, coughed discreetly behind his hand, breaking the oppressive silence, and produced a sealed letter addressed to Sir George, upon a silver salver.

"What's this, heh?" grunted the old gentleman, breaking the wax.

"It arrived first thing this morning, sir—by the carrier from Guildford," replied Charles.

"Ha! An answer to my request, I'll be bound. I told

ye, Gerard, I wrote and asked the Recruiting Officer to take you into the Dragoons—now we shall see what he has to say on the matter!"

Gerard chewed his lip and prayed silently for deliverance, but his prayer was not yet to be answered.

The letter was brief and to the point: Major Sterne presented his compliments to Sir George and apologized for the brevity of his reply, but he was forced to write in haste, as the 3rd Dragoons prepared to move out for embarkation to the Peninsula.

However, he would be more than happy to impress Sir George's son and heir into service as a junior Ensign, and it would not be too late for him to make his way to Southampton and there join up with the remainder of the regiment. He suggested that Master G. Mallory should present himself to Mr. Duckwell, Military Tailor to His Majesty's Officers, at his establishment hard by the barracks, this very morning, and he had no doubt that this worthy gentleman would be able to provide the young recruit with all necessary items of clothing and equipment by the following day. Thereupon, he should make his way to the Red Lion Inn at Petersfield, on the road to Southampton, arriving there by tomorrow night, to make rendezvous with the rearguard of the transport and so continue on his way to the coast . . . Major Sterne assured Sir George of his best respects at all times, and declared himself his obedient servant, etc., etc.

There was a dreadful pause as Sir George finished imparting this information to the company—broken only by a smothered sob from Bella.

"What's that? Did you pass an opinion, miss?" growled her host.

"I was only going to say—it's so dreadfully unfair, so it is—to send a young boy like Gerard off to the wars—"

"Hold your tongue, if you please!" Sir George scowled, folding the letter and fixing Gerard with a baleful glare. "On the contrary—'twill be the making of him. I served under arms when I was no older, and the experience enabled me to become the man I am today!"

Gerard and Bella exchanged unhappy glances, but said nothing.

"Furthermore, I have assured myself, in conversation with Captain Challoner—"

(Now it was Garnet's turn to bite her lip and lower her eyes, but she was determined to remain silent at all costs.)

"—That the Dragoons are to be commanded in battle by a very great military man indeed—Major-General Broccard Savage. You've not heard of him? God bless me, what are young people coming to! D'ye never read the dispatches? Did you not hear how he commanded the Hussars at Corunna? I never knew such ignorance! He's a fine soldier, and a great leader of men, by all accounts. Gerard may think himself honored to serve under him!"

Gerard looked as if this was an honor he could well have forgone, and stirred his teacup moodily.

"Confound it, don't fidget when I talk to you, you young jackanapes! And Major-General Savage isn't one of your high-faluting society dandies neither—he was born and brought up on his family estate in the West Country, I'm told. He can plow a furrow to beat any man in Wessex, he knows how to fell a stand of timber, and he takes pride in shoeing his own horses!"

Under his breath, Gerard ventured to quote: "I am much afeared my lady his mother played false with a smith . . ."

"What's that you're mumbling? Speak up, boy!"

"Nothing of any importance, father; it was a line from Shakespeare that came into my head," replied Gerard, smoothly.

"Shakespeare, heh? More of your damned poetry. Well, you shall soon have all that knocked out of you, I fancy."

Sir George beckoned to Charles to assist him from his chair, and rose to his feet leaning upon his cane.

"You will do as you are bid, and go to the tailor's to be

fitted for your uniform. Then tomorrow afternoon, when your box is packed and you are ready to leave, we shall send you in the carriage to Petersfield, to present yourself to the Recruiting Officer according to his instructions."

"What if I refuse?" Gerard spoke up with more boldness than he felt. "What if I were to disobey you, sir—and run away?"

"Disobey me?" Sir George's complexion purpled dangerously. "May heaven forgive you, you ungrateful dog! If you dare to do such a thing after I've listed you to serve, the Army will hunt you down, sir, and you will be shot—as a deserter!"

Gerard turned pale, and swallowed, and made no more comment.

Sir George's threat might not have been strictly accurate, but it was ominous enough to quell any further argument. The old gentleman glanced at Gerard from under beetling brows, and his tone softened ever so slightly, as he concluded, "But that won't happen. You'll go to war, and be a credit to your family name, I feel sure of it. Here, boy, take this with you—you'll need some expenses for the journey, no doubt."

He dug into his pocket, and produced a worn leather purse, which he slid across the breakfast table.

"Take good care of it, for it contains a hundred guineas. And may God's blessing go with you."

Then he swung round heavily and glowered at Bella. "As for you, young woman . . . The carriage shall take you into Guildford this morning, when your cousin pays his visit to the tailor's shop, and it will deposit you there in good time for you to pack yourself off on the mid-day coach to Bristol—d'ye understand me?"

Bella dabbled at her pretty eyes with a square of lace and cambric, and looked pleadingly at her uncle from under her dewy lashes—but he was not to be moved.

"I fancy you told me when you arrived that you were making your way to Bristol, and then you would take ship back home to Ireland? Very well, we will not detain you any further, and I wish you a pleasant voyage!"

And with that the old gentleman hobbled from the room, helped by Charles.

"Oh, Gerard," Bella's tears began to flow again, as the door closed. "What is to be done?"

"There is no hope for it; he has the whip-hand, and we shall be forced to obey his orders," said Gerard dully.

"I think not," Garnet set down her cup with a little clatter, and lifted her chin, saying, "I have a better plan."

The others stared at her. She had not uttered a single word throughout the meal, and they had almost forgotten her.

"What do you mean? We cannot defy father—" Gerard began.

"We can be too clever for him—which is more to the point."

"Too clever? Garnet, explain yourself!" Bella urged her eagerly. "What is this plan of yours?"

"I suggest that Gerard need not go to Petersfield tomorrow, or to Southampton, or to the Peninsula either. I suggest that he should follow you to Bristol, and there take ship with you across the Irish Sea."

"*What?*" Bella smiled for the first time that day. "Could we, Gerard? Is it possible?"

"I would need money—a ticket for the sea trip would cost me several pounds, I am sure."

"Hasn't he just given you a hundred guineas? You have money and to spare for the journey, and when you reach County Cork I am sure the Delaneys will not refuse you their hospitality—at least until you can establish yourself in some way of earning your livelihood."

"Papa and Mama will be delighted to have you to stay with us for as long as ever you like!" exclaimed Bella rapturously. "And of course I shall do all I can to help you, in every way, you may be sure of that."

"I am quite certain you will, dearest Bella," agreed

Garnet, drily. "For you have done so much for him already . . ."

"But—but—if father finds out, he will cut me off without a penny!" Gerard protested. "And if I run away today with Bella to Bristol he will discover that I have defied him—"

"He shall not discover it," said Garnet. "For you must appear to obey all his orders, today and tomorrow—then, when it is time for you to leave for Petersfield, you will change direction and make for Bristol instead, and meet Bella there."

"Indeed, yes!" Bella's mind was racing now. "I shall arrive there this evening, and stop overnight at the Royal Hotel—and there I will stay until you arrive tomorrow, my dear. Oh, what fun it's going to be!"

She clapped her hands, like a child at a birthday treat, and chattered on, "Then the next morning we shall sail on the packet to Wexford—and once you are out of this country, and beyond the range of Uncle George's anger, you will be a free man!"

"But what of the Dragoons? That officer—Major Sterne —he will be expecting my arrival at the Red Lion in Petersfield tomorrow night. Will he not raise a hue and cry when I do not appear?"

"Leave that to me," said Garnet quietly. "*I* shall go to Petersfield—and I shall make myself known to the Major. I am quite sure I can arrange matters amicably enough, so you will have nothing more to fear."

"Oh, Garnet, could you? *Would* you?" Bella leaned across and squeezed her hand fondly.

Gerard frowned. "But wait a bit—if the carriage that was to take me to Hampshire is now to take *you,* instead, how am I to get myself to Bristol?"

Bella put her finger to her mouth, in dismay. "That's true—and you'll be too late for the daily stagecoach by tomorrow evening. Oh, dear, that's a setback indeed."

"We really need a second conveyance of some sort—"

Gerard began, but Garnet interrupted him, her eyes sparkling.

"*And I have got one!* Don't ask me how or why, but for reasons of my own, I had already arranged that there should be a hire post-chaise waiting by the lodge gates tomorrow evening at six o'clock . . . It was originally intended to go to London—"

"For reasons not unconnected with a certain Captain of Dragoons, I dare swear?" Bella dimpled.

"Never you mind! The fact remains—in all the excitement, I quite forgot about canceling my order for the post-chaise. Isn't that providential? Now it comes to us as an answer to a prayer; you shall take the chaise to Bristol instead, brother, and our problems will be over!"

So the matter was arranged, and Tuesday passed busily enough; Bella and Gerard drove into Guildford, dutifully obeying Sir George's commands, and Gerard saw his pretty cousin off in the stagecoach at noon, on her way to Bristol.

("Don't forget now, lovey, 'tis the Royal Hotel I'm staying at, and I'll be waiting for you tomorrow night.")

Then he proceeded to Mr. Duckwell, the military tailor, and had himself measured and fitted for breeches, dress-uniform, shako, topcoat and every item a young Ensign should require, from riding-boots to epaulettes. It seemed a terrible waste of money when he was, after all, never to wear them, but . . .

He sighed to himself as Mr. Duckwell fussed and pinned and stitched, "Needs must, when the devil—or Papa—is driving!"

So Tuesday passed into Wednesday, and Garnet and Gerard made their final plans. In the morning, Gerard rode once more into town and collected all the kit that he had ordered, then returned to Rosewood for the last time, and set to work, packing a wooden chest that had been plainly stenciled with the legend: "Ensign G. Mallory—3rd Dragoons."

Garnet came into his room, and watched and advised as he folded and packed each item into the box, taking a surprising interest in every detail of the process. When he had finished, he kissed her upon the cheek; it was a brotherly peck, but there was very real affection in the gesture —and deep gratitude.

"Dear Garnet, what would I have done without you?" he asked. "You're quite sure you do not mind going to Petersfield this evening, and speaking to the Major on my behalf? You are positive that it will all be well?"

"I am quite, quite sure of it, Gerard," she smiled. "In fact, I was never so sure of anything in my whole life. Now, all that remains is for us to arrange your farewell with Papa."

At teatime, the family carriage came bowling up the gravel drive to the front steps, and Gerard, wearing a plain traveling dress of brown frieze (for it would have been a great shame to risk spoiling his spotless new uniform upon the journey), made his good-byes to his father and his sister.

"I wish you godspeed, boy," grunted Sir George, clasping his hand and pumping it vigorously up and down. "And I wish you all good fortune in your adventures."

"Heaven knows I shall have need of it, sir," replied Gerard, with a shy side-glance at Garnet, who stood back demurely under the shadows of the portico.

"Heh, what—humph—yes, indeed . . . Well, well, you have my blessing, you know that—and—and come back safe and sound, lad . . ." The old man cleared his throat noisily. "I declare, I believe I shall miss you, for all your tomfool ways—and your damned poetry books!"

He clapped the boy on the shoulder once more, then let him go. "Hurry up—say good-bye to your sister, and then be off with you, for 'tis growing dark already."

"Good-bye, Gerard." Garnet, dressed from head to toe in a voluminous black cloak and hood, stepped forward. "Let me kiss you good-bye inside the carriage, for I should not wish anyone to see me disgrace myself with foolish tears."

And as she spoke, she climbed swiftly into the coach. Sir George frowned—what nonsense was this?—but did not interfere; it would be many a long day before brother and sister would meet again. Gerard followed her, shutting the door behind him; then pulled the blind down to ensure that their last embrace should be entirely hidden.

Sir George huffed and puffed impatiently and tapped his cane as the moments passed, then heard the door upon the far side of the carriage swing open, and slam shut. A voice cried, "Drive on, coachman!" and the vehicle rolled away, crunching over the gravel, and gathering speed as it disappeared into the dusk.

"What the devil? Garnet, come here—" Sir George exclaimed, for at the far side of the drive, a solitary, black-cloaked figure was hurrying away, obviously overcome by emotion, into the shelter of the spinney.

"Tsk!" Sir George clicked his tongue irritably. Oh well, let the wench cry her eyes out in solitude, if that's what she wanted. He shrugged his shoulders, and made his way back into the house.

Inside the carriage, as they turned out of the park on to the high road, Garnet sat back and relaxed, a little smile of triumph upon her lips. Her long journey had begun at last, and she was not afraid, since she knew that at the end of her quest she would find Edmund.

Within the home park, Gerard stayed in hiding among the wintry trees, shrouded in the long black cloak and hood. He waited until it was quite dark, then made a cautious progress—for he dared not be seen by Sir George, or any of the household servants—through the shrubbery, down into the long wood that skirted the walls of Rosewood, and along to the old lodge.

Here, concealed among the bushes where he had left it earlier in the day, was his luggage: a battered trunk and a valise full of his favorite books. He lifted these goods and chattels over the wall and then scaled it himself, dropping down lightly on the far side into a tangle of weeds and a drift of dead leaves. Then he sat himself on the trunk, clutching his bag of books, and prepared to wait.

He did not have to wait very long. The post-chaise arrived promptly at six o'clock, and the driver climbed down to open the door. He raised an eyebrow in mild surprise as Gerard boarded the conveyance, saying, "I was told I was to take a young lady to London, sir—isn't that right?"

"Just two changes in the plan, my good fellow," replied Gerard, trying to sound as grown-up as possible, and lowering his voice an octave. "*I* am to be your passenger now—and the journey is not to London, but to Bristol."

"What's that? Oh, I dunno about that, nobody said nothing 'bout Bristol—'tis a long journey, and—"

Gerard produced a golden guinea and thrust it into the man's hand. "I think you'll find you can take me there, without too much difficulty—can't you?"

The driver examined the coin, bit it, then pocketed it. "Bristol, it is, sir. Right you are—we'll be on our way!"

And he headed westwards instead of to the northeast.

Meanwhile, Garnet continued her journey to the south, counting the milestones that flashed by at regular intervals, and adding up the last few hours that (she felt sure) were all that separated her from her true love.

She was not afraid, although her plan was impossibly daring, and she risked every kind of danger and disgrace if she should be discovered. But she was happy to risk everything for Edmund's sake; and she sat in the family coach now, hugging herself with delight, and anticipating the prospect of their reunion.

She gazed out at the countryside that sped past the windows of the coach; a countryside almost completely shrouded in darkness except for the occasional glimmer of a pond or a stream, or a whitewashed wall that emerged ghostlike from the gloom. Sometimes she saw the lamp-lit interior of a rustic cottage—a woman slicing a loaf, a child reaching for an apple—and once, at a turn in the road, the carriage slowed down and passed a gypsy encampment. She saw a vivid picture, etched in leaping firelight against the night—two young girls leaning forward eagerly by the glow of a bonfire, and an ageing Romany woman with a bright shawl and glittering earrings, scanning their outstretched palms and telling their fortunes . . .

Then the scene disappeared into deeper darkness, and Garnet settled back against the cushions of the coach, musing. She wondered—if she ever had the chance to peep into the future in that way—what she might learn. What lay in wait for her, upon the highroad—not only tonight, but in all the days and nights that were to come?

And what of Gerard, how would he fare in his expedition to Ireland? She almost wished for a moment that she were herself a gypsy, with the power to look into the darkness ahead, and discover what awaited them.

If she had possessed such a gift, and could have had foreknowledge from reading a palm, or a teacup, or peering into a crystal . . . what might she have seen there?

Perhaps it was as well that Garnet had no crystal ball, for the vision of Gerard's future—had she been able to see it—would have alarmed her mightily: not only the distant future, but his immediate prospects, too . . .

At first, everything was to go according to plan for Gerard and Bella.

She was there waiting for him when he arrived at the Royal Hotel, Bristol, very late that night. She had booked an extra room for him, upon the same floor as her own bed-chamber, and she made sure he knew the shortest route from one to the other. The previous night, which she had been forced to spend in chaste and solitary state, had been extremely lonely and now she craved for companionship.

Unfortunately, the long drive from Guildford had proved to be very tiring, and Gerard lay upon his own single bed for a few moments to recoup his energies. He closed his eyes to take forty winks—and when he opened them again it was broad daylight on Thursday morning, and he was still lying, fully dressed in the suit he had traveled in, on top of the counterpane.

At breakfast, when he tried to explain to Bella what had happened, the young lady was very far from pleased, and gave him to understand that she considered herself to be mortally insulted.

However, there was no time to argue the matter, for they had to find their way to the dockside, where the packet-boat to Ireland awaited them. Gerard bought the two tickets, carried their luggage on board, and they set sail soon after.

The voyage was comparatively uneventful, for the weather was kind, and they made a good crossing. Upon arrival in Wexford, Bella pronounced, "Oh, fie, how provoking. It must be market day—the town is crammed with tiresome farmers and their odious fat wives. It's to be hoped they will have room for us at the hotel."

Then she had a bright idea, and announced to her traveling companion, "In case the place is crowded I think I'd better book a *double* room. I'll reserve it in the name of Mr. and Mrs. Smith! Don't forget now—when you come to find me, in half an hour or so, be sure to ask for Mrs. Smith, and if anyone questions you, tell them you're my husband."

"In half an hour?" Gerard's spirits were rising immediately at the prospect of a whole night spent in connubial bliss with Bella, but he asked, "Why do I have to wait till then? Surely if we're supposed to be a married couple, we can arrive at the hotel together?"

"Well, no dearest. I think 'twould be unwise, with you looking the way you do." She ran a critical eye over the fifteen-year-old lad. "They *might* consider I'd married someone straight from the schoolroom, d'ye see. You must smarten yourself up a bit first: buy a top hat to hide those boyish locks, and a tall collar, perhaps, or a scarf, to hide your face? Anyway, I leave it to you. Just do your best to contrive to look a few years older than you are—do you follow me?"

And she walked on into the hotel, and summoned the boots to carry in her luggage.

Gerard scratched his head, and wondered how he could age a few years in the space of half an hour; it seemed so unnecessary, when he already felt perfectly ready to act a husband's role—more than ready, indeed, for the thought of Bella's voluptuous treasures displayed beside him in a double bed was arousing his passions quite remarkably, and his breeches felt uncomfortably tight.

Trying to concentrate on the immediate task in hand, he eyed the windows of the little shops that straggled along the bustling main street of Wexford, and then stopped short.

"Theatrical costumiers—carnival regalia—wigmakers and perruques."

So ran the faded sign, with paint flaking from the lettering, above the poky shopfront. The dusty window was piled high with all kinds of bric-à-brac: ancient swords and bucklers, a crown, an ass's head, a set of masks with gilded faces, and—several false beards . . .

He made up his mind, and strode into the shop, trying to look as if he were at his ease.

Inside, a matronly female was attending to another customer—an imposing figure of a man with the air of a monarch, despite his battered beaver hat and shabby velvet coat with patched elbows.

"Never mind the quality of the cloth, my dear madam," he was saying in sonorous tones that rang around the tiny shop like a trumpet-fanfare. "I do not care to know which mill the material came from, or what type of loom it was woven upon, nor yet the name of the poor wretched chit who tended the shuttles. I am concerned with two questions only, honored lady. One—how will it look under the light? And two—*will it wash?*"

He uttered the last three words in such a vibrant basso-profundo that the crowded shelves rattled, and the good lady behind the counter quivered in sympathy.

"I'll take my oath on that, Mr. Dermot, sir," she said hastily, then turned to Gerard, adding, "Will I leave you to examine the fabric, while I see to this young gentleman here? Because I know you always like to take your time, God rest you—"

"Time—ah, time indeed. What is time?" asked the customer rhetorically, running the bolt of royal blue material through his fingers, while he gazed into the middle distance. "What is this brief span of mortal life? What is the riddle of eternity—and what is the mystic secret of the Sphinx? Speak, oh speak!"

"Take no notice of him, dotey, for he's a theatrical," the shopkeeper explained to Gerard, in a hoarse whisper, for no doubt he was looking more than a little startled. "And what can I do for you, now—would it be wigs you're wanting?"

Gerard reluctantly replaced the chestnut mane of curls that he had been examining upon its dummy head, and replied, "Well—no . . . Not a wig exactly. I'm more interested in—um—well—have you any moustaches?"

"Moustaches, is it? Then you've come to the right place, to be sure!" she exclaimed pulling out a drawer from below the counter. "What size and shape would you be after?"

In half an hour's time, a young gentleman with a slightly tremulous voice, but a magnificent pair of moustachios, presented himself within the main entrance lobby of the Wexford Hotel.

The manager, a seedy individual with a dewdrop at the end of his nose, snuffled and wheezed as he emerged from the recesses of a back parlor.

"Yush?" he asked thickly, wiping his nose on his cuff.

"I—er—I am looking for Mrs.—um—Smith . . ." (Dear heaven—he had almost forgotten the name! How could he be so stupid?) "Yes—Mrs. Smith—is she here, I wonder? You see, I happen to be her—"

The manager snuffled again and broke in, "Then you're in luck, sho y'are—for here she is coming down from her room now. Here they both are—the good lady *and* her husband too."

"Her husband? But—but *I*—"

"Mr. and Mrs. Smith—here's a young gentleman waiting upon you," called the manager hoarsely.

Gerard turned, and saw Bella sailing down the staircase into the lobby on the arm of a tall, broad-shouldered man with a black beard and a pair of fleshy red lips, at present pursed around the end of a cigar.

"Gerard!" Bella broke into a peal of laughter. "What a guy you look! Why ever are you wearing that false hair? Is there to be a masquerade party? Michael, wait here for one wee moment, there's a dear . . . "

She drew Gerard to the furthest corner of the lobby, safely out of earshot, and continued confidentially, "Such a surprise, my dear—what do you think? The moment I set foot in this place, I found an old friend sitting reading his newspaper. It's Mr. O'Brian—you remember me mentioning Mr. O'Brian, I'm sure? Well, here he is, as large as life and ten times as masterful. Would you believe it, he tells me he never meant to treat me so badly; it was all a terrible misunderstanding. And, well, here he is, and here *I* am—it seems almost like the hand of fate, doesn't it?"

Gerard tried to speak, and to his chagrin heard his voice come out in rather a husky squeak. "Yes, but—what about *me?*" he asked.

"Well, my dearest boy, you're safely in Ireland and out of reach of your father, so I suppose you should think yourself lucky. And I'm quite sure you'll find some work or other very soon—and somewhere to live. I'd gladly take you home to Cork, but . . . " She indicated Mr. O'Brian, who stood with his back to them, finishing his cigar, and gazing out into the street, and widened her eyes expressively. "You see how I'm placed, don't you?"

"But the room here—upstairs—you've booked it for both of us—Mr. and Mrs. Smith—"

"Ah, well—as to that. It seems that Mr. O'Brian happens to have a few days at leisure, and so do I—isn't that a coincidence? You must let me introduce you to him before you go. Oh, and do take off that absurd moustache, you look quite ridiculous. Michael, dearest, come and meet my little cousin Gerard."

One hour later, Gerard was seated in the Snug—a cozy little tap-room next door to the lobby—staring into a glass of ale and pondering on the miseries of life. At this very moment, "Mr. and Mrs. Smith" were somewhere upstairs, doubtless rollicking together upon a comfortable double bed, while he sat here with nowhere to go, and nothing to do—except curse his ill luck, and have another drink.

"Another drink," he muttered thickly, draining his glass and pushing it across to the potboy.

"Another drink? That's exceedingly civil of you, my dear sir—I would be more than happy to accept your kind invitation."

"No, I didn't mean—I—"

Gerard stopped, recognizing the stranger who had joined him; the beaver hat and shabby coat might not be memorable, but those resounding chest-notes were unmistakable.

"Oh—yes—all right—we'll have two more drinks," he corrected himself.

"You're a noble-spirited gentleman, sir, I can tell that at a glance." The newcomer introduced himself. "Dermot Maguire, and your humble servant."

He removed his hat with a sweeping gesture, revealing a wealth of greying locks around a bald patch.

"Gerard Mallory," responded Gerard, as they shook hands. "Am I right in believing that you are a—um—member of the theatrical profession?"

"A thespian, sir—born and bred. Remind me to give you my card the next time we meet. It will interest you a good deal, I think, for it lists every one of the crowned heads of Europe, before whom it has been my privilege to perform. Tell me, are you in the business yourself, may I ask?"

"The business?" Gerard wrinkled his brow. "Oh, you mean an actor? Good heavens, no. In fact, I'm not in any kind of business—I only wish I were."

"Is that so? I understand your feelings particularly well, for at the moment my own plans have miscarried, and I am between engagements. You'll forgive my understandable confusion, but I believe I saw you in old Mother Molloy's shop not two hours since, purchasing some whiskers?"

Gerard, who had removed the offending moustache and stuffed it into his pocket, reddened. "Um—yes . . . That's right. But I don't go in for performing or anything like that—not in a professional way, you understand."

"No? More of a literary gentleman, perhaps?" Mr. Maguire eyed the volume which Gerard had been reading to pass the time, one of a selection he had pulled from his book-bag, which now rested beside him upon the battered trunk. "Fond of reading, eh?"

"I enjoy poetry, yes, and plays." Gerard held up the book so that the old actor could read the title upon the spine: *The Merchant of Venice.*

"*The Merchant*—?" Mr. Maguire stared at him as if he were the ghost of Hamlet's father. "Can I believe my eyes? You read Shakespeare? You know—you actually *know*—*The Merchant*?"

"Well, yes, I take pleasure in studying the plays, just for my own amusement, you understand . . . "

"By gad, I do believe you have been sent here from heaven above, to help me in my time of trial!"

"I beg your pardon—?"

The potboy returned and placed two glasses of ale before them; Gerard produced a guinea, and the youth wandered off in search of small change. This simple transaction had not gone unnoticed by Mr. Maguire, either, but he continued dramatically, ignoring the interruption.

"I was about to set out upon a grand tour of the land with my renowned company of players—we have a booking in Waterford, and another in Youghal. And now my leading juvenile has been taken from me at the eleventh hour, due to an over-indulgence in strong liquor and a misunderstanding with the local magistrates. He will not be able to take up the roles of Mercutio, Albany, Laertes or Bassanio for three months at the very earliest."

He lifted his glass and gazed levelly at Gerard across the bubbles of foam. "Tell me, my dear sir, are you familiar with Bassanio?"

Gerard laughed, for he had just been refreshing his spirits with the opening scene.

"Good signors both, when shall we laugh? Say when?
You grow exceeding strange—must it be so?"

Mr. Maguire regarded him dubiously, his head a little on one side, then said at last, "Beggars can't be choosers —you'll do . . . " And took a long swig.

"I don't quite understand—what do you mean, sir? I'll *do*. Do what?"

"Do at a pinch—as a walking understudy. My dear sir, give me your hand, and welcome to the Maguire Touring Company of Thespians. You and I, sir, will travel the length and breadth of the country together—and beyond it, I shouldn't wonder!"

"Beyond? But—but—" Gerard was at a loss for words.

"Why not? 'Come the three corners of the world in arms, and we shall shock them!' Today—Ireland; tomorrow—the wide world!"

But Garnet had no crystal ball and no such glimpse into the future, and so she closed her eyes as the family carriage rattled along on its way to Petersfield, and she slept peacefully—a sweet, dreamless sleep.

9

A New Life

Garnet awoke at last, when the pace of the carriage altered, as they slowed down on their arrival at Petersfield, and then, moments later, turned in under an archway to the inn-yard behind the Red Lion hotel.

With a clatter of hooves upon cobblestones, the pair of horses were reined in, and the coachman jumped down to open the door, expecting young Gerard to alight.

"Why—Miss Garnet—!" he stammered. "I thought—the master told me—"

"All right, Hodge, don't worry," Garnet reassured him as she stepped down. "I am come in Gerard's place, to explain to the Recruiting Officer. Do not trouble your head about it any more. And—Hodge—"

She put her hand in her reticule, and produced some coins. "Whatever you do—keep this intelligence to yourself, please. There is no need for my father to know what has taken place. I may trust you, may I not?"

He accepted the money doubtfully, touching the brim of his old-fashioned tricorne hat. "That you may, Miss Garnet, I'll not breathe a word, but—am I to wait here for you, and take you back to Rosewood?"

"Thank you, no, that won't be necessary. You may travel back at once. I shall make my own way home—in my own time."

Just how much time was, in fact, to elapse before Garnet's homecoming, she could not know; and if she had known, it would probably not have changed anything—for her mind was made up, and she was intent on one objective only. She was on her way to find Edmund, and nothing else mattered now.

"And the box, Miss? Master Gerard's box, shall you want me to take that back again for you?"

"No, Hodge, you will carry it inside, and leave it here—with me. I have a use for it."

So Hodge obeyed orders and shouldered the military chest that contained all Gerard's uniform and gear, following Garnet into the inn.

There Garnet spoke to the landlord—a coarse-featured man with a florid complexion—and asked for one night's accommodation. The man recognized her to be a young lady of quality, and hurried to do her bidding. Within a short space of time, a fire had been lit in one of the rooms upon the first floor, and the bed was aired with the aid of a brass warming-pan full of hot coals. Hodge lugged the wooden chest into the room, tipped his hat once more, and made his way home to Rosewood—still puzzling on this strange turn of events, which he could not possibly understand.

Once he had gone, Garnet locked the bedroom door and took a deep breath—then lifted the lid of Gerard's box . . .

Slowly and carefully, she unpacked each item of clothing, each piece of equipment, and laid it out upon the bed. The moment had come at last, and for a second she shivered in anticipation at the enormity of her action. But she steeled herself: this was her only chance, her only way to achieve the happiness she longed for.

With shaking fingers she began to undress, unbuttoning her bodice, unfastening bows, and untying tapes. One by one she removed every garment that she was wearing, until she stood, trembling very slightly, completely naked, her skin bathed in a soft amber glow from the firelight. She put one hand up to her luxuriant dark ringlets, and felt a pang of regret—but no . . . With her other hand she touched the soft curling fleece that veiled her mount of Venus, almost defiantly. From now on she would wear her hair in matching style; her crowning glory would be sacrificed in favor of short, springing curls, above as well as below!

Swiftly, she went to her reticule and took out a pair of scissors that she had brought from home for this very purpose. There was one poor looking-glass above the overmantel, and—feeling the warmth from the fire upon her legs, like a kind caress across her thighs—she stood close to the glass and set to work with the scissors.

Five minutes later, the job was done. Her elegant tresses lay on the floor at her feet, and a stranger stared back at her, from the mottled reflection: the face of a startled boy, with a boy's cropped head of hair.

She wondered how to dispose of the cut locks—should she burn them in the grate? No, she knew how disagreeably burning hair smelled, and she was afraid that the rank odor might draw attention to the room. Instead, she opened the little window, which looked out upon a flat roof above the bar parlor, and then gathered up the hairclippings as best she could and tumbled them out on to the ledge below. The winter wind would soon blow them away; and perhaps in time some bird or other might make use of them in building a nest . . . She smiled to herself, pleased at the thought.

Then she brushed herself carefully all over, with a hand-towel that hung by the washbasin, to remove any remaining traces of hair. She felt sure that the clothes she was about to wear would be uncomfortable enough, without any extra irritant to chafe her soft skin.

Finally, she returned to the bed, and began to dress herself again—in Gerard's clothes.

First, his under-garments: stockings, undershirt and drawers. The drawers felt very strange, with their opening at the front—she felt oddly exposed and vulnerable when she glanced down at herself. Next she put on his best shirt, finest linen, with a touch of ruffling at the neck, and followed this by pulling on the white breeches. Her legs seemed to be tightly encased after the comparative looseness of a long skirt. Yet, as she moved to pick up the white waistcoat, and took a pace to the head of the bed, she felt a sudden sense of freedom at the easy movement. She could step out boldly now, with nothing to restrict her, and she almost laughed aloud.

She buttoned the waistcoat easily. This wasn't after all nearly as difficult as she had feared.

Next, the boots, of fine black leather. (There were spurs, too, but she had no need to concern herself with those yet; she wasn't going to go off on horseback tonight.) She had considerably more difficulty in tugging the boots on and wished she had brought one of the maids along to assist in this awkward operation, but of course that would have ruined everything. So she struggled on alone. Luckily, Gerard's feet were rather bigger than Garnet's, although brother and sister were more or less of a size in every other respect, and at last she managed the arduous task, and stood upright, a good inch taller, upon Gerard's manly heels.

Now came the jacket, a resplendent garment, short-skirted and bright scarlet, with parallel lines of gold lace across the chest, wide lapels and pointed cuffs in blue and gold. Blue and gold, too, was the striped girdle that nipped it in at the waist, and upon each shoulder was a handsome gold epaulette. A white sash crossed diagonally from the left epaulette to the right hip; and this, with a pair of white gloves that Garnet now drew on, completed the entire picture.

She walked to the mirror once more, and surveyed herself as best she could—the very image of a junior officer in the Dragoons.

All that remained was to discover if her disguise would pass muster. She squared her shoulders, crossed the room once more with a boyish stride, and unlocked the door.

A buzz of masculine talk and laughter floated up from the bar-parlor, as Garnet made her way down the stairs.

The landlord was busy at the farthest corner of the bar, serving tankards of ale, and Garnet kept her face turned away from him as best she could. But the room was crowded with uniformed men, and she hoped he would not notice her among all the others.

One of the young men—a boy of about Gerard's age, she fancied—eyed her with curiosity, and said, "Hello, there! You're a stranger, ain't you? When did you get here?"

"About an hour ago," said Garnet, speaking in as low a register as she could contrive. "I've only just listed—I drove here straight from home."

"Then let me introduce myself," said the other, holding out his hand. "My name's Blades. Richard Blades—Ensign. Glad to make your acquaintance, my friend."

Garnet tried not to wince as he squeezed her hand in a muscular clasp, but responded, "How d'ye do, sir? My name's Mallory—Ensign Mallory."

"Have you seen the chief yet?" asked Master Blades. "Does he know you're here?"

"The chief? I was told to present myself to Major Sterne—"

"That's the fellow—Recruiting Officer—he's in charge of all newcomers like yourself. There he is—over by the counter, d'ye see? Better go and make yourself known to him, young 'un."

Garnet looked and saw the man that Ensign Blades

pointed out, a middle-aged gentleman with graying hair and a pair of spectacles that gave him a rather school-masterly air.

"He's not a great fighting man, by all accounts—blind as a bat, which must be deuced inconvenient in battle, eh? That's why they give him all the office work to do. He's a great one for making up lists and keeping accounts and that sort of farting about," young Blades explained airily.

Farting about? Garnet could not believe her ears; no one had ever used such a phrase in her presence before—she only knew what it meant from a vague recollection of a stable-yard conversation overheard in childhood, when one of the grooms was describing a highly incontinent horse. She realized too late that if she were to go as a man among men she must expect some coarseness of language, but her cheeks burned and she could not disguise her blushes.

Ensign Blades stared at her, "Why, what's up, young 'un? Feeling the warmth of the room, are you? Here, you never told me, what's your first name?"

Confused and off guard, still trying to recover her composure, she heard herself replying, "Garnet," before she could stop herself.

She caught her breath; how stupid of her to let it slip. She had meant to say "Gerard," but it was too late now.

"Garnet, eh? That's an uncommon name, my boy—Ensign Garnet Mallory. Well, come over here, and I'll present you to the major, Garnet."

He led her across the crowded room. Garnet was very aware of several pairs of eyes upon her, and she hoped against hope that the landlord was too busy to single her out.

Major Sterne was cordial, but vague; his day's work was over, and he was taking his ease, and had already consumed quite a few tankards of ale. He shook hands with Garnet, as Ensign Blades performed the introductions, and said, "Mallory, is it? Yes, yes, I think you're upon my list—yes, I'm almost sure of it. I wrote to your father just the other day, it all comes back to me now, Mallory. Let me see, what's your first name, something beginning with G, isn't it?"

With Ensign Blades at her elbow, Garnet was forced to say, "My name is Garnet, sir. Garnet Mallory."

"Oh, really? Yes, no doubt, I made a note of it somewhere, I think. Well, here you are, Garnet Mallory—on the threshold of a new life!"

(How true that was, Garnet thought, he would never know . . .)

"Let me buy you a drink to celebrate the occasion, a drink for both of you, lads, good lads both, I'm sure. Blades, find us a table—mine host, another round!"

Garnet froze as the landlord himself approached to take the order; the man glanced at her briefly, without interest, and his glance slid past her without a flicker of recognition. She realized, with a flood of relief, that she must indeed present a very different aspect from the shy young lady who had entered the hotel an hour ago.

They settled at a corner table, and Garnet listened to the babble of military chatter that swirled around the low-ceilinged parlor.

". . . New Commander—Major-General Broccard Savage, they tell me . . . "

"Old Brock, the men call him . . . Bit of a tartar, so I'm told . . . A real swine for discipline!"

"Anyone else new? Who's his second-in-command?"

"Daisy Deverell, of course—unless some poor bastard pushes him overboard on the way to Portugal!"

"Drowning's too good for the bugger, if you ask me . . . "

Garnet lowered her eyes, and tried not to listen, but Major Sterne was addressing her directly, "Your first night away from the family, lad? Feeling a touch of homesickness, I dare say?"

"No, sir, I—I'm perfectly happy, thank you." She nerved herself to ask the question that had been burning on her lips ever since she arrived. "Do you know—is—Captain Edmund Challoner—here, by any chance?"

"Ned Challoner? Why, is he a friend of yours?"

"He—has connections with my family, sir."

"Does he indeed? Good chap, Ned—one of the best. No, he's not with us—he rode on ahead with the first contingent, set off from Guildford the night before. He'll be in Southampton by now.

"Southampton . . ." She felt a sudden tremor of excitement at the thought. "And we shall be there—when? Tomorrow?"

"Tomorrow, yes, as soon as possible, for we are to make an early start. You'll hear the bugle blowing to rouse you at dawn, lad, and then we'll be on our way directly."

Ensign Blades sighed, "They'd better blow loud and strong for *my* benefit—I'm not over keen on early rising, are you?"

"Oh, I don't mind," she replied. "I shall be quite pleased to get on—the sooner we reach Southampton, the better!"

"That's the spirit, my boy," said the major. "Ah—here's the worthy landlord, with our drinks."

As the man set the tankards upon the table, he winked at Major Sterne, and leaned over, confiding in a hoarse whisper, "By the by, sir; you were asking me earlier about feminine company?"

"Not now, my good man." The major frowned, slightly discomfited, and indicated his two subordinates. "Can't you see I'm rather busy at the moment?"

"Oh, *they* won't pay no heed, I'm sure, sir!" chuckled the landlord. "Old enough to be interested in a pretty skirt or a pair of titties themselves, I'll be bound, eh?"

Ensign Blades dug Garnet in the ribs, and grinned. "It's all right, sir, you can talk freely before us; we're men of the world, ain't we, Garnet?"

"Well . . . What have you got to tell us, landlord? Some pretty doxies in the neighborhood, perhaps?" The major took a pull at his beer and brightened up. "Some young lights-o'-love, willing to join the party?"

"Not exactly that, sir, but . . . If you make it worth

my while . . . I could put you in touch with a certain young lady—who might provide a little bit of fun. If that's what you've a mind to?"

The major coughed primly, and said, "We'll—er—we'll discuss it later, if you please . . . Now drink up, lads—I give you a toast: to King and Country!"

Garnet took one sip of beer, and put the tankard down again hastily. She had never tasted the strong, bitter brew until now, and it was not at all to her taste. But the major, rambling on in a maudlin way about the honor and pride he felt in serving with His Majesty's glorious army, did not notice.

Under cover of this military monologue, however, Ensign Blades nudged Garnet again. "What's up, young 'un? Don't you enjoy strong ale?"

"Well, no, Mr. Blades. At home I wasn't allowed to drink beer, so I'm not used to it."

"Cheer up, you'll soon grow to like it—I did! And for heaven's sake let's drop the formalities, eh, Garnet? I'm Richard, though most of my friends call me Dicky! Now —do you want me to polish off that tankard, when nobody's looking?" he added, obligingly.

"If you would, I'd be very grateful, Dicky," said Garnet.

As soon as she could reasonably get away without giving offense, she made her excuses to the major, and said she was tired after her journey; she would look forward to meeting her companions again in the morning.

She made her way up to her room, her head thick with the fumes of ale and tobacco that had hung around the bar-parlor, and proceeded to undress once more. So far, so good; at least no one here had the least suspicion of her true identity, and tomorrow she would be reunited with Edmund, and her troubles would be over. She looked forward eagerly to an unimaginably bright future, traveling as his companion (his bodyservant, perhaps? For Dicky Blades had told her that many of the ensigns were detailed to wait upon their superior officers in this way) wherever fortune should lead them both. Disguised as a soldier, she would never have to be parted from him again; and once he saw how bold and resourceful she was, and how unlike a demure young lady, she felt certain he would love her with renewed ardor.

She removed her jacket, waistcoat and breeches; then folded them all carefully and hung them over the back of a chair.

The breeches were warm to her touch, and she stroked the rough, male garments with her fingertips. They reminded her of something—she tried to remember what it was.

Climbing into bed (which the warming-pan had left deliciously welcoming to her tired limbs), she blew out the candle upon the table near by, and sank back against the pillow, gazing drowsily into the heart of the fire, where the coals had now turned to glowing embers. She tried to recapture the elusive memory. Something to do with the feel of a man's clothes . . .

Of course, it all came rushing back to her: it was that other occasion, two years ago, when she had had to disguise herself in her brother's attire. She remembered the feel of the coarse woolen breeches, still hot with sunlight. And she remembered Jem . . .

She recalled every detail with crystal clarity, as she had re-created the scene in her mind, time and again since then.

She shut her eyes, and let herself drift back into that long-vanished summer day; they were together, in the cool water of the fishpond, and Jem was teaching her to swim.

"Do you keep your chin well up, missy," he was telling her, standing up to his waist in the clear water. And as she struggled to obey she was aware of the strange sight of his body below the surface, his strong legs spread wide as he took a firm stance, and the even stranger sight of his masculinity, dimly perceived under the ever-changing distortion of the water . . . It seemed to be altering all the time, it seemed to develop and grow and thicken . . .

She felt his hands upon her. First at her waist, holding her up in the water, then one hand sliding towards her bosom. The shock of excitement that possessed her as his fingers cupped her breasts . . . And then the even greater shock, like a revelation, as his other hand traveled further and further down, stroking her hip, moving on to her thigh, and then slipping irresistibly below into the secret place between her thighs . . . The touch of his inquiring fingers had made her shiver with ecstasy. Even now, after all this time, she remembered it still, so vividly.

And at this moment, with a sudden sensation of alarm, she heard the handle of the bedroom door being turned, and the door swung open.

Instantly, she blamed herself. She had forgotten to lock it before retiring to bed—how could she have been such a fool? And in the same instant, she caught her breath, as she recognized her visitor.

"Good evening, my little darling," whispered Major Sterne thickly. "Don't be afraid, my dear girl, I am a friend. Pass, friend—and all's well."

He approached the bed, as Garnet clutched the sheets closely about her.

"A little bird told me you were all alone, dearest one," he continued. He stumbled over the edge of the bedside rug, and Garnet could smell the alcohol on his breath. "Alone—and in need of company, I dare say? A single young lady, traveling alone, has every reason to seek the company of well-disposed gentlemen—like myself. An officer and a gentleman, I do assure you!"

He sketched a mock salute, swayed, and lurched against the edge of the bed. "Allow me to introduce myself, my dearest darling girl," he began, groping with the bedclothes.

"That won't be necessary, Major Sterne," said Garnet, in as deep a voice as she could produce. "I was happy to make your acquaintance over a tankard of ale, sir, surely you can't have forgotten already?"

"What's that?" The major gasped, and peered short-sightedly at the figure in the bed. "Must have left me spectacles down below—what—who are you?"

"Ensign Mallory, Major, the new recruit," said Garnet. "Can it be that you have come into the wrong room?"

"Damn fool of a landlord, gave me wrong directions. Told me there was a pretty young—humph—no, well, never mind . . . These rogues are all the same; not to be trusted. Forgive me for disturbing you, Ensign Mallory. Apologize for any inconvenience . . . Can't think how it happened . . ."

And he retreated sheepishly from the room; Garnet was out of bed in a trice, locking the door after him and thanking heaven for a lucky escape.

Dawn broke all too soon, and when Garnet presented herself, ready for departure in the yard, together with a bleary-eyed Dicky Blades and a dozen other young officers, Major Sterne made no reference to the mysterious events of the previous night.

Another mystery was to be posed later, for when the landlord dispatched one of the chambermaids to Miss Mallory's room, at noon—the young lady not having put in an appearance at breakfast-time—the maid came rushing down again in a great fluster, saying that there was no one in the bedroom—although all Miss Mallory's clothes were hanging up in the cupboard, and she had left a little heap of money upon the washstand, to pay for her board . . . But how could the young lady have vanished into thin air, and apparently totally undressed too? This was a mystery indeed, and one which was still earnestly discussed at the Red Lion, Petersfield, for many a long day—but no satisfactory solution was ever hit upon.

Major Sterne, rather short-tempered and irritable, and far less sociable than upon the previous evening, soon assigned Garnet to a horse for the journey.

"This little chestnut mare should serve you as a mount

—she's not too sturdy, but you're only a pipsqueak your-self, so I dare say you'll be suited to one another. Come, lad, to the saddle with you, up and away, for it's many miles to Southampton, and we must make an early start!"

The column of horsemen set off in fine style, the noise of hooves echoing through the empty streets as the little country town slowly stirred into life. A yawning potboy stood at the door of the Red Lion and watched them go, waving an ironic farewell.

"Off with you—into battle!" he said to himself. "Sooner you than me . . . "

But Garnet's spirits were high as she cantered along on the little chestnut mare. For one thing, this was the first time, since she was a child, that she had been able to ride in the way she loved best; astride the horse, her knees gripping its powerful flanks, and feeling the surging mo-tion between her thighs. Suddenly, the world seemed bright and new, and full of hope—everything was possible. As the Major had said, this was a new life.

She thought of Edmund, with love in her heart, and boundless hope; and then she found herself thinking of Jem, as well.

Perhaps it was because her reverie, lying in bed last night, had been so abruptly interrupted; or perhaps be-cause she saw a pond under some alder trees as she rode by, and remembered that first swimming lesson. Or per-haps it had something to do with the exciting feel of the brute force pounding rhythmically beneath her.

Once more, she gave herself up to the recollection of that long-lost afternoon . . .

At last they had come out of the water, to lie side by side on the grassy bank, drying themselves in the hot sunlight. She could still see the way the last liquid drops sparkled upon his chest, caught up in the curling blond hairs that clustered there; and other water-drops coursed slowly across his flat, muscular belly, to lose themselves in the tangle of that other, coarser hair . . .

Jem followed her gaze, and smiled as he saw she was looking at his rampant nakedness.

"Ain't you never seen a man before? A *proper man?*" he asked.

"No—not like that . . . " she breathed.

"There's a lot as you've still got to learn, I reckon," he said quietly, and rolled over towards her, until they were face to face, lying on their sides.

With surprising gentleness, he began to explore her body; featherlight touches arousing sensations that she had never known before. He caressed her nipples, until they stood up hard beneath his fingers; he traced a long, deliciously slow path from each breast all the way to her navel, and lower yet, to her soft down of secret curls, gradually easing her legs apart, and leading her to open herself to him like a flower unfolding into blossom.

Slowly and surely, he drew her further into the mysteries of sensual pleasure; gradually he turned her onto her back and rolled across her open thighs. She was lost in a kind of delirium, and through her shuddering transports of ecstasy, she was aware of his own growing excitement. She heard his breath coming in ever shorter gasps; and knew that something—somehow—was about to reach a climax.

"Do you help me," he whispered in her ear, panting. "Put your hand here—hold onto me, and guide me—"

Lying beneath him, heedless of anything else except to obey him and please him she let him place her hand down between their bodies and touched warm hard flesh that pulsed violently as she grasped it. She tried to do as she was bidden, and held tightly—

His panting suddenly changed, he gave a frantic moan —she thought for a second he was in pain—then a little cry that she could not interpret at all, and at once she felt a hot, sticky sensation flooding between her fingers . . .

"Too quick," he said at last, when he could speak. "Too soon . . . Better luck next time."

Only there had never been a "next time," and that was why, when Garnet rode off to Southampton to find her love —dressed in uniform and ready to risk everything for his sake—she was still a virgin. When she gave herself at last to Edmund, he would be the first man ever to possess her ... Or so she believed.

But in this life, things rarely work out the way we expect them to, and Garnet was destined to meet with many startling surprises, before she was very much older.

The first surprise came all too quickly, and was a bitter blow.

When the rearguard party of Dragoon Guards arrived at Southampton at last (Garnet took one comprehensive glance at the town, and dismissed it as a very poor sort of place, and far inferior to Guildford), Major Sterne led them to the docks, where they were to take ship for Lisbon.

The young officers dismounted, stretching their legs and easing cramped buttocks after their long ride, and several orderlies appeared as if by magic to take charge of the horses, and ship them aboard the transport.

The sailing ship *Ariadne* lay at harbor, rising and falling gently on the slight swell, and a long line of soldiers were busying themselves with crates, barrels, boxes, loading the vessel with their luggage, like a little army of ants carrying precious treasures into their nest.

Garnet, unaccustomed to such a journey on horseback, felt stiff and tired, and Dicky Blades fell into step beside her as they strolled along the dockside.

"How's your rear-end, young 'un?" he asked sympathetically. "Got a sore bum from all that bouncing up and down? I tell you what, Garnet, I've some special ointment my mother packed in my luggage. When we get on board ship, let's try to share a cabin, and I'll anoint your poor old arse for you, if you like! Capital sort of muck, it'll soon take the pain away."

Garnet tried to persuade her well-meaning friend that

she had no need of his ministrations, and in any event, she hoped to be able to secure a cabin to herself for the journey.

Dicky laughed: "And pigs might fly! We'll be packed in below decks like pickles in a jar, I'll be bound . . . Everyone will have to share."

"Well, if that's the case, I hope I may share with Captain Challoner," Garnet said, trying to keep her voice steady. "I think I told you, he's an old friend of my family."

Dicky stopped a passing orderly, and said, "Hey, you there, is Captain Challoner anywhere about? Is he already gone aboard?"

"He's aboard all right, sir—but not on the *Ariadne*. Captain Challoner sailed in the *Penelope*—that's *Ariadne*'s sister ship—at first light this morning, with the vanguard troops. They'll be halfway to the Bay of Biscay by now, I shouldn't wonder."

This was a desperate blow to Garnet, but she swallowed hard and did her best not to let her emotions betray her, merely nodding—for she did not trust herself to reply—as Dicky continued.

"Well, that's that, so it seems you'll be better off bunking down with me after all, old fellow. I'll have a word with the Transport Officer and do my best to fix it."

Garnet watched dumbly as Dicky Blades bustled off, then she turned away, and walked heedlessly along the sea-wall.

Major Sterne called after her, "Mallory! Don't get yourself lost, young man—we're all to go aboard in the next hour and they hope to set sail on the high tide. D'ye hear?"

Garnet nodded again and carried on walking, not caring where she went, anxious only to be alone with her thoughts. She found herself thinking of the handkerchief that she carried in the bosom of her shirt, next to her heart: a silk handkerchief embroidered with the monogram E.C.—the last souvenir she had of Edmund. She longed to take it out now, to put it to her eyes and dry her tears of disappointment . . .

But of course she would not let herself cry. Whatever happened, she must *never* cry. She had to continue to play the role she had undertaken, and Ensign Mallory must never give way to tears.

Well, it was a setback, but what of that? Soon they would be at sea, and in a few more days they would be in Lisbon, and there she would find Edmund again. It was just a matter of being patient for a little while longer.

Still walking, struggling to control her emotions, she found that she had left the scene of activity far behind. At this point the harbor wall ended, and beyond lay a huddle of brick buildings, warehouses, for the most part, where cargoes were stored.

She went on, past great bales of evil-smelling fiber, and then made her way out of the cold—for there was a chilly breeze springing up off the sea—into one of the warehouses.

It was quite dark inside, and it took a moment for her eyes to get accustomed to the gloom. This was a cavernous place; she was aware of great black shapes looming up around her, huge wheels and shafts of iron, devised for some purpose she could not guess at. Then she heard a loud, brazen clanging; someone was beating upon an anvil . . . This must be some kind of forge—yes, for she recognized the regular swing of a blacksmith's hammer, and the hiss of cold water upon red-hot metal. It reminded her of the stables at home. Somewhere ahead of her, there was a glow of orange light and she felt a sudden wave of heat surge toward her—and stopped dead . . .

Beyond her, upon the wall, was a mighty shadow—the monstrous figure of a creature with the body of a horse and the head and shoulders of a man. She put her hand to her mouth, choking back a cry of fear, and swung around, not knowing what to expect—hardly sure whether she was waking or sleeping.

There stood the forge, with a fire that burned dazzlingly bright, making her shield her eyes against what seemed to be a leaping curtain of flame. In front of the forge was a horse, and beside the horse a man, so their two shadows had been blended into one shadow, half-man and half-beast.

The man, who was in the midst of shoeing the animal, turned to look at her. He wore a leather apron over his breeches, and he was naked to the waist except for a loose jerkin which swung from his broad shoulders. She saw how his sweating brown body shone in the glare of the forge, as if it had been oiled. And she saw his face.

He looked at her for a moment, without speaking, then asked, "Who the devil are you?"

His voice was deep and strong, and resounded under the high roof. If Edmund's voice, the first time she heard it, had reminded her of a violin, this was a very different instrument. When this man spoke, she thought of a trumpet—a clarion call to arms.

"Who are you?" he repeated impatiently. "What do you want with me?"

"Nothing, she replied at last, when she could speak. "I —I'm Ensign Mallory—waiting to go on board the troopship."

"Which regiment?" he asked, and the question cracked like a whip.

"Third Dragoon Guards—sir," she answered.

"Are you indeed? Come closer, boy."

Still bewildered by the stranger, Garnet moved a few steps toward him, and found herself looking into the most remarkable pair of eyes she had ever seen—palest blue, though burning like fire, eyes of ice and flame. But of course she had seen those eyes before, in her dream.

And now the dream turned to reality, and waking and sleeping became one, as he asked her, "Do you know who I am, Ensign Mallory?"

"No, sir," she whispered.

"Then take a good look at me, and learn. My name is Savage—and I am your Commanding Officer."

Recollection rushed through her brain in a frenzy: Major-General Broccard Savage—"Old Brock"—"a real swine for discipline." And she remembered something that her father had said: of course, the officer who took a pride in shoeing his own horses; hadn't Gerard made some sort of joke about it? So this was the man who was to command the Third Dragoons—and control her destiny.

As if he had been reading her thoughts, he added grimly, "Yes, *Old Brock,* I see you've heard of me."

With a swift, surprising movement, he put out one strong hand, and tilted Garnet's chin. "Head up, shoulders back; learn to stand straight, boy. Be a credit to your regiment and to your country. Now get on board ship; be off with you."

He released Garnet, who stood quite still for a moment, as if mesmerized by his penetrating stare.

"You're dismissed, ensign," said the major-general. "Go and clean yourself up—you've got soot on your face."

He wiped his dirty, sweating hand upon his apron, and Garnet turned to go. As she walked away, the man raised his voice, and added one last command, "Know me, the next time you see me."

She ducked her head dumbly, and hurried out, escaping into the cold, wintry air, terrified, and strangely excited.

The horse whinnied and shifted impatiently. The major-general put a hand upon the beast's rump. "There, there. Not long now, my beauty."

But the horseshoe had gone black and cold, and he had to begin to heat it up again. He set to work, but permitted himself one brief moment of amusement, and the hint of a smile, as he repeated under his breath, "Know me next time, Ensign Mallory . . . "

PART TWO

Abroad . . .

1

What Are You Made Of?

"Come on Garnet—don't be shy—drop your breeches!"

"*No!*" She felt herself blushing furiously, and stepped back a pace, but the tiny cabin was so cramped she found herself hard up against the wall. "There's no necessity for that . . . "

"Why, what's wrong with you, lad? I'm offering to help you, ain't I?" Dicky Blades sat on the edge of the upper bunk, looking perplexed. "What are you being so finicky about?"

He had pulled off his riding boots, and stripped off his stockings; his breeches were unbuttoned below the knee and flapped loose above sturdy calves, while his bare feet dangled in mid-air. In his hand he held a jar of ointment —the precious salve that, he insisted, his mother had pronounced to be the perfect antidote to saddle-sores; and he was offering to apply some to Garnet's posterior.

"It's very kind of you, but you need not trouble," she

replied, trying to keep her voice firm and low. "I don't feel any discomfort after the ride from Petersfield, I assure you."

"You're a rare specimen, in that case—what are you made of, young 'un? You must have an arse of old leather, and muscles of whalebone, I reckon."

"I had not ridden at all yesterday, remember . . . You've had a two long days in the saddle," she reminded him.

"Well . . . That's true, I suppose . . . But I felt sure you must have a sore bum too. Heigh-ho—if you don't wish to be anointed—then you can attend to my needs instead."

He slipped down from the top bunk, and began to unfasten his waistband. Garnet looked away hastily, and turned to the door.

"I—if you'll excuse me, Dicky—I want to go up on deck . . . To see the last of England, as we sail out of Southampton water."

She tried to leave, but he moved quickly, his hand upon the latch, blocking the way.

"Oh, no—not so fast, my young bucko! I need a helping hand here, d'ye see? I can't look what I'm doing, can I? There's no mirror in this rabbit hutch of a cabin, and I ain't got eyes in my backside . . . So you'll have to be my body-servant for this once!"

Dicky undid the last button, and let his breeches slide down his boyish thighs, then let his drawers fall too, without the least embarrassment. He turned and bent over, pulling up the tail of his shirt, and presenting his rear view to Garnet's dismayed gaze.

"I don't like—I mean—it seems—"

She hesitated, stammering, as he thrust the jar of salve into her hand. "Come on, look sharp about it—why are you making such a fuss, old son?"

"I've never had to do such a thing before." She tried to explain her confusion.

"What? Never applied a healing lotion to some poor

174

schoolboy after he's been birched? You must have done—"

"I never went to school . . . I was educated privately, at home."

"Oh! That explains why you're so pernickety . . . Well, you'll soon get used to the sight of other chaps in the raw, now you're in the army, Ensign Mallory . . . Come on, get to work, for my poor old arse is stinging quite rotten."

Garnet realized that this was indeed true; "in the raw" was a cruelly accurate description of Dicky Blades' buttocks—for the long hours in the saddle had taken their toll, and his most tender parts were rubbed a violent red. As he spread his legs wider she could see that in some places under his groin the skin was sore and angry, as if it had been flayed.

Gingerly, she put a spot of ointment on her fingertips and begun to massage the painful areas, as gently as possible.

He winced and gave a little gasp of pain at the first touch, but soon her delicate handling, and the cool relief of the medicinal balm, produced more pleasant sensations.

"Ahhhh . . . That's better . . . That's very much better —keep going, young Garnet—you've got healing powers in those fingers!"

Garnet continued obediently, keeping up a regular, soothing movement, and tried not to think about the intolerable situation in which she found herself.

When they first came on board the *Ariadne,* Major Sterne—in charge of the billeting operation—allocated cabins to the officers; the private soldiers and mess orderlies were packed into long dormitories on the lowest deck, and above them their superiors were assigned to better cabins, in order of seniority.

As the most junior of recruits, Garnet and Dicky could have expected very short shrift—they might have had to make do with a pair of hammocks, strung up across a crowded cabin already occupied by four or five senior men—but Major Sterne felt a sense of responsibility to his youngest charges, and decided not to put them in with older, and perhaps more licentious, companions who might set them a bad example. Instead he had reserved the very smallest two-berth cabin on board—little bigger than a cupboard, deep in the bowels of the old sailing-ship—for their exclusive use.

The two young ensigns had stowed away their gear as best they could, and soon heard somewhere above their heads the running of feet and the blowing of whistles. Ropes were being cast off, and they felt the motion of the slow, rolling sea beneath them as the vessel set sail.

There was no porthole, for the little cabin was far below the waterline, and Garnet wished with all her heart that she could be up on deck, to see the land slipping away behind them, and smell the fresh breeze from the sea.

Instead, she was trapped in this stuffy box with a half-naked boy, her nostrils full of the odor of his sweating body and his grubby feet, and the pungent aroma of the ointment which she continued to apply to his exposed flanks.

She noticed with alarm that his male member, which had been hanging limply between his legs, was now showing signs of arousal—and stopped at once.

"There—that's enough," she said quickly, putting the ointment aside. "I hope you're feeling more comfortable. Now I will go up on deck and—"

"Stop! Don't be in such a rush to get away!" Dicky grasped her wrist. "I feel better already—a whole lot better . . . In fact, I'm rather enjoying it . . . And I'm sure you'll feel the same, when I return the favor!"

He swung round, grinning, and made a clumsy grab at Garnet's breeches, fumbling to unfasten the buttons at her waist.

"Stop!" She pushed his hand away, her cheeks blazing. "How dare you—!"

"Oh, don't be such a ninny—you're going to have to

get used to a spot of rough-and-tumble now, you know! That's the worst of not having been sent away to school —you're still so precious bashful, ain't you? Just stop being so prim, and let's get those buckskins off you . . . I'm going to have a look at your little pecker, and see what you've got to be so modest about!"

"Take your hands off me—keep away, or I shall tell the major what you do—" she protested, fending him off as best she could.

"Oh, what stuff—! Old Major Sterne's not your nursemaid, for all he's a bit of an old woman . . . What sort of man are you, Garnet Mallory, that you must run off to nursie's apron-strings? Come—let's see you stand up for yourself—and if you don't know how, I'll soon show you!"

Garnet thrust him away violently, with all her strength, as he made yet another lunge at her, fearing that at any moment her imposture would be exposed.

She was saved by the sound of a bugle, blowing hard and long.

"What's that?" she asked breathlessly. "Listen—is it a shipwreck? Are we sinking?"

"Why, you young jackass—that's the call to the cookhouse! It's time for supper . . . Well, I'll let you go this time—but don't think you're going to get away scot free, old lad! Wait till it's time for bed—I'll soon get to grips with you then, once you're in your nightshirt . . . And we'll find out what you're made of—I'll see what sort of man you really are!"

He pulled up his clothes and dressed himself quickly; Garnet was reprieved for the moment. The two ensigns found their way to the dining saloon, and there Dicky Blades made short work of a plate of bully-beef stew with dumplings. He appeared to have forgotten all about his playful threat, as he laughed and joked with his fellow-officers, and swigged a pint of small beer.

But Garnet caught his eye once or twice across the table, and he lowered his eyelid in a meaningful wink—

and she knew that he intended to tease her unmercifully as soon as they were alone in the cabin once more.

When the meal was over, she contrived to slip out of the saloon while Dicky's attention was engaged elsewhere —a party of young lieutenants were taking wagers on how many days the voyage to Lisbon would last; would it be eight, nine, or ten?—and Dicky was hopefully staking his bet.

On deck, Garnet felt the cool night air like a benediction on her flushed cheeks, and walked as far as she could go, up to the bow of the ship. England lay well astern now, and when she glanced back she could only see a blur upon the horizon: it could have been cloud, but for the occasional tiny pinprick of light from the distant shore. Ahead lay the open sea, and growing darkness, as night fell, and the ship advanced into the unknown . . . An unknown future indeed, for Garnet.

She remembered the voices of the men disputing the wager—could it really be as long as ten days before they arrived in Lisbon? Once there, she felt sure she would find Edmund immediately, and be reunited with him; from that moment on, she would be under his protection, with nothing more to fear.

But in the meantime—how could she survive ten days and nights on board this ship without being shamefully unmasked? How could she share that tiny cell of a cabin with a young man so mischievous—and so obviously lewd and dissolute—as Ensign Dicky Blades, without losing her precious secret . . . or worse?

She thought of throwing herself upon his mercy, and telling him the whole story, begging him not to tell anyone else . . . He might agree to that, indeed—but at what price? She recalled the rakish twinkle in his eye, and the lusty prowess that was evident in his young loins; and she knew that she could not hope to pass ten nights with him in such close proximity—or even one night, for that matter—without some gross indelicacy upon his part. He

178

would take advantage of her defenseless situation, she felt certain of that.

Still she paced the deck, until it was quite dark, and the stars came out overhead, glittering in stray patches of sky, among drifts of gathering cloud. She paced, and worried, cudgeling her brain to find some way out of this horrible dilemma.

Now the masculine attire that she had put on so eagerly, only a mere twenty-four hours ago, seemed like a trap that had closed upon her. The thick material of the breeches seemed to drag at her legs in a coarse embrace; the fine jacket, buttoned across her chest, felt as if it stifled her in its grip—she had done her best to flatten her breasts, tying a linen band tightly over her bosom, to disguise her natural curves, and the sensation now felt unbearably constricting.

She resented "Ensign Mallory" and longed to throw off the uncomfortable masquerade and be herself again . . . A young woman, in women's clothing—soft, and pretty, and feminine . . .

A footstep close by, in the shadows, made her start, and she caught her breath. Had Ensign Blades pursued her?

"Who goes there?" asked a deep, resonant voice.

She knew instantly who it was: those vibrant tones were unmistakable. She had been joined by Major-General Broccard Savage, her commanding officer.

"Ensign Mallory, sir," she replied.

"Who? Oh—it's you, is it?"

He stopped beside her, and put a strong hand on her shoulder, swinging her round to face him. "Don't you know you must stand to attention when addressing a senior officer, Ensign?"

"I—I'm sorry, sir . . . " She faltered, and did her best to obey.

"Not a very military bearing, young man—I've had occasion to speak to you about that before, I believe?"

"Yes, sir."

"Stand upright—so—chin up, head back, shoulders square . . . That's better."

Roughly, he pushed and pulled her into some semblance of a soldierly posture, with his hands upon her upper arms, then said, "Why, you're shivering, boy . . . What are you afraid of? Is it me? Look at me when I speak to you, Ensign!"

She summoned up all her courage, and stared him full in the face.

The clouds had thickened now, and the night sky above was almost pitch-black; but in some strange way his eyes seemed to glow with a brilliant inner light of their own . . . Palest blue—ice and flame, that froze and burnt at the same time.

She had noticed at suppertime that he was not present with the other officers in the saloon, and guessed that he preferred to dine alone, in his own cabin. She wondered now what he was doing here, walking the deck.

At the very same moment, his words chimed with her thought.

"What are you doing out on deck, young man?"

"I . . . I came to get some fresh air . . . sir."

"What's wrong? Is the motion of the ship disturbing your stomach? Feeling queasy, is that it?"

"No, sir—not at all," she replied honestly—for in fact she had scarcely noticed that the sea was growing rougher now, and the vessel had begun to pitch and toss as they forged ahead through the black, oily waters.

"That's as well—for it'll be worse in the Bay of Biscay, they tell me . . . But if you're not ill—what's the trouble? Is it a different kind of sickness that upsets you? Home-sickness perhaps?"

"Not that either, sir."

"No? Tell me—how long is it since you left home? How long have you served with the Dragoons?"

"I left home yesterday evening, sir."

"I see . . . I thought as much." His lips twitched once;

then he put out his hand and, very lightly, lifted her head with one finger below her chin.

At the instant that his fingertip touched her, she trembled—feeling an electric current pass between them. She wondered if he felt it too, but his face gave no sign.

In the same brusque tone, he continued: "Is that what brings you here, alone in the darkness, when you should be getting some rest? You can't sleep, eh—for thinking of the family you left behind? Is that the problem?"

She had a sudden wild impulse to tell him what the problem really was—to confess the whole truth to this stern, masterful stranger—she tried to imagine what he would say . . . But he withdrew his hand, and stepped back slightly, with a curt nod.

"Well, you'll learn to live without your family in time. Better men than you have had to do so, and you'll be no different from the rest. You can survive without your loved ones, you'll find. Now take yourself off, and get some sleep . . . That's a command!"

He turned sharply, and strode off into the darkness as abruptly as he had come. With a sense almost of relief, Garnet realized that she could never have unburdened herself to him, or laid bare the details of her innermost emotions . . . He was the very last person in the world she would ever confide in.

To him, she was one tiny, insignificant detail in a vast military maneuver; an unimportant lackey, to be commanded and bullied and forced to obey orders as swiftly as possible. Nothing more than that.

Reluctantly, she set herself to obey his latest injunction, and made her way below decks to the tiny cabin, dreading the encounter that she knew must lie in wait for her there.

When she opened the door, the room was in darkness; she hoped desperately that Ensign Blades might still be amusing himself with his fellow-officers, drinking and gambling—but a smothered noise from the gloom quickly dismissed this thought.

"Garnet—is that you—?"

"Yes—are you in your bunk? Were you asleep?"

"No—I'm ill . . . It was that damned bully-beef . . . Or the d-d-dumplings . . . Or—oh, good gad—the sour beer!"

And he broke off, to emit a horrifying retching noise, then gulped. "Quick, young 'un—fetch me a basin, before I puke on the floor—!"

Somehow Garnet managed to light a candle and procure a wooden washing bowl and a ragged towel. As the ship plowed on into the Bay of Biscay, and the sea became ever more violently rough, she discovered with relief that she was a naturally good sailor. As—unluckily—poor Dicky Blades was not.

She held his head as he vomited, and cleaned him up afterward, putting a damp cloth upon his fevered brow; then pondered this unexpected development and the ironic reversal of their roles. There was no more teasing or tormenting now, and she did her best to make the unhappy youth as comfortable as possible, under the circumstances. She no longer feared or disliked him; all she felt was an overwhelming sense of pity that any human being should undergo such misery. When dawn came, he fell into an uneasy sleep; she blew out the candle and crawled into her own bunk at last, to try to snatch a few moments of rest.

Up on deck, Major-General Savage climbed to the captain's bridge, his adjutant, Major Sterne, at his heels.

They found the ship's captain surveying the horizon grimly, as it rose and fell; the windows of the wheelhouse were lashed with driving rain.

"What's the outlook, sir?" asked the major-general. "Is there any sign of this weather abating?"

"Not as far as I can tell, sir," replied the old seaman. "It looks to be set in for the next day or two, I'm sorry to say."

Major Sterne, who had passed a disagreeable night in

company with several fellow-officers who had all succumbed to nausea at one point or another, grimaced.

The sea captain misunderstood his expression of displeasure, and added: "Aye, sir—you'll be disappointed at the reduction of our speed, but 'tis bound to hold us back . . . This south-easterly is blowing against us, and the journey cannot help but be slow, I fear."

"I was thinking of our men, Captain. They've not gained their sea-legs yet—and they're in a good deal of discomfort, below decks."

Major-General Savage nodded agreement, and as they staggered awkwardly down the companion-way, clinging to the rope that served as a handrail, he added: "Not only the men, Major . . . I've no doubt it will come hardest to the new recruits. There's one I met last night, looking as if he was too young to be taken from his mother's knee . . . Ensign—Mallory, I believe the name is—d'ye know the feller I mean?"

"Yes, sir—I've spoken to him once or twice."

"The boy's so pale and delicate—why, his voice isn't properly broken yet! I couldn't help wondering how he'll survive this rude weather—and the rough life he's been flung into . . . A strange, odd sort of lad, I thought him—don't you agree?"

Major Sterne gave it as his opinion that a youngster like Garnet Mallory, plucked from the bosom of a wealthy family, must inevitably find his first initiation into military life somewhat of an ordeal.

"I suppose so . . . And yet—there's something about that young man, Major—I can't say why, but he troubles me, somehow . . . Yes—he troubles me . . . "

So the voyage dragged on. Ensign Blades was confined to his cabin for the entire duration of the trip. When it became known that he was so unwell, and that Ensign Mallory had taken it upon himself to nurse his young companion, Garnet was excused from other duties, and made Dicky Blades' welfare a full-time job.

Not that there were many other chores for the officers on board the *Ariadne*. The cavalry horses, which were quartered in the hold, had to be fed and watered daily— and exercised, as well as possible under the circumstances; but this was a labor assigned to the lower ranks.

Once, Garnet made her way down to the hold, and for the rest of her life she would never forget the impression that the spectacle made upon her. Eight or ten brawny soldiers, stripped half-naked, for it was overpoweringly warm and stuffy in such close confinement, dimly seen by the flickering light of a few lanterns, taking four horses at a time and walking them back and forth, back and forth, in the narrow space that ran between the makeshift stalls: male torsos and shining horseflesh glittering alike in the fitful lamplight.

At other times she took her recreation from the sick-room by walking on deck. The rain stopped on the third day, though there was little to be seen except the vast expanse of grey sky and greyer sea below. Once, she glimpsed the huge, black bulk of a whale breaking the surface half a mile away, and a sudden waterspout erupted from it, as the helmsman somewhere aloft shouted the traditional cry:

"There she blows!"

And on another day, a group of porpoises appeared, frolicking round the ship for all the world like a party of children let out of school and playing tag.

But these were rare diversions, and for the most part Garnet's voyage was passed below decks, tending to Dicky, trying to coax his feeble appetite with cups of soup or tots of brandy, and combing his tousled hair or bathing his hot, sweating arms and legs.

Dicky, of course, had not the slightest suspicion as to Garnet's true identity; indeed, he was entirely preoccupied with his own misfortunes, and showed no interest whatsoever in her as a companion during the long days and nights. Inevitably, he sometimes kicked off his blanket, or threw off his shirt, exposing himself without any self-consciousness—until she became almost accustomed to the sight of his naked limbs and private parts.

As for herself, she decided to remain clothed in shirt and breeches throughout the journey, and only risked removing her lower garments when the candle was extinguished at night and the little cabin was in total darkness.

Dicky Blades was unlucky in more ways than one, for the rough passage at sea delayed the vessel considerably, and although he had staked a bet on the voyage lasting ten days, it was not until the eleventh that *Ariadne* finally sailed majestically up the river Tagus and into the harbor of Lisbon.

Garnet had run up on deck as soon as she heard the news and gained her first sight of Portugal from the ship's rail. She returned to the cabin soon afterward, and gave Dicky a report on what she had discovered.

"It's a beautiful city—from all I could see—built on several hills, and all the houses painted white . . . The sun came out to welcome our arrival, Dicky, and every building seemed to shine so brightly . . . They say we'll be going ashore in half an hour or so—do you think you'll feel well enough?"

"Did you catch a glimpse of any girls on land while you were at your lookout?" Dicky asked, sitting up and showing signs of interest for the first time.

"Oh—I believe so—there were so many people along the harbor wall—the women are dressed in black, mostly—"

"Who cares what they're dressed in? It's *undressed* they interest me!" retorted Dicky, throwing aside his bedclothes and perching on the edge of the upper bunk. "I feel quite my old self again—and my poor John-Thomas is impatient for exercise—eh, old fellow?"

He pulled up his shirt, and made an obscene gesture, to demonstrate his eagerness to assert his manhood. Garnet lowered her eyes and turned away, her face pink. Even her recent enforced intimacy with Dicky could not inure her to such a priapic display.

Dicky saw her expression, and at once his mood changed. He scrambled down and stood penitently before her in his shirt-tails.

"Sorry, young 'un . . . I was forgetting—you're shocked by my loose ways, ain't you? Well, I have to own that you've behaved like a regular brick this last week or so—my own mother couldn't have taken better care of me! So I swear that from now on, I shan't rag you any more, Garnet. I'll be your best friend, and help to look after you—as you looked after me."

He clapped Garnet on the shoulder, and thrust out his hand.

"There—shake upon it, old fellow . . . And now help me get dressed, for I can't wait to see what lies in store for us in the city of Lisbon!"

Garnet too felt a thrill of excitement, though for a different reason; this was where she would find Edmund, and she looked forward with all her heart to the moment when she would see him again.

At last the *Ariadne* was made fast alongside the harbor wall, and a gangplank run out. The officers were sent ashore first, while the other ranks followed with the horses and baggage.

Major Sterne told the two ensigns that the younger officers were to be greatly honored by having their billets in the royal palace—for of course the Portuguese were loyal allies to the British in the war against Napoleon's invading army.

They set out along the narrow streets of the city, and Dicky Blades soon protested: "Beautiful, did you say? You call this place beautiful? Pooh—it stinks like a cesspit!"

Garnet had to admit that, upon closer inspection, Lisbon was something of a whited sepulcher; for the inhabitants clearly knew nothing of hygiene, and—as in medieval England—all the household slops and ordures were flung from the houses into a stream of filth that ran down the center of each street. The smell was extremely unpleasant, and she had to take great care where she walked.

As for the royal palace—that too was something of a disappointment; true, the brigade's horses were accommodated in the prince's own stables and riding-house—a superb edifice, where the animals walked upon floors of finest tile and took their hay from mangers of gleaming white marble. But the British officers accompanying the beasts were quartered in the old attics above, which were normally the province of the Portuguese stable lads—horsehair palliasses laid out in rows on the hard wooden floor, twenty or thirty men to a room.

The young captains and lieutenants grumbled angrily at this inhospitable reception, but they had to make the best of it. When they came downstairs again, Lieutenant Edgecombe, who gave himself airs, and considered himself something of a dandy because his father was a London banker, said with heavy sarcasm: "Damme if I don't change places with my horse for the night—I swear the animals are treated with more respect than we are!"

Garnet couldn't help agreeing that he had some reason for the gibe; but she was glad that the little chestnut mare was so snugly settled, after the long ordeal of the sea voyage. Once she was sure that her mount was well-housed, and properly victualed, her thoughts turned again to Edmund, and her pulse quickened . . . It would not be long now!

On the first evening ashore, the officers were expected to dine together, in the mess. A handsome old house, in the pleasantest part of the city, had been requisitioned for the use of the senior command. It had once been a ducal residence, and there were several suites of comfortable rooms at the disposal of Major-General Savage and his staff.

There was a large reception room on the first floor, and this had been converted to the officers' Mess. At seven o'clock, Garnet and Dicky—having spruced themselves up as well as possible—followed Major Sterne into the long paneled room lit by branched candelabra.

Garnet looked about her swiftly, searching for a familiar face among the little knots of uniformed men in their scarlet, blue and gold . . . But she could not instantly pick out Edmund.

There seemed to be fewer officers present than she had expected; and most of them were men she recognized from the *Ariadne*. At this moment, she heard Major Sterne ask: "Why—where's the advance guard, then? What's become of Major Clowes—Hawkins—Challoner—?"

Major-General Savage was in conversation with some of his chiefs-of-staff, by the imposing marble fireplace where some logs burnt brightly, throwing up a stream of golden sparks.

Now he turned and replied: "We shan't see them tonight, Major . . . And I fear I do not know when we shall see them again. I have just learned that they have been called to support Wellington in the field, and they rode off to join in the siege of Ciudad Rodrigo the first thing this morning . . . By all accounts, they will be flung into battle immediately—their situation is very desperate."

A log shifted and fell in the grate—and Garnet felt the room spinning around her. As everything went black, she swayed and collapsed and would have tumbled headlong, but just before she swooned Broccard Savage caught her in his arms.

2

A Change of Orders

When Garnet came to, she found herself lying on a bench in a dimly-lit room. A military cape had been rolled up and put under her head as a makeshift pillow, and an old greatcoat was spread over her body in place of a blanket. Other coats and tunics hung around her on the walls, and she realized that she was in the outer lobby which served the officers' Mess as a cloakroom.

As she stirred and looked about her, Dicky Blades, perched on a chair nearby, leaned forward hopefully.

"Garnet! I say, old fellow—are you all right?"

"What? Oh . . . Yes—yes, I think so . . . What happened?" she asked, in an uncertain voice.

"You collapsed, young 'un—keeled over like a falling tree! Took us all completely by surprise, I can tell you." He moved across and knelt beside her, a worried look on his young face. "Do you want a glass of water? A drop of brandy, perhaps? How are you feeling now?"

189

"I don't want anything . . . I'm trying to remember—I came in to the Mess with you and Major Sterne." She put a hand to her head as the memory began to drift back. "And then the major-general said—he said—oh, heavens . . ."

She closed her eyes, with the pain of the recollection.

"Here—you're not going to pass out again, are you?" Dicky wrinkled his brow. "Shall I call someone in to look after you?"

"No . . . No, I shall be perfectly well . . . It was just—for the moment—" She broke off, for she could never confess to Dicky Blades the heart-stopping shock she had received when the commanding officer had revealed—almost casually, it seemed—what had become of Edmund.

To be so near to reunion with her love, and then to have her hopes so rudely shattered . . . Edmund in battle—Edmund in danger, under fire, facing the enemy . . . The thoughts raced through her brain.

"How did I get here—after I swooned?" she asked, distractedly.

"Major Sterne and I carried you out of the Mess, between us. He said I was to stay with you till you recovered a little, and then I was to see you back to the billet . . . We can go as soon as you feel strong enough."

"Oh . . . Very well . . ." From being ghostly pale, her complexion now crimsoned, as she pictured the scene of her humiliation. "To fall down in a swoon—in front of a room full of officers . . . What must they have thought of me?"

"Oh, don't trouble yourself with that—there's a lot of sickness about, out here in Portugal, so they say. Chaps are dropping down like flies with all kinds of plague and pox . . . I say, you don't think it might be catching—whatever you've got?" he added as an uncomfortable afterthought.

Despite her unhappiness, Garnet found herself smiling faintly.

"No, Dicky—I don't think it's catching . . . You need not worry."

"That's a relief . . . And anyway, you *didn't* fall down —I mean, not in a heap on the floor, if that's what's bothering you. Oh, you probably would have done, but old Brock saw what was happening and he caught you as you started to go down . . . I must say, he moved like greased lightning!"

"Major-General Savage caught me?" She stared at him incredulously. "What are you saying? How? Why?"

"He was standing only a pace away; I suppose he noticed you'd turned a bit green—he grabbed you as you fell. He's got the strength of an ox, that man—he held you in his arms as easy as if you were only a baby."

She caught her breath. The idea of being held by Broccard Savage somehow frightened and disturbed her.

"Then what?" she asked at last, when she could control her voice. "What did he do next?"

"Oh, he passed you over to old Sterne and myself . . . 'Get this boy out of here, he's too young to be allowed to stay up to dine,' he said—joking, you see. 'It's a long way past his bedtime' . . . So we carried you in here, like I said."

"He made a *joke* about me?" Garnet clenched her fists. "How *dared* he?"

"He didn't look as if he thought it was funny," said Dicky. "In fact, he seemed quite put out . . . I heard him saying something about it being monstrous they should send youngsters like you and me to war . . . All nonsense, of course—but I suppose if you're not well—"

"I am perfectly well!" Garnet sat up. "Come, I am ready to go now."

"All right, old son—we'll make our way back to those precious stables . . . As for being sick or well—we shall soon find out, one way or the other, tomorrow morning."

"What do you mean?" She rose to her feet unsteadily, and Dicky put his hand on her arm to help her. "What is happening tomorrow?"

"You are to be sent to the military surgeon, for a physical examination . . . Old Brock's orders!"

"What?" It was as well he was holding her, otherwise she might have fallen again. "No—that's impossible—"

"He says he's not wasting pay and rations on any man who's not strong enough to pull his weight. If the medico says you're not fit—they'll pack you off home to England."

Garnet hardly slept a wink that night.

It was not because of the uninviting horsehair mattress she lay upon, nor the presence of twenty or more men stretched out in rows alongside her, in uncomfortable proximity—she could hear the sounds of their bodies twisting and turning, their heavy breathing and snores, the indistinguishable words or the eerie moans they uttered in their sleep—nor even the fact that she was ravenously hungry, for she had eaten no supper.

She lay awake in real terror at the prospect of seeing the army doctor in the morning. True, medical examinations, both for the military and for civilians, were sketchy affairs at best. Ladies never disrobed for a doctor unless it was completely unavoidable, but contented themselves with describing their symptoms, in the vaguest possible terms, so as not to transgress the bounds of modesty.

And even gentlemen, Garnet believed, would not normally be required to do more than put out their tongues, or suffer the doctor to listen to their breathing or count their pulse rate—at least, that is what she hoped. But suppose this man were to insist upon her undressing? Suppose he was determined to make a detailed examination of her anatomy?

She could not bear to consider such a horrifying possibility. She decided that when they told her where to find the surgeon's quarters, she would contrive to mislay the directions . . . She would never present herself at his office; instead she would lose her way, and say nothing about it.

Alas for her plans. When the next day dawned and

the young officers rose and went down to the stable yard, where they washed and shaved at a trough of water by a pump, Garnet's hopes were dashed yet again.

She stood waiting her turn to wash her face and hands —no more than that; for she was still dressed in the shirt and breeches that she slept in, and as anyone could see, her smooth cheeks had no need of a razor—when Major Sterne bustled in to give the orders for the day, and began to assign the captains and lieutenants to their various duties.

". . . Captains Hooker and Larwood to the parade-ground, in charge of pack-drill for the men . . . Lieutenant Edgecombe—you will take a picquet to exercise the horses. Ensigns Blades and Mallory—ah, yes, you are both excused duties this morning; you are to go to the military surgeon's office, Dr. Norton . . . I will give you instructions how to find the address."

Garnet and Dicky looked at one another, then Garnet said: "Surely there is some mistake, sir? It is only I that is to be sent for a medical examination, not Mister Blades."

"Blades is to accompany you and bring you back— those are the orders," said the major testily. "Now look sharp, all of you—there's a lot of work to be done to-day; a lot of work."

Garnet thought of trying to enlist Dicky's support, and suggesting they should disobey and play truant, but she knew he would never agree to this. And how could she make him understand why she was so alarmed at the simple prospect of seeing the doctor? She even thought wildly of giving him the slip as they walked along the narrow Lisbon streets after breakfast; of running away, deserting from the regiment, and trying to make her way alone to find Edmund . . . But that would be madness . . .

There was no escape. At nine o'clock precisely she knocked upon Doctor Norton's door, and a voice mumbled. "Come in . . ."

Beseeching a speedy deliverance, she opened the door

and walked in, leaving Dicky in the outer room cleaning his fingernails with a penknife, totally unconcerned . . . Lucky Dick, without a care in the world!

The doctor looked up. He sat at a desk—a thick-set man with jowls of fat tumbling over the edge of a grubby neck cloth, and a two-day growth of stubble on his chin. His eyes were bloodshot and watery, and his hands shook a little as he beckoned Garnet forward.

"Come closer, boy . . . Let's have a good look at you . . . You're Ensign Mallory—is that right? Yes, yes, of course—I have a chitty here, signed by the commanding officer . . . He wants me to give you a thorough examination."

He picked up a brief note, which trembled in the air as he held it in her direction . . . "Very well then—get undressed."

"If you please, sir . . . " Garnet stood rigidly at attention, in the position that Broccard Savage himself had imposed upon her. "I would prefer not to remove any of my clothing . . . For personal reasons."

"Eh? What's that?" The doctor had very thick, beetling eyebrows, and now they seemed to be climbing up to pursue his receding hairline. "What are you saying, young man?"

"I—I don't wish to undress, sir."

"Why not, in God's name? Don't be shy with me, soldier—I've seen enough naked bodies in my lifetime, I assure you. One more isn't going to make much difference . . . Now stop talking nonsense and take off that uniform."

"I'm sorry, sir. I must beg to refuse." Desperately, Garnet tried to think up some kind of explanation. "You see, sir—it was my mother's last wish . . . She made me promise—before I left home to join the army—that I would never disrobe except when I was entirely alone . . . In order to ensure that I would never be led astray by unchastity or licentiousness . . . "

194

"Damme—d'yu think *I'm* going to lead you astray, you young puppy?"

"No, sir—of course not—but you see, I gave her my word . . . I can't break that sacred promise now."

Garnet made a mental apology to her poor mother's memory; she regretted having to take her name in vain, but she hoped that in her present desperate circumstances, she might be forgiven.

There was a pause, and then the doctor rose to his feet, a little unsteadily.

"I see . . . So that's how it is." He seemed to be mildly amused. "Well, I've heard some queer tales before now, but . . . We'll say no more . . . So be it, Ensign Mallory; you shall retain your modesty."

"Thank you, sir."

Garnet tried not to flinch as the old man shuffled round the desk and approached her, but remained at attention, her arms tightly at her sides.

"We'll have to do the best we can, I suppose . . . Put out your tongue, lad."

Garnet obeyed, feeling foolish.

"Hum . . . Bowels satisfactory? No constipation? No diarrhea?"

Dismayed by such frankness, she shook her head dumbly.

"Good, good . . . shut your mouth now . . . Take a deep breath in . . . And out . . . Once again—in—and out . . . "

He stood facing her, practically nose to nose, and as she breathed in, Garnet was almost nauseated by the whiff of brandy that he exuded . . . So that was why his speech was slurred, and his hand shook; he had been drinking—and at this hour of the morning, too!

Then he put his hand upon her shoulder, and said, "I shall require to listen to your heart and lungs, boy."

"Yes, sir?" Garnet frowned, unsure what he meant by this.

"Don't be alarmed, it won't hurt you." He put his

hand upon her again, and to her dismay his fingers moved on to her collar, and she felt him commence to unfasten her tunic.

"No, sir—remember—you said you would not require me to—to—"

"I don't want you to undress, but I must open your jacket, boy. How can I listen to you through these layers of cloth?"

Fumblingly, he began to undo the tunic, loosening the gold-braided frogs, until her scarlet jacket hung open, revealing the shirt beneath.

She held her breath; surely he would stop now? But no—the doctor's hands continued to busy themselves, undoing her shirt-buttons.

She knew that only the plain linen bandage that strapped up her bosom now lay between her and discovery, and she closed her eyes.

"Hullo? What's this, eh?"

She looked down to find that he had a silken kerchief in his hands with the initials E.C. embroidered upon it . . . Of course—she had completely forgotten Edmund's handkerchief, which she always carried next to her heart, hidden inside the linen band, between her breasts. Quickly, she snatched it back.

"I'm sorry, sir—my handkerchief—"

She stuffed it into the pocket of her tunic, and prayed that her ordeal might soon be over. But the old doctor had not finished yet.

Slowly, he began to unfasten the linen band. With a cry of despair, Garnet clutched at his wrists as his hands closed over her breasts.

"Good God . . . And what have we *here*—?" he asked, his eyebrows climbing even higher.

She was discovered, and there was no more hope of concealment.

A few minutes later, fully-dressed and trying to fight back her tears, she confessed the entire story to the old doctor, and begged him not to betray her.

He said nothing at all for a long time, but sat at his desk, drumming his fingers and considering the matter. She stole a glance at him; his expression was enigmatic, but she thought she detected a twinkle in his eye.

"Please, Doctor—say nothing—send me back—and tell them there is nothing wrong with me . . . Say that I am in good health—for that is the absolute truth."

He sighed, and said at last. "I suppose I could report that you are in excellent physical shape, for God knows that is what you are!"

She saw that he was smiling, and clasped her hands pleadingly: "Oh, dear Doctor—you are the kindest and best of men. Only keep my secret and I swear I will always be grateful to you . . . " She ventured to add: "To prove my gratitude—I'll go out and buy a bottle of the best brandy in Lisbon and send it to you—I promise!"

He chuckled. "Very well, Ensign . . . I shall be like one of the three wise monkeys . . . I hear nothing, I see nothing, and I say nothing . . . And I wish you all the luck in the world, for the quest you are upon is a dangerous one indeed."

When Garnet and Dicky got back to the royal stables at last, and climbed up to their shabby attic lodgings, they found a hue-and-cry in progress. All their fellow officers were present, and everyone appeared to be talking at once: arguing, swearing, accusing or defending one another.

"What is it? What's the row about?" Dicky demanded, but it was some time before he could make himself heard.

At the heart of the disturbance was the dandified Lieutenant Edgecombe; his uniform unusually crumpled, and his face white with anger.

"Some fellow's going to swing for this, I tell you—take my word for it!" he shouted angrily, brushing a lock of hair out of his eyes. "I'll not put up with this sort of treachery—by God, I won't!"

"What's the matter?" Dicky repeated. "What's Edgecombe in such a bate about?"

"Graham Edgecombe has had his gear looted," answered one of the others. "He says there's twenty guineas missing—and a gold watch, and I don't know what else besides."

"Well, don't look at *me*—never touched his rotten money!" snapped another officer.

"It's hardly likely to be one of us responsible for your loss," pointed out Captain Hooker. "For heaven's sake—are you accusing us of turning to petty thieving?"

"All I say is—the watch and the money are gone—my purse—and a locket I had from my sweetheart—and a pair of kid gloves, and—"

"You keep adding to the list each time you tell the tale!" retorted Captain Hooker. "There'll be a small fortune missing at this rate, before you've done!"

"Damn your eyes, Hooker—are you calling me a liar?" Lieutenant Edgecombe scowled. "I tell you the things have disappeared! And they didn't take to legs and walk off all by themselves! One of you must be responsible, and if someone don't own up and return what's gone, I shall report it to the commanding officer!"

"You can't do that, Edgecombe," said one of his friends. "Old Brock set off at first light—he's ridden off to Ciudad Rodrigo, to support the advance troops. We shan't see him again for some while, I'm thinking."

"I don't care . . . I'm not going to sit back meekly and say nothing—" Graham Edgecombe was almost choking with rage. "I'll get the truth out of you swine yet—"

"It's simple enough to prove your point one way or another, surely," said Captain Hooker. "We can all turn out our pockets, here and now. Then we shall see if anyone's got something in his possession that don't belong to him."

"Pockets aren't enough!" cried Edgecombe. "What's to stop one of you having the swag tucked inside your shirt? I demand that you strip to the buff—every man-jack of you, one at a time. Then we'll see who has anything to hide!"

"No—!" The exclamation sprang from Garnet's lips before she could stop to think. The entire roomful of young men stopped arguing and turned to stare at her.

"What's wrong with you, nipper?" asked Captain Hooker.

"The boy's got a guilty conscience, perhaps," said Captain Larwood.

"That's not true—I—we—" Garnet stammered, and Dicky came to her rescue.

"What he means is, there's no need for us to be searched, for we've been out ever since breakfast. We weren't even here when the things disappeared."

Garnet heaved a sigh of relief, but Edgecombe grumbled, "I only discovered that I'd been robbed half an hour ago . . . The thief could have been at work last night for all I know . . . Anyone could have gone through my gear while I was asleep, and I'd have been none the wiser."

"Well, I vote we don't have to submit to a body-search —the weather's too cold for that kind of diversion," said Captain Hooker. "However, as I've said, I have no objection to turning out my pockets if it will make you any happier . . . Here you are—I'll make a start."

He began to empty his pockets onto his mattress as he spoke, and the rest of the officers slowly followed his example. Edgecombe watched closely, as tobacco, coins, banknotes, pocket-watches and purses tumbled out, one after another.

"Well, Mallory?" he prompted, meaningfully. "Don't hang back—do as the others do."

"Yes, come on, Garnet," Dicky urged. "The sooner we get this game over, the sooner we'll get away . . . Buck up, there's a good lad."

So Garnet, grateful to be spared the humiliation of public exposure, joined in and began to tip the contents of her pockets onto her bedding.

Almost at once, Edgecombe pounced.

"Hullo! Where did that come from? I've never seen you flaunting that fancy kerchief before . . . Silk, by gad—"

One of his friends picked it up. "And initialed, as well . . . What's this? G.E.? That don't stand for Garnet Mallory—but it does fit Graham Edgecombe!"

Garnet could have wept with despair . . . To have escaped discovery this far, and to be tripped up now over such a small matter! What a fool she had been—why didn't she remember that Edmund's handkerchief was monogrammed?

Everyone gathered round, accusingly. Even Dicky's face betrayed some measure of suspicion, she noticed.

"Well, you little thief, what have you got to say for yourself?" snapped Captain Larwood. "Where's the rest of your booty? Come on—where's the gold watch?"

"Please listen—" she began, desperately, as they began to close in upon her. "I haven't stolen anything—this isn't Captain Edgecombe's handkerchief—it belongs to me . . . I brought it with me, from home . . ."

"G.E.?" Nobody believed her, obviously.

"You're making a mistake—it's not a G, it's a C—E.C.—for Edmund Challoner . . . I told you, Captain Challoner's a friend of my family. He is a particular friend of my sister, and—and she worked this handkerchief for him . . . She asked me to convey it to him when we meet . . . as a keepsake."

There was a moment of uneasy silence, and then another voice drawled: "What a charming notion . . . How thoughtful of your sister, dear boy."

Everyone looked round. In the open doorway, Lieutenant-Colonel Hugo Deverell directed his monocle at the assembled group of officers. He had come up the stairs during the argument, and stayed to watch and listen.

"I'm not so sure—" Graham Edgecombe continued uncertainly. "I suppose that *could* be a 'C' and not a 'G' . . . I don't know, but . . ."

"You must know if the kerchief belongs to you, surely?" said Captain Hooker.

"Well—to tell the truth, I cannot recollect whether I have brought any with my initials on them or not . . . A chap can't be expected to keep every little detail in his head."

"Gray, you're a fool," said Hugo Deverell, walking into the room. "This is what I came to tell you . . . There's no thief here, I'm happy to say—the culprit has been found elsewhere. Come, take your little treasures, and let's hear no more nonsense."

He tipped a heap of valuables into Edgecombe's hands: the watch, the gloves, locket, purse and all.

"I take it these trinkets do belong to you, my dear?"

"Yes—what—why—where did you find them?"

"They were returned to me by the sergeant-major—together with a dozen other items. Corporal Morris had them hidden inside his knapsack; he was left here on guard this morning, while you were all out on duty, and it seems he went through the entire place, picking up unconsidered trifles."

"Morris? The blackguard—what will happen to him?"

"What do you think? He'll be flogged . . . Tomorrow at dawn, on the parade ground . . . It's all arranged."

The next morning a wintry sun rose in a hazy sky, and there was a sulphur-yellow light over the city. The roofs and towers stood out darkly against this sinister glow, and Garnet, as she hurried along with Dicky Blades to the parade ground, could not help shivering.

"What's the matter, old chap? Feeling the cold, are you?"

"No—no—it's not that . . . I just wish we didn't have to go and witness this poor wretch being flogged."

"Oh, is that all . . . I know what you mean—it does seem devilish rough before breakfast, on an empty stomach," Dicky shrugged. "Still, it couldn't be left any later, for we're all due to ride off into the mountains at eight o'clock. The whole regiment's on the move today."

"Into battle! I know . . . " Garnet sighed, with a sound that combined anxiety and satisfaction. "Active service at last."

Dicky gave her a sidelong look. "Are you scared, young 'un?"

"A little . . . Not much . . . No, I think I'm rather looking forward to it," Garnet replied truthfully . . . she could not wait to catch up with the advance party—and Edmund. She hoped and prayed that he was still safe, and had come through Ciudad Rodrigo unhurt.

"Well, you're a cool customer, and no mistake," Dicky said ruefully. "I can't say I look forward to it exactly . . . According to old Sterne, being in battle is always uncomfortable—and he says the only time you can forget the discomfort is when you're face to face with the enemy . . . And then the real fighting is such an awful shambles, you don't have time to think of anything else."

"Oh, don't alarm me any more!" Garnet exclaimed. "It's bad enough to have to watch the flogging this morning! I feel quite sick already at the thought of that."

"Why, bless you, what a funny, contradictory cove you are . . . " Dicky shook his head and laughed. "You look forward to going into action, and being shot at—and you're nervous at the idea of some thieving hound getting the punishment he deserves . . . I don't understand you sometimes, Garnet."

Privately, Garnet was desperately anxious not to disgrace herself at the punishment to be meted out to Corporal Morris. She knew that she dared not risk fainting yet again; she had to watch the appalling scene, and appear to show no emotion whatever.

Lieutenant-Colonel Deverell was in charge, and he gave his orders with as little concern as if he had been issuing invitations to a *soirée*.

The entire brigade was drawn up in the form of a hollow square, facing inward; it was imperative that every available man, from the first officer to the youngest drummer-boy, must be present, so that all might mark and learn from this salutary warning.

Corporal Morris, a small, wiry Welshman with thick black hair and sideburns, was brought out of his cell by two orderlies, and led to the middle of the parade ground.

A wooden triangle had been fixed up, where everyone could see it clearly, and now Deverell gave a languid nod to the sergeant in charge of the proceedings.

As if in some archaic heathen ceremony, the men went through the appointed ritual. The Welsh corporal, who was dressed only in shirt and breeches, quickly pulled his shirt over his head, and stood naked to the waist. The two men by his side stepped forward smartly and, taking his wrists, fastened them with iron shackles to the extreme ends of the triangle so that he stood with his arms wide apart, as if he were being crucified, but with his back to his persecutors.

Garnet noticed that his body was covered with matted, black curls, even on his shoulders, and that a line of shining black hair ran down his backbone like a mane.

The sergeant picked up the rawhide whip, and flexed his muscles, then looked inquiringly at the officer.

"One hundred lashes," said Deverell, quietly and calmly.

A low murmur ran through the ranks, and was swiftly hushed.

The punishment began. The sergeant's brawny right arm rose and fell and rose and fell again, each time producing a crack that rang out like a pistol shot.

At first Morris gave no sign or sound of pain; his face was completely expressionless, except that his whole body shuddered under the force of the repeated blows. Garnet watched—longing to be able to take her eyes off the man's terrible ordeal, but knowing that she, too, had to endure it somehow.

She saw the thin line of the lash raising livid weals across his flesh—and soon the cruel strokes broke the skin, so that tiny trickles of crimson rolled down his back, mingling with the matted fuzz of dark hair.

As the flogging continued, the Welshman's stoic bravery began to crack, and he started to cry out—the sounds wrung from his lips, until he was almost sobbing.

"Poor Evan—poor Evan—pity me—God a-mercy on poor Evan . . . That it should come to this . . . God help Evan Morris—!"

At last, when his back was flayed and bleeding like a carcass of raw meat, he began to scream and fling himself about in his agony, until he overturned the triangle and fell headlong in the dust.

Impassively, the two orderlies hauled him up and set the triangle in position again; Morris hung onto it now as if it were a gibbet, his feet unable to support him, and his breeches stained with the blood that coursed down his body.

At long last, the hundredth lash fell, and it was all over. The offender was lifted up and dragged off to his cell once more, to recover as best he could. The parade was dismissed.

Garnet tried not to show her feelings, but even Dicky Blades looked completely stunned and revolted by the barbaric spectacle; they avoided one another's eyes and said nothing.

Garnet hoped that after this, even in battle, she would be able to endure any scene of inhuman butchery, having survived this experience. It was time to go and saddle up, to ride off on the long road that led northward up into the mountain passes.

As they walked toward the stables, a voice called out.

"You two—Blades—Mallory—come here one moment, please!"

They wheeled round obediently, as the lieutenant-colonel hailed them. He screwed his eyeglass in tightly, and surveyed them.

"By the way—you two are to report to Major Sterne. You are to proceed with him to the base camp at Castelo Branco; latest orders."

"Base camp—?" Dicky stared at him. "You mean— we're not going to fight—?"

"Not yet . . . Cheer up—you'll live to fight another day, my young cock-sparrows!" Hugo Deverell looked them up and down appraisingly. "When you have a little more meat on your bones, perhaps."

"I don't understand, sir—we were told everyone was going to Ciudad Rodrigo, in the forward lines—it was posted in company orders—"

"Well, there's been a change of orders, my dear boy . . . The major-general himself has left word. You should think yourselves fortunate."

"But sir—it's not fair—I want to go ahead and join the—the others—in the advance party—" Garnet blurted out indignantly.

"No doubt you do . . . But you are here to obey orders, Ensign . . . However, I can give you one scrap of information that I'm sure will console you a little. I see from this morning's dispatches that your friend Edmund Challoner has come through the siege with flying colors. He is safe and well, and has distinguished himself admirably."

"Oh—thank God!" breathed Garnet impulsively, before she could restrain herself.

"Quite so . . ." Lieutenant-Colonel Deverell smiled and nodded. "Sometimes I begin to wonder who cares for the dear fellow more—you, or your sister?"

3

A Spanish Triumph

So the young ensigns were forced to obey orders and follow Major Sterne—not into the battle area, up in the mountain passes that crossed the frontier between Portugal and Spain—but safely out of danger at the regiment's base camp, far from the actual fighting.

Castelo Branco was a small town perched on a hill near the upper reaches of the River Tagus, and there the two ensigns were billeted, together with the major, in a private house that had been requisitioned from a local money-lender.

The house was comfortable enough, though after the first night Garnet spent in a Portuguese bed, she awoke to discover that she had been attacked by an army of fleas which were obviously long-established residents in the mattress and bedding. On checking with her colleagues at breakfast, she discovered that they had suffered similar onslaughts—but whereas the two men preferred the luxury of soft upholstery and blankets, and were prepared to put up with the consequences as the price that had to be paid—Garnet quickly elected not to risk a repeat performance, and from that night on she made her bed upon an old oak chest, covering herself with her cape and greatcoat.

It was not exactly sumptuous, but it was clean, and she would undergo hardships a great deal worse than that rather than endure the torment of itching and scratching that so cruelly punished her soft skin.

"For pity's sake, Mallory," Major Sterne reasoned with her once or twice. "Why are you so finicky about a few insects? Go and wash yourself free of the pests under the pump in the back yard, as Blades does . . . That's the way to deal with them!"

But Garnet could not and would not resort to such a remedy; and Dicky—who knew how modest his companion was about such personal matters—defended this point of view.

"It's a matter of taste, sir," he explained. "Garnet don't choose to take a cold shower every morning—that's all . . . And there are some days when I'm in agreement! We're getting more than our share of cold showers in this neighborhood, I reckon."

Certainly the weather was unfriendly. It was the rainy season, and spring seemed to be a long time on the way. Day after day, the skies were grey and heavy with low cloud, and a cold wind blew down from the mountaintops. Sometimes there were storms, and they all listened to the rolling thunder echoing round the hills and valleys. And then, occasionally, the rumble took on a deeper and more ominous note.

"Gunfire," said Major Sterne, listening intently with his head on one side. "That's the sound of the heavy cannon . . . Poor devils—we're well out of it, and we should count ourselves lucky."

But Dicky and Garnet could never accept this philosophical attitude. Dicky chafed over the long weeks of inactivity—weeks that dragged into months; and Garnet waited for news of Edmund—and longed to see him again.

Sometimes, when she lay at night upon her hard, spartan bed, and pulled the thick greatcoat up to her chin for greater warmth, she found herself thinking of Major-General Savage, too, and wondering where he was at that moment . . .

She gave herself a sharp reproof—what on earth was she doing, wasting time in remembering the man? The man who had scolded her, who had mocked her weakness when she collapsed, who had punished her by sending her out of the battle area, and sentenced her to this dreary round of endless boredom?

She decided that if there was one man she really detested above all others in his majesty's glorious army—that man was Major-General Broccard Savage.

Life at Castelo Branco, though not in any way a hardship, was certainly frustrating. They had quickly fallen into a daily routine; rise—wash—breakfast—and after breakfast the two youngsters would ride down the hill to the nearest encampment of troops, to collect or pass on the latest overnight dispatches.

They would return at noon with these documents, and spend the rest of the day seated at a long wooden table, assisting the major in collating the lists of dead, wounded or missing, and keeping a tally of the number of men lost, or the number of prisoners that had been taken.

Each day Garnet scanned the long roster of names with dread, fearing to find Edmund Challoner among them; and each day she gave thanks that he had been spared once more. Other news reached the base camp by rumor and gossip, through the inexplicable agency of the military grapevine.

One evening after supper, Dicky lay back on the sofa, kicked off his boots, and said, "Do you know what I heard today? Old Brock is a black-hearted devil, and no mistake."

Major Sterne, polishing his spectacles at the far end of the room, reproved him mildly.

"That is no way to speak of our commanding officer—kindly do not let me hear you talk so in future, boy."

"But what has he done?" Garnet wanted to know.

"He's such a stickler for discipline—you'll never guess what his latest order is!"

"Go on, tell me."

"Well . . . Believe it or not, but it's God's truth I'm telling you—the old—" He broke off and grimaced in the direction of the major. "I beg your pardon—our beloved commander—has given instructions that any man in the regiment caught wearing his greatcoat unbuttoned is to be flogged without mercy!"

"What?" Garnet was horrified.

"Isn't that monstrous? Where does he think we are, on Church Parade in Guildford on a Sunday morning? Those men are in battle, and all he cares about is a smart turnout!"

"You've only heard half the story—and so of course you've got it all wrong, as usual," said Major Sterne, packing up his papers and journals at the desk.

"What do you mean, sir? It's true—I can swear to that—"

"Yes, it is true—but not for the reasons you suppose . . . The fact is, a great many of the other ranks had been passing off counterfeit coins to the Spanish peasants as English money . . . They were pulling the buttons off their greatcoats and flattening them out with a hammer, then calling them English guineas! Old Brock—ahem—I should say, Major-General Savage was forced to take some action to put a stop to it."

"And so he punishes anyone with buttons missing?" Garnet looked thoughtful. "That was rather clever of him, I suppose."

"Rather clever? The man's a military genius . . . Don't underrate him, whatever you do."

The major tucked his book under his arm, replaced his spectacles on the end of his nose, and headed for the door.

"I am off to bed. I shall see you both in the morning. Good night to you."

"Good night, sir," they murmured, and as the door closed behind him, Dicky yawned.

"Good night, Granny . . . Honestly—he's such an old woman . . . I still say old Brock enjoys thinking up new excuses to have the men flogged! He takes an unholy delight in it."

"Do you think so?" Garnet shivered, remembering those ice-blue eyes that had seared her very soul.

"I'm certain of it . . . like Daisy Deverell—there's another one of the same breed—two of a kind, they are . . . Cruel buggers."

Garnet pursed her lips. "I don't know what you mean . . . Lord Deverell was very obliging and polite, each time I've seen him."

"Well—you beware of him, young 'un—that's all! Once Daisy sets his sights on you—you'd better take to your heels and run for it, old son—and the faster the better!"

"You're just talking nonsense—he seems to be both an officer and a gentleman, and there aren't many I've met that can be described so . . . And I do not know why you give him that silly nickname—why do you call him 'Daisy'?"

"Oh, because he gives himself airs and graces—you must have noticed he's a terrible dandy—!"

"In that case I'd have thought you might call him a dandelion—rather than a daisy!" Garnet was pleased with her little joke.

"You simply don't understand, do you? That's another lack in your education, from not going away to boarding-school," sighed Dicky. "The trouble about Daisy is he—he's more like—what he wants is . . ."

He broke off, embarrassed and annoyed. "Oh, you're such a *baby,* Garnet Mallory—there's no telling you anything! Just you give the old sod a wide berth if he ever crosses your path again, that's all . . . Now *I'm* going to bed, too."

And he took himself off to his room, rather sulkily.

So the long, chilly springtime wore on, and at last the skies cleared, and the blossoms began to break through on the fruit trees: almonds, then apricots, lemon and oranges.

The temperature started to climb, and as the sun shone the mood of the British army began to brighten as if to match the weather. The hard winter of struggle was over, and they were rewarded with victory.

The first real news came in a dispatch signed by Broccard Savage, and addressed to the commander-in-chief himself—the Duke of Wellington. Major Sterne and the two ensigns made out a copy of the triumphant message, to be sent home to his majesty's ministers, in Whitehall. A list of the number of prisoners that had been taken in every battle . . . Two thousand at Ciudad Rodrigo, five thousand at the Garrison of Badajoz, and now, an unparalleled record—twelve thousand at Salamanca . . . It was a major triumph for the British and their allies; and once in receipt of this news, Wellington—away to the northeast, at Valladolid—decided that the time was right for a major onslaught upon the capital city—Madrid itself.

The various arms of the attack would come together and concentrate upon one determined push into the very heart of Spain.

"Well, boys—pack up your gear, for we are on the move at last," said the major. "And pray God that the Iron Duke knows what he is doing."

Garnet's spirits rose. At last something was going to happen—the blank, grey days at Castelo Branco that now seemed like a prison sentence, were over, and they were heading for victory . . . And a reunion with Edmund.

It was a slow advance across the mountains, and over the Spanish frontier. Days of hard riding, and a scarcity of rations—and even harder nights, sometimes passed in remote, unwelcoming hamlets, where there was no accommodation for them, and they were forced to spend the hours of darkness under the stars, rolled up in fur rugs, sleeping in the clothes they traveled in, huddled together for warmth . . . For at those altitudes, the nights were still bitterly cold, once the sun had set.

The main body of the Third Dragoons was a full day's journey ahead when they reached El Escorial, a village in the High Sierras; and that night they heard deafening reports of cannon fire, and saw the velvet-black sky pierced again and again with flashes of fire.

Dicky fretted at their helplessness, and wished that he could be up there at the front line, in the thick of it. Garnet imagined Edmund in action, going through the dreadful ordeal of shot and shell—but as she thought of him, his face seemed to waver and dissolve, like the face of someone from a dream, and she found it hard to picture what he looked like.

She felt ashamed; true, they had not met for a very long time, but how could she be so faithless as to forget that face—the face she loved so well? Try as she could, all she could conjure up in Edmund's place was a square-cut visage that seemed to be carved from seasoned oak, with palest blue eyes.

Another explosion, somewhere on the road ahead, drove these fancies from her mind, and she shuddered, drawing the fur rug more tightly around her.

The next morning, the sun rose on a scene of peace and tranquillity. A dispatch-rider galloped back and gave them the good news; the enemy had been routed, during this final struggle, and the last barrier had fallen. The highroad into Madrid now lay wide open to the victorious army, and the Duke of Wellington had requested that the Dragoon regiment should accompany him, as his personal escort.

Dicky and Garnet turned and without a word flung their

arms about each other in a transport of joy. As she felt the boy's rough, warm embrace, she tensed for a moment—dreading that he might detect the outline of feminine curves beneath her uniform—but he was far too excited to notice.

"Victory at last! And we're to take the city of Madrid in triumph!" Dicky exclaimed. "I say—what larks!"

"Now just you stop playing about, boys—we still have a lot of work to do—and a long way to go, to catch up with the rest of the regiment," Major Sterne reprimanded them. "Saddle up your horses, for we must make a start at once."

After one more day in the saddle, they finally rejoined most of the main body of Dragoons by evening, at the outskirts of the city.

Madrid had no suburbs, but a high city wall, with a wide gateway at every one of the roads leading into the center of the capital, and as they passed through the Escorial Gate, they came upon a group of fellow officers, sitting drinking at a nearby café.

"Major! Come and join us in a celebration!" shouted Captain Hooker. "And you two, my young bucks—come and have a glass of wine to drink Wellington's health—and damnation to old Boney!"

They dismounted, and drew up extra chairs at the café tables on the little terrace.

"Do we have to drink with the children?" asked Lieutenant Edgecombe, with a sneer at the two ensigns.

"They deserve a share in the celebration," said the major. "Over these past months, they have done very good service, in their own way."

"Fetching and carrying your billets-doux?" smiled Edgecombe. "Doing their sums and their schooling? Oh, yes—brave boys indeed."

Dicky Blades flushed with anger, and pushed back his chair.

"If you're saying we wanted to run away from the real fighting, I'll prove you wrong, sir!" he challenged the lieutenant. "I don't give a fig for your superior rank—I'll take you on any time you like—"

"Now, now, gentlemen, please!" the major entreated them. "This is a day of rejoicing, not a time for squabbling . . . Behave yourselves, do!"

"Well . . . The young rip needs to be taught a lesson—" muttered Gray Edgecombe resentfully.

Garnet pulled Dicky down into his chair, whispering: "Take no notice, Dick—can't you see he's drunk too much already?"

And certainly it seemed clear that the other young officers had been celebrating the fall of Madrid for some while.

All around, the city opened its arms to greet them like a lover; the hated French invaders had been put to flight, and the citizens of Madrid gave the British a hero's welcome.

Every house was illuminated with scores of candles at the windows, and from the casements, lengths of bright cloth—flags—bunting—tapestries—were hanging out into the streets, as a mark of patriotic joy.

"They certainly seem pleased to see us here," Dicky commented, throwing back his first glass of Spanish wine in fine style.

"Yes . . . Where are the others?" Garnet asked, looking around. "The officers of the advance troops—Major Clowes—Captain Challoner—"

Edgecombe laughed.

"Gad, the boy's forever pestering about Challoner—you haven't changed at all, you young shaver! Ned Challoner ain't with us—he's been removed to a higher sphere!"

"What?" Garnet clenched her hands until the knuckles showed white. "What do you mean?"

"He means that your friend Captain Challoner is one of three or four Dragoon officers who have been picked out by the Duke of Wellington," explained Captain Hooker, more kindly. "He's chosen them as his personal entourage while he's in Madrid—I hear they're all to be presented at the royal palace tonight . . . They're moving in very exalted circles!"

"I see . . ." Garnet breathed again. This was only a minor setback. Soon—very soon now—she would see Edmund. At any moment he might put in an appearance; he was somewhere in this glittering city tonight, close at hand—and that was comfort enough, for the moment.

After two or three more glasses of wine—which Garnet managed to refuse, for the first taste had not been to her liking—the officers became impatient to move on. Night was falling, and as the lamps were lit, they felt impelled to go into the town and explore its delights in more detail.

Garnet and Dicky went along with the party, Garnet keeping a sharp look-out, in case she might suddenly come across Edmund at any street corner.

Madrid by night showed itself off to advantage; it was a magnificent city, with imposing houses and wide, tree-lined avenues. The little band of officers passed by the royal palace, and Captain Hooker pointed it out to the others. Garnet gazed at the high stone façade, and wondered if Edmund were within at this very moment—perhaps only a few yards away, on the other side of those thick walls . . .

"And here's a theater! Why don't we go in and amuse ourselves by watching the play? It'll serve to pass the time, even if we don't understand the lingo," suggested Captain Larwood.

"Good idea—there's bound to be some women there," winked Edgecombe. "Deuced fine women, too, these Spaniards . . . Let's go and see what we can find!"

So they threw a few gold coins to the theater manager, who sat at his desk in the foyer, bowing and smirking, and made their way in to the auditorium.

The play was already in progress, and the English group were not very popular as they made their way to some vacant seats in the amphitheater, talking loudly as they did so. Hissing and hushing broke out, until the visitors were settled at last, and the play could continue without interruption.

Garnet found it hard to follow the plot; she had seen very few theatrical performances before, and those she had seen, at home in Guildford, had not prepared her for anything like this.

It was a comedy—that was plain enough from the screams of laughter that arose from the audience at regular intervals. And it was concerned with marriage—or cuckoldry—for there was a complacent fat husband with a red face, and a pretty young bride with a roving eye . . . Who kept giving her husband the slip and darting off to join a young gallant in some secret tryst behind a screen, or among a grove of flat wooden trees, or even at last—oh, for shame!—in the marital bedchamber, where the sinful lovers finished up on the floor, beneath the bed, in each other's arms.

Garnet felt herself growing crimson with embarrassment, and wished that she had not joined the theater party —but the rest of her companions seemed to be enjoying themselves well enough.

The climax was reached when the little minx ran off with her Lothario at last, and the fat, foolish husband discovered that he had been betrayed. He did not rage or rant, or threaten vengeance; instead, he took the news with a weary shrug of resignation, and said something unintelligible—the words were gibberish to the English onlookers, but the meaning was somehow clear—to the effect that when all else failed there was still one natural function that would never leave one unsatisfied . . .

And with that, he pulled a chamber-pot from under the bed, and proceeded to lower his breeches, presenting his backside to the delirious audience as the curtain fell.

Garnet was horrified, and said as much. When they regained the street and were strolling back along the quiet by-ways of the city, she complained hotly.

"No playhouse in England would ever put on such a

disgusting spectacle! How could you all bring yourselves to laugh at such a display?"

"It's only a bit of fun—" Dicky argued, but Edgecombe cut in: "You're so high-and-mighty, young Mallory—what's wrong with you? Ain't you got a bladder and guts like everyone else? Or are you too genteel ever to unbutton your breeches and take a piss?"

He was fairly drunk by this time, certainly; but most of the officers had been drinking heavily—and when the lieutenant turned his words into action and unfastened his fly, the others began to chuckle, copying his example.

"By gad—that's a good notion—I've a mind to water the garden myself, old man," said Larwood, unconcernedly exposing himself in the light of a street lamp.

Everyone did likewise except Garnet. Even Major Sterne followed suit, though he did turn his back, through some vestige of primness; the others stood in line, and laughed as half a dozen jets of steaming urine described curving arcs in the cold night air.

"What's the matter now, Mallory? Don't you want to go? Or ain't you got a pecker at all?"

Garnet's heart sank, and she turned away to hide her discomfiture. This had always been a problem, ever since her long masquerade began; whenever she was forced to obey the call of nature, she had to wait—sometimes for an agonizingly uncomfortable time—until she was alone, or able to duck out of sight behind a convenient hedgerow or under a bridge . . . Or, more often, to endure the nauseating stench and abomination of a Spanish privy or earth-closet. She envied the young men who were able to relieve themselves publicly, in this offhand way—and she felt like a freak because she could not do the same.

"Oh, leave him alone, Edgecombe—for God's sake!" exclaimed Dicky, buttoning his trousers when he had finished. "He's been better brought up than the rest of us, that's all—it's not his fault if his manners aren't as vulgar as yours!"

"Why, you young dog—" Edgecombe became truculent, but his friends restrained him.

"Come now, old man—no quarreling tonight . . . Forget it—let's go and find another drink!"

Major Sterne decided that he had had enough, and would retire from the party at this point; his head was spinning, and he wanted to take a stroll in the cool night air.

As the older man walked away, Graham Edgecombe snapped his fingers, a gleam in his eye.

"Damme—I know where we'll go! Follow me, lads— we'll have a high old time!"

"Where are you taking us, Edgecombe?" asked Garnet. "I think perhaps I should leave you as well—I'm tired, I want to find a bed for the night."

"Don't you worry, Master Mallory—there's plenty of beds where we're going . . . That's the beauty of having arrived in town ahead of the rest—I have the entrée to all the best places . . . This way!"

He led them along a narrow street, and turned off into a still more narrow alley-way. There was a small doorway in the wall, with a lamp burning above it—a lamp that had been painted red.

He pulled at the bell, and they waited for a moment as the clanging echoes died away. Garnet noticed some of the others were whispering, and nudging each other, and pointing at the red lamp—but she could not catch what they said.

Footsteps approached, and the door was thrown open by a very large lady in a voluminous black gown. She had hennaed hair piled up in a bright orange coronet upon the top of her head, and her cheeks were thickly powdered and painted.

"Oh, it is you, Señor!" she beamed, flashing a smile that showed several gold teeth, and ushering Gray Edgecombe in. "And you have brought your friends—good boys all, I can see—come in, señors—make yourselves welcome . . . My house is your house!"

219

Garnet was startled by the appearance of their hostess, and even more amazed by the sight of the house. What had seemed a small, insignificant dwelling from outside, on closer inspection proved to be something very like a palace—a vast reception room, under a glass dome raised by classical pillars, and an assortment of elegant sofas and armchairs, with odd pieces of antique sculpture dotted about, among pots of fern and gently tinkling fountains that emptied into gilded basins.

"Is it an hotel?" she asked Dicky.

Dicky, who was looking decidedly bleary-eyed by this time, giggled and winked at her playfully.

"It is a *sort* of hotel," he whispered. "Ain't you never been to a house of fun before? No—of course you wouldn't . . . Well, you've got to start some day, and I reckon this is as good a time as any!"

She stared at him, trying to make sense of what was going on, and then noticed that the officers were all behaving in a very casual manner—taking the good lady at her word indeed, and behaving as if they owned the place. Edgecombe flung his shako into a corner, and started to unbutton his tunic, Captain Hooker clapped his hands and called for more wine, and Captain Larwood actually flung himself down on one of the sofas and began to pull off his boots.

"Are they all mad?" Garnet asked in dismay. "We shall all be asked to leave!"

But on the contrary. The hostess was nodding and smiling as if this were quite a common occurrence in her house, and she even called for her maid to assist Captain Larwood, who was having some difficulty with one of his boots.

The maid appeared—and Garnet gasped . . . Was she dreaming? Could this be really happening? For the girl who answered her mistress's summons was dressed in a semi-transparent chemise, with her hair unbraided upon her shoulders, as if she had been roused from sleep.

The young officers welcomed her with whoops of approval, and as she knelt to help remove Captain Larwood's boot, he pulled her roughly toward him and embraced her.

At the same moment, other girls appeared—some older, some younger; one or two dressed from head to toe in high fashion, arrayed in frills and furbelows and pinchback jewelry . . . Some in various states of undress—one in the briefest of Grecian togas, like a figure from some mythological frieze . . . And one girl wearing nothing at all but a pair of black silk stockings and crimson garters.

Garnet put her hand to her face, to cover her confusion. She realized at last what sort of house this was . . . She had once eavesdropped on two of the menservants at Markwick, when they discussed just such a place as this; she was hiding behind the green baize door of the kitchen wing, and they did not know they were overheard.

" . . . A house of ill-repute," one had called it, "where you can get any girl to give you a good time—one or two, or as many as you choose—if you've got the cash to pay for your pleasure . . . It's what they call in foreign parts a *bordello*."

A bordello—and here she was! Garnet Mallory, trapped with no hope of escape, in one of the lowest haunts of vice in all Europe . . . What was she to do?

Instinctively she turned toward Dicky for help in this crisis—but Dicky's own desires had been aroused by the sight of so much feminine allure, and he was determined to satisfy his appetites after so many months of enforced celibacy. She saw him beckoning the prettiest girl in the room: a voluptuous Spanish beauty with long black ringlets and a mouth like a ripe, purple plum . . . As she swayed slowly toward him, Dicky's excitement mounted, and Garnet could see very clearly that she could expect no help from that direction.

Gradually, all the men were choosing partners, or having partners found for them by the ample Madame in charge. To Garnet's horror she suddenly heard the older woman say: "And the little one . . . Who is to take care of the little soldier boy?"

She tried to force a smile. "I—I don't need anyone, thank you, madam . . . I will sit here—and wait."

"Oh, but no, it is not possible! We must find you a friend, little man . . . Good God above—can it be that this is your very first time—no?"

Garnet felt herself blushing, and hung her head.

Edgecombe caught the end of these remarks, and called across: "That's the idea, Madame—young Mallory's a pure young virgin—it's up to you and your troupe to remedy that defect before the night is over!"

"Do not distress yourself, little one, we will be very gentle and you shall have the best time of your whole life—I promise!" wheezed the plump brothel-keeper, grasping Garnet's arm in a beringed hand. "Come with me . . . We give you extra-special treatment!"

The other officers saw Garnet being dragged inexorably toward the grand staircase that led to the upper floors—and burst out laughing, not at all unkindly. It was a necessary part of everyone's experience, and—as Dicky had said earlier—this was as good an opportunity as any other.

But Dicky himself had forgotten all about Garnet by now; he was already making his way into a dimly-lit bedroom—and the luscious Castillian was breathing in his ear: "Go in—get undressed—and climb into bed . . . I will be with you very, very quick!"

He hurried to obey, intent on what promised to be an unimaginably thrilling experience. Boots, breeches, tunic, were all flung hither and thither; he pulled his shirt off with such speed that one of the seams ripped below the shoulder. Leaving his clothes scattered on the floor, with his virility fully aroused and throbbing impatiently for relief, he leaped into bed.

A moment later the door opened, and a figure cloaked in a black negligée slid silently into the room. Dicky raised his head from the pillow to enjoy the sight of his beautiful partner as she disrobed—but alas! At the same instant, she blew out the bedside candle, leaving them in total darkness. He began to complain about this—but the soft hiss of silk falling to the floor, and the scent and warmth of naked flesh as she slipped into the bed beside him, quickly distracted him.

He put his arms around her—and recoiled . . . Surely the lovely Spaniard wasn't so enormously well-built—so vastly proportioned—? He put an exploratory hand up to her head . . . No long ringlets flowed down over her fine shoulders; instead, a coronet of hair was piled up on top of her head . . . With a cry of despair, he realized that he had been tricked.

"Do not distress yourself, soldier boy . . ." hissed Madame in his ear. "I give you a very good time—you wait and see . . ."

He tried to argue, but already her practiced fingers were playing upon his body, and he felt her wet lips sliding down over his chest, across his stomach, and still farther down . . . The sensations she aroused were irresistible, and he could not fight against them for long . . . He surrendered to her skill, and began to enjoy himself.

Meanwhile, Garnet was in a very different situation.

Still fully dressed, she sat on the edge of a huge four-poster, surrounded by mirrors. This was the very best apartment in the house, with—an extraordinary luxury—its own dressing-room adjoining, and in this dressing-room was a vast circular tub of shining pink marble, sunk into the floor. The tub was filled with perfumed, soapy water, and the Castillian beauty tipped another vial of bath oil in as she looked through the open doorway invitingly, and called to Garnet.

"Come, little one . . . Undress . . . let me bathe you first . . . No?"

Garnet shook her head, desperately trying to think of some way to escape discovery.

"You are shy—I know that. But you need not be shy with me . . . Come—we will undress together . . . Like brother and sister! Then you need have no fears . . ."

The girl came back into the bedchamber, smiling, and

unfastening the sash round her waist. She only wore one garment—a long, pleated robe of purple taffeta, that echoed the color of her shining mouth. As the sash slipped to the carpet, the robe fell open, and Garnet could see the girl's figure, revealed in all its glowing nudity.

"Come and kiss me, little soldier," she said. "My name is Melita . . . What is yours?"

She held out her hands, and shook the robe from her shoulders. It tumbled down behind her in a froth of purple, and she stood completely naked, her arms open wide.

"My name is—Garnet—" said Garnet, finding it difficult to speak, in face of this magnificent display.

For there was no question about it; Melita had the most perfect body Garnet had ever seen. Her breasts were firm and young, tip-tilted, with cherry-red nipples; and her thighs were smooth and shining as if they had been carved from two polished columns of ivory. Her pubic hair was closely curled, and—as Garnet later discovered—delicately perfumed. Melita was a girl who paid great care to every detail of her toilet.

"Kiss me," she pleaded again. "Let us be friends, Garnet . . . Yes?"

Garnet moved toward her slowly, as if hypnotized, and allowed Melita to put her slender hands about her waist; their lips met in a long, sweet, yet oddly passionless kiss.

Melita released her at last, and stood back for a moment, still smiling, but a little puzzled. "What is the matter, Garnet? Don't you like girls?"

"I like girls—how can I help liking them? When I am a girl myself!" said Garnet, recklessly.

She knew that she could not delay the moment of truth much longer, and so hastened to bring the whole confused business to an end.

"What? Speak slow—I do not understand the English so good—"

"I tell you—I am a girl . . . Look—if you don't believe me!" And Garnet quickly threw off her tunic, unbuttoned her shirt, and loosened the linen band that enclosed her bosom.

Melita stood transfixed, staring at the beautiful apparition that faced her—almost like a mirror-image: bare breasts pointing at bare breasts. Then she began to laugh.

"It is impossible—a woman in the British army? But *why?* No wonder you are so shy . . . When we kissed—I should have guessed at once . . . Oh, I must tell some of my friends—"

"No—*please!* I don't want anyone to know . . . If the other officers ever find out, they will send me home to England, and I don't want to go . . . The man I love is here, in Spain, and I must find him!"

"What? The man you love? Which man? Tell me his name—perhaps I know him!"

"His name is—" Garnet's mind went totally blank for a moment. It began with a B, surely—no, of course not . . . Edmund, that was it . . . How could she have forgotten it? "His name is Edmund Challoner . . . Has he been here?"

"An Englishman—Edmund—no, I would have remembered . . . But don't worry, Garnet—your romantic secret will be safe with me—and I promise you that my friends can be very discreet . . . Only let me call them—quickly!"

So, half an hour later, Garnet found herself lying back lazily in the huge circular marble tub, luxuriating in the bliss of warm, scented water, and telling her story to a rapt audience of five Spanish harlots—who laughed, and cried, and sighed sentimentally, and declared that it was as good as a play . . .

Melita's slim, supple fingers worked up a lather of suds, and soaped Garnet's back with gentle, relaxing movements.

Then she said: "Come—it is time we took you downstairs to your friends the officers, or Madame will come to ask what is going on—and people will begin to suspect something . . . Fetch the warm towels, Carmencita—and Aldonza, make ready the uniform—for our new friend must turn back into a soldier again!"

Garnet climbed reluctantly from the bath, and impulsively put her arms around Melita; for a moment their two naked bodies clung together in sincere embrace.

"Thank you . . . I thought that this was going to be the worst night of my life, Melita—and you have made it one of the happiest."

Melita looked into her eyes, and smiled. "We are friends, then—you and me?"

"Friends—always."

As they parted, for a fleeting second Garnet thought of that other night when she had shared a bathtub with Bella Delaney, at Markwick, and marveled at the difference between that mischievous unsatisfied girl, and this radiant creature whom she was proud to call her friend.

But Melita could be mischievous too, in her own way; for when at last Garnet was fully dressed and ready to rejoin her comrades in the hall below, Melita brought her companion down too, and proceeded to explain to all and sundry that she was sorry to keep them waiting so long, but it could not be helped . . . Young Ensign Mallory was so *very* demanding—

"Time and again—there is no stopping him! And when he had had enough of me, he went on to Aldonza—*and* Carmencita—*and* Maria—*and* Estrella—isn't that right, girls?"

The Dragoons looked—and admired—and marveled at Garnet's unexpected prowess.

Captain Hooker dug Gray Edgecombe in the ribs, and said: "It seems your idea of a joke on the boy misfired slightly, wouldn't you say? Still, he's obviously enjoyed it hugely—so all's well that ends well! Don't you agree, young Blades?"

Dicky—who looked quite cross-eyed with exhaustion —or was it contentment?—merely blinked and yawned.

"Three cheers for good old Garnet, say I . . . Now let's

go out and find somewhere to drink the good fellow's health—before all the cafés shut up for the night."

So they paid their dues to the Madame, who was now purring like an overfed cat full of cream, and departed, with many promises to return again at the first possible opportunity.

There was one café still open on the main avenue at the center of the city, and a sleepy waiter served them one last round of drinks.

Dicky staggered to his feet, raised his glass, and proclaimed: "Here's to Garnet Mallory, and his newly-discovered talents as a young lecher—all the spunk of a mule, and the sticking-power of a buck rabbit! Long may he live to do it again—and again—and again!"

The others laughed and joined in the toast. Garnet, half shocked and half amused by this unexpected turn of events, was forced to reply to Dicky's complimentary words. They dragged her up to stand on a chair, amidst cries of "Speech—speech—you randy young devil!"

She tried to think what to say, but before she could begin she sensed a change of mood. A chill fell across the noisy group, and she discovered that they were no longer smiling. They all stared past her, at the open door of the café, and Hooker and Larwood were doing their best to struggle to attention.

She looked round. There in the doorway, framed against the darkness beyond, stood Broccard Savage, watching and listening to the disorderly scene.

Shamed and humiliated, she scrambled down from her ridiculous position, and waited for him to say something. But he remained silent. Was it her imagination—or did he ignore the others and single her out for his particular inspection? She felt his eyes—those eyes—burning into her; and the look he gave her was one of disgust and disappointment and black anger.

Then, still without a word, he turned on his heel and strode off into the night.

Larwood cleared his throat and said uneasily: "Making a public exhibition of ourselves, gentlemen . . . We shall be for it in the morning."

Garnet tried to think back over what had been said in the last few minutes—and wondered how long he had been standing there . . . And wished she were dead.

4

My Body-Servant

While the Dragoons were quartered in Madrid, their horses were housed in a livery stable and indoor riding-school, a short distance from the center of the city.

The following morning, Garnet rose early and went straight there, before breakfast; she had been a little concerned during the previous day's ride that her chestnut mare seemed to be slightly lame, and she wanted to make certain of this at the first opportunity.

Also, she had not slept very well; her rest had been continually broken by thoughts of the ludicrous exhibition she must have presented at the café last night . . . And memories of the thunderous glance that Old Brock had cast in her direction. She would have given anything not to make such a fool of herself in front of him, of all people.

She walked into the huge riding-school, where the regiment's horses were temporarily stabled. The animals were

229

loosely haltered and tethered to posts along both sides of the enclosed space. In the center there was a long expanse of tan bark, scuffed and trodden into a crazy pattern; a promenade that provided easy going for novice riders, or a soft landing-place if they should be thrown from their mounts.

As she approached the chestnut, the beast scented her, and gave a little whinny of greeting—and the sound echoed strangely under the high roof of criss-crossed rafters.

"Hullo, my girl . . . let's have a look at you, then," said Garnet soothingly, patting the shining flanks, and letting the velvety wet mask nuzzle against the side of her face. "Let's see your off foreleg, shall we?"

She examined the forlock; there seemed to be no soreness there, or any undue strain in the tendons. As she proceeded with her careful examination, a quiet, deep voice said:

"What seems to be the trouble?"

She started—almost guiltily—knowing who the newcomer must be even before she turned to look at him.

"Good morning, sir," she replied, letting the horse's leg fall and stiffening into the position of attention.

The major-general was dressed in a rough working uniform, with a leather apron over it; at first glance anyone might have taken him for a groom or a stablehand . . . Except for the indomitable thrust of his square jaw, and the fiery gleam in his eye that proclaimed him to be a leader of men.

As she looked at him, with her heart pounding, Garnet found herself remembering the first time she had ever set eyes upon this man—at least, in her waking moments. She recalled that chilly afternoon at Southampton, and her first sight of him, shoeing one of his horses in the forge at the dockside warehouse. And her mind went back still further, to that odd, inexplicable dream, when she had conjured up his image from nowhere . . . Then, strangely enough—for why should such a triviality bother her now?

—she noticed for the first time that there had been a discrepancy between the man she had dreamed of, and the living being standing before her. In her dream, he had had a fierce scar, running from his left temple up into the roots of his hair: in real life his face was unmarked, except by lines of experience. Why, she wondered, had her vision played her false on this one particular detail?

But she had no time to pursue this question, for Brock was speaking again—not to her, but to the mare . . . Speaking in more gentle, sympathetic tones, than any she had heard him utter before.

"Easy, lass . . . There's my beauty . . . We'll soon find out what's amiss, and set you to rights, never fear . . . "

He stooped, lifting the horse's hoof and inspecting it. Then he beckoned to Garnet to come closer.

"Look here . . . There's the trouble—a loose shoe . . . When did you last check her shoes, Ensign?"

"Oh—I forget, sir—the day before yesterday, I think—"

"Never neglect to do so every single day. Remember the old adage? 'For want of a nail, the shoe was lost . . . For want of a shoe, the horse was lost . . . For want of a horse—' " He broke off and shrugged. "Let us hope we have caught this particular omission in good time; the duke would not be pleased if he were to lose a battle—all for the sake of your little chestnut mare!"

"No, sir." She took courage and dared to ask: "It's not likely, sir, now—is it? After such a victory as we have had recently?"

The officer straightened up, and his face darkened.

"The war is not over yet, lad. We still have far to go before we drive the French out of this country altogether." Then he changed his mood again, indicating the horse: "See that a blacksmith is found as soon as possible to give your beast a new shoe. We don't know when we may have to travel on, and these Spanish roads are long and hard."

"Yes, sir. I'll see to it, sir."

She saluted, and waited for the man to move away; but

at the last moment, a thought occurred to him, and he turned back to ask: "By the by, Ensign Mallory . . . Were you very drunk last night?"

She bit her lip, knowing that her cheeks were scarlet, and despising herself for betraying her feelings so openly.

"Not very drunk, sir . . . A little . . . Enough to make me talk rather stupidly, perhaps."

"So I imagined . . . Don't make a habit of it, boy . . . It don't become you."

And with that, he walked off to the farthest corner of the building, and busied himself with the care of his own black charger.

Relief and mortification mingled in Garnet's heart, and she made her escape as quickly as possible. On her way out, she found a sleepy orderly, and gave orders concerning the horseshoe that was to be replaced; then left the building and walked swiftly back to her lodgings . . . Her ears were still ringing with the major-general's icy disapproval.

What right had he to take such a lofty, patronizing attitude? Who did he think he was, to give her such orders? Because he was her commanding officer, that did not allow him to take charge of her every action, every word, every thought . . . Did it?

She felt as though she were a child, and he the teacher; a puppet, and he the puppet-master who pulled the strings; as if he only had to snap his fingers, and she must jump to do his bidding . . . Odious creature! She resented the terrible power that he held, and fought against it.

When she returned to the house where she was billeted, together with some of the other officers, she found them already at breakfast.

"Come on, Garnet—your eggs and bacon will be cold —a British breakfast at last! We thought you were going to miss it," chattered Dicky, making a place for her next to him at the table.

"Or would you prefer porridge, perhaps?" asked the landlady.

"No, thank you, ma'am . . . Bacon and eggs will suit me very well," replied Garnet.

Very late on the previous evening, after their unfortunate encounter with the major-general, the little party of officers had repaired to this house in a quiet residential avenue; it was an address that had been passed on to Major Sterne—a rooming-house, run under the personal supervision of a respectable Scottish widow, Mrs. McBey.

Even at one o'clock in the morning, that worthy soul had made the British army very welcome. Garnet and Dicky shared a small room up in the attic, and Major Sterne and some of the others were lodged on the various floors below.

"More coffee, gentlemen?" Mrs. McBey inquired, wiping her hands on a spotless apron. "I apologize for the lack of tea, but what with one thing and another, there's been a wee bit o' scarcity of that commodity around the shops in these parts."

"Coffee, please, ma'am," said Garnet, pushing a cup across to the good lady. "This is the best breakfast I've tasted for many a long day."

"And so say all of us," agreed Dicky, while the other officers murmured their approval.

"You're not the only Dragoons under my roof, you know," Mrs. McBey continued, as she poured the coffee. "I have another officer here—just above; he's taken the first floor set of rooms for himself and his man servant . . . A lieutenant colonel, I think he is."

The others exchanged glances and Captain Hooker said, "Don't tell us that we are to be honored with the company of Daisy Deverell at table!"

"No, no—though his name is Deverell, sure enough—but I *think* he said his first name was Hugo . . . And according to what his valet told me, he's one of the nobility—a lordship, no less!"

"Dear me . . . And is Hugo, Lord Deverell to join us for breakfast?" asked Major Sterne, who was something of a snob.

"No, sir, he won't be doing that. He keeps to his own chambers, you see—he explained that he would have his man, Mr. Pilling, to serve him all his meals there . . . He's not what I'd call of a sociable persuasion—well, it's hardly to be expected, is it?—with him being a blue-blood . . ."

Dicky began to make a critical comment on the blue-ness of Lord Deverell's blood, but was quickly silenced by his superiors.

Aware of the landlady's presence, Captain Larwood changed the subject.

"I wonder if we'll be called out to give an account of ourselves to Old Brock this morning—"

"I must ask you to speak more respectfully of our commanding officer, sir," said Major Sterne plaintively. "It sets a bad example to the others . . . And anyway, why should Old—why should the major-general call you out?"

"You don't know, of course—it happened after you left us all last night . . . We had a little—um—party, and our esteemed commander happened to come across us in one of the cafés, painting the town red."

"Oh, for shame—" Major Sterne glanced uneasily at the landlady, but Mrs. McBey was making her way majesti-cally from the room.

"If there's anything further you require, gentlemen, just call for me . . . Now I shall leave you to breakfast—and your conversation—undisturbed."

She went out, ad Captain Hooker chuckled.

"What Larwood omitted to mention was that we'd all been drinking—and whoring—and we were still in the highest of high spirits when the old boy caught us."

"You know what he's like," said Larwood. "We'll be in for a severe reprimand, if I'm any judge."

"I don't think you need worry," said Garnet. "I saw him just now—at the stables . . . He reprimanded *me*—

but from his tone, I got the feeling that he will not raise the matter again."

"Well, well! So you were the scapegoat for the lot of us?" Larwood smiled. "Hard luck, Mallory . . . Did he give you a cut across the bum with his riding-crop? It's a habit of his, when he's out of temper."

"No! He never even touched me," said Garnet indignantly. "He—he just told me not to make a fool of myself again."

"He must be getting lenient in his old age," retorted Hooker, swallowing the last of his coffee. "Come, gentlemen—the day is wasting; let's set forth."

"Certainly, there's a great deal of work to be done—a great deal," Major Sterne chimed in. "I have a copy of the daily orders here—Captain Larwood, you are to take charge of stable duties, Captain Hooker, there's to be a ceremonial parade at noon, and all ranks will be required to turn out for drill practice at eleven o'clock . . . "

"Will the whole regiment muster for that?" asked Garnet. "All the officers and men?"

"All—except for the special party chosen to accompany the commander-in-chief," replied the major. "Lord Wellington's advance squadron are to leave the city this morning; he is taking them to head an attack on the French garrison at Burgos—some hundred miles or so to the North, I understand."

"So—Captain Challoner—?"

" . . . Has given you the slip again! This isn't your lucky day, young 'un!" laughed Dicky. "Anyone would think the wretch was trying to run away from you!"

The other officers joined in, teasing Garnet about her "family friend," the gallant—but elusive—Captain. They were, it seemed, destined never to meet.

Garnet hardly heard them. Puzzled, she examined her own feelings, and wondered—why did this latest bulletin seem so much less of a disappointment than usual? Was it because she was becoming accustomed to setbacks by now? Oh—it was a blow; of course it was—but she accepted it with equanimity. If she didn't meet Edmund to-day—there would be plenty of other days, and she would see him again eventually, no doubt . . . Curiously, it didn't seem to matter quite so much, after all.

Breakfast being over, the officers dispersed to their apartments, to prepare for duty.

As the last to arrive, Garnet was the last to quit the breakfast-room, and so she was going up the stairs alone when—on the half-landing at the top of the first flight —she almost collided with someone coming down.

"Hold hard, man! Look where you're going—it's taken Pilling half an hour to get the shine on my boots just so —if you were to tread on my toes now, I fear the poor fellow might cut his throat!"

She snapped to attention as she had been taught. "I beg your pardon, sir."

She made room for Lord Deverell to get by on the narrow stairway, pressing back closely against the wall, but he seemed in no hurry to pass on.

"Hello, dear boy—so it's you, is it? Little Ensign Mallory . . . Well, this is quite a surprise, I must say." He screwed his monocle into his eye and raked Garnet with a close scrutiny. "I had no idea that we were sharing the same residence . . . How very fortunate."

"Fortunate, sir—?"

"Yes, indeed—for I had promised myself that I should become better acquainted with you, Master Mallory, when the opportunity presented itself. And now it seems that the Fates have smiled upon us—for here we are, so to speak, at close quarters . . . Delightful!"

He made a move as if to draw Garnet toward him— then checked himself. "No, no—we both have work to do, I feel sure, and there is to be a parade at noon . . . But I shall make sure that we resume this interesting conversation, my dear. I shall look forward to seeing you again—later."

"I hope so, sir," said Garnet politely, a little puzzled.

"Oh, I shall insist upon it . . . Be sure of that."

And he clattered down the staircase and was gone.

When Garnet reached the attic bedroom, she found Dicky brushing his unruly mop of hair at the glass, and said: "I've just seen Lord Deverell on the stair."

"Talk of the devil—! I hope he didn't see *you*."

"Oh, but he did—we exchanged a few words. He was extremely civil—I can't think why you are so unpleasant, every time you speak of him."

"Unpleasant? I'm trying to warn you for your own good. Steer clear of him, young 'un—or you'll be in for the shock of your life, I promise you!"

"What nonsense . . . He's most gentlemanly and charming—and I don't want to hear any more of your slanders against him."

"Don't, then—and when you come crawling back on your hands and knees, with a sore arse—don't expect any sympathy from *me!*"

"Hold your tongue, Dicky Blades—for I won't listen to another word!"

Garnet grabbed her shako and cape, and slammed out of the room before Dicky could reply. She hadn't the faintest idea what Dicky's crude warning might mean, but supposed that, in some silly way, he must be slightly jealous that Lord Deverell should always make himself so agreeable to Garnet, while he ignored Dicky completely.

The day passed without any special incident; the victory parade through the streets of the city was a great success—the citizens cheered, while their wives threw rose petals at the Dragoons as they rode by on horseback.

Somewhere a long way ahead, in the vanguard of the procession, Garnet caught an occasional glimpse of Broccard Savage; he was mounted on the black charger, his back as stiff as a ramrod, looking neither to right nor left, and making no response to the plaudits of the crowd. In complete contrast, Lieutenant-Colonel Deverell cantered along easily, smiling and bowing, and even—on occasion —kissing his hand to a pretty señorita at an upper balcony, and so won all hearts.

When the day's duties were over, and the horses bedded down for the night, Garnet and Dicky returned to Mrs. McBey's establishment.

"Hey—what do you say to the idea of another visit to Madame this evening, young 'un?" asked Dicky. "You could see your gorgeous Melita again—and all the rest that you pleasured—"

"No, no, not tonight," said Garnet hastily.

"Between us, I'm sure we could raise the cash. I tell you what, I'll sell my ivory-backed hairbrush—that should be good for a guinea or two . . . "

"No, really . . . You go if you wish, but leave me out of it . . . I am rather tired."

Dicky grinned understandingly. "After last night's performance—yes, by Jove, I suppose you must be . . . Well —some other night, perhaps."

As they entered Mrs. McBey's house, they found Lord Deverell standing in the hall—surveying, with an expression of quizzical distaste, a water-color of Loch Lomond.

"Delightful—!" he smiled, as he acknowledged the two boys.

"You admire the painting, sir?" said Garnet.

"No, the painting's deplorable . . . I was referring to the company . . . I shall require you to present yourself in my rooms on the first floor, Ensign Mallory. I have matters to discuss with you . . . As for you—what's-your-name?—you may be dismissed; you're not needed."

"Oh, but—" Dicky stammered uncomfortably, trying to signal to Garnet. "We've got to go out again, Garnet— immediately . . . Don't you remember?"

"You go if you wish," said Garnet coolly. "I told you— I'm staying here."

So Dicky was forced to retire, as Garnet accompanied Lord Hugo to the first-floor apartment.

The officer threw himself back onto a divan, and eyed Garnet up and down with approval.

"Yes, yes—very good—neat, trim and presentable . . . You'll do very well, I'm sure."

"I'm sorry, sir—I don't understand—"

"Then let me explain. I have just sent my man, Pilling, off to Burgos with the advance squadron. Poor chap—it's been some while since he's seen active service, and I really mustn't be selfish . . . He deserves an opportunity to cover himself with glory, don't you agree?"

"I suppose so, sir," said Garnet, completely bewildered.

"So—since I've had to make a sacrifice and let the good fellow go—that leaves me in the devil of a hole, you see . . . I have no one to wait upon me. And *that's* why I decided you would be the ideal replacement. I'm going to appoint you, my dear—as my body-servant."

Garnet blinked, then said cautiously: "Thank you, sir. But what exactly would that entail?"

"It entails your loyalty—your service—your obedience in all things. And in return I shall see to it that you are well provided for, too . . . It is an arrangement that should work to our mutual satisfaction, Master Mallory . . . You look after me—and I will certainly look after you."

"Yes, sir . . ." Garnet brightened. It didn't sound too bad at all . . . "But what I really meant was—what will it entail, in practical terms?"

"You will valet me—care for my clothes, and see that I am immaculately turned out at all times . . . I have a high standard to maintain, you know. You will provide food and drink and everything necessary for my physical well-being . . . I hope I make myself clear?"

"Do you mean—I'd have to cook your food?"

"When we are on a campaign, in the field, that is quite possible; at present, of course, the excellent Mrs. McBey provides my repasts. Your job is simply to serve them up. And I suggest we should make a start right away. There is the dinner-table—the food is under those covers—let us see what sort of waiter you prove to be, my dear boy."

As he said, there was a small square table with a long white cloth, laid with cutlery and glasses for one, and on the sideboard was an array of dishes, kept hot under silver covers.

"Take a napkin, and begin . . . First, the wine."

The bottle was already uncorked, Garnet noticed with relief, and all she had to do was pour a glass for Lord Hugo. This wasn't difficult, although her nervousness made her fingers tremble slightly, and one tiny spot of red wine landed upon the snow-white cloth.

"Clumsy of you, Mallory," said Lord Hugo, smiling slightly. "Try not to let it happen again—for your own sake."

He sipped the wine and pronounced it excellent.

"So good is it, in fact, that I am prepared to break all conventions—and invite you to share it with me, my dear . . . A bouquet such as this is far too fine to enjoy alone . . . Drinking should never be a solitary vice."

He pushed another empty glass across and waited while Garnet filled it. She tried to argue that she was not accustomed to strong drink—but he would not listen to her.

"Pooh, what stuff and nonsense! Taste it, and let the delicate aroma steal into your brain . . . Go on—drink deep!"

She was forced to do as he said, and discovered thankfully that this was not the raw *vin du pays* she had sampled on the journey across Spain—this was a vintage wine indeed.

"Now the soup . . . And while you serve it, you must tell me—for I am really very interested—about your passionate friendship with Ned Challoner . . . Dear Ned is one of my closest companions, and I long to hear what you think of him."

"Why—sir—he's really more of a friend to my sister,

than to me . . . " Garnet tried to correct him, fearing to get tripped up in the confusing explanation.

"So I remember—there was even some talk of him marrying the girl, surely? But you can be frank with me . . . You have a special affection for the gentleman, do you not? Don't deny it—I can see from your face that it is so . . . "

He tasted his soup, and laid down the spoon with a clatter—a few drops flew from the plate and marked the cloth again.

"Oh, vile—Mrs. McBey can fry eggs and bacon, but her soup is plebeian beyond belief . . . Take it away— and give me some more wine—and take a little more yourself."

Garnet hurried to obey, trying to clear away one set of plates and replace them—to dish up some sort of chicken stew and peppers, swimming in gravy; to replenish the wine-glasses—and at the same time to steer her way through this maze of questions and insinuations about Edmund, anxious not to give herself away.

"Oh, come—don't be bashful, my dear—I know very well how you hero-worship the captain . . . Why, you even carry his handkerchief with you as a keepsake—because of course all that tomfoolery about your sister didn't deceive me for a moment . . . You have a secret *tendresse* that you dare not openly admit—tell the truth now—!"

"Well—sir—I have—I am—I like Captain Challoner very much indeed—" Garnet felt the strong wine beginning to take effect, and her voice shook when she replied —just as her hand shook when she refilled the glasses.

"You're being stubborn, boy, and I won't allow that," said Lord Hugo, his smile fading. He looked down at the tablecloth, and his eyebrows lifted in dismay. "What's this I see?"

His monocle swung from its silk ribbon, as he pointed to the marks on the cloth. "More drops of wine, and some soup stains as well!"

Garnet tried to excuse herself. "My hand trembled, sir —I'm sorry—but as for the soup—I think you did that when you dropped the spoon—"

"How *dare* you criticize me?" Lord Deverell seemed to have changed in an instant from a smiling friend to an implacable enemy. "I'll give you one last chance, boy— behave yourself now, or else I shall have to punish you severely . . . Every man who works for me has to learn that lesson!"

He tapped the wineglass, making it ring.

"Come here at once, and fill this glass to the brim . . . And if you spill one more drop—you shall be beaten!"

Garnet was suddenly terrified. She remembered Dicky's words of warning, and wished—too late—that she had paid more heed to them. "Excuse me, sir—I don't think I wish to be your body-servant after all—I have to go now —I'm sorry—"

She made for the door, and grasped the handle . . . Only to discover that the door was locked. Lord Hugo must have turned the key when he brought her in, and then removed it . . . She was trapped.

"I said *come here,*" he repeated, very quietly, but with such menace that her blood ran cold. "Fill my glass this minute, you young jackanapes—do you hear?"

Slowly, she approached the table. He held the glass close, so that she had to walk round and stand next to him as she poured from the bottle. Very carefully, she measured out the wine, and watched—holding her breath as the level mounted to the brim . . . She was leaning slightly forward, as—

Lord Hugo's right hand suddenly slid up her legs, and fingered her bottom . . .

The inevitable happened. She gave a startled cry, and the bottle jerked wildly in her grasp: a shower of ruby-red liquid splashed over the tablecloth.

She put the bottle down, awaiting the outburst of fury that must surely follow, and looked fearfully at the officer.

He was smiling. Dimly, she realized that this was what he had intended to happen; this gave him the excuse he needed . . .

He rose to his feet, and said: "Come in here, boy. You've had your chance—let us see if actions may speak louder than words."

He took her by the collar, flung open the door into the adjoining room, and dragged her across the threshold.

When she realized she was in his bedchamber, she began to struggle and cry out: "No—please—let me go—stop—"

"Oh, no, Garnet Mallory—I shall not stop until you receive the punishment you deserve."

He flung her away from him; she staggered, and fell back across the bed and watched, wide-eyed with horror, as he picked up a slim, vicious-looking cane that lay on the bedside table.

"Now then . . . Get your clothes off, boy—and take what's coming to you!"

"No, sir—you can't—you mustn't—"

"It's high time you learned some discipline!" he continued: she noticed that his lips were wet, and a dribble of saliva was running down his chin. "Take off that uniform—or by God I'll rip it from you!"

As she lay helpless, unable to move, he put aside the cane and suddenly threw himself upon her like a wild animal, snarling and cursing as he tore at her tunic and breeches. She tried to defend herself, but it was impossible—although she fought back with all her strength, she felt the buttons give way—buckles and laces ripped apart —her shirt was torn from her body, and her breeches were being dragged down her thighs . . .

At first she could not understand what he wanted; her knowledge of sexual matters did not extend so far—but almost at once she realized with horrified clarity what it was he wished to do to her; and her whole being rebelled against this obscene outrage.

She tried to cry out for help—but her voice was smothered by the feather pillow—and who was there to come to her rescue?

She could feel the intensity of his perverse appetites—this was not love, in any shape or form—this was unmixed hatred . . . Hatred for her personally—or hatred of womankind as a breed—or even, in some dark and unimaginable depth of his soul, a hatred of humanity itself.

Through this act of violation, he was achieving some kind of mindless revenge upon his fellow-men—and all his pent-up venom and envy was being directed upon her helpless body.

She felt a sudden surge of overwhelming pain, and thought that she was going to faint—hoped, indeed, that she would do so, for at least, in unconsciousness, she would be spared the full knowledge of the ghastly consequence. As she welcomed the waves of darkness that seemed about to engulf her, as if from far away, she was aware of a hammering noise, louder even than the pounding of her heart . . .

Someone was banging at the locked door.

Hugo Deverell paused in his crazy attempt, and caught his breath. "The devil take you—whoever you are—" he snarled between his teeth. "Go away—leave me alone . . . "

He tried to ignore the interruption; but then a voice began calling: "Sir—your lordship—please come downstairs, sir—you're wanted!"

Garnet recognized that voice at once, and began to take hope. It was Dicky Blades; and she was sure he would not be easily put off.

If he had not been crazy with lust, he would have noticed sooner, but his own excitement was overwhelming by this time, and he was already beginning to pull off his uniform by the time he realized the truth.

She lay spreadeagled across the bed, her garments torn aside, her lovely breasts quivering and her most private parts exposed to his astonished gaze.

He looked down at her—and gave a short, disgusted

bark of bitter laughter. "A girl . . . A *girl,* by God—and I never guessed!"

"Please, sir—now you see me as I am—let me go—", she gasped.

But he was breathing very hard now, and the look in his eyes was completely beyond reason, as he shook his head.

"Oh, no . . . " he panted. "I'll have you publicly court-martialed—I'll have you shipped back to England like the common whore that you are—I'll have you—"

In a sort of frenzy, he continued to fling off his clothes.

"Oh, yes—I'll have you . . . I've gone too far to stop now—*I'll have you,* you little bitch—!"

And he threw himself upon her.

5

My Aide-de-Camp

This, was, without doubt, one of the most terrifying moments in Garnet's whole life. It was even more horrible than Jem Bolt's frantic attack upon her, that night in the summer-house in Markwick . . . For she had in some sense understood and sympathized with Jem's desperate love which had forced him to that pitch of desire —whereas Hugo Deverell's insistent lust was something cruel, inhuman, and without any precedent in her experience.

She could sense that, to him, she had ceased to exist as a person. He had an idiosyncracy of referring to the other ranks as "bodies"—and that is what she had become for Lord Deverell, at this instant; a body—a piece of warm, struggling flesh, to be used for his pleasure, and thrown aside when his needs were satisfied.

She tried to fight him off, but he had thrown his whole weight across her, and she was helpless. By now he had stripped off most of his clothes, and she could feel his skin pressing nakedly upon her own—and smell the acrid odor of male sweat, combined with the latest and most expensive toilet water—and hear the sound of his quick, hard breathing as he drove his loins angrily against her, in rapid thrusts.

But this was still not the worst moment of all.

That happened a few seconds later, when he took her by the shoulders, and gripped her roughly, panting: "Turn over, you whore . . . Roll over, I say—*do as I tell you!*"

He tugged at her, heaving convulsively, turning her body beneath his own. Then he gave a grunt of satisfaction, and with one merciless hand, dragged her legs apart, so that she lay spreadeagled beneath him, face down in the pillow, half-suffocated.

As if to prove the point, the banging on the door was redoubled, and Hugo Deverell was forced to stop again.

"God damn, it, man—how dare you address an officer in that way! Go to hell!"

"Sorry, sir—can't do that," Dicky responded cheerfully from the other side of the door. "I tell you, you're wanted downstairs immediately, sir . . . By the major-general!"

"What?"

This had its effect. With a sulphurous curse that Garnet had never heard before, the lieutenant-colonel released his hold upon her, and scrambled up from the bed.

"Get your clothes on, you bitch," he muttered. "You heard what the boy said—I have to go."

"Yes, sir." She could not move at first, her body was trembling—she could not yet believe she was free.

"Look sharp about it!" he added furiously, as he began to pull on his uniform.

Garnet said nothing, but looked at him with scorn.

In truth, he cut a sorry figure now—his male member, which had been rampant only an instant ago, was now quite discouraged, and hung forlornly between his legs, as he struggled to hoist his silk drawers and buckskin breeches. His clothes were creased and rumpled—a far cry from the usual dandified image of Hugo, Lord Deverell.

He felt her contempt, and turned away, saying thickly: "You'll suffer for this, you little strumpet . . . I'll make you pay for it, in my own time and in my own way . . . Never fear!"

"You—you will not report me to the commanding officer? Have me sent home to England—in disgrace?" she asked, dismayed.

"No . . . Not that. If I sent you away, how would I ever contrive to punish you—as you must be punished? Your hour will come, Garnet Mallory. I'll have my way with that soft, smooth body of yours when the time is ripe . . . Just wait and see."

He pulled on his tunic, and squared his shoulders, looking at his reflection in a long mirror on the wall.

"Now get out of my sight, woman . . . You disgust me . . . "

Garnet scrambled into her clothes as quickly as possible, and he flung the key at her. As soon as she turned it in the lock, Dicky pulled the door wide open—and she almost fell into his arms.

He looked at her disheveled appearance and white face, and said nothing; they exchanged a single glance that said it all.

"The senior officers are to report for duty down below," Dicky said, repeating the order he had been given, then added in a lower tone: "I'll see you up in the attic—presently."

Half an hour later, Dicky climbed the last flight of stairs and came into their little bedroom to find her lying back, motionless, upon her thin mattress. She had hardly stirred since she flung herself down upon the bed, reflecting on her narrow escape.

"Well, old fellow?" Dicky asked quietly. "I won't say I told you so—though I did . . . was it as bad as I said it would be?"

"It was worse . . . worse than I'd ever imagined." Garnet turned her head away. "But you did warn me, Dicky —thank you for that."

He sat beside her on the narrow bed. "And what happened? Did he have your cherry? Did it hurt much?"

She bit her lip. "It was beginning to hurt a great deal —but before he could—before he completely—" She broke off, and touched his arm. "That's when you knocked at the door . . . Thank God for your interruption, Dicky —or else I should certainly have been lost."

He put his hand upon hers, with surprising gentleness.

"I know what it's like, young 'un . . . One of the top prefects tried it on me at school . . . Some of the chaps said you get used to it after a while—but I know *I* didn't . . . "

"It was providential that the officers should have been called for duty at that particular time." She remembered what he had said. "Is the major-general still downstairs?"

"Yes . . . That's what I came to tell you . . . It seems there's trouble at Burgos . . . Somewhere away to the North—a hundred miles or more."

"Yes, I know—that's where the Duke of Wellington went, with the advance party . . . "

"Your precious Captain Challoner—that's right." Dicky grinned. "Well, they found themselves in trouble when they got there, apparently. The Frenchies were on the run until they reached Burgos—but now they've decided to turn and face our troops, and fight it out . . . Sounds as if they're all set for a first-class battle."

"Oh, dear God . . . " Garnet's heart sank. "Poor Edmund—"

"Lucky Edmund, you mean. He'll be in the thick of it—distinguishing himself in the fray, as usual. Well, this time, the rest of us will have a chance to shine as well."

"What do you mean?"

"That's what Old Brock came here for—an emergency staff meeting with the senior officers. Wellington needs reinforcements, and he's sending every available man up to Burgos tonight."

"Everyone? You and me—?"

"Me, certainly. I've got to start packing my gear right away. I don't know about you, young 'un . . . He asked me to send you down to see him in Mrs. McBey's parlor, as soon as the staff conference is over."

"He asked for me—by name? Are you sure?"

"No doubt about it . . . 'Send me Ensign Mallory,' he said. 'I particularly want to speak to him' . . . And he was looking straight at Daisy Deverell when he said it . . . Our dishonorable lieutenant-colonel turned quite green about the gills, I can tell you."

"I don't understand—the major-general cannot possibly have known what occurred between Lord Deverell and myself—"

"He doesn't *know* anything; but I dare say he's got a pretty shrewd idea . . . Dirty Daisy's little ways are pretty well-known, and a young shaver like you is just his favorite meat . . . Come on now—pull yourself together, and go down to see what Old Brock wants."

She did her best to obey, trying to summon all her strength for this latest ordeal. Being sent for by the major-general reminded her of the infrequent occasions, at home when something she had done displeased her father, and he had summoned her to the library to account for her misdeeds.

She stopped and thought . . . Was that why she disliked Broccard Savage so much? Was it because, in some strange way, he reminded her of her father?

She had left Markwick and one bad-tempered and embittered tyrant, and put herself under the rule of yet another. But whatever reprimand he had in store for her, there was no running away this time. She made her way downstairs and knocked hesitantly at the parlor door.

"Come in," said the deep, familiar voice.

She entered and stood to attention, her eyes fixed on a

spot above the major-general's head. He sat at his ease, in a comfortable armchair, studying a map that was spread out upon a low table.

"You sent for me, sir," she said.

"So I did. Stand easy, Ensign. You are not on parade now."

She tried to relax and allowed herself to steal a glance at his face.

He looked serious—but not severe.

"I expect you have already been informed that I am sending almost every available officer and man to the relief of the advance squadron at Burgos?"

"Yes, sir . . . Do you wish me to start packing up my gear?"

"Not tonight. I said 'almost every available man' . . . I am myself forced to stay on in Madrid for a while."

"Sir—?" She did not understand.

"As the senior British officer remaining in the capital, I represent King George—and must put in an appearance at the Spanish court tomorrow, to pay the usual courtesies between monarchs. It is a damned disagreeable obligation, frankly; I'd give a thousand guineas to be out of it, and off to pursue Bonaparte—but I have to do my duty . . . Just as you shall."

"Me, sir?"

"Come closer, boy." She advanced a few steps, and the major-general studied her intently for a moment. "You look pale—are you not well?"

"I am perfectly well, sir."

"That's good. Because I shall require you to put in some long hours, and work as hard as may be necessary, in the next few days."

"I'm sorry, sir—I don't know what you mean."

"All the other junior officers are needed in the field; but I must have some sort of attaché here with me in the city—and also when we set forth on the road, to follow the army northward. I have decided to appoint you as my personal *aide-de-camp,* Ensign."

She stared at him, speechless, unable to believe her ears.

"I see you are dumbfounded . . . As well you might be—" and surely she saw a twinkle in his eye? "It is an extraordinary honor for one so young and inexperienced . . . Quite frankly, boy—I made up my mind that you will be less of a liability here with me, than in battle, facing the enemy!"

He was laughing at her again . . . She clenched her fists.

"Very well . . . That is all I have to say. You are dismissed. Go to your room and try to get a good night's sleep, for we shall be busy tomorrow, you and I."

So her audience with the great man was ended. She returned to the attic, where Dicky was frantically trying to pack all his belongings into knapsacks and shoulder-bags that suddenly seemed much too small—and told him her news.

He shrugged and sympathized. "I dare say the old man thinks you're too green to be under fire—hard luck, young 'un . . . Still, your turn will come, sooner or later, don't worry. I bet we'll soon meet again—at our next famous victory!"

The next two days passed quickly; as the major-general had warned her, they were very busy—paying ceremonial calls upon various princes and dignitaries of the court, and attending a formal *levée* in the king's throne-room.

But Garnet herself barely caught a glimpse of all these activities; she felt she was nothing but a glorified pageboy, riding behind Broccard Savage as he cantered through the streets of the city, and then waiting long hours in a series of ante-rooms while he went in to offer his credentials and engage in long, diplomatic exchanges.

She hardly saw her lord and master at all . . . It was extremely boring.

But she thought about him a great deal; and at night when she retired to bed, she let her imagination roam . . . Things could have been so much more enjoyable if she had been able to accompany him on his official rounds . . . Talk with him, walk with him—even—for there was a ceremonial ball at the palace that night, and Broccard had told Garnet she might take the evening off, while he went to the soirée alone—even to dance with him, with his arms around her, his hand upon her waist . . .

She sat up in the narrow bed with a start: what was she dreaming of? How could she possibly dance with this stern, overbearing man—when he was a senior officer, and she disguised as a boy under his command? And besides, she was in love with Edmund—wasn't she?

And even more complicated than that—even if she were *not* in disguise, and *not* affianced to Edmund Challoner—what possible reason had she for thinking that Major-General Broccard Savage would ever wish to dance with her?

But she could picture the scene so clearly . . . She could not resist letting herself drift into the mists of a rose-colored fantasy—the vast, glittering ballroom, ablaze with lights; the sway and swirl of the music that captured their senses with its insistent rhythm . . . And Brock's strong arms about her, and his blue eyes smiling down at her as they whirled away together, on and on forever . . .

She felt her body stirring with passion at the thought, and her blood beat hotly in her veins, as she lay back against the pillow . . .

No—no—*no!*

She scolded herself violently, this was madness—what was she doing, letting herself even consider such a thing? What was happening to her? She turned over, punching the pillow into another shape, and tried to fall asleep. But it was a long time before she could banish the thought of Brock Savage and those penetrating, smiling eyes.

The next morning, when she presented herself for duty, she found the major-general already attired in his service uniform, with his saddlebags packed.

"Good news, boy," he said, with satisfaction. "Our job in Madrid is ended; we are free to take the highroad toward Burgos. Go and make yourself ready, for we ride out in half an hour."

They had a long journey ahead of them; first an uphill climb into the high Sierra de Guadarrama—and then across the wide, rolling plains of Old Castile, through a vast area of open cornfields and vineyards.

The sun beat down, and as they rode, Garnet kept the chestnut mare a good dozen yards behind the major-general's black charger. After her disturbed and disturbing night, she was not anxious to get into conversation with this unsettling man, but preferred to keep him at a distance.

At last he must have realized that she was hanging back, and reined in his horse until she could catch up with him.

"What is wrong? Is the heat of the day too much for you?" he asked, quite sharply. "Why are you dawdling?"

"I'm sorry, sir . . . I'll try and keep up."

"Please do so. We are not here to take our leisure and admire the view, you know."

She said nothing, but her heart thumped as they continued along the dusty road. Why should this domineering man have the power to agitate her so, with a few simple words? His voice echoed in her head; it was not so much the things he actually said, but his vibrant tones that resounded in her ears, and set her pulses racing.

So they traveled on, barely exchanging a word, until the sun set at last, and the day came to an end. They reached a village so small that it did not even seem to have a name; but there was a wayside shrine, and a cluster of wooden hovels—and an inn.

"Come, Ensign—we have covered enough ground for one day," said Brock Savage. "Let us see if there is accommodation for us here."

Half an hour later, the two horses were stabled, and the officers had been provided with rooms.

It was not a place with any pretension to grandeur;

apart from themselves, the guests were all gentlemen of the road—peddlers, hucksters, or rogues. But the house itself seemed clean and respectable enough, and when the daylight dwindled outside the windows, and the purple Castilian night crept across the landscape, a guitarist somewhere below plucked strange gypsy melodies from his instrument. Garnet stood at the open casement, looking out at the first handful of golden stars as they appeared in the sky, and yearned for something . . . And did not know what it might be.

A knock at her bedroom door made her pull herself together.

"Yes?" she responded, wondering what was happening.

"Are you dressed and ready to dine?" asked Brock Savage.

"Why—yes, sir—yes, I'm quite ready—"

She opened the door. He was standing in the narrow passage, with his head slightly bent, for his tall frame fitted uneasily into this low-raftered building.

"Come with me, then," he said. "Dinner is served."

He led the way along the corridor to another door—the door, Garnet realized, to his own bedchamber. She hung back uncertainly on the threshold, but he urged her forward.

"What are you waiting for? We mustn't let our supper get cold."

She walked in—and stopped short.

There was a small table, laid with a long white cloth and two sets of cutlery and glasses . . . And a bottle of red wine, already opened.

Brock mistook her hesitation for shyness, and said: "You don't object to eating with me, I hope? I took a swift survey of the company below, and it seemed to me we'd do rather better up here, on our own . . . Don't feel nervous, boy—we're not on duty now, and you may relax."

"Thank you, sir," she replied in a low voice, watching

256

carefully as he shut the door. But she noticed that he did
not turn the key in the lock, and she breathed again.

"The food will be sent up directly," Brock continued,
"but I thought perhaps we might permit ourselves a
glass of wine while we wait—what do you say to that?"

"Thank you, sir," she repeated, flatly.

He paused in the act of pouring two glasses.

"You don't say very much, do you, young man? I
noticed today—I hardly had half a dozen words from
you on the journey. Are you always so tongue-tied in
company?"

She shook her head, unable to explain.

"And you were hanging back a good deal of the way—
as you hung back just now when I opened the door . . .
One might almost think that you had some rooted aver-
sion to my company, from the pains you take to avoid
me." He smiled, trying to win some warmth in response.
"Is Old Brock really such a dragon?"

He held out one of the glasses, and she took it—still
silent.

"Come, let us drink a toast to the future . . . The
future of this confounded war—may it soon reach a successful conclusion!"

They raised their glasses and Garnet tasted the wine.
This was a local brew; strong and raw, but with a rich,
inner glow that made her tingle.

"And now another toast—to you and me, Garnet Mallory . . . And may we come to know one another a little
better . . . "

She stared at him, and slowly put her glass down upon
the table. He frowned: "What is the matter? Have I offended you in some way?"

"No—sir—but—"

She could not tell him how she longed to drink that
particular toast with him; longed for it, and yet dreaded
it . . . Dreaded to make the discovery that he was not
the man she believed him to be . . .

257

He put his own glass aside and walked toward her.

"You are avoiding me again . . . Don't be afraid of me, Garnet . . . For I want you to trust me."

Trust! As he spoke, he put his hands on her shoulders, and she found herself falling helplessly into the depths of those blue eyes . . . She was on the point of forgetting everything, and giving herself up completely to his power —and then . . .

His firm hands slid around her shoulders, and he drew her closer to him.

"Let go of me!" The words were torn from her in a kind of agony.

Now her worst fears were realized; this was what he wanted from "Ensign Mallory"—the events of her horrifying intimacy with Lord Deverell were being repeated, like a nightmare that recurs again and again . . . She remembered something Dicky had said about Brock Savage and Deverell—"they're two of a kind" . . . And Larwood asked if he'd whipped her with his riding-crop—"it's a habit of his" . . .

"Why—Garnet—what is wrong?"

"Don't touch me—I know all about your sort of man —I won't let you near me—"

To her amazement, he began to laugh.

"Oh, my dear Garnet—my very dear Garnet—you have misjudged me completely . . . Have no fear—I nurse no shameful desires."

She stepped back a pace, ready to defend herself.

"I don't believe you . . . You're lying—you and Lord Deverell—"

He tried to interrupt, telling her that she was mistaken, but she would not listen; almost defiantly, she continued to talk, determined to put an end to this false, humiliating situation.

"But what you don't realize is that it's all for nothing— you cannot have your way with me, for I am not a boy— *I am a girl!*"

She stopped at last to regain her breath, and in the silence that followed she could hear from the courtyard—but it might as well have been a thousand miles away—the plaintive music of the guitar.

Then Brock Savage laughed, very quietly; and there was a gentleness in his laughter that she would never have expected—but when he spoke, his words put every other thought from her mind, for he said simply: "Yes, Garnet . . . I know."

"You *know?*" She stared at him, open-mouthed, and the whole world seemed to turn upside-down.

"How could you know? Who told you—when—?" Suddenly she remembered the one person who could have betrayed her secret. "It was that doctor, wasn't it—what was his name?—*he* told you . . ."

Brock smiled slightly. "Quite right . . . Doctor Norton."

"And I made him promise he would not—I even sent him a bottle of brandy to pay for his silence—"

"But I gave him half a dozen bottles, to persuade him to confide in me," said Brock.

"Oh, that was vile—men *are* vile—" Garnet was in despair.

"Don't blame the doctor too much. You see, I guessed even before he told me; I only sent you for the medical examination to confirm my own suspicions."

"You cannot have known—"

"Oh, but I did . . . The evening when you fainted, and I caught you as you fell; I was quite certain that it was not a boy I held in my arms . . . And even earlier, on board ship—when I touched your face—so—"

He held out his hand, and tilted her chin with one finger.

"Did you not feel it too? The electricity that passed between us? Can't you feel it even now?"

She slapped his hand away, her eyes blazing.

"How dare you? How dared you play games with me—pretending—tricking me—humiliating me—"

"Never that, I swear to you—"

"Don't say any more. I think you must be the worst

man in the world . . . I've never been so insulted in my life—please let me pass—"

He stood aside automatically as she swept from the room, like a miniature whirlwind.

"Garnet—" he began to call after her, but she was gone, and the door slammed shut in his face.

Confused and excited by her show of spirit, he began to chuckle to himself, then picked up the wine, pledging one more toast with an ironic gesture: "To Garnet Mallory!"

Afterward he looked at the empty glass he was holding, the smile dying from his lips; he gazed around the empty room, at the table still laid for two.

In a sudden burst of anger, he hurled the glass against the whitewashed wall, and watched the fragments explode across the bare boards. Then, slowly, he sank into a chair, and put his head in his hands.

"Oh, God . . . What a mess I've made of it."

Somewhere downstairs, the guitar went on playing.

6

Good News and Bad

Garnet slept very little that night, wondering what was to become of her, now that her secret was known to the commanding officer. She told herself that she despised the man, for the way he had deceived her and for his patronizing airs—and therefore she did not care what action he might take. If he sent her home—all well and good; at least she would never have to set eyes on Brock Savage again. . . .

And as for his unforgivable familiarity . . . She could still remember the feel of his strong hands upon her, and the quizzical condescension of his smile. If he ever again had the temerity to try and take advantage of her plight in that way, she would report him to the Duke of Wellington as a lecher and a libertine—and the devil take the consequences!

She rose early; it was going to be yet another scorching hot day, and there was a fine heat haze over the wide cornfields when she stepped out of the back door, to go and attend to the little chestnut mare.

No one else was about at this hour—or so she thought, until she walked into the stable and found Brock already there before her, grooming the black charger.

He glanced at her briefly, his face expressionless, and then resumed his task with brush and curry-comb.

"Good morning," he said quietly.

"Good morning—sir," she said, with a tiny flash of insolence.

She turned her back, and busied herself with her horse, waiting to see what else he might say.

After some time, he began again: "Last night . . . was an unfortunate misunderstanding," he announced.

"I'm sorry, I must beg to differ," said Garnet. "I assure you that there was no misunderstanding on my part . . . Once you had explained that you had been deliberately making a game of my situation—I understood perfectly."

"I did *not* make a game of—"

"All I would like to know now, sir, is what you propose to do about me, in the light of your knowledge. Perhaps you would be courteous enough to tell me what you intend."

"I should of course send you directly back to Lisbon, to board the first available ship home to England . . . That is my duty, clearly enough."

"So I imagined. The game is over, and you cannot play your charade any longer—so I am to be dismissed . . . Quite so."

"You are too hasty, Miss Mallory. It would be wise if you were to pause long enough to let me finish . . . At least hear what I have decided."

"Well, sir?"

"I was going to continue by saying—although that is my duty, I have concluded for once in my life that there are other considerations of greater importance. I do not wish you to go back to England."

"What?" She dropped the piece of harness that she was about to buckle upon the mare, and swung round to face Brock. "What do you mean?"

He remained with his back to her, speaking over his shoulder and appearing to devote most of his concentration on grooming his mount's coat to a high black gloss.

"I wish you to remain in this country—for three reasons . . . Firstly, because I am a busy man with very many more vital matters to occupy me in the immediate future. To have to put in a report on this business, detailing how you came to be here, and how I discovered your true identity—this would be a great waste of time for everyone concerned."

"And I am not worth taking trouble over—no, of course not."

He ignored this. "The second reason is that you would always be quite convinced that I had thwarted your plan out of sheer vindictiveness. No—don't interrupt me—you have already given ample proof of that by your childish reference a few moments ago to the 'game being over' . . . You would certainly ascribe the lowest possible motive to my actions."

"With some reason, I think—"

"No . . . But we will not argue about that."

"As for this talk of thwarting my plan—what can you know of my plans?" She asked, indignantly.

"Doctor Norton did not simply give me a report upon your physical condition . . . He also told me something of your story—there is a young officer serving with the Third, to whom you are betrothed—am I right?"

She picked up the tackle she had dropped, to conceal her mortification, and said hotly: "It is none of your business, sir. You are mocking me again!"

"I promise you I am not. In fact—that is the third reason why I shall not have you sent home. I find your devotion to this young man faintly admirable: your quest has been very foolish, of course, but it is also more than a little heroic . . . And I should be sorry to think that your efforts to find your lover might all come to nothing—on my account."

There was a pause, and she heard herself say, reluctantly: "Thank you, sir . . . For that, at least."

"This may well be the greatest mistake I have ever made—but I have decided, in view of all these considerations, to try to forget everything I know of your case. As far as I am concerned, you will be returning to duty with the junior officers of the Third at the earliest opportunity; today, if possible."

"I see . . . So—you do not wish me to continue to act as your *aide-de-camp*?"

"Under the circumstances, I think we must regard that as a highly undesirable—in fact, an improper—situation . . . And I shall therefore wash my hands of you, Ensign Mallory. You must take your chance—and I see no reason for us to meet again."

"Very well." She lifted her chin, drew herself up, and saluted. "I am ready to leave as soon as you give the word, sir."

After a hurried breakfast of rolls and coffee, they set out once more; once again, Brock Savage led the way, and Garnet remained a good twenty yards to the rear. But this time he did not reprove her, or appear to notice the gap between them, and they rode on without communication.

By nightfall, they caught up with the Third Dragoons; they met them along the highroad, and one glance at their bedraggled uniforms—at bandaged and bloodstained arms and legs—at their grey, exhausted faces—told the unhappy story.

The French had thrown in their heavy artillery to relieve the besieged city, and the Dragoons had come under an unmerciful cannonade. They were forced at last, by their losses in both cavalry and manpower, to fall back, defeated, and it was a retreating army that Garnet now met upon the road.

They pitched camp for the night, and the major-general withdrew for a conference with his chiefs-of-staff.

To her relief, Garnet found Dicky Blades alive and unhurt—though very shaken by his first encounter with the enemy. He had seen horrible sights, and stood by helplessly as some of his colleagues were blown to pieces . . . Gray Edgecombe had been one of the first to fall.

Garnet closed her eyes, as Dicky told her the details of his death. She had disliked the vain young lieutenant and feared his cruel tongue on occasion—but she could never have wished an end such as this for him. To have half his body ripped to pieces by a shell that burst almost under him.

She shuddered, and said: "Don't tell me any more, Dicky . . . I cannot bear to hear it."

"I know how you feel, young 'un . . . I shall see the look on his face as he went down until the day I die . . . And hear the sound of his horse screaming . . . I wish to God I could forget it."

Luckily, there was a lot of work to be done, and as always Major Sterne was there, urging the boys on; there were tents to be put up, bed-rolls to be unpacked, food and stores—such as there were left—to be prepared for supper . . . There was little time to reflect on what had happened; their immediate future was of more concern than the recent past.

Gone were the smooth sheets at Mrs. McBey's or the more simple comforts of the village inn; Garnet was back to the harsh realities of active service, sharing a tent with half a dozen young officers, and sleeping on the hard, unwelcoming ground.

So the time dragged on, as one day followed another, and the days lengthened into weeks.

It became apparent that the major-general's strategy was to deploy their forces in a two-pronged attack upon the French. They were to divide up and circle round Burgos, pushing still farther northward, toward the coast.

There was a shortage of victuals, and life for the Third

Dragoons was Spartan indeed during that long, hot summer. Garnet began to wonder if she would ever again know the bliss of a soft bed, or a properly cooked meal, or a lazy delicious bath in clean water . . . Meanwhile, Edmund remained in the special squadron attending the Duke of Wellington, somewhere on the other side of the mountains—and farther out of reach than ever before.

As for Brock Savage, he had been as good as his word, and their paths had never crossed again. Once or twice Garnet saw him in the distance, always grim and unsmiling, always surrounded by a group of senior officers, making and remaking plans of attack. It was as if their brief time together had been nothing more than a dream; she felt certain that he had put her from his mind quite coldly and deliberately . . . And she told herself that she was very glad of it, for the last thing she wanted now was Brock Savage's insolent, smiling arrogance.

Then, one afternoon, she was out riding in a patrol with half a dozen of the young officers; they were supposed to be reconnoitering the terrain, somewhere in the vicinity of Vitoria, but their efforts had borne little fruit, and they had not seen any sign of the enemy forces. Once again, it was a blazing hot day, and the sun beat down upon them relentlessly.

The horses slowed from a canter to a walk, and they rode in single file down a narrow path into a valley where there were a few spindly trees, and the promise of some shade—and, best of all, the sight and sound of a river, gurgling and splashing among the burning rocks.

Garnet consulted the map she carried in her saddlebag.

"This must be the river Zadorra—it runs right up to Vitoria—"

"Who cares what it's called? It's cool and wet—that's all that matters!" exclaimed Dicky as he dismounted. "Let's give the poor beasts a drink, for pity's sake."

The horses were led to the water's edge, and needed no second bidding. They advanced into the swiftly-flowing river, and curved their graceful necks, lapping the water eagerly.

"Come on—let's follow their example," called Dicky. "I haven't had a decent bath for weeks—this is a fine chance!"

As he spoke, he began to undress, unbuttoning his tunic and breeches, pulling off his boots, and flinging his clothes left and right—almost as impatient to dive into the clear crystal flood as he had been anxious to achieve sexual relief at the bordello.

Garnet remembered the bordello all too clearly, and felt the same sense of acute discomfort as she watched all the young men beginning to remove their uniforms. On active service, there was little reason for the officers to dress or undress, each night and morning; they spent long stretches of time living and sleeping in the clothes they stood up in, and it was rare for Garnet to see any of her companions in a state of *deshabille*.

Now, quite suddenly, it was as if time had rolled back and she was Eve in the garden of Eden—surrounded by a crowd of lusty Adams, who had not yet tasted the forbidden fruit, and so were happily unaware of their own nakedness.

But Eve had sampled the apple, and in her shame she did not know where to look. On all sides, the young male bodies openly exulted in their freedom, and seemed almost to flaunt their virility in her face.

She lowered her eyes and turned away, sitting on a patch of grass beneath the trees, waiting, as men and horses enjoyed the unaccustomed delight of the cool, refreshing water.

Naturally, it was not long before the others noticed that she remained aloof, and they began to call out.

"What's wrong, Garnet? Come in and join us! What's the matter—can't you swim? Are you afraid of getting wet?"

"It's all right—I *can* swim—but I don't wish to . . ." she replied, lamely.

Yes, she could swim . . . She remembered with startling clarity the first lesson she had had from Jem; his strong body pressed against her, as he carried her into the waters of the fishpond . . . But he had been excited and aroused, whereas these swimmers were frolicking together in care-free pleasure, like the dolphins she had watched from the deck of the *Ariadne*.

"Oh—come on—don't be such a spoilsport—come on in, you'll enjoy it!" shouted Hooker, and Larwood added: "If you don't—we'll come out and get you—!"

"Oh, no—don't be silly—". She stood up nervously, and began to protest. "I tell you I don't want to bathe today—please—"

But they wouldn't listen to her. Even Dicky, she realized with dismay, was laughing and joining his voice with the others. There was no malice in them; they genuinely be-lieved she was missing all the fun, and wanted her to share in it . . . So they all scrambled out of the river and advanced upon her, making jokes and mock-threats.

"Come along—no excuses now—off with your clothes, young Mallory—"

Dicky reached her first, and as she tried to retreat, he grabbed her wrists.

"Oh, no, you don't get away so easily, young 'un—you're coming for a swim, whether you like it or not . . . All right, chaps—let's strip off his uniform . . ."

Garnet struggled helplessly, almost in tears with frus-tration and shame; but it was no good. Six muscular young men, all as naked as the day they were born, but rather spectacularly better developed, flung themselves upon her, toppling her back onto the grass. It was only a moment of horseplay to them, and they had no idea of her real feelings as they closed in upon her. Their power-ful torsos all shining and slippery with water, and their hands busy at every point, unbuttoning, unlacing, unfas-tening . . .

She gave up all hope of deliverance, awaiting the first

startled cry of astonishment as her secret was revealed, and she would be exposed forever . . . But before that could happen—

She thought for a moment that a thunderbolt had fallen.

There was a blinding flash of light that seemed to fill the sky, followed by a deafening explosion, and a rush of air like a scorching wind . . . Air that smelled sickeningly of gunpowder.

Instantly all other thoughts were swept from their minds.

"Cannon, by God!" said Captain Hooker. "The bastard Frenchies are shelling us . . . "

The officers left Garnet instantly, and rushed to retrieve their own clothes; still wet, they pulled on their uniforms as best they could, and then ran into the river to pacify the frightened horses. During this diversion, Garnet managed to dress herself completely, and then she too jumped into the water up to her thighs, as she went to the aid of the chestnut mare.

A minute later, a second shell exploded with another thunderclap, landing in the river about a hundred yards away, and sending up a great fountain of spray.

"Quick, lads—get on your horses and ride up out of this valley—they've got our range!" ordered Captain Larwood breathlessly.

In fact, as they discovered much later, the French artillery had not the faintest notion that their shells had come so near to wiping out a squadron of Dragoon officers; they had fired the cannon in self-defense, and the shots had fallen wide of their intended mark . . . For the advance assault party of the British and Spanish forces had surprised the main body of the French, some three leagues to the west of Vitoria—and a pitched battle had begun.

Garnet and her companions rode up the valley path for all they were worth, and when they reached the brow of a hill, she had an unbroken view of the spectacle that lay before them.

A huge body of the enemy troops—eventually estimated to be some seventy thousand strong—were deployed on the far side of the River Zadorra; one flank was protected by the mountain foothills, the other by the river itself, partially screened by thick woods. In the center of their position, an artillery brigade kept up an unceasing fire on the British, and Garnet at first thought that there must certainly be another massacre, as at Burgos —for the British were drawn up in the open plain, and appeared to be totally defenseless.

But she had reckoned without the skillful strategy of the Duke of Wellington and Major-General Savage.

Wellington appeared at first to be concentrating his forces upon the center of the French lines—but, Garnet soon realized, the British were studiously following the old adage: "Divide—and conquer."

Under the command of Brock Savage, one division began to scale the foothills and harass the enemy from their right flank, while Garnet found herself—together with another division of Dragoons—making an assault upon the river, to the left, and driving the French back upon the city of Vitoria.

This was her baptism of fire, and at first the thrill of the chase possessed her utterly; she felt no fear for her own safety, nor even—for everything happened so quickly—concern for those men she saw fall in the struggle. It was all one great, surging movement—onward and upward to victory; and she felt drunk with elation as she spurred on the chestnut mare.

But the initial impetus soon waned, and when it came to the river-crossing, at a place called Gamarra Mayor, at the entrance to the city, the initial rush halted . . . The British artillery were moving in now, and in order to get the big guns across the bridge it was necessary to go ahead and clear the bodies of men—some dead, some dying—who lay strewn upon the narrow bridge, blocking the way.

Garnet watched, horrified, as these bleeding, mutilated men were unceremoniously rolled over the bridge and dropped into the running water below, like so many carcasses of meat . . . And when the way was open, the heavy artillery were able to move ahead, the huge wheels of the gun carriages rolling in the blood of the men who had died there.

By evening, it was all over, and the enemy was in full flight.

Vitoria fell to the British advance, and the Dragoons rode in, in triumph.

Garnet found herself alongside Dicky, and smiled with relief to see that the boy had come through the day's ordeal without injury.

"I was lucky . . ." said Dicky, but he sounded a good deal less confident than usual. "God knows I could have been blown to perdition a hundred times—you and I are the lucky ones . . . Major Sterne told me that we lost two thousand today, counting both killed *and* wounded."

"Where is the major now?"

"Gone into the city to search out quarters for Wellington and the chiefs-of-staff. I wonder where we'll have to sleep tonight . . ."

"It doesn't appear that we will have much choice," said Garnet quietly, looking about her.

For certainly the city of Vitoria had suffered severely during the French retreat. Many houses had been shelled; doors and windows hung off their hinges, and roofs had lost their tiles, exposing gaping holes and bare rafters to the evening air.

One imposing mansion, however, seemed to have escaped any real damage, though its inhabitants had prudently packed up and removed themselves from the scene of the fighting long before. This was the building that Major Sterne had requisitioned for the officers' quarters, and by the time Garnet and Dicky arrived, several of the commanders were already esconced there.

"You can bet that there'll be no room for us with the top dogs," commented Dicky bitterly. "I dare say we'll finish up pitching a tent in the back yard . . . "

However, they stabled their horses, and made their way in, across the patio, to the main building.

Even after such an appalling day, Garnet was amazed to discover that she could still feel hungry and thirsty, and she sniffed longingly at the aroma of frying ham and onions that wafted across from the kitchen quarters, and looked forward to suppertime.

Some of the officers were already in the dining-room. Their military boots clicking upon the bare, shining floor, and their English chatter sounding a little out of place within these alien surroundings of wrought-iron screens and polished tiles.

"Mmm—a good, full-bodied sherry . . . " purred a voice that made Garnet's gorge rise.

She looked round, and saw Hugo Deverell sitting at a long refectory table, one leg elegantly cocked over the arm of his chair, taking a sip of sherry from a tall glass.

He saw her at the same moment, and his lips twisted into a smile. "Why—if it isn't the dainty little Ensign Mallory . . . " he sneered. "Come and pay your respects to your elders and betters, my dear."

Garnet glanced at Dicky—who muttered under his breath, "Tell Daisy you hope he rots in hell . . . "

But there was no help for it; Garnet was forced to go forward and salute the lieutenant-colonel.

"That's more like it . . . Glad to see you've survived so far, dear lad . . . " And he accented the word "lad" with the faintest possible touch of sarcasm. "I must say I was sorry to hear of your poor friend's misfortune."

"What?" She frowned, aware that others were listening. "Do you mean Captain Challoner? What's happened to him?"

"No, no, dear boy—nothing's wrong with Ned Challoner, as far as I know . . . I was referring to our revered major-general—old Brock himself . . . Isn't he your new protector? I heard you'd been pressed into service as his personal aide . . . "

"What do you mean?" She stared at the cruel, tormenting face, and almost shouted: *"What's happened to him?"*

"Oh, didn't you know? The poor fellow was wounded— it seems some French swine fired a pistol at his head . . . Old Brock's on the sick list now—upstairs in bed, I'm told . . . I felt sure you'd be the first to know of it, my dear . . . "

Perhaps Garnet should have disguised her feelings, and pretended to indifference; but she could not help herself. She turned without a word, and pushed past Dicky—she saw the look of surprise on his face, as she ran by—and raced on, out of the dining-room and up the stairs to the floor above, where she stopped a passing orderly and tugged at his arm, demanding:

"Where is he? Where is the major-general—?"

Vaguely, she was aware of being instructed which room he was in, and ran on blindly, pushing open the door without even stopping to knock . . .

Brock Savage lay back against a bank of pillows, a bandage partially covering his skull and his left eye. His face was an unnatural color: he had lost a good deal of blood, leaving his normally tanned complexion almost olive-green. But he had paper and a pen to hand, and was struggling to write out his report on the day's exploits.

He glanced up as Garnet burst in. She stood quite still, staring at him, and then gasped: "They told me—you were hurt . . . "

He gazed at her for a long moment, as if he had never seen her before, and then said in a strange, unfamiliar voice: "Garnet . . . Shut the door . . . And come here."

She did as he bade her; the door slammed shut, and she moved toward him—then, suddenly, without knowing how it happened, she found herself on her knees beside the bed, with tears rolling down her face, and her arms around him . . .

Holding him close and repeating over and over: "Thank God . . . Thank God . . . "

The official report, unfinished, slid in all directions, and the pen fell on the floor, as Brock put his hands to her face.

"My dear girl . . . What are you trying to say to me?"

She could not speak, quite choked with tears, and he shook his head in bewilderment, asking gently: "Why should you care what happens to Old Brock, in God's name? I thought you despised and detested me?"

"I thought so too," she managed to blurt out at last, between her sobs. "Only tell me—are you very badly hurt?"

"It's nothing . . . A scratch—a head-wound—the doctors assure me I shall be up and about again very soon."

"But—your eye—"

"Too soon to say yet how that may be affected; I must be patient till they take the bandages off . . . Don't cry, Garnet Mallory; it's not worth crying about."

He brought her face close to his own, and put his lips to her cheek, tasting the salt tang of her tears, kissing her smooth young skin, then pressing his mouth upon hers.

As they embraced, Garnet forgot every other kiss that she had known; this was the first time in her life that she had ever felt totally at one with any man. His mouth was firm yet soft, determined but yielding too. The kiss lasted for only a few moments, but within that short space of time she experienced a joy that some are never fortunate enough to know in a whole lifetime . . . Giving and taking, male and female, becoming one body and one soul.

At last they broke apart, looking at each other in amazement.

"And I never knew . . . " she breathed. "How could I have been so stupid?"

"My dearest Garnet . . . " He tightened his embrace around her shoulders for an instant, then released her. "Don't say any more now. We are both tired and a little light-headed, I expect; not quite in full possession of our

senses. We will talk again, later—tomorrow perhaps . . .
But until then, I think we should—"

He broke off, listening; they both heard footsteps approaching in the corridor outside.

"Make yourself presentable, for we are about to receive visitors," he said quickly, and as a knock came at the door, he added in a louder voice: "One moment, please."

Garnet stood up, dashing the tell-tale signs of tears from her face, and straightening her uniform. She nodded briefly at Brock.

He called out, "Very well . . . Come in!"

Major Sterne entered the bedroom; he was mildly surprised to find Garnet there, but assumed that she had been sent to carry out some errand for the major-general.

"All right, boy—you may go now," he said, dismissing her, and then turned to his commanding officer.

"Sir—the Duke of Wellington is below. He presents his compliments and best wishes for your speedy recovery."

"Very good of the duke; thank him for me, major, and tell him I'm much obliged . . . " Brock began.

His voice faded as Garnet slipped from the room and made her escape, her mind in a whirl.

What was happening? What was the magic that this extraordinary man possessed—that he should hold such power over her? She had thought she knew what love was, in all its various forms; the happy delirium she had felt in Edmund's arms, the thrilling excitement as Jem had first explored her body . . . But this feeling she had, that now overwhelmed her completely—this was something completely new, involving all her other emotions and yet transcending them. It was as if she were alone on the threshold of a totally new world, without maps or charts to guide her . . . And yet at the same time not alone; for she knew quite certainly, from the moment that she felt Brock's strong arms about her, that she would never be alone again.

Downstairs, in the dining-room, many more officers

275

were now assembled, most of them grouped in an in-
gratiating semi-circle round one man . . . A spare, angular
figure with a Roman nose and high cheekbones—the
commander-in-chief himself.

Someone said politely: "You must feel very gratified,
sir . . . It has been a glorious day for you."

"Yes," said the Duke of Wellington. "We have got all
their artillery."

He moved out of the little group, which immediately
fell back to let him pass.

"I am going to bed," he announced. "Some of you—
tell Brock Savage that I shall march the army off myself,
in the morning."

A voice asked: "Sir—at what hour?"

The great duke stretched his arms and yawned prodigi-
ously, then replied:

"When I get up . . . "

And with that he strode out of the room. A buzz of
conversation broke out as soon as he had gone, with
everyone talking at once.

". . . Brilliant man . . . Old blood-and-thunder . . .
Capital fellow . . . Damned play-actor . . . The finest
soldier I ever hope to serve."

This last phrase stood out, sharp and clear, and Garnet
started violently. She looked to see who it was that spoke
—then saw, across the room, half hidden by a knot of
fellow-officers, the face of Edmund Challoner . . .

At the same instant, Dicky was at her side, nudging her
and saying: "There he is at last—your precious captain!
Ain't you going to go and speak to him, after all this long
time?"

"Yes . . . Of course—but—" Her thoughts raced; she
played for time, trying to decide how to deal with this
situation. If Edmund should see her suddenly, without
warning, he might well ruin everything by his reaction;
she felt she had to prepare him a little for the revelation.

Quickly she dug into the inner pocket of her tunic; this

was where she now carried his monogrammed handkerchief, for safety. She drew it out and gave it to Dicky, saying: "Do me a service, Dick . . . Take this across and give it to the captain quietly . . . Tell him it comes from a friend who is nearer than he imagines."

"All right—if that's what you want . . ." Dicky scratched his head and grinned. "My stars—you're a rum cove, young 'un, and no mistake."

He took the kerchief and crossed the room. Garnet watched, and held her breath as she saw him wait for a suitable break in the conversation, and then respectfully claim the captain's attention, whispering in his ear and passing over the keepsake.

Edmund looked at it—recognized it—frowned—and then smiled, saying cheerfully: "I think I can guess who gave you this . . . Young Ensign Mallory—am I right? I remember now, the youngster was being packed off into the army by his father—where is the boy?"

He began to search for a familiar face in the throng, and Garnet's heart beat faster, as he continued talking to Dicky.

"I know the family well—for I'm engaged to be married to the daughter of the family—a lovely creature, by the name of—"

And at this instant his eyes met hers, and he stopped dead as he uttered the name:

"*Garnet* . . ."

Luckily, Dicky misunderstood, and assumed that he had simply broken off to announce that he had spied his future brother-in-law across the room.

"Yes—you're right—Garnet Mallory gave me the handkerchief for you, and there he is;" he agreed. "Well, sir—now you've met one another again, I'll leave you both to talk. You'll have plenty to say to each other, I'm sure."

He strolled off, and Edmund walked up to Garnet like a man in a trance.

"Garnet . . ." He repeated at last. "I cannot believe the

277

evidence of my own eyes . . . For the love of heaven—
tell me I am not going mad—what are you doing here?
And in such a guise—?"

"I came to find you, Edmund," said Garnet, simply.
"It has taken a very long time, but at last I have been
successful."

"But *how*?" He broke off, adding: "This is madness—
we can't talk here . . . But I have been provided with accommodation within these premises, on the second floor. I
suggest we should repair to my room, and there you shall
satisfy my curiosity . . . Come, let us go—we shall not
be missed in this crowd."

So they slipped away quickly and easily, and went upstairs.

But Edmund was mistaken on one point; their departure had not gone completely unobserved.

At the far end of the room, Daisy Deverell rose slowly
from his chair, with a tiny half-smile upon his lips—and
prepared to follow them.

7

Dishonor — and Death

Edmund led the way upstairs, with Garnet close at his heels, and on the second floor of the house he opened a door which led into a rather unusual room.

"This is where I have been quartered," he explained, as they went inside. "As you see it's hardly a bedchamber, but none the worse for that."

He had laid out a bed-roll on the floor, with blankets and a pillow; but apart from this the room was sparsely furnished, without even a chair, and only one small wooden table, covered with oil paints and jars of brushes. An artist's palette, daubed with all the colors of the rainbow, showed that this unconventional room was normally used as a studio; and the open window commanded a view of tiles and chimneys, over the huddle of outbuildings behind the house. A flat roof immediately outside was clearly connected to the laundry, for sheets, shirts and petticoats still hung there forgotten, from a spider's web of criss-crossed washing lines.

"You see how the inhabitants of this mansion must have decided to abandon it at very short notice—everything is as they left it," Edmund continued. "When the assault upon the town began, they simply dropped whatever they were doing, and bolted."

"Yes . . ." Garnet admired a canvas that hung, unfinished, from two stout hooks in the rafters—an attempt to re-create the view from the window. "I wonder who the painter was . . . He puts my poor attempts at watercolor to shame."

They looked at one another, and smiled for the first time, remembering the summer afternoons at Markwick that now seemed so long ago: the polite tea-time conversations, and the formal inspection of Garnet's artistic handiwork in leather-bound albums.

"We're a long way from Surrey now . . . " said Edmund. "I still can't believe that you are really here."

"There were times when I thought I would never see you again," said Garnet. "But now—at last . . . "

She left the sentence unfinished, and turned back to the landscape on the canvas, comparing it with the reality beyond the window. Already it was getting dark; the Spanish twilight quickly faded into night. She drew a pair of curtains across the casement, as Edmund lit a candle, shielded within a rough lantern that hung from the beams in the ceiling. A warm yellow glow sprang up and drew them within its magic circle.

"You must have a great deal to tell me . . . And I long to hear every word of your story, my dearest Garnet," said Edmund. "I would ask you to sit down, but as you see there is no chair I can offer you."

"I am very used to living in rough-and-ready conditions, I assure you," said Garnet. "We can sit on the bed and make ourselves comfortable there."

Suiting the action to the words, she threw herself down

on the thin mattress that was spread out on the uncarpeted floor; Edmund gazed down at her, still bemused by her appearance as she lay back and smiled up at him—one knee crossed over the other, her weight supported on her elbows . . . Every inch the young ensign.

"It's amazing," he said. "You seem to have turned into a boy so completely—it still takes my breath away to look at you."

"I am not changed so *very* much," she retorted, demurely. "Only in outward appearance, you know . . . "

"But when—how—*why* did you undergo this incredible transformation? Begin at the beginning, and don't leave out one single detail."

"When? The day after you left the barracks to go to Portsmouth, I formed the notion—partly to enable Gerard to escape being pressed into service, which he wished to avoid at all costs—but even more, so that I might follow you and find you again."

"You are an extraordinary girl," he declared. "What have I done to deserve such devotion?"

She bit her lip, and looked away for a moment, unable to answer this question as truthfully as she should. There would be time later, she thought, to deal with this problem.

"First let me tell you as much as I can remember about my escape from Markwick . . . Sit down beside me, Edmund; this is no time for formality between us!"

So he obeyed, and curled up next to her on the bedroll, looking with wonder at this bewildering creature in boy's clothes, and listening eagerly to her adventures.

She gave a very full account of the first few weeks—her sea voyage, her enforced companionship with young Dicky Blades, the arrival in Lisbon, and the ensuing period of boredom, serving with Major Sterne at the base camp. Then Madrid, and the setback of Burgos, leading eventually to the grand triumph today, in Vitoria.

And yet, although she told him a great deal, she left

out the most important fact throughout her narration; for Major-General Broccard Savage was never once mentioned, from start to finish.

He was in her mind all the while, and his name continually trembled upon the tip of her tongue; but she never referred to him at all. Only—as she looked at Edmund's handsome face, so close now to her that she could reach out and touch him, if she had wished to—she saw only Brock's blue eyes, Brock's stern but understanding gaze, Brock's smile that seemed to penetrate the very core of her being . . . And she kept thinking of him on his sickbed, doubtless suffering a good deal of pain—only such a short distance away; and yet she could not run to him, as she longed to.

"Tell me about yourself, Edmund," she said at last, with an effort. "For I am quite exhausted with so much talking . . . How have you fared, since you came to the Peninsula? I know of course that you were selected to ride ahead with the Duke's own advance party—and I prayed continually that you might escape danger."

"I have been very fortunate; your prayers must have been heard, my dearest . . . For I have come through the whole campaign until now without so much as a scratch . . ."

Impulsively, he put his hand upon hers, and pressed gently.

"But I was doubly fortunate in having such a girl as you to care for me . . . As brave as she is beautiful."

And he leaned forward and took her in his arms.

She struggled instinctively, and he mistook her reaction for natural modesty, saying in soothing tones, "Don't be alarmed, my dear love—for as you yourself pointed out, there is no need of formality between us now . . . You have dared so much to be with me, and I have longed for you so many times while we have been apart . . . let us put an end to our unhappy separation at once, and make up for all the time we have wasted."

His arms tightened about her, and she felt his hands upon her body, urgently exploring and demanding.

She recollected a thousand lonely nights when she had longed for just such an embrace as this, and the way her skin had tingled at the mere thought of this man . . . And now she lay here, in his arms, and she felt nothing at all. Nothing but a cold, unhappy numbness, and a complete inability to respond to his touch as she would once have done.

All the time, a pulse in her brain was pounding with an insistent rhythm, that repeated over and over the one syllable: "Brock . . . Brock . . . Brock . . . "

She was aware that he was beginning to undress her; his fingers had unfastened her tunic, and slipped into her shirt, stroking and caressing, closing gently over her breasts, fondling her nipples . . . She tensed at once, and he interpreted the sudden tremor as the onset of passion.

"Yes—yes—very soon, my darling—" he whispered in her ear; and his hands moved down to her waist and began to explore further. She knew that she would soon be completely undressed and helplessly vulnerable, and she knew that she had to stop him before it was too late.

"No—Edmund—please—not that, not now—" she gasped.

"There is nothing to fear, dearest—I will be gentle and patient with you—but this is what I have dreamed about for so long . . . And now I am certain of your love, for you have proved yourself so loyal—"

"Edmund—you must listen to me—" She tried to hold him off. But despite herself, she felt her own body responding to his ardor, and she knew she was slipping all too easily on the giddy downward slope that could only reach one conclusion. "Listen—there is something—I have to tell you—"

"Later, my love . . . Tell me later . . . Tell me afterwards . . . "

His hands seemed to be everywhere at once, and she

fought to control her emotions, despising her body for its wanton weakness—but his mouth closed upon hers, and she felt his tongue pressing between her lips, insistently. She could not speak, or protest, or defend herself any longer . . .

"*Shameful* . . . The most shameful spectacle I ever witnessed."

A door shut firmly, and the lock clicked.

Edmund and Garnet sprang apart upon the bed, looking up in dismay at the interruption.

"The next time you wish to practice the abominable sins of Sodom, I suggest you should take the precaution of locking the door first," said Lieutenant-Colonel Hugo Deverell—and as he spoke, he withdrew the key and slipped it into his breast pocket.

"Sir—!" Edmund struggled to his feet, trying to explain: "You don't understand—"

"I understand the evidence of my own eyes, Ned . . . And I am shocked beyond measure to find you capable of such debauchery . . . Two officers of his majesty's glorious army—engaged in perverse and carnal intercourse . . . " Hugo smiled, and his smile was like the blade of a cutthroat razor. "Words fail me, my dear."

"Sir, only let me correct you—and beg you to forget what you think you have seen—"

"I only wish I could—but alas! I fear it will be engraved upon my memory for the rest of my life . . . And I always considered you to be such a noble, upright young man—how grossly I was deceived."

"Sir, I insist that you must know the truth . . . Garnet here is not what you imagine—"

"He already knows perfectly well who I am—and what I am," said Garnet with disgust. "He is simply playing a game with you, Edmund."

"What? He *knows?*"

"You impose upon my indulgence too much," Hugo purred. "Some time ago I made the startling discovery that Ensign Garnet Mallory was not really a boy—and out of the kindness of my heart I agreed to conceal my knowledge; in fact, I have tried to forget the incident altogether . . . Therefore, as far as I am concerned, Ensign Mallory must still be a young man—but now I find him engaged in an obscene embrace with another junior officer —am I expected to wipe this incident from my mind also? No, no—you cannot ask me to overlook *all* your shortcomings, Garnet Mallory . . . This time you have gone too far!"

Garnet had been adjusting her uniform during this whimsical speech, and now—more self-possessed, and feeling a little more confident—she asked: "And what do you propose to do about the situation, Lord Deverell? Am I to be sent home to England in disgrace, after all?"

"Disgrace would be too slight a word for the weight of public obloquy that would fall upon you in such circumstances," said Hugo, and he began to pace the room thoughtfully, savoring the situation to its utmost. "If I were now to expose you as the little slut that you are— lewdly parading in men's clothes, for the purpose of following your lover and fornicating with him—"

Edmund stepped forward, his face hot with anger and his fists upraised, but Hugo turned and silenced him with a single glance.

"Don't interrupt me, my dear . . . I am your lieutenant-colonel, and if you were ever unwise enough to forget that fact, I should have you cashiered instantly . . . To resume—you came to Spain and inveigled yourself into the British army, Garnet Mallory, for the sole purpose of coupling with this unfortunate officer . . . And I should certainly make sure that every man, woman and child in the British Isles would come to know of your depravity."

He took a breath, and looked Garnet up and down with withering contempt before continuing.

"That is what I *should* do . . . That is my bounden duty, in fact . . . But in view of your tender years I am inclined to be merciful."

"Merciful? *You*?" Garnet's contempt easily out-matched his.

He ignored the interjection.

"As I said, I have agreed to overlook your anatomical deficiencies; you are, to all intents and purposes, an ensign in the Dragoons—and as such, you and your paramour must take the consequences of your actions. Captain Challoner, as the older and—one hopes—the wiser of the two, you must shoulder the major blame for this unspeakable indecency . . . Do you agree?"

Edmund stared at him, and answered one question with another. "Come to the point, sir—what are you suggesting?"

"Once again—I know where my duty lies. Duty dictates that I should report your behavior and have you court-martialed . . . Thereafter, you would undoubtedly lose your commission and be expelled from the regiment with dishonor . . ."

Edmund's face was expressionless; he stared straight ahead, but a muscle twitched at the angle of his jaw.

"However—I am, I repeat, a merciful man. I would not wish such public humiliation upon you—if it can be avoided . . . And I think I can suggest an alternative."

Edmund still said nothing, and Garnet asked quickly: "What do you mean? What alternative?"

It was Edmund who replied, in a flat voice, drained of all emotion: "He means that he will punish me himself—and keep his mouth shut. He's done it before, with other ranks who have stepped out of line, and he's made them pay for their mistakes."

"I don't understand—what sort of punishment—?"

"Rather than put anyone to the unpleasantness of judicial proceedings, I prefer to take the law into my own hands . . . Judge, advocate, and jury—and I even carry out the sentence myself," said Hugo, lightly.

"In other words—he thrashes me," said Edmund.

"Oh, no—no, Edmund—that's horrible—" Garnet was

appalled, as she began to understand Hugo Deverell's little scheme.

"Why not? You both deserve to be punished—and I consider this is the most lenient penalty I can exact . . . What do you say, Ned?"

"Do I have any choice?"

"You have three choices—as I thought I'd made clear . . . Public exposure and shame for this young female, or court-martial and disgrace for yourself . . . Or a simple taste of the lash, at my hands."

There was a pause; Garnet tried to protest once more, but Edmund stopped her.

"Don't say anything more, my love . . . This is between Deverell and myself . . . "

"Quite right, dear boy; in fact, I would almost venture to say that this is a confrontation which we both knew must take place, sooner or later . . . Are you prepared to accept my sentence?"

Edmund drew himself up very straight, and said quietly: "I am . . . Send Garnet away, and I will take whatever is coming to me."

"Oh, no—the girl must stay—she has to be the witness of your castigation; for that will be *her* punishment too . . . And besides—I shall need her assistance in this little ceremony."

He looked round the room, and snapped his fingers.

"Very well, Ensign Mallory—you can begin by taking down the picture that is hanging from that beam. Put it aside, facing the wall—carefully now, for one must take great care when handling works of art . . . "

Garnet was totally bewildered, and very apprehensive, but she had to obey.

"Splendid . . . Now, Ned—you will oblige me by removing your tunic and shirt. Do not be embarrassed; I'm quite sure our young ensign has seen your classic torso before."

In silence, Edmund did as he was told, flinging his

287

clothes upon the mattress, and then stood before Lord Deverell, stripped to the waist, his skin shining slightly where a thin film of sweat broke out upon his body.

"Good, good . . . Now place yourself below that rafter, and raise your hands above your head."

Edmund moved slowly, almost as if he were an automaton going through a routine of prearranged actions. Without surprise, he stood patiently in position as Hugo Deverell took the two cords that had supported the painting, and secured his wrists to the hooks in the beam.

"Excellent . . . Lastly—Ensign, you will remove the captain's leather belt and hand it to me."

"Oh—no—" she hesitated, but Edmund said, "Do as he bids you . . . There is no help for it—the sooner we get this over, the better."

So she unbuckled the heavy belt, and removed it from Edmund's waist; his breeches sagged slightly, settling upon his hips. Hugo took the belt from her hands, flexed it, then cracked it in mid-air once or twice.

"Yes . . . I hope you will appreciate that this is not the instrument I would have chosen, Ned, but we have nothing else immediately available . . . Now then, my dear—brace yourself . . . "

He raised his right arm, and the leather strap whistled through the air like a knife, cutting viciously across Edmund's shoulder-blades. Garnet put her hand to her mouth, stifling an involuntary cry.

Again and again the lash rose and fell, leaving angry stripes across Edmund's back. Garnet bit her knuckles, remembering the man she had seen flogged in Lisbon, dreading the moment when the blows would at last draw blood, and striving to be as courageous as Edmund himself—for although his body rocked with the force of the beating, his face never changed, and he never uttered a sound.

After a few moments Hugo paused, breathing heavily; clearly, he was not satisfied with the response he was getting.

"This is no good," he said thickly—and Garnet noticed

with a little chill of terror that his lips were moist with saliva. "He needs to be stripped—*you, Mallory!*—take his breeches down . . . At once—d'ye hear?"

"No! I won't do it—"

"You will obey orders, Ensign—!" snarled Lord Deverell, and he struck Garnet full in the face with the back of his hand.

She recoiled from the blow, which almost knocked her off her feet, and heard Edmund saying between his teeth: "Do it . . . Whatever he tells you—do it, for God's sake —or he'll make you suffer all the more . . . "

So she complied, loathing herself for her cowardice, and loathing Hugo Deverell for his abnormal tyranny . . . Her hands shook, and it was only with great difficulty that she finally brought herself to unfasten Edmund's breeches and slide them down his thighs. His drawers were dragged down at the same time, and she made an instinctive movement to pull them up and cover Edmund's nakedness— but Deverell grasped her arm.

"Leave him alone . . . let's see what sort of a figure he cuts—without a stitch to shield him . . . let's see how he takes his punishment *now!*"

In truth, Edmund had never appeared more noble in Garnet's eyes; for now he was beyond all humiliation, and although his manhood was completely exposed he stood straight, proud and defiant, in contrast to the inhuman sickness of his persecutor. Lord Deverell had made a sneering reference to Edmund's "classic torso"—and it seemed to Garnet that he now resembled some godlike figure from an antique sculpture, his body so perfectly formed, and so splendidly displayed—while Hugo Deverell's bid for revenge was as meaningless as a lunatic's attempts to deface an imperishable work of art.

But Hugo, Lord Deverell had not finished yet; and as he was about to continue the flogging, he suddenly paused, changing his mind.

"No . . . " He smiled, and Garnet felt sick at the sheer malevolence in his expression. "Before I proceed any

289

further—I feel it's only right for the prisoner to be given some consolation . . . And from your fair hands, young Mallory . . . So you will pleasure him, pet him—fondle him . . . Try to forget I am here, and give him all those little secret delights you used to, when you were alone . . . *Do as I say!*"

She stared at him in horror. He was mad; there was no question of that. She was locked in a room with two men —one completely helpless, and the other insane.

She looked into Edmund's face, and he tried to reassure her. Whatever happened now—it didn't really matter any longer. All he cared about was that he and Garnet should get out of this room alive. He nodded, imperceptibly.

As if she were hypnotized, Garnet forced herself to obey, putting her hand upon Edmund's body, brushing him with trembling fingers, feeling his warm flesh respond to her touch, and so continuing—caressing . . . stroking . . . arousing . . .

Bang!

In that small, enclosed space, the sound of a pistol-shot was deafening. For an instant Garnet could not understand what was happening—her head was spinning with the noise, and a flash of light almost blinded her . . . And then she saw Hugo Deverell lying stretched out upon the floor, where he had fallen across the mattress, and she knew immediately that he was dead.

"Quick—untie my wrists—for God's sake—" gasped Edmund.

She released him, as quickly as she could, her thoughts in a turmoil.

"What happened? I don't understand—"

"The window—it was someone outside the window— take the key from his pocket, and run to fetch help," Edmund said, massaging his chafed wrists, and pulling up his breeches.

Garnet dropped to her knees by the body, and could hardly bring herself to touch it—but she knew she had to do as Edmund said. As he stumbled toward the window, still half-naked, and then climbed out onto the flat roof, she forced herself to roll the body over onto its back, and put her hand into the breast pocket where the key was hidden . . . A patch of blood was spreading quickly across the fine silken shirt, and when she withdrew the key, her hand was stained and wet.

But there was no time to be lost.

She pulled herself together, opened the door, and ran out along the passage. Already in the distance she was aware of a babble of voices; the shot had alerted the whole house, and people were coming to investigate.

As she flew down the first flight of stairs, she met a party of officers coming up to meet her—Dicky Blades among them.

"What's the trouble? Who started shooting?" he asked her.

"An accident—" she stammered, without stopping to think. "There's been a terrible accident—"

And she ran on, to the room where she knew she would find help and strength and reassurance.

She flung the bedroom door wide, and burst in upon Brock Savage, who was still propped against the pillows. He looked up, curious to know what all the noise was about—but when he saw Garnet in the doorway, his face changed.

"Good God—what's the matter? You're as white as a sheet . . . And there's blood on your hands . . . "

She threw herself into his arms, and sobbed like a child.

Meanwhile, only a few yards away, on the flat roof of the laundry, Edmund was playing a deadly game of hide-and-seek under the night sky.

Somewhere among the lines of washing that now flapped like pale, disconsolate ghosts in the darkness, there was a murderer—with a gun. He tried to find his way through the maze of ropes and drying linen, half expecting at any moment that another shot would follow the first and put paid to his search forever.

Then he stopped—and listened . . . And heard the sound of harsh, painful breathing, very close at hand.

Slowly he lifted the edge of a damp bed-sheet—and found himself face to face with Lord Hugo Deverell's one-time body-servant, Pilling, who was crouching in the shadows, with one of his lordship's duelling pistols still in his hand.

"You—?" breathed Edmund, incredulously.

"Yes, sir . . ." Pilling raised his head, and wiped his lugubrious, drooping moustache—and Edmund realized with a shock that he was crying. "I had to do it, sir . . . I *had* to—didn't I? . . . It was bad enough when he sent me away—when he didn't want me waiting on him no more, so he got rid of me by sending me into the front line . . . But I didn't care—I felt sure he'd take me back one of these days . . .

"And today—after the battle—I thought that was my chance . . . I came here this afternoon, and asked him to take me in . . . I swore I'd do everything he needed—wait on him hand and foot, like I always did—and then I took his pistols off to clean them, and I washed his best shirts and linen, and hung them out to dry with the rest of the laundry . . . I'd have done anything for that man, sir . . .

"But just now—while I was outside here—I looked through the window and I saw what was going on . . . Well, sir—I had to put a stop to it, didn't I? Because he deserved to die . . . I suppose I always knew that really . . . He had to die—and now it's my turn to follow him . . ."

And before Edmund could move, he turned the pistol upon himself—and pulled the trigger.

8

Wild Strawberries

In Brock Savage's room, the second shot rang out loudly, interrupting Garnet as she tried to tell Brock what had happened.

"Another—?" The major-general pushed aside the bedclothes. "That settles it—I can't stay here, propped up in bed like an invalid . . . I shall go and find out what the devil is happening."

"No—you can't, you mustn't—you're a sick man, you've got to rest—"

"Poppycock!" snapped Brock, gritting his teeth. He swung his legs over the side of the bed and slid to the floor with an effort. "Fetch me my robe . . . And stop arguing!"

"But—" She was still protesting, even while she instinctively put out a hand to support him.

"You heard what I said, Ensign Mallory . . ." he growled, but he leaned upon her a little, as he stood upright, swaying very slightly. "Am I or am I not your commanding officer?"

She waited until she was quite sure that he was steady upon his feet, then said quietly: "Yes, sir . . . Always."

And she went to fetch the old *robe-de-chambre* that had been flung across the back of a chair. It was of worn sand-colored velvet, trimmed with rough brown fur at collar and cuffs, and had obviously seen many years of service. As she helped him slip his arms into the sleeves, the thought flashed through her mind that many another man would have appeared ridiculous in this situation—standing barefoot, in his nightshirt, with a great white bandage covering half his head, fumbling into his gown—but somehow Brock's dignity was unassailable. He looked, she thought, like an old lion, preparing to leave his den and take his rightful place as the king of beasts.

"Now show me the way to Captain Challoner's room, if you please," he said, breathing a little heavily after his efforts.

"Are you sure you can manage—? Can you see well enough?"

"I can see better with one eye than most people do with two!" he snapped, and made for the door.

There was a little knot of officers hanging around the open doorway of the studio room when they reached the second floor, but they all fell back at the sight of the major-general; and as he gestured impatiently for them to stand aside and stop gaping, they made way for him to pass through, with Garnet at his side.

"Shut the door, Mallory," he ordered, and Garnet obeyed quickly.

Edmund, still stripped to the waist, was climbing in through the open window; he stopped short on seeing his commanding officer, and stood to attention.

"At ease, sir," muttered Brock, and concentrated upon the lifeless body of Hugo Deverell, which lay sprawled across the bed-roll on the floor. A spreading stain of blood seeped through the crimson shirt front and made a small pool upon the floorboards. Garnet turned her head aside, and felt a wave of nausea.

Brock seemed to sense this, and rapped out another command.

"You—Mallory—go and stand by the door, to keep guard. I don't wish to be disturbed on any account, you understand?"

"Yes, sir." She moved away, relieved to be able to take her eyes from the grisly spectacle.

"I'm informed that the lieutenant-colonel was killed by some sharp-shooter outside the window—I take it you have been out onto the flat roof to investigate?"

"Yes, sir, I did—and—I found the marksman."

"What? We heard another shot—did he try to attack you too?"

"No, sir. He made a confession and told me what he had done—then before I could stop him, he fired again, and took his own life."

"Good God. Who—?"

"Pilling . . . A private soldier—he had been Deverell's body-servant for several years."

"I seem to recall the man slightly. I was under the impression that he was devoted to his master," said Brock.

"He was indeed. I believe that was why he took such a desperate measure."

Brock passed a hand across his face; he suddenly seemed very weary.

"I see . . . Where is the other body?"

"Outside . . . I was coming to fetch help—it will need at least two of us to carry him in through the window."

Brock flicked a glance at Garnet, and Edmund misinterpreted the look, adding hastily: "No, sir—not Mallory —he is not strong enough . . . I will find someone else."

"Not strong enough—and not man enough for the task, either, perhaps?" said Brock smoothly, with the faintest gleam of humor.

Edmund looked from one to the other, uncertainly.

"It's all right," Garnet said, taking a step nearer the two men, but keeping her voice low in case of eavesdroppers on the other side of the door. "The major-general knows my secret . . . He is one of the very few people who knows the truth."

"What? You never told me that—" Edmund stared at her, then turned to Brock. "I didn't know myself until this evening, sir . . . What do you intend to do now?"

Brock leaned against one of the posts that supported the rafters; he was beginning to feel dizzy—the doctor had warned him against trying to get out of bed too soon, but he would have died rather than confess his weakness.

"Well, Captain . . . If you are referring to the unfortunate deaths of these two men—I can do nothing except report the facts to a higher authority. Plainly the manservant was temporarily deranged, and killed his master in some fit of madness . . . It is all most regrettable, but there is no further action that can be taken; the incident may, I think, be regarded as closed."

He took a deep breath, feeling his heartbeat thudding uncomfortably beneath his rib-cage, then looked across at Garnet—and his voice softened a little.

"As for the problem of yourself and your fiancée—for I understand that you are engaged to be married, Captain? . . . I can only offer you my most sincere congratulations —and felicitations to Miss Mallory on this satisfactory conclusion to her long quest. She has been most diligent in her search for you, and she deserves to be happy . . . As I am sure you both will be."

"Thank you, sir." Edmund smiled with relief, but Garnet said nothing.

"I shall not officially recognize Miss Mallory's true identity, you understand—there is no point in creating an unnecessary sensation by making her story common knowledge—but rest assured that I shall use my best efforts to see that you are both returned to England at the earliest possible moment, so that you may be married and live happily ever after."

He squared his shoulders, and took Garnet's hand, clasping it gently as he asked: "Isn't that how all the best stories should end?" Then he made for the door, saying: "Now, Captain—I shall leave the disposal of those two unhappy wretches to your good offices. Go and procure any assistance that you require."

"Sir!" Edmund saluted smartly, and opened the door.

The little crowd of officers who waited in the passage gathered around him as he stepped out, eagerly asking what had been happening, and all talking at once.

Under cover of the noise, Brock stayed for one last word with Garnet.

"I gather—from the captain's appearance—that you were both surprised by the arrival of Lord Deverell at a moment of some sensitivity?" he asked. But his bantering tone belied the look in his eyes.

Garnet saw that he was in pain, and stammered unhappily: "Yes—I mean, no—that is to say—not exactly—"

"Don't be embarrassed, my dear . . . It is very natural; I am only sorry that your first reunion was so vilely interrupted . . . But from now on, I am quite sure all will be well."

"You don't understand—it's not—*I'm* not—what I mean is—"

He would not let her finish.

"I understand perfectly. The things you said to me, half an hour ago, are already forgotten. You were overwrought and tired—you did not know what you were saying—I think perhaps I even understood that at the time. But now you and your husband-to-be are together again, and I am very happy for you both."

She wanted desperately to argue, to explain—but she could not find the words. In any case, a small group of men, led by Edmund, were now making their way into the room.

"I must obey my doctor's orders, and return to bed . . . Good night to you," Brock concluded and marched out, with his head held high.

After that night in Vitoria, which had seemed such a turning point in Garnet's life—and what later proved to be so indeed—life seemed curiously flat and colorless. Day followed day uneventfully, and time passed slowly.

The French troops, in retreat, were falling back on their last two strongholds in the northeast of the peninsula: Pamplona and San Sebastian. Wellington ordered his foot-soldiers to pursue the enemy onto the higher ground, while the Dragoons moved on toward the north coast, where they linked up with reinforcements sent out by troopship from England, arriving at Bilbao.

"Let the infantry do the climbing—these broken foot-hills of the Pyrenees are no terrain for cavalry," the duke declared.

So the Third Dragoons took the coast road, and advanced steadily toward the French border, as the weeks lengthened into months.

All this time, Garnet was under canvas again, sharing a tent with Dicky Blades and some fellow-officers, but rarely seeing Brock Savage, even at a distance.

For his part, the major-general, when he thought of Garnet at all—and he was generally far too busy—or too prudent—to allow himself such an indulgence—assumed that she would be spending all her available leisure in the company of Captain Challoner. They were together at last—living and working side by side, he imagined—which was as it should be.

In fact, this was not the case. They met at meals, in the officers' Mess, perhaps; sometimes they rode out on patrol with a dozen other men, in forays along the sea coast, but when they were both off duty, and could snatch a few moments of ease, it seemed that Edmund always had plenty of other matters to occupy him. He was, in as tactful a manner as possible, avoiding Garnet.

She did not object to this; she even thought that she understood the reason for it. After all, their last encounter was scarcely idyllic—their reunion had been, as Brock Savage said, "vilely interrupted," and their enforced intimacy under duress must have left a humiliating scar on Edmund's self-respect . . . Small wonder that he did not wish for any fresh reminder of that outrage.

But it was a strange situation that Garnet now found herself in, and an unhappy one. Even Dicky Blades remarked upon it.

"Well, your friend the captain don't seem as friendly as you told me he would be! After that long while you were hunting for him, now you scarcely seem to pass the time of day with the fellow!"

"Oh—he's a busy man . . . We're all busy . . . There's still a war to be won, you know!" Garnet tried to explain.

"Not for much longer . . . From all I hear, the Frenchies are about ready to throw their hand in, any day now," grinned Dicky. "Rule Britannia—and may Old Boney roast in hell, I say!"

"Hell" was not a bad description of San Sebastian, when they at last arrived at that fair city . . . A fair city no longer, for the French troops had defended it with all their failing power, and every inch of the territory had been fought over. The long crescent of silver-sandy beach facing the Atlantic ocean was littered with corpses, bloody debris, and every kind of horror, and the fine streets of imposing houses were blocked or barricaded with rubbish. Worst of all, the retreating army had made a last attempt to delay the British pursuit by setting fire to many of the buildings, and when the Dragoons rode in to take possession, greedy tongues of flame were still licking at blackened beams. Through open doors or broken window, they could see the burnt-out shambles within, still glowing with red-hot ashes . . . This was "hell" indeed.

So the advance moved in; the Dragoons rode through the little seaport of Passages, and then—a few miles farther—they saw a long, low building, that had once stood guard across the highway, now in squalid ruins, with a pair of broad gates torn from their hinges and thrown aside onto a rubbish-pile, ready for a bonfire.

"What's that place?" Garnet asked Major Sterne, who happened to be riding beside her.

"That was the frontier post," he told her. "This must have been the main route across the border between France and Spain."

"So that means—" Garnet looked back at the wreckage over her shoulder as they passed along the road. *"Now—we are in France?"*

They were not at all sure what sort of reception might await them, as occupying troops entering enemy territory; but they need not have worried.

Their destination—the first township within France—was St. Jean-de-Luz, a fashionable little seaport, as fresh and gay as San Sebastian had been dead and defeated.

There was no trace of warfare to be seen here—and no sign of any hostility either, for the inhabitants of this southwest corner of France were, for the most part, Royalists, and secretly opposed to Bonaparte's republic. Furthermore, they considered themselves to be Basques rather than French, and so welcomed the English troops almost as if they were an army of liberators. Pretty girls lined the streets and held out posies of flowers to the officers as they rode by; it all reminded Garnet, inevitably, of their first entry into Madrid—and yet St. Jean-de-Luz, though so much smaller, seemed even more fashionable and worldly than that great grey city.

The shops were full of smart clothes—luxurious lengths of silks and laces—frivolous bonnets and pretty parasols. Garnet let the others ride on ahead and slowed the little chestnut mare to a walking pace, as she gazed into the shop windows . . . Such elegant clothes—such style, such charm . . . For the first time in many, many months, she felt a stab of envy, and longed with all her heart to throw off her rough, male attire, and become a young woman again . . .

"Are you feeling homesick?" Brock's deep voice broke into her daydream, and she started, as he reined in his black charger, and paused beside her.

He indicated a display of fine lace in a little *boutique,* with a half-mocking smile. "Don't despair, Garnet Mallory . . . It won't be long now, I promise you!" he said, then added: "Indeed—I have some news for you and Captain Challoner. Be good enough to present yourselves at my tent this evening, before dinner, will you?"

He spurred his horse, and rode on without waiting for an answer.

That night, Edmund and Garnet did as they were told, and found the tent which Brock Savage used as his bedchamber, study, and headquarters. An orderly showed them in, then left them alone with the commanding officer.

"Don't stand on ceremony—pull up a couple of those folding stools, and make yourselves as comfortable as possible," Brock said, seated behind a plain wooden map table. "And you can talk freely—we shan't be overheard here."

He broke off, and glanced sharply at Garnet, who was staring at him in amazement.

"What's wrong now? You're looking at me as if I were a ghost . . . Is something troubling you, Miss Mallory?"

She swallowed, and then managed to blurt out: "You—your bandages—they've taken off the bandages—"

"Oh, yes! Thank heaven—it's a relief to be rid of them, I can tell you."

"And you're suffering no ill-effects from your wound, sir?" asked Edmund.

"Nothing worth bothering about—except a bit of a scar . . . Oh, they say I may have to put up with a few headaches—but what of that? My eyes are undamaged, praise God—and that's all I care about. Well, Miss Mal-

301

lory—aren't you glad to hear I'm off the sick list at last?"

"Oh—yes, sir—of course—only . . ." She shook her head, unable to continue. "Yes—I'm very glad indeed."

How could she possibly tell him what an extraordinary shock she had just received, when she recognized that livid scar, which now ran from his left temple into the roots of his hair? How could she ever explain that she had seen him with that self-same scar, long, long ago, in a dream?

But Brock was busy with a package that lay upon the table; a package wrapped in pale pink tissue and tied with a ribbon of deep rose.

"Here—you'd better take this, young woman . . . It's more suitable for you than for me, I fancy."

He pressed the parcel into her hands, and then turned to Edmund, saying awkwardly, "I hope I don't breach any etiquette, Captain, by making a wedding-gift to the bride before the groom?"

Speechless, Garnet unwrapped the tissue paper and took out the finest shawl she had ever seen—made of French lace, as white and light as a cloud of snowflakes.

"I hoped it might suit you—as a bridal veil, perhaps?" Brock suggested.

She did not know whether to laugh or to cry; in a voice choked with emotion, she managed to say; "Thank you —oh, thank you, sir . . . It's quite beautiful . . . The most beautiful thing I ever saw . . . Oh, Edmund—just look!"

"You're very kind, sir," said Edmund gruffly.

"Not at all. It's by way of being a farewell present, so to speak."

"Farewell—?" Garnet caught her breath.

"Yes, indeed. For you see—that shall be my other wedding gift to you both. I have made arrangements for you to take passage back to England upon the first ship that sails for Portsmouth from this harbor—which should be within a week, I'm told."

"To England—? But—my duty to the Dragoons—the war—" Edmund began.

"There is no war." Brock rose to his feet, hesitated, then said at last: "The news is not officially published yet, but—by tomorrow the whole of Europe will know of it, I've no doubt . . . Bonaparte has capitulated; the war in Spain is over."

Garnet and Edmund looked at each other, wide-eyed.

"After all this time—all this terrible fighting—is *that* how it happens? So easily?" she asked.

"It seems Napoleon Bonaparte has decided he does not wish to play the game of war any longer," Brock nodded. "He's gone off to sulk, they say—according to the last report, he summoned his chiefs-of-staff and scolded them, saying, 'Now look at the fix we are in—peace has broken out!' "

"So . . . We are all to go home—?" Edmund spoke as if he could scarcely believe it yet.

"Some of the others may have to wait a little longer—there is to be an occupying force sent on to Toulouse . . . But you two will return to England as soon as possible."

"And you, sir—what about you? Are you going to Toulouse?" Garnet asked.

"No, not I." Brock stretched his arms wide, exercising the muscles of his broad shoulders. "I'd be no use as an occupying commander—I'm a fighting-man, not a diplomat . . . And I won't go home, either; the Third Dragoons will be put out to grass for a while, in England—and that's not my style . . . Besides, half my old comrades are gone now; it would be a melancholy situation for me."

"What will you do then?" she asked.

"I'm off to America tomorrow afternoon, Miss Mallory. I can't say I relish the idea of a long sea trip, but needs must."

"*America*?" she exclaimed. "But—why?"

"There's another war out there which has to be finished, and I've been given a new command . . . They seem to think I'll find enough work there to keep me occupied. The frigate *Enterprise* sails on the afternoon tide —first to the Azores, then to Bermuda, and so on to

Chesapeake Bay . . . Wish me godspeed, won't you?"

That night, Garnet had to say another farewell—to Dicky Blades; for he was to be one of the party who were to occupy Toulouse. She told him that she was to be sent home—together with Captain Challoner—and hoped he would not think this was too odd.

But Dicky shrugged it aside. "Yes, I dare say you'll be happier back in dear old England—after all, you never were too keen on warfare and bloodshed, were you, young 'un?"

"Were *you*?" she asked.

"Well—not exactly, no . . . But then there's a devil of a lot of fun to be got out of life afterward, as long as you've still got all your arms and legs and other vital organs!" he winked. "They do say the girls in Toulouse are as luscious as ripe peaches—and all ready for the plucking, too!"

He began to pack up his knapsack for the last time, ready to ride off in the morning.

"Still—even if we're both going our separate ways, Garnet—let's hope our paths might cross again one of these days . . . For I must own—and I'm not codding you when I say this—I'll never forget you, young 'un . . ." He scratched his head, and stared into her face with that look which always reminded her of a puzzled terrier puppy. "I don't know what it is, but there's something about you—in some peculiar way, you seem different from any other fellow I've ever met!"

She put her hand upon his for an instant, and smiled: "Do you know, Dicky—I believe you're right."

The next day, most of the Dragoons set off on their travels again, and Garnet and Edmund were left behind, feeling a little lost.

"Come on, let's go for a ride," Edmund exclaimed at last. "It's going to be another fine sunny day—too good to sit around here, doing nothing . . . Let's go up into the hills, and explore the countryside."

So that is what they did, and by midday they had

ventured high upon a steep hill, several miles inland, over-looking the town.

Edmund's prediction was right; the early haze soon cleared and the late summer sunshine was hot upon their backs, as the horses labored up a rocky path.

"Shall we give the poor brutes a rest?" he asked—and they turned off the path into an open meadow. At one end, a little grove provided some welcome shade, and here they tethered the horses, letting them crop the grass beneath the trees.

"We shall have an intermission too," Edmund continued, and he took off his tunic, tossing it upon the ground. "Come—sit down, my dearest—and let us make plans for our future."

"Perhaps we should do that," Garnet agreed. "We don't seem to have talked to one another for a long time."

"No—well—there have not been many opportunities until now. But since the war is over, and we are going back to England—we have a great many things to talk about."

"What sort of things?" she asked, lying back upon her elbows.

He looked down at her, and smiled.

"Oh—little things like weddings, and homes, and families . . . But you make it very hard for me to concentrate when you look at me like that!"

He put one finger very lightly upon her lips, but she frowned, and turned her head.

"No—be serious, Edmund . . . I *do* want to talk to you—very seriously."

"Upon such a heavenly day, too! Don't be so solemn, my love . . . Look at me . . . And smile—a little."

She would not; she was trying to find a way of telling him the truth, and she did not know how to begin.

The landscape fell away below the meadow and it seemed as if St. Jean-de-Luz was a model town lying at their feet; rooftops, spires and turrets, all in miniature, and beyond them an ornamental pond with toy sailing ships bobbing upon sparkling blue water . . . And in one of those toy ships, later today, Brock would be sailing half-way across the world . . .

She tried to collect her thoughts, and began again: "Edmund—listen—I have to tell you—"

"I say, look here!" he interrupted. "We've picked a good spot for a picnic, without knowing it—see what I've found."

He held out his hand, showing her half a dozen wild strawberries. There were plants half hidden among the grass all across the meadow, some with little star-shaped white flowers, and some bearing those sweet, miniature strawberries that always tasted so much better than all the rich, ripe fruit cultivated by market gardeners.

She took one from his outstretched hand and sampled it, but strangely enough, it seemed to have very little flavor, and she was disappointed.

Edmund laughed: "You've got a tiny drop of juice on your chin . . . let me clean you up."

With his handkerchief—the one embroidered with his initials—he dabbed at her mouth, and then, leaning closer, impulsively moved forward to kiss her red lips.

It was a long, tender kiss; and as unexciting as the taste of the wild strawberry. She remembered the times, at Markwick, when he had kissed her, and she had longed for him to take her completely—but not any more.

He sensed at once that she did not respond to him, and put his arms round her, trying by the force of the embrace to arouse some passion in her. It was no good: at last he let her go.

"I know—you're afraid of me now—I understand that . . . But do not be alarmed, my dear love—for I shan't make any demands upon you; I shall not press my attentions upon you until after we are married."

"No, Edmund," she said, dully.

"Oh, I realize what you are thinking. You are remembering the night after Vitoria, when you came to my strange studio room, and I tried to possess you . . . I lost my head—but that won't happen again, I promise . . . It was a single moment of frenzy; I had been starved of any love or affection—I shall never try to take advantage of you in that way again—"

"I know you will not," Garnet said. "And I wasn't remembering that night at all. My mind was going back much earlier—to the last time I saw you at Markwick . . . "

"When we said goodbye?"

"No, it was after that . . . I thought you had gone forever, and I went to the little upper room above the barn, where I could cry as much as I wanted to, all alone . . . At least—I thought I was alone."

He frowned uneasily. "What do you mean? I don't understand."

"Then I heard voices—laughter—down below—and I looked to see who was there . . . And I saw you with the two servant girls, Lucy and Rosie . . . "

"You *saw* us—?" He was very pale.

"Yes . . . I watched you—for a little while—until I couldn't bear to watch any more . . . That was another 'moment of frenzy,' Edmund—wasn't it?"

He could not answer at first, but averted his face, unable to look at her.

She said quickly: "Dear Edmund—I'm not accusing you—I don't blame you for taking your pleasure with them—I was only sorry that you could not have told me how you felt—about those other girls . . . Or about me . . . "

He did not move, and she put one hand upon his shoulder.

"Please don't feel guilty. When I'd had time to think about it sensibly, I decided that I must come and find you, and tell you that I understood—I really did understand—and I wanted to be the kind of girl you needed . . . I believed I could—that's why I followed you from England—"

Edmund spoke at last, and his voice was thick and husky, as he tried to explain his feelings.

"I don't know how to tell you . . . It's always been like that, for me—ever since I first knew about women . . . Never the young ladies I met in the drawing-room, at tea parties or *soirées* . . . Always the serving maids—the laundresses, the kitchen girls . . . I wanted them—nobody else—"

"I knew that really, Edmund . . . I suppose I almost guessed from the first moment we met, when you thought I was one of the servants."

"But you *didn't* know—how could you?" He still wouldn't look at her. "I wonder how it happened—how it began . . . All I know is *when* it started; I was about thirteen or fourteen, and it was midsummer . . . Strangely enough, it was strawberry-time then, as well."

As he dredged back into the past, wrestling with his memories, his voice took on a firmer tone.

"I was alone in the house—the family had gone off somewhere, I don't remember where; I'd been left behind on my own—as a punishment, perhaps . . . I was always getting into scrapes at that age . . . And I was wandering around the home farm, looking for something to do . . . Then I went into the dairy.

"Abigail, the dairymaid, was there—nobody else. She was a beautiful girl—oh, a little on the plump side, perhaps, but full of fun and with such bold, laughing eyes . . . She seemed quite grown-up to me, though I suppose she can't have been more than seventeen at the most.

"Anyway—there was a big bowl of thick cream on the dairy table—and a cabbage leaf, like a dish, full of ripe strawberries.

"I said to her: 'Abby—you're a wicked girl and you'll never get to heaven—you've been thieving strawberries when the gardener wasn't looking' . . . And she said: 'Well, why not? I've got all the cream I need—I only took a few strawberries to go with it . . . Besides, why should I care about getting to heaven? I have all the fun I want,

here and now!' . . . And somehow I knew what she meant
—for I'd heard the servants gossiping about the way Abby
carried on with the under-footmen . . . "

He took a deep breath and continued:

" 'You'll care soon enough,' I said, 'when I tell Papa
what you've been up to—he'll have you whipped for
stealing his best fruit.' And then she smiled, and said to
me: 'Don't tell on me, Master Ned—have a strawberry . . .' And she picked one up and popped it in my
mouth. I can still recall what it tasted like—so sweet, so
juicy it was . . . And she put another strawberry between
her lips, and I thought she would eat it, but instead—
when I'd swallowed mine, she turned to me and leaned
very close, and—and she fed it into my mouth, from her
lips to mine . . . And we stayed like that, close together,
with our faces touching, and the warm smell of her body
against mine, and the feel of her fresh clean skin, and
the mischievous laughter in her eyes . . .

" 'Now you won't tell, will you, Master Ned? You
won't make trouble for poor Abby—for if you hold your
tongue, Abby'll teach you a trick worth two of that . . .'
That was when she pulled loose the ribbon of her bodice
and her dress fell open, so that I saw her breasts—and
she took my hand, and drew it into her bosom, to touch
and feel . . . "

He fell silent, remembering that moment as vividly as
if it had happened only yesterday. He remembered how
he had clutched at her body hungrily, and she had
laughed, and told him to be patient—for there was no
sense in hurrying things—and how she had schooled him,
step by step, helping him to remove her clothes, piece by
piece, and at the same time unbuttoning his breeches,
and exploring his own body, touching, tickling, caressing
and quickening his uninitiated flesh—until they were both
naked in each other's arms, and they sank to the rag rug
on the floor, threshing about in a sudden convulsion of
ecstasy . . . Then with one shudder of delight, young

Ned kicked out against the table leg, and the bowl of cream overturned and drenched them both.

For a moment, he had been appalled by his own clumsiness, and expected Abby to scold him—but she pulled him closer still, and laughed.

"You know what they say—'tis no use crying over spilt milk—nor cream neither—"

Then she set to work to clean him up, licking the cream with her little pink, probing tongue, from every corner of his body—and teaching him to perform the same service upon her . . .

With an effort, Edmund shook himself from his reverie, and glanced sideways at Garnet as she basked in the French sunlight, concluding: "It was a long time ago —but I shall never forget Abby . . . "

"Of course . . . And I understand that. For something a little like that happened to me too, when I was young."

"But it won't make any difference to us, I'm sure," he went on quickly, rolling over to face her. "Because I love you, and you love me, and I will never behave dishonorably after we are married—I'll take my oath upon it—I am determined to go through with our marriage, and I will never let you down—"

Garnet turned and smiled faintly.

"No, Edmund . . . Don't make such promises—for they aren't necessary . . . Let us be frank with one another—I don't love you, and you don't love me, and there's an end of it. Why should we pretend any longer? I shall always be very fond of you, and very grateful, because if it were not for you, I should never have discovered the truth about myself. But now we both know the truth, there is no need for any nonsense about engagements or marriages . . . It's all off, my dear—and I give you your freedom—very gladly."

She picked up the remaining wild strawberries that he had dropped, and before he could speak, she popped them into his open mouth.

"There—enjoy your strawberries . . . And go and find another Abigail to give you all the cream you want . . . But I cannot stay to keep you company; because I know now what I must do."

With his mouth full of the subtly flavored fruit, he tried to argue, or to dissuade her, but it was useless; she was on her feet in a single bound, and a moment later the little chestnut mare was untethered, and Garnet had swung up into the saddle.

"Garnet—come back—" Edmund cried after her; but Garnet only shook her head, tossing her springing curls as she cantered off down the path.

The church bells of St. Jean-de-Luz were striking four o'clock as she rode through the town, past the market-place and out onto the harbor wall.

At the far end, the frigate *Enterprise* was in full sail upon the glittering sea, dazzling against the afternoon sunlight. Some sailors were lugging a few last bales of hay and wooden casks up the wide gangplank, as Garnet dismounted, and led the mare toward the ship.

"Where d'you think you're off to, my lad?" asked one of the seamen.

"I'm coming on board—bound for America," said Garnet.

"You can't do that—you've no business on this voyage," he began to protest, but she tossed the horse's bridle to him.

"Oh, yes, I have . . . See that the mare is fed and watered, and stable her in the hold—"

As she ran up the companion-way, whistles were blowing, and orders were being shouted on all sides to hoist the anchor, and cast off forward and aft.

Garnet made inquiries, and at the moment that she felt the timbers lurch under her feet, as the vessel swung out from the quayside, she knocked upon the door of the principal stateroom.

"Come in . . . " said Brock Savage.

311

She went in without a word. Brock was alone, studying a map of North America. He looked up—and blinked—and looked again, incredulously.

"Ensign Mallory reporting for duty, sir," said Garnet, rather out of breath. "I'm sorry to say I've left everything behind me—family, friends, all my wordly goods—I've nothing but my horse to ride, and the uniform on my back . . . And—oh, Brock—" she gave a little sob of laughter—"If you want me to have a bridal veil, you'll have to find me another!"

Then she was in his arms, and his sweet strong mouth was upon hers, and they set sail upon their new life together.

PART THREE

America . . .

1

Interlude in the Sun

The smooth, sandy beach was hot under Garnet's back. She stretched contentedly, and gave a little purr of pleasure.

Beside her, Brock's voice murmured, "Were you asleep?"

She opened her eyes—half-blinded by the brilliant light —and saw his face close to her own. His hair was tousled and still wet with sea water, his face bronzed by the sunshine of Bermuda . . . More handsome, she thought, than ever.

And here she was, alone with her lover, both basking naked on the sands after a swim in the ocean, far from civilization, or prying eyes, or any workaday anxieties. For Garnet, it was like a dream that had come true at last, and she said as much.

"No, I wasn't asleep . . . But I have to pinch myself to make sure that this is all real!"

He smiled down at her, and very gently took the tip of her nose between his finger and thumb.

"Allow me . . ."

She laughed and brushed his hand away; he shifted slightly, rolling over onto one elbow, and then slid his forefinger under her chin, tilting her face toward his own.

"Garnet . . . Give me your mouth."

She responded at once, and their lips met joyously; she tasted the brine upon his tongue, and smelled sand, and sea, and sunlight on his skin—and gave herself up totally to the moment of delight.

"I love you, my love," he breathed—and she could feel his voice, his chest vibrant against her.

"I love you," she repeated, in a whisper. For there were no other words to be said.

He sat up, and flexed his arms, looking down at her slim body.

"You will get burnt if you expose yourself to this blazing sun for too long," he warned her. "And what will become of your reputation, young lady, when you return to England at last—as brown as a gypsy, with a tan over every inch of your shameless skin?"

She put her hand upon his broad shoulder.

"Don't—don't talk about returning to England . . . I never wish to go back—I shall stay with you, always."

He gazed into her eyes with longing, and said, "If only that were possible . . ."

"Of course it's possible! For I am *not* a young lady—I am Ensign Mallory, and your personal body-servant—I will go wherever you go, for I belong to you."

She indicated the pile of her clothes—her uniform—that lay tangled with his own in a little heap nearby, and sketched a mock salute.

"I am here to serve you, sir—for the rest of my life."

He sighed, and turned his face away, deep in thought.

She wondered what it was that bothered him. For everything had gone so smoothly, from the very first moment that she had stepped into his cabin on board the *Enterprise*.

He had tried briefly to protest—to argue that this was madness, and she must return to England as arranged, to marry Edmund Challoner—but she told him that her engagement to Edmund was broken, and there was no other man in her life . . . No man except Brock Savage.

Even as he took her in his arms, while the ship rose and fell on the first surge of the tide, moving out from the shelter of the St. Jean-de-Luz harbor and meeting the long, strong roll of the Atlantic breakers—they both knew there was no going back now.

"So . . . You will have to accompany me as my *aide-de-camp* once more," he said—and his eyes danced at the prospect.

"Not your *aide-de-camp* this time, sir . . . Your body-servant," she corrected him, then clasped both hands around him on a sudden passionate impulse.

That was when he had said—for the first time—"Give me your mouth, Garnet" . . . And there and then, in the low-ceilinged stateroom with its sloping window looking out onto the deep peacock-blue sea that stretched away to an endless horizon, they fell into an embrace that drew their twin souls together until they became one . . . One heart, one mind, and one love.

They were interrupted by a knock upon the door, and Brock cursed under his breath as they moved apart.

"What the devil—? Who is it?" he demanded.

"Captain's compliments, sir, and he begs you will do him the honor of dining with him . . . Supper will be served in twenty minutes, sir," said the sailor on the other side of the door.

"Oh—very well . . ."

They heard footsteps retreating, then looked at one another—and laughed.

"So much for romance!" Brock remarked. "We can't live on kisses, my dear . . . We must go and dine with the good sea captain."

"Both of us——?"

"But of course. I shall explain to him that you are my personal attaché."

And so, twenty minutes later, they presented themselves in Captain Anderson's cabin, and Brock performed the necessary introductions.

"Mr. Mallory——I am pleased to make your acquaintance," the captain declared, clasping Garnet's hand in a vise-like grip that almost made her cry out. "Benson——lay another place at table."

The steward hastened to obey, and Brock apologized for having upset the arrangements.

"No need for apologies, sir," said Captain Anderson heartily. "Always glad to have more company——fresh faces . . . But the fact is, I hadn't been informed you would be traveling with any staff . . . I'm afraid we have made no provision for extra accommodation——I'm not quite sure where we shall find suitable quarters for the young gentleman."

"That need not present any problem, Captain," said Brock easily. "For I shall be happy to share my cabin with Mr. Mallory . . . There are two bunks——we shall be perfectly comfortable, I assure you."

"Oh——?" Captain Anderson raised one eyebrow——a little taken aback. "Well——if you are quite sure it will not inconvenience you——"

"Not in the very least. In fact——" Brock improvised speedily: "Since my recent head-wound, I have been advised by the doctors always to sleep with an attendant within close call . . . In case of any sudden relapse, you understand."

"Ah——quite so, quite so . . . Nasty scar, I see; doesn't do to take chances." And the captain nodded sagely, quite satisfied.

Dinner was served directly and the Captain commenced by pouring very large tots of rum all round. He passed one to Brock, then offered the second to Garnet——who shook her head politely.

"Thank you, sir—but no . . . I never touch strong liquor—I must beg you to excuse me."

"What—a growing lad, old enough to serve in the army —old enough to set sail across the Atlantic Ocean, and won't take a drop of rum? What's the world coming to?"

Brock intervened: "I pledged my word that the boy should not come to any harm while in my service . . . let him have a glass of lime juice instead, if you please."

Over dinner, the conversation took a more serious turn; Garnet sipped her lime juice and remained silent, listening to the two officers as they discussed the war with America.

"I thought that trouble was all over and done with, after '76," Captain Anderson exclaimed.

"And so it should have been, sir—I agree with you. This is a damned unnecessary war, in my opinion. It's been brought on by stupidity, and encouraged by sheer stubborn pride . . . And the sooner we can put paid to it, once and for all, the better."

"But the American privateers have been harassing our ships very grievously," said Captain Anderson. "Bastard outlaws, the lot of them!"

Brock glanced quickly at Garnet, to discover how she would react to such strong language—but she continued her meal demurely and gave no sign of discomfiture.

"They had the confounded impudence to attack our supply ships, which were carrying stores out to your troops in Spain—yes, making raids on the British navy, and almost on our own doorstep too! As for the American seaboard, God knows how many of our vessels they intercepted over there."

"I believe the Americans would claim there were faults on both sides," Brock pointed out. "There has been continual fighting along the Canadian border—"

"That's another thing! These rebels actually have the gall to try and claim Canada for their own—as if they didn't hold enough territory already! They need a sharp lesson, in my opinion."

Brock shrugged. "Well, sir—now that the war with Bonaparte is over, perhaps we can turn our full attention to the problem. At least part of the trouble stems from British blunders at a diplomatic level—even though America has been an independent nation now for nearly thirty years, our government still treats her with contempt and patronage, like a poor relation . . . A new agreement must be found; there's no question of that."

"And you are to push through such an agreement—at the head of a contingent of soldiers?" asked Anderson.

"I hope we may achieve a satisfactory outcome by common-sense and good intentions . . . But I am not in charge of the entire campaign, you understand. When we reach Bermuda, I am to be joined by General Ross—he will be the supreme commander—and two admirals of the fleet, who will be responsible for all naval operations . . . It will be my task to assist these gentlemen in every way I can."

"Well, I wish you luck in the venture," said the captain. "For as you rightly say—the sooner it is settled, the sooner we may all sleep in peace at night."

Eventually the evening came to an end, and Brock and Garnet retired to their state-room . . . But not yet to sleep.

Brock shut the door firmly, and turned to her.

"Well?" he said at last. "You have passed several tedious hours, I'm afraid."

"Oh, no—I wasn't bored. It was all very interesting," she said.

"You need not be diplomatic with me," he smiled. "However—it's over now, and you may relax. Stand easy, Ensign Mallory."

She looked at the two bunks, and asked: "Do you prefer me to sleep in the upper berth—or the lower?"

He held out his arms to her.

"Isn't that what is described as an academic question? Come here, my love . . . Come to me."

She moved into his embrace, and he kissed her again.

"If you knew how I have been longing for this moment throughout the evening—all through that tiresome discussion!" he murmured in her ear. "I wanted you all to myself . . . "

"I have been thinking the same thing," she confessed. "Those few hours seemed to last an eternity."

"I love you for that," he said, and then added: "We have wasted too much time already . . . let us go to bed."

She shivered, in a spasm of nervousness, and he asked: "Are you cold? Or afraid, perhaps?"

"Neither cold nor afraid," she replied truthfully. "But I confess . . . I feel a little shy . . . I am not in the habit of taking my clothes off except when I am alone. When I was in Spain, and sharing a tent with my fellow-officers, I always slept in shirt and breeches."

"Very prudent . . . And you shall not change your custom for my sake—"

"What?" She was about to unbutton her tunic, but stopped short. "You don't wish me to undress?"

"No . . . Because tonight, Miss Garnet Mallory, you may leave that trifling task in my hands . . . let me assist you."

As he spoke, he took hold of her jacket and unfastened it, slipping it from her shoulders.

"And now your boots . . . Sit on the edge of the table, and let me be your bootboy."

"No!" She smiled, but she felt a little shocked nevertheless. "It's not right that you should kneel—to me—"

"It will be my pleasure, I assure you."

He looked up at her with such a wealth of love in his expression that her protest faded on her lips, and she allowed him to pull off her leather boots. Without moving from his position, he let his strong hands slide up onto her legs—stroking her thighs—and loosening the waistband of her breeches.

"Now stand up," he said. As she did so, he slid the breeches down and helped her to step out of them—then followed this by rolling down her stockings and slipping them off.

She stood before him, barefoot, in her shirt-tails, blushing a little.

"I must appear rather ridiculous to you . . . Half-undressed—in a boy's shirt—"

"You appear to me to be quite enchanting," he said gravely, and rose to his feet. "I have never seen a lovelier sight."

He drew her toward him, and began, one by one, to undo the buttons on her shirt.

Moments later, she was naked in his arms, and he was covering her with potent kisses. Then, as if she were a child, he picked her up effortlessly, and carried her onto the upper bunk.

He blew out the candle that illuminated the cabin, and in the light from the window, where the waves glittered brilliantly and made a path of silver that led toward the full moon, she watched him stripping off his own uniform.

Unclad, his body looked even more heroic in the glittering moonlight, and for an instant she was almost afraid . . . She had never known a man's body in the act of love, and he was so massive—so powerful . . .

Then he climbed up to lie beside her on the narrow bunk, and she forgot all her fears.

For, with all his rugged strength, he was also the most tender of men, and proceeded with infinite patience to lead her, step by step, through the mysteries of sensual passion.

He caressed and kissed her body again and again—her breasts, her hips, her thighs—turning her this way and that in his arms, and teaching her things about her own body that she had never even guessed.

Not only in the most private and sensitive places—but he could also produce thrills of excitement from the way he ran his finger down the length of her spine, or softly tickled the back of her knee, or even—very lightly— kissed the lobe of her ear . . . She writhed with pleasure, and pressed herself against him hungrily.

Then, with his left hand, he began to explore the precious secrets of her womanhood; fondling, cherishing, stimulating—tantalizing and satisfying, both at once—until she felt the innermost part of herself set free in a sudden flood of passion, and she lay back, unfolding her love to him.

"Give me your mouth . . . " he said again, and then: "Give me yourself . . . "

And as he put his lips upon hers and his tongue thrust within her, he entered her body.

She cried out once—but it was not pain, or not pain alone. Joy and wonder were in the cry also; and a sublime satisfaction that she had never known before, as he slowly roused her to a wilder frenzy, in a steadily increasing rhythm of desire that mounted again and again to higher and yet higher peaks of ecstasy.

They melted together in a long moment of perfect harmony, clinging in a breathless embrace, as if they could never be parted again.

This was love . . . And Garnet knew that for her there would never be any other, as long as she might live.

Some hours later, they lay side by side at last, their arms about one another—temporarily sated, and tingling with the total fulfillment of their passion.

"Oh, Brock . . . " She stroked the thick, springing hair upon his chest as she spoke. "Is it always like this?"

She heard him sigh, and turned; his face was silhouetted in profile against the window, and she could see that he was content.

"Never for me . . . Never before—not like this," he said.

"I'm glad . . . " She thought for a moment, then asked: "But you must have known love so many times before—with many other women—"

"So many women . . . But I have never known love; not as we found it tonight, together . . . Once I believed I had caught love—but it was only a bird of passage, and she did not stay."

Garnet felt a sharp pang of jealousy.

"Who was that? Tell me about her."

"She was my wife."

Garnet started, and sat upright.

"Your wife—? You never told me—"

He pulled her down to him again, his arms warm and reassuring around her.

"Don't be alarmed—I have no wife . . . It was ten years ago—and the marriage lasted barely ten months."

"What happened?"

"She was taken from me . . . One day—out for a drive —the carriage went into a ditch and overturned . . . She was killed instantly . . . Poor Lydia."

"I see . . . I'm sorry. Did you love her very much?"

"I thought so—then. But ten years is a long time. Do you remember?—I told you once, when we talked on board the *Ariadne*—you learn to survive without love, after a while."

She nestled closer to him.

"You'll never have to do that . . . Not now . . . Never again . . ."

"My dearest girl—you're still so young; so very young . . . Do not build your hopes too high," he said softly.

"What do you mean? I'll never leave you—"

"Well . . . We won't talk of that now. Let's not think of the future, let us make the most of this present moment— for it will never come again."

He drew her toward him, and began to kiss her breasts; and their ardor—which had seemed to be appeased— burst into flame once more.

So the voyage passed all too soon; the long weeks at sea went by in a flash, and Garnet wished the time might never come to an end. She had never known such sublime happiness, and indeed there was only one thing to mar her joy.

One afternoon, some weeks later, she sat on deck, dressed in her uniform, and watched Brock as he studied a map of the American coast and made some notes in his pocket-book.

There was no one else in sight, and Garnet was emboldened to ask: "Brock . . . Tell me something."

"Anything, my love."

"Well . . . That's what I want to ask you . . . You call me your love, but—what is to happen to me? What is to happen to *us*—when this old war is over, and we are able to go home to England?"

He looked up at her. "What do you want me to say? What would you wish to happen?"

"I want you to tell me . . . I want to know what I may expect."

"Oh—you'll put on a skirt at last, I've no doubt, and go back to see your dear Papa, and find your dear brother again—and tell them what an instructive and enlightening vacation you have spent—"

"Stop it!" She couldn't bear it when he teased her. "You know I won't do that . . . I can't leave you, Brock—I told you, I belong to you now—"

He put down his book, and his face was serious.

"My dearest—I cannot expect to keep you forever."

"Why not? If it's what we both want? Why shouldn't we get—"

She hesitated, unable to continue.

"Married? Is that what you were about to say? Oh, no, my love—I can never ask that of you. I have been married once—and I know what a tragedy marriage may be . . . Besides—it would not be suitable; I am twenty years older than you. Imagine how you would feel—when you are in the prime of life, tied to this doddering old fogey . . . No, the idea is disgusting—I refuse to consider it."

And he would not let her say another word on that subject. Instead, he broke off, and rose to his feet, pointing: "Look—land ahead!"

Bermuda lay before them, and soon most of the men aboard the troopship hurried up on deck, thronging the rails and staring eagerly at the long, low coastline as it came into view. Flowering trees and white houses sprang up from the island in the sun, and when the vessel came alongside the Devonshire Dock at last, there were many local girls—both white and colored too—dancing a little dance of celebration on the greensward, to welcome the British army ashore.

Garnet watched the scene—and despite the cheerful air of festivity, her heart sank. Very soon now Brock would be absorbed in his duties again, and their brief idyll together would be at an end.

She still had a short respite, however, for the frigate *Tonnant*—which was to bring the senior officers to rendezvous with the *Enterprise*—had not yet arrived, and for a little longer Brock was forced to wait, and pass the time by investigating the delights of Bermuda.

Delights indeed! He hired an open landau with a genial colored coachman, and made a tour of exploration with Garnet—from the elegant colonial houses of St. George's, down to the village settlements of Southampton and Somerset at the far end of the island.

The next day, they both elected to ride out unaccompanied, and took their own horses; the animals soon found their land-legs after the long sea voyage and exulted in the fresh air and sunshine.

Now the black charger and the little chestnut mare were tethered in the shade, under some tall cedars and palmettos, while their riders lay naked upon the burning sands under a cloudless sky.

"This must be the most beautiful island in the whole world," said Garnet, surveying the scene.

The whole of the south shore was scattered with similar peaceful little creeks and inlets, where white sands met blue water, in a riot of semi-tropical vegetation—the climbing morning-glory and the tall spikes of yucca seeming to enclose each bay in its own secret paradise.

"Oh, Brock—we are so very lucky."

She sat up and studied him as he lay stretched out beside her. His brown skin gleamed in the sunlight, and his fleece of body hair had begun to bleach a little; she traced the line of curls from his chest, down across his flat, hard stomach, and then let her fingertips wander in the bush of hair that sprang up between his thighs.

He flexed his legs a little, and smiled.

"You will arouse deep, carnal desire in me if you continue upon that course," he warned her.

She ignored him—and continued to toy with his hair, and to tickle and tease the most responsive parts of his lusty body. He gave a grunt of pleasure, and she watched his male strength quickening into life.

Impulsively, she bent her head low, and kissed him there—at first lightly, a little uncertain of his reaction, and then with real fervor. He closed his eyes, giving himself up to these new and unexpected sensations, and let her soft lips and darting tongue play upon his body as if it were an instrument and she a musician, drawing out such sweet music . . .

He tried to hold her, and pull her down to him, but she eluded his grasp.

"No—let me—" she breathed, her own excitement mounting to match his.

She climbed over and spread her knees wide, sitting across his thighs—and with instinctive skill proceeded to take the initiative, while he lay back upon the hot sand and felt his blood pounding and his inmost senses soaring to a climax under her guidance.

Soon—all too soon—it was over, and they lay together, feeling the slow ebb-tide as their shared passion abated.

She looked at him, and smiled: "Well—my lord and master? Was it well done?"

But his eyes were still closed, and he did not reply.

She eased herself away, and said at last, "I shall go and bathe—to refresh myself."

She hoped he might join her; they had had one swim together already, and she would have enjoyed his company in the water, and the feel of his limbs thrusting against hers beneath the waves . . . But he made no response, and she ran into the sea alone.

Looking up at the sky, she saw that a cloud had crossed

the sun; it was not quite so warm now as it had been earlier. She dived into the deep, cool water, and gave herself up to the magical spell of the ocean.

When she emerged, some ten minutes later, the change in the weather was very marked: more clouds had gathered, and the sun had disappeared—there was a strange, unearthly light in the sky, and the landscape seemed unnaturally still. There was not a breath of air, and Garnet was sure there must be a thunderstorm on the way.

Shaking the water drops from her body, she made her way up the beach, and said: "We must get dressed . . . I think it's going to rain."

She glanced at Brock—and stopped short.

He was sitting where she had left him, but now he was huddled over, with his chin upon his hands, and as she watched, he lifted his head and looked up at her—and his face was the face of a stranger.

He gazed at her with an expression of sheer hatred, his eyes frighteningly cold and clear—and then he said, weighing every word:

"You lied to me . . . "

"What—? What do you mean?"

"You told me you had never slept with any man before our first night on the ship—you said you were completely innocent—*and I believed you*—!"

He raised one arm as if to strike her.

She did not flinch, but replied steadily: "I was speaking the truth."

"*Don't tell me any more lies!* That can't be true . . . What you did—just now, here on this beach—who taught you those tricks? For God knows you didn't learn them from me . . . How did you discover the secrets that draw a man inside out, and send him half-mad with desire—?"

It was as if he had struck her; she sank onto her heels in one swift movement, with the breath knocked out of her.

"Oh, God . . . " she said at last, when she could speak. "Is *that* all—?"

And now he roused up as if he really meant to attack her.

"All—?" he repeated thickly. "*All*?"

"I swear to you I have never done such a thing before, as heaven is my witness," she said. "Believe me, for it is the simple truth . . . Yes, I admit that I learned more than an innocent girl should know—while I was living side by side with my fellow-officers . . . No—" she hastened to add, before he could interrupt—"not because I ever put such ideas into practice . . . But I have lived with men long enough to understand what pleases them; I heard them talking to one another, as men do, and comparing notes on their experiences . . . At the time I was shocked and horrified, but now I am glad that I listened, because it enabled me to give you pleasure . . . And that is all—I swear it."

There was a long silence, then Brock stood up, putting his hand to his brow again, and muttered: "This damn thunder . . . It makes my head ache . . . I can't think . . . "

He walked across to the pile of clothes on the sand, and began to get dressed, with his back turned to her.

Moments later, she followed suit, for the first big raindrops began to fall, and by the time they were both ready to mount their horses and ride off the storm had broken. They were soaked to the skin when they arrived back at the ship.

During the ride they had not exchanged another word; it would have been hard to talk in any case, for the drumming of the rain was deafening, and occasionally there was a flash of lightning and a crash of thunder that startled the horses, accustomed to gunfire though they were.

Another ship lay at anchor in the dock alongside *Enterprise*—the frigate *Tonnant* that they had been expecting. With a nod and a curt word, Brock excused himself and went straight to the captain's cabin.

Half an hour later, after Garnet had toweled herself dry and changed into fresh clothes, he came back to the stateroom, put his arms round her, and said, "Forgive me . . . I should not have spoken to you as I did."

"You were angry—I know, and I realized why—it must have seemed very—"

"Don't say any more." He put a finger on her lips. "Let's not speak of it again . . . I didn't know what I was saying, my love; it must have been the storm—this damned head of mine felt as if it would split . . ."

"How do you feel now?" she asked.

"I—I'm perfectly well again, don't worry about that," he said, but she could see that his face was pale beneath the tan, and his eyes were haunted. "I'm only sorry that I spoiled our day by the sea . . ."

"It doesn't matter. There will be other days—perhaps we could go back to that little beach again, tomorrow—"

"I wish I could—but it's impossible. Now the *Tonnant* has arrived, I must start work. They have called a preliminary staff meeting after dinner tonight, and every moment will be occupied from now on."

He kissed her once; and she knew from the strain and tension in his body that he was still in pain.

"This has been an interlude in the sun," he said at last. "But now the storm clouds have gathered again; our little holiday is over, and I must be about my business."

2

Keeping Up Appearances

That evening, Garnet sat up late, waiting for Brock's return. She had something to occupy her, for she had found that the shirt he had been wearing during their expedition to the beach had become slightly torn, and needed mending.

She remembered, as she threaded a needle and set to work, how he had tugged off his clothes as soon as they were safely alone together; in her mind's eye, she saw again his tanned, lithe body as he dragged his shirt over his head, and let his breeches fall—the eagerness in his blood already apparent, his hard masculinity standing proud and erect . . .

She sighed, bent over her sewing, and longed for him to come back to her.

There was a knock at the door, and she glanced up at once.

"Who is it?"

"Captain Anderson . . . May I come in?"

"Of course."

He opened the door and entered the stateroom, looking around him curiously: it was the first time he had been inside this room since Brock Savage and his young attaché had come on board.

"Good evening, Captain—I'm sorry, the major-general is not returned—"

"I'm aware of that; that is why I am here," replied Anderson. "May I join you for a moment, young man?"

Without waiting for an answer, he settled in the one remaining armchair.

"Please do not let me interrupt you . . . Carry on with your needlework by all means," he continued pleasantly.

"Oh . . . Thank you." She bit her lip, slightly put out to be found busy with such a feminine task. But what of that? Men in service had to turn their hands to all kinds of chores—and after all she was Brock's personal body-servant.

"I have a message for you, Mr. Mallory," the captain went on, after a moment. "A sailor from the *Tonnant* just came aboard—to tell us that the staff meeting over there is likely to go on for the best part of the night—so there's no telling when the major-general will be returning . . . I felt you would wish to know that."

"Oh—yes, indeed—I'm grateful to you, sir . . . " Garnet hesitated, then added: "But you need not have troubled yourself to come in person to tell me—you should have sent one of the ratings—"

"Ah, but I'd been wanting to have a word with you in any case, you see . . . And this gave me a capital opportunity."

Garnet looked up—alerted by something in his tone.

Captain Anderson was a heavily-built man, with ponderous jowls that bulged over his collar, and rather sleepy eyes, half hidden in pudgy wrinkles. But now those eyes were wide-awake, fixed upon her very intently.

"I'm sorry—I don't understand—" she began.

"I have been meaning to tell you . . . Perhaps you didn't know that one of the junior officers on board has been taken ill? We have had to put him ashore, for medical treatment more skilled than anything that would have been possible on this ship."

"I'm sorry to hear that, sir, but—what has it to do with me?"

"Simply this, Mr. Mallory. His cabin is now vacant, and likely to remain so. Of course, it's below decks, and not as agreeable as this stateroom, but it does contain everything necessary for a single man . . . In other words, I'm in a position to offer you accommodation all to yourself, at last."

She continued sewing for a moment, her thoughts racing, then said: "That is very good of you, Captain—but I don't know what the major-general will say—he particularly requested me to share these quarters, as you know—"

"Oh, yes, I hadn't forgotten that . . . But I believe it might be in his best interests—and yours—if you were to make the move."

"Why do you say that?" she asked, a shade too quickly.

Captain Anderson's face was serious, but not unkind, as he replied, "Life on board ship can be very like a women's sewing-bee in some respects—did you know that? When men are cooped up together with nothing to do but talk about one another—that talk can sometimes be malicious . . . There are rumors buzzing—or so I'm told—which could do harm to the major-general's reputation . . . Not to mention your own."

Garnet put down her work indignantly.

"I hope you know better than to pay attention to such gossip!" she said, feeling her face flush with anger—and a touch of guilt.

"I, Mr. Mallory? It is no concern of mine," said Captain Anderson, smoothly—and he indicated her handiwork, where it lay upon the table. "I must congratulate you on the delicacy of your mending. You sew a very fine seam, young man . . . Though I've known some seafaring men who were equally adept—at such things."

She understood the implication, and resented it.

"Sir—I have done nothing that I am ashamed of . . . "

"I'm very glad to hear it. But the question is rather more what others might say. I'm speaking in the major-general's best interests; I hope you realize that. And I'm sure you have his interests very much at heart. That's why I feel that it would be wiser if you were to remove to this other cabin I mentioned . . . Don't you agree?"

She paused before replying cautiously: "If you really think that—my presence here—might do his reputation harm in some way . . . "

"I think it's a question of keeping up appearances. Let's say no more—I will leave it to your own good sense and judgment." The captain rose to his feet with surprising agility for so bulky a man. "Think on what I have said . . . And good night to you, Mr. Mallory."

"Good night, sir."

She thought it over for a long time that night as she lay alone in her bunk, and the dawn crept up across the sky before she fell into an uneasy sleep.

She was awakened by the door opening once more; as Brock himself, looking haggard and grey-faced, walked into the stateroom.

"Still asleep? It's getting late—the sun has been up for these past two hours or more," he said, and walked over to the bunk where she lay, only half aware of what was happening.

"How can you look so confoundedly beautiful, even when you've got sleep in your eyes, and your hair tousled?" he asked, with a spark of humor in his tired gaze. Then he bent and kissed her on the mouth: a long hungry kiss.

Her hands closed about his neck, and she drew him down to her as he made a move to break away.

"Don't go—" she whispered. "I waited for you so long . . . Come to bed now . . . Please."

"My dearest girl—I wish I could." He freed himself from her embrace, and straightened up. "But I have no time. The damned meeting lasted all night—and now I am only here for five minutes . . . Just long enough to pack up all my gear and return to the *Tonnant* . . . I have to shift my quarters to the admiral's flagship, you see."

"What—?" She sat up—wide awake at last.

"The chiefs of staff are expected to be on call, close at hand at all times . . . To dance attendance on Admiral Cochrane."

He began to pack his belongings, filling the military chest that always traveled with him.

"You're moving on board the *Tonnant*—?" she asked, slipping out of the bunk. "Then I must pack too—it won't take me long—"

"No . . . There's no need for that." Brock stopped and looked at her. "You're not to come with me—you're staying here."

She stared at him in dismay.

"No—we agreed, I go wherever you go—you know that—"

"Not this time, my love. I have to travel alone on this voyage."

She grabbed his arms, and clung to him.

"Don't say that—don't send me away—I can't bear it—"

"I'm not sending you away. You shall stay here, on the *Enterprise*—you will be perfectly comfortable—"

"I don't care for *comfort*!" She spat out the word. "Why are you treating me like this? You're angry with me—is that it? Or you're ashamed—ashamed to be seen with me!"

"Don't talk such nonsense," he said briskly, disengaging himself. "But I shall become angry if you don't behave sensibly—and do as I tell you . . . You know that I love you very much, but now circumstances demand that I must change my plans. We are sailing today—for Chesapeake Bay, on the American coast—and for the time being, we must travel separately . . . No—don't argue—I shall expect you to do your duty—just as I have to. Be good—be patient—and wait until we may be together again."

"When will that be?" she asked, dully.

"I do not know. But I ask you to wait patiently." He moved closer, and lifted her chin with one finger in the old, familiar gesture she loved so much. "Will you do that?"

She swallowed, and tried to keep her voice steady as she answered: "I will wait for you . . . "

The voyage to Chesapeake seemed to last an eternity. Garnet went through the motions of daily life as if in a bad dream; the weather was warm and the sky was cloudless, but she did not notice it. She felt more lost and alone than ever in her life before.

All those golden days and nights with Brock, that had been such a revelation to her, now seemed to have vanished forever, leaving nothing but memories—and a deep, unsatisfied yearning.

She allowed herself to be moved into the small vacant cabin—it would hardly have been fitting for a junior ensign to occupy the best stateroom on the ship—and spent the nights lying awake, feeling her body burning with desire for the man she loved.

By day, she stayed on deck, watching the other vessels around and ahead of them as they sailed in convoy—for now they had been joined by several more troopships, carrying still more battalions—riflemen, artillery and marines—toward the American shores. She tried to pick out which of the many sails and masts must be the *Tonnant* —and imagined that, somewhere there, Brock would be pacing the deck as she did, and thinking of her . . .

At last the unhappy journey was over, and the British flotilla anchored in Chesapeake Bay. Once they had established their positions, the various ships began to communicate—by flag signals, and by putting out small dinghys, taking messages or supplies from one to another.

Garnet made up her mind; in the cabin, she still had Brock's shirt—for she had not finished sewing it when he moved out. Now she packed it carefully into a neat parcel, and at the first possible moment asked Captain Anderson if she might be taken across to the *Tonnant,* where she rode at anchor, a quarter-mile away.

The captain eyed her thoughtfully for a moment, then gave his assent.

Half an hour later, Garnet was scrambling up a rope ladder and clambering onto the deck—the parcel stuffed into her half-open tunic.

Two of the *Tonnant*'s crew helped her over the ship's rail, but she hardly noticed them in her excitement. She was dimly aware that one of them—a well-built young sailor with a curly blond beard—was staring at her very fixedly—but she soon forgot that, as an army sergeant stepped forward to meet her, and demanded to know her business.

"I have something here to deliver to Major-General Savage," she explained. "Where is he?"

"Give it here, and I'll see he gets it." The man held out a hand for the package.

"No—I must give it to him personally . . . It is very important," she said firmly. "Please take me to him at once."

The man hesitated—then said: "Very well . . . If that's the way of it—come with me, sir."

And he led her away along the deck. At the rail, the broad-shouldered, bearded sailor watched them go—his eyes still fixed on Garnet.

The sergeant knocked on a door, and flung it open.

"Messenger for Major-General Savage!" he announced in a hoarse bark, and stood back to let Garnet go in.

In the admiral's cabin, a meeting was in progress. Four men sat at a long table—Brock at the end farthest from the door. His expression changed as he saw Garnet.

"What's this?" The senior man present, who was obviously the admiral in command, looked up, displeased.

"I thought I made it clear that we were not to be disturbed?"

"Parcel to be delivered in person to the Major-General, sir," rapped out the sergeant. "Matter of great importance."

"Well, Savage?" The admiral turned to Brock.

Brock rose to his feet, his face darkening.

"What are you doing here, Ensign?"

"I—I've brought something for you, sir—something you left on board the *Enterprise* . . . " she faltered under his stern gaze.

He frowned. "What is it?"

She took a deep breath, but heard her voice sounding thin and childish as she replied: "Your second-best shirt, sir—washed and mended . . . I thought you might be wanting it."

The other officers exchanged glances, and smiled amongst themselves.

"I see . . . Thank you." Brock's tone was cold and cutting as steel. "I will talk with you later, Ensign Mallory. Sergeant—you will conduct the young man to my cabin."

"Very good, sir."

The sergeant clicked his heels, saluted, and showed Garnet out.

She sat miserably in the cabin for an hour, knowing that her bright idea had misfired very badly, and hating herself for having made Brock appear at a disadvantage.

When he finally joined her, he closed the cabin door with care, then said quietly: "Was that little diversion meant to entertain me?"

"Oh, Brock—" She tried to throw herself in his arms, but he held her off, looking down at her with serious reproach in his eyes. "Don't scold me—I couldn't help it—I never meant—"

"I told you to wait for me . . . This is not the time nor the place for us to be together—surely you must realize that."

"I had to see you . . . I missed you so badly—and I

remembered that I still had this shirt—I truly thought you might be glad of it . . . I didn't know you were in a meeting—I thought you would be alone—"

"It was a stupid mistake on your part. I must ask you not to do such a thing again."

"I won't—I swear it—"

He passed his hand across his brow, and sighed.

"You could not know . . . I shouldn't be harsh with you—it's this infernal weather, so close and sultry . . . "

This was certainly true; Garnet herself felt prickly and uncomfortable in the heavy, humid climate of the American coastline.

"Is your head troubling you?" she asked, longing to take him in her arms, but not daring to risk such a familiarity in his present mood.

"Not especially," he said, turning away, and she knew that this meant "Yes."

"Perhaps the ship's doctor could give you something to ease the pain—" she ventured, but he snapped: "I have more urgent matters on my mind at this moment! These damned navy men are planning strategies on land and they don't know what they're talking about!"

He paced the cabin as he talked, as much to himself, Garnet suspected, as to her.

"That was Admiral Cochrane who spoke to you; the other two are his colleagues, Admiral Cockburn—and General Ross, who's in charge of our military forces, and my commander-in-chief . . . Cochrane's a wily bird—but his hatred for all things American makes his judgment unreliable. His brother was killed at Yorktown in '81, and Cochrane's had an obsession to be revenged upon America ever since.

"Cockburn's not got that devil driving him—but he's a rough, tough, impetuous man—goes at everything with his head down, like a bull at a gate . . . You can't reason with him.

"As for General Ross—he's the exact opposite. Cautious to the point of indecision—never seems to know his

own mind; consequently, the two navy men make short
work of him when it comes to plans of campaign . . .
And it's my job to try and keep the three of them in
line—God help me!"

He turned and threw Garnet a smile for an apology,
over his shoulder.

"That's why I'm not at my best and brightest today . . .
I'm sorry."

Emboldened by this, she moved closer to him and took
his hand.

"Don't be sorry . . . You need never apologize to me.
I was the one who made things worse—by coming here
and interrupting you—"

"No . . . Not really." His arm slid around her shoulders
and pressed her to him. "At least our plans are made now
—for good or bad. We must press on, and hope for the
best."

"Am I allowed to know your plans?"

"There's no special secrecy—within a very short time
every man in Chesapeake Bay will know the next move . . .
There is a contingent of the American navy anchored not
far away—you've seen the mouth of that estuary almost
directly ahead? Well, that's the Patuxent River, and that's
where their ships are lurking . . . We intend to follow them
up river and destroy their flotilla."

"I see . . . When do we set sail?"

"As soon as Admiral Cochrane can give the order. That
is why you must not be here. The *Tonnant* will be in the
vanguard of the attack—so you must get back on board
the *Enterprise* as soon as possible."

He turned her to face him, and kissed her once—holding her tightly, as if their bodies might melt into one with
the force of his passion.

"Now you must go . . . Good luck, my dearest one—
and God grant we may soon be together again, when
this sorry business is over."

He opened the cabin door, and she walked out . . .

Walking blindly, for her eyes were swimming with tears.

She heard the door shut again behind her, and paused, not knowing which way to go. One thing was certain, she could not go out on deck like this. If they had to "keep up appearances," Ensign Mallory could not risk being seen weeping when she left the major-general's cabin! She hung back in a dark corner under the companion-way, and waited, trying to compose herself.

Some minutes later, she heard voices, and the sounds of whistles piping on deck; then running feet—and a rattling, rumbling noise that she could not identify.

The swing of the timbers beneath her feet made her realize what was happening: the *Tonnant* had hoisted her anchor, and they were setting sail.

She raced up the steps to the deck, and her fears were confirmed. They were moving at a fast pace now, toward the American shoreline, and it was too late for her to attempt to leave the ship.

She wandered aimlessly, wondering what on earth she should do, and passed a knot of men busy coiling lengths of sodden rope. One of them, she noticed, was the fair young sailor with a beard who had helped her aboard. She gave a half smile as she walked by, but he did not return it. Instead, he gazed at her, as if he had seen a ghost; he seemed transfixed.

She puzzled over this, and glanced back as she turned the corner of the deck . . . He was still standing there, motionless, staring after her.

Garnet brushed this odd incident aside, and concentrated on finding somewhere to conceal herself—a hideaway where she could remain out of sight for a time. Almost at once she found a likely place; one of the deck houses had an open door, and she slipped inside. It was a sail locker, where the huge canvasses could be stored—but now it was half empty, for the *Tonnant* had crowded on sail to make for the river-mouth with all possible speed.

She positioned herself by the tiny porthole, where she

could see and hear what went on—and prepared for a long wait.

The Patuxent River was like a corkscrew, which wound its way in lazy curves through thick forests. As the *Tonnant* led the line of ships up the narrowing waterway, the wooded banks seemed to close in upon them, and from her vantage point Garnet was sometimes able to look back on the vessels that followed, and watch their masts gliding between the tall trunks of trees—so it almost appeared as if some of the trees themselves were on the move.

The sultry, overcast weather became more and more oppressive, and the air was very still, except for the piping of bosuns' whistles—not only from nearby, but from the ships farther off, fading into the distance—and the shouts of the sailors in the bows who were continually reporting back to the helmsman as they took soundings. They were in unknown waters now, without charts to guide them, and the only way they could be sure of navigating the changing deeps and shallows was to check the depth of the river by dropping lead weights overboard as a measure. Garnet heard the calls being repeated—some near, some far—in the traditional phrases that all river-pilots understood . . .

"Starboard lead there—and look sharp about it!"

"We are drawing nine . . ."

"Drawing nine—*de-e-ep* four . . ."

The bosuns' pipes sounded piercingly among the trees, like the calling of birds, that echoed and reechoed.

And still the long file of ships slid on, farther and farther into the deep, wooded countryside, as the light faded, and dusk fell.

Suddenly, a sound very close at hand broke in upon Garnet's thoughts, and she turned to see the door of the sail-locker opening behind her.

A sailor walked in. She held her breath as he pushed the door to, and then stood with his back against it.

It was the man who had been staring at her; and now here he was, regarding her in the same, eerie way . . .

Tall, broad-shouldered, with his shirt half unbuttoned,

and a thatch of blond hair on his chest that mimicked his short, curling beard . . .

She stared back at him, and something stirred in the recesses of her memory—some resemblance—

"Well, Miss Garnet . . . En't you a-going to say hello to an old friend—now that I've found you?"

Her heart turned over, and she thought for a moment she was going to faint.

"*Jem . . . Jem Bolt . . .* I didn't recognize you—"

"But I recognized you all right, Missy . . . Oh—not the first moment, p'raps—I couldn't believe me own eyes when I saw you climb aboard—but after . . . The more I looked, the more I knew I was right. There weren't no mistaking you."

"I never knew you had gone to sea, Jem—"

"I had to do *something* with my life after I ran off, didn't I? You didn't expect me to starve, did you? Or kill myself for love?"

He was laughing now, and she tried to smile, as he moved forward; he seemed to tower over her.

"It—it's good to see you, Jem . . . A surprise—for both of us . . . "

"Aye . . . That's what it is . . . I wasn't never so surprised in my life—seeing you there—dressed up like you are . . . " He laughed again. "And going into that chap's cabin the way you did . . . But you always were partial to soldiers—eh, Miss Garnet?"

She realized the danger she was in, and said quickly: "Jem—listen—you must help me keep my secret—nobody must know who I really am—it's essential—"

"But *he* do know, I'll be bound . . . That soldier with the gold ribbons on his coat—I wager he do know your precious secret! Be you his fancy woman, then? Traveling with him—to have a bit of fun—is that how it is between you?"

He came closer still, and she could feel his hot breath as he stood looking down at her.

"Mind your own business, Jem—leave me alone—"

"Oh, I'm not a-going to let you go, not now I've found you . . . But I'll keep your secret, p'raps—if so be you make it worth my while," he grinned.

"What do you mean? I can't give you money—I have almost nothing—"

"Who's talking of money? There's something I do prize far more than money . . . " And his huge hands closed around her, as he continued: "For now you en't a-going to refuse me—are you? You *can't* refuse me nothing, not now!"

She struggled helplessly, gasping: "Let me go—I'll call for help—I'll have you punished—"

But he laughed all the more, in triumph, as his greedy fingers began to explore her body.

"No fear of that, Missy . . . 'Tis Jem Bolt who gives the orders this time . . . From now on—you'll do as I tell you!"

He took hold of her tunic, and tore at the fastenings, ripping them apart in his impatience.

And then, all at once, the cabin seemed to tilt sideways; Garnet felt the ship lurch dangerously, and heard an ominous sound as the keel scraped against the river bed.

Jem hesitated—alert and listening—then a cry went up.

"We've run aground! All hands on deck!"

And the boson's whistle shrilled again, urgently.

He let her go, and ran for the door, muttering an oath. She followed a split second later, trying to rebutton her tunic as she hurried out.

On deck, it was growing dark, but even by the light of the ship's lanterns it was clear what had happened. The river ran into flats and shallows at this point, and without an experienced pilot who knew every twist and turn of the waters, it was impossible for the British ships to proceed any farther.

The officers were already at the rail, discussing the situation; throwing caution to the winds, Garnet ran straight up to Brock and touched his arm.

"Sir—excuse me—I must speak to you—" she began breathlessly.

He swung round instantly, and his face was livid in the flickering lantern-light.

"*How dare you . . .* " he said, quietly and clearly—and every word was like a knife in Garnet's heart, but she persisted, trying to explain.

"You don't understand—something's happened—"

"I know exactly what has happened," he interrupted her, aware of his fellow-officers who were openly listening. "You disobeyed my orders, Ensign Mallory . . . Sergeant—put this man in a dinghy and have him confined to his own quarters on the *Enterprise*. He's under arrest."

3

Under Arrest

"Confined to his own quarters . . ."

From that moment, Garnet was technically under arrest, and she could not argue any longer, or protest against the sentence Brock had imposed upon her.

The "quarters" were, of course, her small cabin below decks on board the *Enterprise*—and it was there that the army sergeant conducted her, as soon as a dinghy could be launched to transfer her from the *Tonnant*.

She was provided with a plain evening meal, and a carafe of water; her punishment was coolly impersonal, though not harsh—but the sound of the key as it turned in the lock, imprisoning her in the cabin, struck her like a whiplash.

She tried to swallow some food, and found it difficult, then pushed the platter aside . . . She was too unhappy to eat.

Punishment and loss of liberty were hard enough to

bear—but the worst thing of all was the memory of the anger in Brock's ice-cold eyes as he banished her from him.

She knew very well that he was in an impossible situation; by pestering him as she had done, in the presence of his superiors, she had exposed him to ridicule, and he had to take some disciplinary measure. She knew too that he was very worried about the strategy that the British forces were embarked upon, and that he had to give his whole mind to his task as a military commander. She also realized that the unbearably close, humid climate was aggravating the pain of his head-wound, so that his temper was dangerously explosive.

Even so, she kept asking herself—had she made him hate her? Could he forgive her for that moment of rashness and folly? Or had she lost him forever?

Looking back, it seemed almost incredible now that she should have been anxious to the point of desperation over Jem Bolt and his threat to her safety. Already that problem had become irrelevant; she might never see Jem again—it didn't matter so very much after all . . . Nothing mattered except her love for Brock. And when would she see *him* again?

At last she took off her clothes, crawled into her bunk, and spent a miserable night, tossing and turning, throwing aside the blanket, and tormenting herself with these questions, over and over.

She awoke from a fitful sleep, some time before dawn, to the sound of the door being unlocked.

She sat up, instantly on the alert, as the sergeant—who appeared to be acting as her gaoler—marched into the cabin, carrying a small lantern in which a candle burned with a mellow flame.

She groped for the blanket to cover herself—and realized too late that it had slipped onto the floor: she was dressed only in one of Gerard's old shirts, darned and patched after long wearing, which she had relegated to use as a nightgown.

Her legs were bare, and she struggled to pull the shirt as far down her thighs as possible, while the sergeant glanced at her curiously.

"Good morning, Ensign Mallory," he rapped out, in his usual clipped cockney style. "Time to rise and shine, young sir . . . It'll soon be first light, and we must be on our way."

"On our way—where?" she asked.

He grinned, and unfastened the collar of his tunic, then threw himself down upon the single wooden chair.

"Mind if I make meself comfortable? We've got ten minutes before we're due on shore."

"I don't understand . . . Where are we going?"

"On the march, young sir . . . Up river. The powers that be 'ave decided we can't sail no further, for the river's too shallow and too dangerous from 'ere on. So we travel on land now: like the good Lord intended! This 'ere sea-faring lark ain't no good for military men like you an' me, lad."

Garnet interrupted: "But I'm under arrest—I can't go anywhere—"

The sergeant winked. "You're in luck, ain't you? Orders is orders—every available man in every battalion is being marched off today . . . Well, that includes *you,* don't it? We ain't going to waste another serving soldier to stay behind on this ship just to keep guard over *you,* lad— stands to reason!"

"I see . . . But the major-general said—"

"You don't want to worry your 'ead about what 'e said —you listen to me, young sir, and you won't go far wrong."

He cocked an eye at Garnet's legs again, and added: "Tell the truth, lad—I've taken a shine to you, and that's a fact . . . So you'll come with me, on the advance party; I'll look after you, and see you don't get into mischief!"

He winked again. Garnet bit her lip, unsure what the man's intentions were. He was, perhaps, about Brock's age, and quite personable, in a rough-and-ready way, with cropped hair of grizzled grey, and a square-cut weather-beaten face.

"White's the name, young sir . . . Sergeant White—known to me mates as Chalky . . . Put yerself in my 'ands, lad, and you'll come to no 'arm."

"Thank you," she said uncertainly.

"Get yerself dressed now—and look sharp, for we ain't got time to 'ang about." Sergeant White jerked a thumb at the table, where Garnet had folded her uniform when she undressed. "You carry on, lad—don't mind me."

Garnet reluctantly slid from the bunk, taking great care not to expose any further areas of her anatomy, then stood in her shirt-tails, facing him.

"Excuse me, Sergeant—" she began.

"Chalky, lad—we're not on parade now—don't stand on ceremony."

"Chalky . . . " She repeated nervously. "Might I ask—if you've no objection—I prefer to make my preparations . . . in private . . . "

There was a pause; then the Sergeant rose to his feet and nodded.

"Right you are, young sir . . . I understand . . . Lor' love yer, I got a son about your age, back home in Shoreditch . . . 'E's just the same—everlasting wanting to be on 'is own, 'e is; shy as a bloomin' vestal virgin—gawd knows where 'e gets it from . . . Never you mind—I'll leave yer in peace. But be sure you're dressed and ready to go ashore in five minutes, or there'll be trouble!"

He gave Garnet a playful, not unkindly slap across her shoulders, nodded once more and marched out.

She breathed a long sigh of relief, and set up a prayer of thanks for Sergeant Chalky White's unknown and fastidious son . . . And began to dress herself as fast as possible.

As the sergeant had explained, she was detailed to ride ahead with him as part of an advance party, to try and blaze a trail which the troops of infantry and artillery would be able to follow. Within half an hour, dawn was breaking, and the first two riders set off along the shore of the river.

It was going to be another oppressive, sultry day, and Garnet was glad that she did not have to make her way on foot, laden with her gear and equipment. The going was hard enough on horseback, and the little chestnut mare picked her way with difficulty through the lush undergrowth and swampy foliage by the riverside.

There were trails of a sort here, but no beaten track of any kind, and Garnet realized that it would be a slow and difficult journey for the foot soldiers.

"Are there no roads in this part of America?" she asked the sergeant, looking back over her shoulder, for she was riding several yards ahead.

"I reckon the folks in these parts must travel by boat most of the time," he called across to her. "Look there— we're coming to a village . . . But there ain't no proper road—just a few old river-barges moored up alongside."

They made their way into the village; a signpost proclaimed the name—"Benedict, in the State of Maryland."

Garnet looked about her with interest as they rode along the main street; frame and shingle houses—a general store—a saloon—a little wooden church . . . It was like a toy village, and like a toy it was empty of life.

"Where is everybody?" she asked.

Chalky White shrugged, and spat at a white picket fence as they rode by.

"Must've 'eard that the British were on the way—and they've all locked themselves indoors—'iding under the beds, I dare say," he remarked.

"It doesn't seem so to me," Garnet disagreed. "That house has its front door left half open—and the washing's still hanging out to dry in that backyard . . . It looks as if they just dropped everything and ran off . . . I saw a town in Spain that was left at a moment's notice, rather like this."

"Well . . . I'll stop awhile and take a closer look round," said Chalky, reining in his horse, a plodding old grey.

"You ride on a step farther, lad, and I'll catch you up presently."

He dismounted, and began to tether the grey to the picket fence, as Garnet continued on her way.

The main street soon petered out into weeds and overgrown moss, and then reverted to a wild, grassy trail once more, as the trees closed in upon it.

Garnet proceeded cautiously, very much aware now of being on her own. Although the sun was high in the sky by this time, there was a thick heat haze, and it was difficult to see very far ahead. The heat made the air shimmer, and two or three times, as she peered into the undergrowth, Garnet thought she saw a movement—but it was only a trick of the light that deceived her eyes . . .

She rode slowly on, and the trees grew still closer together, as if to crowd her off the narrow path. Their heavy branches overhead cut off the daylight, and she felt as if she were riding underwater—at the bottom of a green, greasy river.

The chestnut mare suddenly pricked up her ears and stopped dead, making Garnet catch her breath.

"What's the matter? What's wrong, old girl? What have you seen?"

The horse stayed motionless—listening—waiting.

Garnet heard the sound of her own heart beating, and then the snap of a twig, only a few yards away—and a soft footfall.

She whirled round, and found herself face to face with a figure from a nightmare . . . A man in rags, who had stepped out of the forest, with his hand stretched toward her . . . A man with a grey face, and some hideous disease that disfigured him horribly. Instead of a nose, he had two blood-red holes for nostrils, and half his jaw appeared to be crumbling away.

Garnet recoiled instinctively, and the man spoke.

"Don't be afraid," he said, in a dry, cracked voice with an unfamiliar twang to it. "I won't touch you—but keep your distance, for God's sake."

She stared at him as if she were mesmerized, unable to take her eyes from that ravaged face, and she smelled the sickly-sweet odor of corruption and decay.

"Ha'n't you never seen a leper before?" asked the stranger.

"No . . . " She whispered. "Never . . . "

"Have no fear, I won't pass it on to you, brother," he said. "But I need help . . . That's why I stayed behind, when all the other folks ran off . . . You're a Britisher, ain't you?"

She nodded dumbly, feeling a cold trickle of sweat down her spine.

"I thought so . . . All the rest of Benedict township done took to their heels—but not me . . . I stayed on—'cos I need your help to save me . . . A British doctor mebbe could save my life . . . I'm *beggin'* you to help me, brother."

Garnet made up her mind, and said huskily, "Very well—you must follow me . . . I'll lead the way—we'll do the best we can."

She turned the horse and they set off back along the path toward Benedict. After a quarter of a mile or so, she spied Sergeant White riding out to find her—and was very glad to meet him again.

Quickly, she explained the circumstances, talking in low tones, and glancing back at the leper who stood waiting patiently some distance away.

"Poor devil," muttered Chalky. "I don't give much for 'is chances, and that's a fact . . . Still—while there's life, there's 'ope, so they say—and in the meantime, 'e might be able to do us a good turn, perhaps."

"A good turn? What do you mean?"

"You say he's a local man—and that's what we need . . . For you and me is strangers in these parts!"

He went forward—though keeping a judicious distance from the man—and proceeded to parlay with him, finally striking a bargain. In return for medical treatment from the British military surgeons, the leper agreed to act as guide to the advance party and lead them safely up river to Marlboro.

Upper Marlboro was to become a turning-point for the British, thirty miles from the sea, and twenty miles from the transport ships anchored just below Benedict. The commanders of the combined forces met there in General Ross's tent, to discuss their next move.

Admiral Cockburn was outspoken in his opinion.

"I say we press on. Damme, we're nearer Washington now than we are to the sea—and we've not set eyes on the American troops yet. As for their precious navy—they've gone off to skulk in some safe hideaway, and we're no nearer to destroying their fleet now than we were when we started. We can't march back to our own ships empty-handed. For heaven's sake let us make a bold move, and strike at the capital!"

General Ross, as always, saw both the advantages and disadvantages of this advice.

"We don't know the territory—we're working in the dark, and the farther we go inland, the more stretched our lines of communications must be from the base camp at Benedict. We have no cavalry—except for the few horses that some of the officers have brought with them—and little enough artillery. We have no knowledge of the disposition of the enemy; I would be very reluctant to put my head into a noose upon such scanty information."

Brock Savage massaged a vein that throbbed in his forehead, and said: "I agree that it would be foolhardy to take any decision without more intelligence. With your permission, sir—let us send for Sergeant White, who has been dealing with the one wretched informer that we have so far discovered."

The sergeant was sent for at once, and stood rigidly to attention, his toes turned out and his shoulders back.

"Sir!" he snapped, in response to Brock's questioning. "The American feller is very sick, and not to be relied upon—but 'e gives it as 'is opinion that their troops 'ave been retreating all along the line, and are now falling back upon their three main bases of Washington, Annapolis, and Baltimore."

"His *opinion?*" Brock glanced at his two colleagues. "I could have made an equally reasonable guess myself, with no more certainty to go upon. Why should we trust this man's opinion, gentlemen?"

Admiral Cockburn thumped the map table with his fist.

"It sounds highly probable to me—look at the lie of the land . . . The Americans will have split their forces—here, here and *here* . . . " He planted a stubby forefinger upon the city of Washington. "A mere twenty miles away. I say let's chase them back there and give 'em a run for their money."

"Does the American informer know the roads between here and Washington?" asked Brock.

"I believe so, sir—I'll 'ave to ask 'im, to make quite sure. But Mallory told me 'e'd been to Washington when 'e was a boy—"

"*Who?*" Brock looked up, transfixed.

"Ensign Mallory, sir—who found the man originally—'e's got quite friendly with the poor bastard, and they've 'ad several long talks—"

"Are you telling me that Mallory is *here*, at Marlboro?" Brock cut in, and the vein at his temple pulsed angrily. "I thought that Ensign Mallory had been confined to quarters, on board ship?"

"Begging your pardon, sir—I couldn't make meself responsible for 'im there *and* do my duty on the march. So I took 'im along under escort in the advance party, where I could keep an eye on 'im . . . Strictly speaking—'e's still under arrest, but on a loose rein as you might say."

"Is this your young *aide-de-camp* again, Savage?" asked General Ross quizzically. "He seems to cause you a deal of trouble, don't he?"

Before Brock could reply, Admiral Cockburn interrupted impatiently.

355

"We're wasting precious time . . . Do we or do we not march upon Washington? We are waiting upon your decision, General."

General Ross sighed, then said evasively: "In any case, I cannot act without the direct permission of my superior. Admiral Cochrane is the commander-in-chief of this expedition—"

"And Admiral Cochrane is safely on board the *Tonnant,* twenty miles down river! *He* can't make up your mind for you—!"

"Sir . . . I must ask you to choose your words with a little more care," frowned the general, with a tilt of the eyebrow toward Sergeant White, still standing passively by: "I am simply saying that it is my duty to inform the admiral and ask his permission to proceed—"

"Then inform Admiral Cochrane by all means," said Brock, thinking fast. "Write a letter, sir—and we will have it dispatched to him at headquarters, as soon as possible . . . Sergeant—find Ensign Mallory, and bring him here immediately."

Five minutes later, Garnet was escorted into the tent. She looked once at Brock—but his face was carefully controlled and without any expression, telling her nothing. She felt as if her heart would break, and fixed her gaze at a point above his head. She was sure that if she had to suffer the ordeal of his cool, level stare, she would betray herself irrevocably.

"Well, Ensign . . . " Brock said quietly. "You have traveled farther than I expected."

"Yes, sir." She still would not look at him.

"But by a happy accident, this now enables me to give you a mission which needs to be carried out as quickly as possible. Here is a letter from General Ross, which must be delivered to Admiral Cochrane on board the frigate *Tonnant.* I want you to take it to him."

Garnet stepped forward, accepted the sealed envelope and stepped back again, like a mechanical figure.

General Ross, who had been watching and listening to

this exchange, asked: "Do you have any questions, boy?"

"Just one, sir. What am I to do when the letter is delivered? Bring back the admiral's reply?"

Brock replied before the general could speak. "You will stay on board the *Enterprise*—as you should have done all the time—and await further orders."

"But sir—"

"No more questions, Ensign. Do your duty—and wait with all the patience you can muster—until you are sent for."

She dared to look at him at last; and she knew that—although to all outward appearance his face had not changed—his expression had softened ever so slightly, and his eyes held the ghost of a smile.

She saluted, turned about, and left the tent, her spirits soaring. He had forgiven her—and he would send for her again, some time, somewhere . . . Nothing else mattered.

The ride back to Benedict was long and hard—but now it seemed almost like a pleasure trip, for she knew that Brock still loved her. She realized that he was contriving a way to keep her on board ship, far from the theater of war, for her own safety—and though she hated to be parted from him, she accepted that he meant it for the best.

Because the trail to Benedict was now a familiar one, the chestnut mare took to it willingly, and Garnet made good time on the journey. There was only one bad moment—when the heavens were suddenly split by a series of colossal explosions. She did not know how far away they were, or what they meant—could the Americans after all have laid a trap for the British forces? Was this the sound of battle breaking out?

She waited tensely, but at last the noise died away, and was followed by a long silence. Whatever it had been, it seemed to be over, so she spurred the shivering horse, and rode on.

It wasn't until she had passed through the village of

Benedict—still without any sign of life, and as quiet as the grave—and had dismounted on the riverbank, preparing to run up the gangplank to the deck of the *Tonnant,* that she remembered Jem Bolt . . .

How stupid of her not to have thought of Jem until now . . . If he saw her return, he would certainly try to intercept her; to come on board his ship was asking for trouble. But she had no alternative; the letter had to be delivered.

She looked cautiously left and right as she walked across the deck to the admiral's cabin—but there was no sign of Jem. So far, so good . . . She knocked and entered.

Admiral Cochrane—a corpulent man with the face of a benevolent Roman emperor—glanced up as she walked in. "Ah—I know you, don't I, young man?" he asked. "Brock Savage's young *attaché*—I remember . . . What are you doing here?"

She explained her errand, and handed over the letter. The admiral read it swiftly, and his face clouded over with preoccupation. He seemed almost to have forgotten her presence.

"Is there—is there anything else you wish me to do, sir?" she asked after a few moments.

"Eh? What's that? Oh—no, thank'ee . . . " The admiral rubbed his chin thoughtfully, his mind still upon the contents of the letter, as he added:—"Do you have further orders?"

"Only to return to my quarters aboard the *Enterprise,* sir."

"Then you'd better do that . . . Very well, Ensign—you're dismissed."

She left the cabin and made her way back to the path along the riverbank, wondering what to do next. She could try to hail a dinghy to ferry her out to the *Enterprise*—which was standing to, some quarter-mile out, in deeper water . . . Or she could wait until next time some of her crew came ashore, and persuade them to take her back on board.

Pondering this, she found herself strolling along the bank, drawn back irresistibly to the deserted village of Benedict.

There was something fascinating about those silent, lifeless houses. She noticed that the washing still hung as she had seen it before, forgotten on the clothes lines. She peered into the window of the saloon—dirty glasses and a half-empty bottle stood upon a table. It was amazing that the British troops had passed through here without taking advantage of the unprotected goods and chattels left wide open to them—but of course they had been on the march, under close scrutiny, and the British policy was "no civilian bloodshed—no looting of civilian property."

She wandered on, feeling that she was in a dream; the little church stood just as it had been left—there were still flowers upon the stones in the graveyard. A swing hung from the bough of an apple tree, unmoving, and a child's paper kite, caught up in the topmost branches, fluttered feebly in the heavy air.

She reached the house that she had noticed particularly upon her first passage through Benedict—the one that had the front door half open . . . Somehow, it seemed to be inviting her to set foot inside.

It was as if she were wearing a cloak of invisibility; she could walk into these houses, and satisfy her curiosity about the people who lived there—unseen, undiscovered . . .

She couldn't resist it. She walked quickly up the trim garden path, pushed the door a little further ajar, and walked in.

The door opened straight into a neat, simple parlor, with a table laid ready for a meal, and sprigged muslin curtains at the windows. There were flowers in a vase—unfamiliar flowers that she did not recognize—but they had begun to droop for lack of water, and the petals were falling. She took another step toward them, to look more closely—and heard the door shut quietly behind her.

"I been following you, Missy," said Jem Bolt. "I knowed as I'd find you again, sooner or later . . . And here you be."

She overturned the vase of flowers in her sudden terror, and stared down at the scattered blossoms stupidly, then moved automatically to pick them up.

"Leave them!" he said sharply. "They don't matter . . . We got no time for flowers now . . . You're a-coming with me."

He moved toward her, his bulky body between her and the door, and she knew that escape was impossible.

"What do you mean—?" She stammered. "Where are you taking me?"

He grasped her wrists in his strong hands.

"Upstairs," he said.

At the same moment, thirty miles to the north, encamped outside Marlboro, Admiral Cockburn walked briskly into General Ross's tent, where he had been discussing the strategic situation with Brock Savage.

"Well?" asked the General. "What news?"

"I've just learned the cause of those explosions, gentlemen," said Cockburn, in high good humor. "Good news for us!"

"What's happened?" asked Brock.

"The American fleet was under the command of a certain Joshua Barney—and he'd withdrawn the ships up river to a place called Pig Point . . . A crude designation —but then what can you expect of simple colonials?"

"Never mind the name—what were the explosions we heard?" demanded General Ross.

"According to my information, when Commander Josh Barney heard we had come so close, he decided that discretion was the better part of valor . . . He blew up his own ships, rather than risk their falling into our hands—

and has now departed, together with four hundred sailors, to rally round his illustrious President James Madison, in his time of trial."

"He's retreated to Washington?" asked Brock. "Are you sure?"

"Absolutely certain . . . Now, General—what do you say? Do we strike while the iron's hot? Do we chase them and destroy them—once and for all?"

Brock tried to interrupt, but General Ross had been fired by Cockburn's enthusiasm at last.

"Yes . . . We can't afford to risk waiting for Cochrane's reply . . . You're right . . . Give the order, gentlemen . . . We march on Washington!"

. . . While in the deserted village of Benedict, far from any kind of help, Garnet found herself being driven up a narrow wooden staircase—half-pushed, half-carried onward by the urgency of Jem's demands.

She almost fell into the little room at the head of the stairs. A bedroom, with a plain four-poster bed in it, and the bedclothes flung back, as the last occupants had left them.

Jem slammed the door shut behind him, and chuckled.

"You picked out a good house to visit, Missy," he said. "Couldn't have chosen better meself . . . Almost like as if it was here waiting for us—eh?"

She backed away, her hands ready for self-defense.

"What—what do you want of me—?" she asked, and her lips were trembling.

"You don't need to be asking me that," he replied. Already his hands were busy, unbuttoning and unfastening his blue uniform.

She sank onto the bed, her thoughts racing desperately.

"No, Jem—no, please—"

But even as she spoke she knew that it was inevitable. She was a prisoner in this little room, and there was certainly nobody to come to her rescue this time. His face was set and flushed with excitement—it would be impossible to dissuade him. If she tried to fight him off by sheer physical force, he would be bound to overpower her eventually—and in so doing, she could be seriously, even permanently, injured . . .

Now stripped to the waist, he undid the buttons of his bell-bottomed trousers and let the flap fall. She saw that his manhood was already strong and hard, as he took a step toward her.

"Don't be a fool," he said, breathing fast. "Do you be sensible, and you won't get hurt . . . Take off your clothes, Miss Garnet . . . "

Slowly—hopelessly—she began to obey.

4

Defeat—and Victory

He stood and watched her as she undressed. She felt his eyes upon her, and instinctively turned away, shielding herself from his gaze, but he grabbed her arm roughly, and pulled her round to face him. She knew then that she could expect no mercy from Jem Bolt.

"Is this what you want?" she asked, with all the dignity she could muster. "To see me stripped—humiliated—?"

She removed her last garment; the trim, white shirt of military cut, and dropped it to the floor, standing before her adversary, completely naked.

He had been smiling lewdly as he watched the slow process of her undressing—amused by the items of masculine attire that were removed one by one to reveal the feminine beauties hidden beneath . . . But now the smile faded from his lips, and he stared at her in a sort of wonder.

She had never looked lovelier as she stood there—helpless and yet courageous; her head was held high, and her arms hung straight at her sides. She made no further attempt to cover her nudity—her ripely rounded breasts, each with its rose-pink nipple standing out boldly—her gently molded waist and the creamy curve of her hips; and between her thighs, the very essence of her womanly mystery—veiled in soft chestnut curls.

Jem himself was completely naked—and his own rugged maleness was the exact counterpart to her beauty. Even at this moment—hating him as she did and fearing the imminent assault that she knew must follow—she found herself almost admiring the firm, strong lines of his splendid body. Against her will, she noted his broad chest, with its fuzz of blond hair that led down across his muscular stomach . . . The tight, narrow buttocks, and sturdy flanks . . . And his manhood, throbbingly erect as he took a pace toward her.

"I do love you so . . . " he said huskily.

"You don't understand what love means—you want my body to use for your pleasure—nothing more than that . . . "

"No! It en't true—'tis love, I tell you!" he asserted, and his huge hands closed around her shoulders, as he eased her back onto the bed. "And I think as how you do love me too—p'raps."

"Never in a million years," she said with bitter scorn, holding his eyes in a long level gaze. "I despise you, Jem Bolt. Do what you like—and afterward I shall only hate you the more . . . I will never love you!"

"Shut your mouth, girl—I won't listen to you!" he snarled, then threw himself upon her savagely.

The weight of his body almost took her breath away, and she gasped helplessly as she struggled beneath him. After the passionate delights she had known with Brock, whose ardor combined strength and sensitivity in perfect balance, she knew she had to endure real physical hardship at Jem's hands, and steeled herself to expect the worst.

She was resolved not to cry—or plead for help—or make a sound, however painful the ordeal might be. She would concentrate entirely on her hatred of this man, and do nothing to add to his selfish pleasure. All the time that he had his way with her, she would be cold, remote, aloof . . .

Only—strangely—it didn't happen quite like that.

Oh, yes, he was hungry for her body, and grasped her limbs crudely, forcing himself impatiently upon her. But he had learned enough in sexual experience to make things easier for himself, by preparing her gradually for his violation.

Even as he forced her legs apart, urging his thighs between hers, he began to cover her with kisses . . . His mouth was upon hers, his eager lips and tongue seeming to have a quicksilver life of their own as they moved from her mouth to her chin, her neck, nuzzling into her shoulder, nibbling the lobe of her ear . . . She had never before been kissed by a man with a beard, and the harsh sensation of his bristling cheeks upon her skin was oddly stimulating . . . And always, at the same time, she could feel the insistent pressure of his thick, hard masculinity hot against her.

His hands were everywhere—her shoulders, her waist, the small of her back—sliding across her bosom, stroking and titillating her breasts, massaging her nipples until she felt a tingle of excitement thrilling through her . . . And then his right hand slid down to her soft body hair, and began to explore every inch of her most private, her most vulnerable area; touching, teasing, probing—and with such surprising gentleness, too.

To her dismay, she felt her body responding to his skill—her own treacherous passion betraying her. Try as she would, she could not keep her resolve to remain cold and aloof—desperately she sought to control her emotions, but it was useless . . . Wave upon wave of overpowering desire flooded through her, and she was helpless in his arms.

Hating him—hating herself almost more—she felt herself surrender; her innermost secrets opened up to him, and the pounding shaft of his virility plunged deeply within her, again and again.

Shuddering with ecstasy, she abandoned herself to the moment—forgetting everything in the torrent of love that swept her away.

And at the moment of climax, love, lust and hatred mingled together in one overwhelming consummation . . . and she burst into tears at last; bitter, angry tears that wracked and scalded her.

"Oh, Garnet—it was good—it was so very good," Jem panted in triumph. "Was it the same for you?"

She could not speak at first; in this instant of frenzy, she could only revenge herself upon him physically.

She buried her teeth deep into his neck, biting with all her strength—wanting to hurt and bruise his body, as her soul had been hurt and bruised.

"You little devil!" He yelped with pain, and jerked back involuntarily, withdrawing from her in one violent movement. "Look what you done—you've drawn blood!"

"I'm glad!" She flung the words in his face with venom. "That will be something for you to remember me by."

The taste of blood was on her lips, and she wiped her mouth furiously with the back of her hand as she continued: "I hate you more than any man in this world . . . And if you ever dare to approach me again—I shall let your superior officers know what sort of animal you are . . . No matter what the cost may be to myself—I shall have you arrested and punished, Jem Bolt . . . Now get out—and leave me alone."

He looked at her for a long moment, as if he would say something—as if he wanted to plead with her. It was an ironic reversal of their roles, for now it seemed that she had all the power, and he had none.

But he said nothing; there was nothing he could say. Instead, he groped stupidly for his clothes, and scrambled into his uniform. At the door, he turned for one last look at her—one mute appeal—

Garnet closed her eyes, and rolled over, burying her face in the pillows. When at last she looked up again, he had gone.

He ravished me, she thought, trying to pull herself together. Yes—this is what they mean by the word—I have been ravished . . . Betrayed by my own mindless emotions . . . And so I have been untrue to Brock—untrue to myself—untrue to my love . . .

In despair, she began to cry again, quietly, and eventually sobbed herself into a deep, exhausted sleep.

When she awoke, she did not know for a moment where she was; the daylight had gone, and the room was almost dark. It was evening already.

Sadly and automatically, she dressed herself, and—with some lurking feeling of guilt toward the unknown householder whose domestic privacy had been so shockingly invaded—she took the rumpled and stained sheets from the bed, folded them, and put them in a linen basket that stood nearby, ready for the next wash.

She went down the narrow staircase, and at the front door took one last, unhappy look back at the little house . . . The scene of her most poignant defeat . . . Then she walked out, and this time she closed the door behind her —shutting it away forever, into the past.

When she reached the riverbank, where the *Tonnant* was still anchored, a sailor on deck called out—and she started, fearing for an instant that it might be Jem.

But it was a stranger: black-haired, and with black mutton chop whiskers.

He called down to her: "Ensign Mallory? Admiral's been sending out search parties for you these past three hours—we've been looking high and low for you, sir!"

"Oh—I'm sorry—I was . . . out—walking," Garnet replied awkwardly.

"Then you'd best come aboard right away and explain to him yourself, for he's been in a rare old taking about you . . . This way, young sir—look sharp!"

Garnet hurried up the gangplank, and a moment later was entering the admiral's cabin once more.

"So there you are!" Admiral Cochrane glared at her from beneath beetling brows. "Where on earth have you been?"

"I went for a walk, sir—and afterward—I fell asleep . . . I'm sorry."

"Sleep, eh? You'll need all the sleep you can get tonight, my boy—for at dawn tomorrow I shall require you to set off once more, with a dispatch for General Ross."

"Oh, but—I thought—I was told to stay here until further orders."

"These *are* your further orders, young man! Don't I make myself clear? I've written a letter replying to General Ross's last missive—and you're the only one here who knows where the General is encamped now, so you must take it. Your horse will be rested by morning, I hope—ready for another journey?"

"Yes, sir—certainly." Even in her present mood of despair, Garnet's spirits revived a little at the prospect of seeing Brock again. And he could not be displeased with her this time; she had no choice but to obey the admiral's orders.

"Very well, then. Take this letter, and deliver it into the hands of General Ross at the first possible moment tomorrow . . . Now get to your quarters, and catch up on your sleep, Ensign . . . You are dismissed."

To begin with, everything turned out as the admiral had planned. Garnet spent one last night in her cramped quarters aboard the *Enterprise,* and as the first rays of dawn striped the night sky, she set off on the chestnut mare.

She rode through silent Benedict and along the now familiar path that followed the Patuxent River northward; through another deserted township—Nottingham—and so at last to Marlboro, where she had last encountered Brock and the chiefs-of-staff.

But here things began to go wrong . . . For—instead of waiting for Admiral Cochrane's dispatch—General Ross had begun the advance toward Washington on the previous day, and when Garnet arrived she found herself staring blankly at empty fields where the army had been encamped.

At first, she wondered if she had lost her way and come to the wrong place—but the odd items of litter left behind by the British soldiery soon convinced her.

This was the place—but where was the army?

Then she found the marks of horses' hooves and the heavy track of artillery wheels, and began to follow, wondering where the trail might lead her.

In fact, the British forces were now drawn up about five miles to the east of Washington, outside the town of Bladensburg, on a tributary of the Potomac.

They had progressed so far without any kind of opposition from the American troops. Once they moved into the environs of Washington, the going was much easier, and they marched along well-marked roads, without let or hindrance.

As Sergeant Chalky White remarked to his cronies, "It's like a reg'lar holiday outing—a fam'ly picnic!"

Then, at midday, they topped a small hill and looked down upon the Potomac River—and the lines of green-jacketed American soldiers, deployed below the town of Bladensburg, in three widely-separated lines.

"What's our best way, Yankee?" Sergeant White asked the leper, who was still acting as their guide and informant.

"That's but one way you'll get through," rasped the American, mopping his brow. "You see that narrow bridge 'cross the river? You'll need to take the bridge, I reckon—'cos there's no other way around."

This intelligence was swiftly passed back to General Ross and Brock Savage.

Brock suggested: "It might be wise to begin by making a feint down there—toward the troops on the left flank. A diversion could have the effect of drawing off their fire and uncovering their main force in the center—and it will certainly give us the opportunity to muster all those infantry who are still strung out upon the road behind us."

"Fiddlesticks!" snapped Admiral Cockburn, mounted with some degree of discomfort upon a white farm horse which had been commandeered from a meadow earlier in the day. "We can't sit about here waiting for reinforcements—let's strike at once, General—slam-bang in the center . . . We can take that bridge before they know what's hit 'em!"

Brock began to protest as diplomatically as possible that perhaps the admiral was not entirely familiar with military strategy on dry land—but to his dismay, General Ross forestalled him.

"Quite right! I agree with Cockburn—give the order, Savage—we attack immediately."

"Surely, sir—it would be prudent to wait at least until our position can be consolidated—"

"Prudence be damned," said Cockburn. "Board 'em, sir —board their guns!"

"As if"—Brock reported to Garnet, long afterward— "he were attacking a warship."

The attack was foolhardy in the extreme, and did not deserve to succeed; indeed, it might well not have done so, except for the fact that the Bladensburg defenses were sadly undermanned.

The American forces were small, and unprepared for the British attack; a scratch militia had been hastily raised from Washington when the alarm was sounded, and these were largely a force of civilians, pressed into service and inadequately armed, under the command of one General William Winder—a Baltimore lawyer, with little or no experience of warfare.

In the event, American inefficiency was attacked by British stupidity . . . and routed.

Brock could hardly believe his eyes as the first wave of British soldiers advanced upon the narrow bridge, to be met by a salvo from the American guns. A second assault followed—and the Americans began to waver, but their artillery barrage continued.

The officers themselves rode in among their troops, to put heart into the men, and Brock could see Cockburn— as violent and clumsy as 'a sailor on a horse' is traditionally supposed to be—windmilling his arms and shouting obscenities as he pressed ahead.

Then an unlucky bullet found its mark, and Brock felt the big black charger jerk violently beneath him. The beast reared up as Brock dug his heels in and tried to cling on—and then collapsed, with the weight and force of a falling tree. Brock lay, one leg trapped under the horse's side, unable to move, as the stricken animal convulsed in its final agonies.

Minutes before this, Garnet had overtaken the straggling lines of infantry upon the dusty road, and now galloped over the breast of the hill and down toward the scene of battle.

She arrived just in time to pick out Brock's figure, as he rode into the thick of the *melée* upon his great black horse . . . Then even as she watched, she saw the beast rear up, and both horse and rider disappeared into the tumult.

There was no time to be afraid or anguished; putting spurs to the chestnut mare, Garnet never hesitated, but flew like the wind across the battlefield, then dismounted and knelt at Brock's side, where he lay half-crushed beneath the charger.

He was covered with blood—and Garnet's heart stopped. For an instant, she was quite sure that he was dead.

But he shook his head, as a swimmer does when he surfaces from a dive, and wiped his face with one hand, even while he drew his pistol from its holster with the other.

"Brock—" she gasped.

He looked up at her—without registering any surprise —and said simply: "Stand clear . . . This won't take a moment."

Then he pointed the muzzle at the horse's head and pulled the trigger, putting the creature out of its misery.

The wave of fighting rolled on, and there was a brief lull in the din of battle. Garnet and Brock were marooned in a sea of blood and mud, with a dead horse, and a handful of wounded—or dying—men.

"Help me up," he ordered.

She did the best she could, heaving at the horse's heavy carcass, and with an enormous effort managed to raise the dead weight by a fraction of an inch—just sufficiently for Brock to drag himself free, and massage some life back into his leg.

"You're hurt—wounded—" she began breathlessly.

"A little battered, but none the worse for that." He grasped her hand, and staggered to his feet. "Don't worry —I shall live!"

"But your face—your tunic—all that blood—"

"From the poor beast . . . I'm not even scratched. The wretched animal was shot from under me."

"Thank God—promise me you are not seriously injured—"

"I'm not—though it's no thanks to General Ross!" Brock flexed his knee painfully. "Tell me—in heaven's name—how do you come to be here? Always popping up like a jack-in-a-box when least expected."

"I was sent under Admiral Cochrane's orders, sir," said Garnet. "With a dispatch in reply to the general's last letter."

"Then you've had a wasted journey, for the reply comes too late—whatever it may say. As you see, our general and his seafaring colleague have taken matters into their own hands."

Garnet strained her eyes to see through the drifting smoke.

"The enemy are in retreat, I think. We have won the day."

"Oh, yes—it's been a mighty victory indeed! At the cost of—what? three hundred men or more . . . Whereas there was no need to lose more than fifty at the most . . . And now I suppose we are to go blundering on into Washington . . . Though how I'm to get there without my poor brute of a horse, I do not know."

Garnet acted instantly, plunged away and returned in a moment, handing over the reins of the little chestnut mare.

"She's not the kind of steed you're accustomed to, but she won't let you down," she said.

"And neither will her young rider," said Brock, with such quiet sincerity that Garnet could have sobbed with happiness. "Very well—I will accept the loan of your horse, under these circumstances, for I must ride on ahead with my lords and masters . . . But what is to become of you, in this predicament?"

"Don't concern yourself with me, sir," said Garnet. She longed to throw her arms around him and tell him how much she loved him—but there was no time to be lost, and in any case they could well have been observed. "I will follow behind with the infantry . . . I will see you in Washington."

"Excellent . . . Take care of yourself, for God's sake—and meet me in Washington before nightfall."

"I will be there."

She took a pace back and saluted, as the man she loved vaulted into the saddle and rode off—mudstained, bloody, but invincible.

Only a mile or so ahead, the American troops were falling back in disorder, retreating as fast as possible to the safety—as they imagined—of the capital. Among them was a very distinguished figure, the American president, James Madison.

President Madison had left his wife at home in Pennsylvania Avenue, earlier in the day, and had ridden out to Bladensburg with General Winder to see the final outcome for himself—confident of victory.

Now, a sadder and wiser man, he returned in the gathering dusk, and as he rode along the highroad, he discussed the desperate situation with his private and confidential secretary, Harry Vanderburg, who cantered along briskly by his side.

"We must evacuate the city, Harry—as fast as possible. These Britishers will stop at nothing—the first necessity is to remove our women and children, and get them out of harm's way."

"But Mr. President—nothing is ready, no one in Washington will be expecting such a move," argued Vanderburg, a fat-cat burgher of Dutch origins. "Your good lady was planning a banquet tonight—in honor of our expected triumph over the enemy . . . And my wife has made plans to go to the theater this evening, I seem to recollect . . . This will throw them all into a fine turmoil."

"That cannot be helped. Our duty is to protect the inhabitants of the city—and we can best do that by packing them off, away from any area of danger. To turn back and fight would only be asking for further bloodshed—I cannot risk putting more innocent lives in jeopardy. A careful and controlled evacuation of the civilian population—without panic or hysteria—is the only course open to us now."

"In that case, Mr. President, I will carry out your orders, of course . . . You may rely upon me," said Vanderburg, and rode off at top speed.

Despite the President's well-meant plans, the city of Washington was already in a state of frenzy by this time, for the first news of the crushing defeat at Bladensburg had already reached Capitol Hill by mid-afternoon, and the word spread like wildfire.

"Our defenses have fallen . . . The city is wide open . . . The British are advancing!"

On all sides, a mass exodus was under way, as householders bundled up their most precious belongings into carriages, or upon hand-carts, and prepared for instant flight.

At the presidential mansion, everyone seemed to be quite stunned by the news—and the servants gazed at one another in blank disbelief.

There was the grand banqueting-room all ready and waiting for a splendid *soirée*—the long table laid with the best silverware and crystal, with places for two-score guests: the entire Cabinet and their wives, the senior military officers, and many more. The wine bottles were already in the coolers—and now it seemed that all these preparations had been in vain.

"What are we to do, ma'am?" the butler asked the president's wife—charming and fashionable Dolly Madison.

Dolly was at her writing desk, occupying her time at this desperate moment by penning a long letter to her sister.

"Will you believe it?" she wrote. "We have had a battle near Bladensburg, and I am still here—within sound of the cannon! Mr. Madison comes not . . . May God protect him."

Soon afterward, Harry Vanderburg arrived with the news of the president's express commands—and became very impatient when Dolly insisted that, if she had to abandon her home, she was certainly not going to leave behind the portrait of George Washington which hung in a place of honor on the dining-room wall . . . a portrait that had been screwed into position.

Everyone had to wait while the butler, the door-keeper, and one of the under-gardeners eventually broke the frame and removed the historic canvas. Then Dolly Madison swept up all the portable treasures that she could carry in her reticule, and climbed into the carriage to obey her husband's orders and remove herself to a place of safety, in Virginia.

As the carriage was about to drive off, Dolly said

through the window to Mr. Vanderburg: "Harry—what is to become of your wife? Would you not like me to take Esther with me, and look after her?"

Harry Vanderburg frowned, his fat lips pursing into a scowl.

"It's good of you to think of it, ma'am—but I can't allow you to run any further risks . . . You must leave this minute . . . And in any case, I don't rightly know where Esther is at the moment . . . She was intending to go to watch some play at the theater tonight—heaven only knows what she'll be doing now!"

Dolly sighed. "Pray God she's already left town . . . All right, tell the coachman to drive on."

As the presidential carriage bowled rapidly out of town, Dolly—even in the midst of her concern and preoccupation—noticed that men were at work outside the Ford Theatre, slapping stickers across the playbills which announced:

"Tonight's performance of 'The Lily of Killarney' has been canceled."

Inside the theater, on the darkened stage lit by one lamp only, an imposing figure was hurriedly packing theatrical costumes into a wicker basket. His shabby coat and beaver hat had seen better days, but his manner was majestic, and his voice rolled round the empty auditorium like a battlecry.

"For the love of dear, sweet heaven—" declaimed Dermot Maguire, with all the power of his Irish brogue. "Will no one come and give me a hand?"

"Coming, Dermot," came an answering call. "I'm on my way—what's the trouble now?"—and a young actor stepped out of the wings.

"The trouble is, you lazy puppy, that the girls have gone off in a state of mortal terror—the stage manager's getting drunk over in the saloon—the rest of the company are dispersed to all corners of the city—and there's no one to give me a hand, packing up the props and costumes, at all."

"There's no hurry, old man," said the youngster, perching himself nonchalantly on the corner of the basket. "Haven't you canceled tonight's performance anyway? Why don't you just go off and have a nice quiet snooze somewhere, and come back when all the shouting's died down?"

"And leave the entire inventory of the Dermot Maguire Touring Company to be pillaged and looted by a horde of English barbarians? Never—I'd sooner defend it with my life's blood!"

"Oh, come now—I can't think that the British army are going to take much interest in a few moth-eaten old robes and some wooden swords," smiled the young actor.

"Your compatriots, my dear boy, are not to be trusted . . . Liars and thieves, the lot of them—and I'm not giving them the chance to rob me. We must get packed up and leave town as fast as possible."

"Oh, no—not I!" The young man stretched luxuriously. as if he had all the time in the world. "You go if you like—I'm staying in Washington tonight—for I have an assignation, and it would be ungallant to break it."

"An assignation? What are you talking about—with whom, pray?"

"A gentleman never kisses and tells, but in this case I'll make an exception . . . I'm promised for supper to a certain Mrs. Esther Vanderburg, for her husband's off on important business somewhere, and she's feeling neglected. And after supper—well, I simply can't disappoint the dear lady, can I?"

"You shameless young buck—d'ye mean to tell me you'd stay here and risk your life for the sake of a woman's favors?" asked Dermot Maguire.

"I certainly would," said Gerard Mallory.

5

Washington Is Burning

"Then the devil take you—for I'm shocked and horrified by your reprobate ways . . ." The old man tried to continue with his labors, but his hands were shaking in a combination of fear and fury.

"As if it wasn't bad enough," he continued, "the way you've been making up to my two pretty nieces this long while, kissing and carrying on whenever I took my eyes off you . . . Now you must go fornicating with every loose woman and cheap whore that comes your way."

He tugged at the corner of King Lear's cloak, which Gerard was accidentally sitting on.

"Lift yourself, can't you?—you're crushing the nap of the velvet!"

Gerard laughed. "That velvet long since lost its nap— why don't you admit it's threadbare, like all the rest of the costumes and draperies?" But he raised his slim hips obligingly, and added: "And for your information, Mr.

Maguire—Esther Vanderburg is a lady of the highest position in the city . . . Her husband's got some important post, working for the president—so mind what you say of her!"

"If she flings herself at *your* feet, she can't be very particular," muttered old Dermot, over his shoulder.

Gerard stood up, carefully adjusting the line of his elegantly tight trousers over the largesse with which a benevolent Nature had endowed him.

"It ain't my feet she's interested in," he replied, cheerfully.

Dermot slammed the lid of the wicker basket shut, in a sudden fit of temper.

"Get out—go on—get out of my sight, you—you—libertine!" he roared, and his sonorous voice echoed through the empty theater. "You're dismissed—discharged—I won't have you in my company a moment longer!"

"You really mean that?" Gerard had the grace to look a little abashed. "You're giving me my marching orders?"

"Indeed I am. . . . And it was a bad day for the Maguire Touring Thespians when you first crossed my path in Wexford."

"Oh, come—I haven't served you so badly since then, old man—from Bassanio to Iago—not to mention a gallery of damfool squires and lords and seducers in all these tuppence-colored melodramas you love so much . . . Thank God, whatever happens to me tonight, at least I don't have to spout that old rubbish about 'Death or dishonor—take your choice . . . '!"

Almost purple with rage, Dermot Maguire exploded.

"I won't hear a single word against 'The Lily of Killarney'—it's a very fine play—and it always fills the pit at every performance! It tells a powerful, pious tale—and you'd be a better man if you believed in some of those moral speeches you had to 'spout' as you call it . . . Not to mention being a much better actor!"

"Now you're becoming personal," said Gerard, drawing

himself up. "Pray, what's wrong with my acting, might I ask?"

"Oh—I'm not complaining—you're a draw with the women—a good profile and a bulging pair of calves—you show off to advantage in tights—but looks ain't everything, and when all's said and done, you're an amateur, my boy—and you always will be!"

He fumbled in his pocket for a worn leather purse, produced a couple of gold pieces, and flung them contemptuously upon the bare boards of the stage.

"There—that's all the money owing for your salary, sir . . . Now take it and go—and bad 'cess to you!"

With all the dignity he could muster under the circumstances, Gerard stooped to pick up the money.

"Very well, Mr. Maguire . . . So, this is farewell—forever!" he declaimed, theatrically—slightly spoiling the effect by adding: "Oh, and by the way—give the dear girls a kiss, won't you? From yours truly."

Then he turned, and left the stage—and began to regret his impetuosity a moment later.

As he stepped from the safe shadowy world within the stage door into the bustle and clamor of the city streets, his heart sank a little . . . What on earth was he to do?

He had nothing—except the gold coins that jingled in his pocket, the clothes on his back, and a few more items of apparel and some clean underwear at his lodgings. Now it appeared that conditions in Washington were growing more and more desperate—on every side, agitated citizens were hauling carts or whipping up their pack-horses—all intent upon fleeing from the approaching British army.

"Where will I go? What shall I do?" Gerard asked himself.

Certainly, he had come many a mile since that faraway afternoon in Wexford, when he had first met Dermot Maguire in the Snug, and very soon after, had joined the troupe of strolling players. A great deal had happened to

Gerard since then; he had experienced all kinds of adventures, and learned many lessons—and he had fallen in and out of love . . . But that is another story.

One lesson he had studied diligently, and by now he was proficient indeed in the arts of love.

He reflected upon Esther Vanderburg's opulent charms —and at once his loins quivered expectantly at the thought, responding to the alluring image in his mind's eye. Despite the predicament he was in, he suddenly felt hopeful again, and turned his steps resolutely toward the Vanderburg's residence. Whatever else might befall him, there would be a sumptuous supper awaiting him there tonight . . . And an even more sumptuous diversion to follow the repast.

The outlook wasn't completely black after all, he decided.

The front door was opened to him by the good lady herself.

"Why, Mr. Kean—I declare, I was just this minute thinking of you!" she exclaimed, and drew him into the house.

Even after all this time, Gerard still felt a brief shock when he was addressed as "Mr. Kean." When he first joined the Maguire company, he had decided prudently to adopt a stage name—and since the tragedian Edmund Kean was then beginning to make a huge success at Drury Lane, old Dermot had elected to capitalize on his fame, and even let it be hinted that young Gerard Kean was a distant relative of the great man . . .

"Come in, Mr. Kean—come in at once—I must apologize for being so rude as to open the door to you myself, but the fact is—my servants have all taken fright, poor silly creatures, and run off to save their skins . . ."

"If only they resembled their mistress—they would have a skin worth saving," said Gerard, allowing his hand to hold hers for a moment longer than propriety would dictate.

"Why, Mr. Kean—you're a terrible tease!" Mrs. Vanderburg too was in a state of tension—but Gerard sensed that it was not only the national crisis that made her nervous. "I don't know what to say to you . . . I couldn't decide what to do for the best."

She led him into the parlor, offered him the best armchair, and settled herself upon a plump, overstuffed sofa.

Gerard hesitated for an instant, then smilingly sat beside her.

"Forgive me . . . This looks more inviting," he explained.

She fanned herself vigorously with an ivory fan, and returned his smile, a little tentatively.

Esther Vanderburg was certainly a very handsome woman; past her first youth, perhaps, but as richly bountiful as an overblown rose, with deep brown eyes that suggested both passionate sincerity—and an irresistible wickedness. Gerard found the combination very attractive indeed, and felt his trousers tighten at the automatic arousal of his desires.

"What I mean to say—" Esther let her eyes drop for a moment, and drew an involuntary breath, then continued as steadily as possible: "To say is—I wasn't sure whether I should see you tonight or not. Everything is in a state of chaos—I discovered that your engagement at the theater had been canceled . . . I wasn't even certain whether you might already have left town, Mr. Kean."

"Leave town—without even saying goodbye to you? Never!" exclaimed Gerard, inching nearer along the sofa. "Such conduct would be unthinkable . . . " He put one hand gently upon hers. "Besides, you were gracious enough to offer me supper, after the performance . . . Or has that invitation now been withdrawn?"

"I would never withdraw any invitation I gave to *you,* Mr. Kean," said Esther, demurely. As she spoke, she clasped her hands to her breast, seeming not to notice that his hand was still fondling her own. Gerard let his

383

fingers stray onto the smooth silk and lace of her corsage, as she continued talking. "A cold collation was prepared for you by the staff before they took to their heels—it awaits your pleasure, in the dining-room . . . That is—if you are already hungry?"

"I am in no special hurry," replied Gerard. "We actors are accustomed to take our meals at a late hour . . . Tell me—if all the servants have left—and your husband is away on business—"

"You have guessed correctly . . . I have to confess to you—we are quite alone in the house," said Esther Vanderburg, gazing at him wide-eyed over her fan.

Gerard's fingers ventured still farther into the ample delights of the lady's bosom.

"In that case might I suggest that we follow the usual custom, madam, and eat as originally planned . . . *after* the performance?"

Without more ado, Mrs. Esther Vanderburg opened her arms, all her defenses totally down—and welcomed the invader.

At the same instant, Washington itself was being violated; the city's defenses crumbled, and with barely any sign of opposition, the enemy forces rode in to take possession of the American capital.

General Ross, Admiral Cockburn, and Brock Savage led a small advance party into the empty streets as dusk was falling—Brock still mounted upon the little chestnut mare.

There was one momentary interruption, when a spatter of rifle fire greeted them—but the shots all went wide.

"Snipers—holding out in that house on the corner of the square!" Brock pointed. "Sergeant, take two men and put a stop to any further impudence."

"Very good sir." The men hurried off, and Cockburn called after them: "Set fire to the house when you've done—teach the blackguards a lesson!"

"We are under orders not to destroy any civilian property unnecessarily," Brock reminded him, but Cockburn said doggedly, "I consider it to be a necessity, sir . . . General Ross—I hope you agree?"

As usual, the General equivocated: "Our task as I see it is to negotiate—to come to some form of agreement with the American leaders—"

"Impossible, General!" Cockburn rose in the stirrups, easing cramped muscles after his unaccustomed ride on the borrowed farm horse. "Look around the city—ninetenths of the citizens have already deserted it . . . There's no one here to parlay with. Make an example of the place —set fire to every building—show 'em who's the victor!"

"Sir—that is against every rule of warfare—" Brock protested.

"Yes . . . I agree—at least in part," said the General. "We shall not attack any private dwellings—only buildings of military or national importance. Give orders, Admiral, that our men are free to burn and destroy any arsenals, barracks and suchlike—and the legislature—the House of Representatives, the Capitol, and so forth."

Brock knew that further argument was useless; he was in a subordinate position to the two senior officers, and he had no choice but to accept their commands without question. But his deepest convictions were offended, and he raged inwardly as he saw the British troops set out upon their long night of destruction and arson.

Cockburn rode off to encourage the men to their task, and it was the General and Brock who entered the presidential mansion in Pennsylvania Avenue, at the head of a small contingent of soldiers.

"Good God—look at that—!" exclaimed Ross, in amazement.

The mansion was empty, but in the gathering dusk, they surveyed the great banqueting room . . . The only sign of disarray was in the broken, empty frame upon one wall, where a painting had evidently hung until very recently. Apart from this, the long table was immaculate with white damask, laid with crystal and silver for forty guests who had never arrived.

"Light the candelabra," ordered Ross, and the men were quick to obey his bidding.

It was an eerie, unforgettable scene in the golden candlelight; even the wine coolers were stocked with bottles already chilled, and trays of empty glasses waited nearby.

"Here's a health to His Majesty—and the Prince Regent!" said the general, pouring himself a generous measure. "Gentleman—I give you the loyal toast!"

The men were not slow to follow his example, and the wine was soon dispatched. Then General Ross gave the order.

"Now—proceed through the rest of the building—and consign everything to the flames."

He took the lead by picking up one of the branched candlesticks, and hurling it at the window curtains. Within seconds, the mansion was on fire.

Brock Savage watched—sick to his stomach at the orgy of vandalism that ensued. The troops moved through the mansion like locusts, piling the furniture up for one mighty bonfire, or pillaging any minor trinkets they could lay hands upon—an embroidered silk scarf—a pair of shoe-buckles—even the wretched president's most private and confidential correspondence: the love-letters he had written to his wife.

Soon the night sky was glowing red from the light of the conflagration; the city was ablaze.

In the Vanderburg house, Esther left the double bed, and stood naked at the window—even her boundless sensuality distracted for a moment by this awesome spectacle.

"Gerard . . . See here—Washington is burning . . . " she said, as if stupefied. "Oh, what shall we do?"

"The fire is many streets away, don't worry." Gerard lay back, almost relieved to have a brief respite from their bouts of passion. "They're only attacking the government buildings—we're safe enough here . . . Come back to bed, my angel . . . "

"You really think they will not attack this house?"

She returned to him, wanting to be convinced that she had nothing to fear, and sat beside him; her hand traced the outline of his knee, his thigh, his masculinity—as if it moved of its own accord.

He slipped his arm around her, pulling her closer.

"Forget about the war . . . Forget everything else . . . Do you know that old poem—about gathering roses while ye may?" He stretched up to kiss her, and felt the stirrings of renewed excitement once more.

"Again—? Oh, Gerard—you're a darling, darling boy—but—do you really think we should—?"

"Of course . . . " He put his lips to her full, voluptuous breasts. "Who is to disturb us here—?"

In answer to his question, they heard the slam of the front door shutting, from the floor below—and they were both transfixed for an instant, as if turned to stone.

"The British—" said Gerard, hearing heavy footsteps climbing the stairs.

"Worse than that—it's my husband!" gasped Esther.

When Harry Vanderburg walked into the bedroom, his wife was alone in bed, the sheets modestly drawn up to her chin.

"You're still here?" he demanded incredulously. "Why in God's name didn't you get out while the going was good?"

"I didn't know what to do, Harry," she answered, breathing rather quickly. "I decided to—to stay here—and wait for you . . . "

"And go to bed?" he inquired, gazing round the room.

"Well—yes—I felt a little tired, you see."

"Oh, yes, I see . . . I see very well . . . The servants have all packed themselves off, I suppose? Left everything in a mess, no doubt?"

"Why, yes, Harry—they've all gone—"

The thickset Dutch-American paced at the foot of the bed for a moment.

"Sure, sure . . . Gone off and left the place untidy . . . Will you look at this? One of the footmen must have thrown his old boots in here before he went—couldn't even stop to pack a bag, I guess!"

And with his toe, he prodded at a bulging heap that was not quite concealed beneath the long crocheted bedspread . . . Not only a pair of boots, but breeches too—a shirt—a jacket—

"A whole change of clothes, dammit! Ye Gods—the rascal doesn't deserve to get them back, for his slovenliness . . . I reckon we'd do well to consign the whole lot to the British soldiers, and let 'em add this rubbish to their bonfires!"

As he spoke, he gathered up the bundle of clothes, opened the window, and flung them out into the street below.

"Why, Harry—what—what are you saying?" Esther stammered, turning very pale. "I don't understand—"

"Don't worry, my dear—because *I* understand, very well indeed . . . I understand everything."

Harry took two steps to the closet, and flung the door open. Inside, among a profusion of dresses, silks and satins, Gerard stood helpless—as naked as the day he was born.

"And who might you be?" demanded the injured husband, pleasantly. "I don't think I've had the honor of your acquaintance, sir."

"This is Mr. Kean, Harry—Gerard Kean, from the Irish players—and it's not at all what you think—I can explain—truly I can—"

"I don't really believe any explanations are necessary, do you, madam?" continued Harry Vanderburg. "I suggest you should take yourself off downstairs—I'll deal with you later . . . In the meantime, I'll have a few words with Mr. Gerard Kean . . . "

Esther began to scramble out of bed, and grabbed at her robe to cover herself, still babbling:

"Harry—please—let me tell you how it happened—"

"Oh, I think I can figure how it happened—all I don't know is, how often?" said Harry, smiling his fat pussycat smile. "Now get out, Esther, and leave us alone . . . You're beginning to bore me."

"But I—"

"I said get out!" he snarled with sudden venom, and she didn't wait any longer, but fled in disarray, wrapping her robe around her.

They listened to her stumbling downstairs, and then Mr. Vanderburg said with smooth—almost deferential—courtesy, "Won't you oblige me by stepping out of there, young man? It's hard to carry on a conversation with someone inside a clothes-closet."

Gerard, feeling extremely vulnerable, and not a little foolish, did as he was told, murmuring, "If I could put some clothes on, perhaps—"

"Unfortunately you have no clothes; I've just thrown them out—didn't you hear?"

"Yes, but—there must be something I can wear—I mean—anything at all—"

"Oh, there is . . . All in good time. But it won't hurt you to expose yourself just a little longer, I'm sure . . . I've no doubt you're very proud of your manly charms—since you take such pleasure in exercising them."

"Sir—! I admit you have every right to feel offended, but I see no reason why I should stay here and listen to your insults." Gerard squared his shoulders, defensively folding his hands before him at the same time. "I intend to leave this house immediately—"

"Like that?" Harry Vanderburg inquired politely.

"I shall find some garments elsewhere in the building, no doubt—and if you are foolish enough to try and stop me, I think I can give a good account of myself—unprotected as I am—"

"But what you don't seem to realize, Mr. Kean, is that you are in a very dangerous situation . . . Very dangerous indeed. For I shall not let you go so easily—"

"You can't stop me, Mr. Vanderburg—"

"Oh, I guess I can . . . I've got what you might call a trump card."

Harry took his right hand from his jacket pocket—and Gerard found himself looking down the muzzle of a pistol.

"It is loaded . . . And I hardly think anyone would raise any query if your body were found tonight, with a bullet in it—in the middle of so much carnage . . . Do you?"

Two seconds earlier, Gerard had been sweating with embarrassment; now, suddenly, he felt the sweat turn ice-cold upon his skin . . . He knew that Harry Vanderburg was not joking.

"What are you going to do?" Gerard asked him.

"I'm very tempted to dispose of you once and for all—just by squeezing the trigger, Mr. Kean . . . But I have a duty to my country—to my president—and I believe I can put you to a better purpose," he said.

"What do you mean?"

"You are an Irishman, I understand—but you're English-speaking—you could pass for English, I've no doubt?"

"Yes—of course—but why?"

"I'm glad to hear it . . . For you can make yourself useful. We need to know what the enemy plan to do—we need to find out their strategy, and you will obtain that information for us."

"You mean—you expect me to spy on the British—?"

"I don't expect it, Mr. Kean . . . I insist upon it . . . " He raised the pistol slightly, to press the point home. "When you leave here, you will make your way into the enemy lines, explaining that you are English—that you have been left behind in foreign territory, and that you need assistance. You will obtain all the intelligence you can, and you will report back to me with such intelligence within three days from now."

Gerard stared at him.

"Why should I report back to you? You can't make me—"

"Because, dear Mr. Kean, if you do not, I shall take great pleasure in informing the British command that they have a spy within their ranks—an Irish rebel in English guise—and you will quite certainly be shot, as a traitor."

"They won't believe you . . . " said Gerard uncertainly. "I shall tell them I'm an English gentleman—why should they believe that I'm in disguise?"

"Simply because you will be . . . They're hardly likely to credit the word of a man dressed up in woman's clothes . . . It's fortunate you're of a fairly short stature, Mr. Kean—you'll have no trouble, fitting into my wife's clothes . . . Come—no more talk—choose one of her gowns, and get yourself dressed . . . For you have work to do!"

Gerard was speechless. He tried to argue—but the words would not come. He realized that Harry Vanderburg had caught him in a trap from which there could be no escape.

Refuse—and be shot down in cold blood . . . Obey—adopt a female disguise and run the risk of exposure, disgrace and, in all probability, execution.

"Don't keep me waiting, Mr. Kean—I suggest that dove-grey silk will suit you very well . . . It will bring out the color of your eyes . . . "

Harry Vanderburg sat on the edge of the bed, the pistol aimed at Gerard's heart, as he continued: "You can say that you are the wife of a British officer who has become separated from her husband in the confusion, and is searching for him. With any luck, they might even believe your story. For your sake—I certainly hope so."

Like a doomed man, slowly—automatically—Gerard took the dress of dove-grey silk down from the peg . . .

The infantry were the last to arrive in Washington, and it was quite dark by the time Garnet reached the city center. For half a day she had been marching alongside the men, and now she was tired and frightened.

In spite of the late hour, the streets were bright with the glare of fires, and the troops—eager to join in the free-for-all—were impatient to be turned loose upon the wide-open city.

At the word of dismissal, they dispersed quickly, hastening off in all directions—in search of food, loot, liquor, or even, they hoped, women . . .

Garnet wandered on disconsolately, feeling very much alone, and totally lost.

Suddenly there was a blinding flash, and the ground shuddered beneath her feet. Then, a split second later, a series of deafening explosions—louder than any she had ever heard through all her experience of warfare in Spain. It was like an earthquake and a thunderstorm rolled into one. She threw herself flat upon the dirt road, and expected every moment to be her last, as the long crescendo of explosions continued, deafening her, echoing and re-echoing between the buildings. She put her hands over her ears, trying to blot out the noise, and shut her eyes against the blinding light of the flames that seemed to reach up and lick the sky. She remembered the devastation of San Sebastian, which had appeared to her as a city of hell. But if that had been hell, this was the inferno itself.

At last the noise abated, and the final echoes rolled away.

Totally panic-stricken, she scrambled to her feet and began to run—she did not know where—from one unknown terror to another—running blindly, without even looking where she was going . . .

Darting from one street to the next, she turned the corner, and charged headlong into a man who was standing under the portico of a private house.

"Hold hard, youngster—where d'ye think you're—"

He broke off—and then his arms closed around her, supporting her, bearing her up.

It was Brock. At the instant that she most needed comfort—reassurance—safety—here he was. She clung to him, her breath coming in great sobs.

"I didn't know where you were—or where I was—or what was happening . . . I've been so—so frightened . . . "

He held her tightly for a moment, then said quietly: "You're safe now . . . Good lad—take courage, for you're among friends."

Belatedly, she began to realize that he was not alone, and tried to pull herself together.

"I'm sorry—sir—I beg your pardon—I didn't think what I was saying . . . "

A small squad of British soldiers stood close at hand, escorting a stranger with one arm in a sling—a tall man, in the uniform of an American naval officer.

"This is Commodore Joshua Barney," Brock explained quickly. "The commodore realized that he must accept defeat after Bladensburg, and so surrendered himself to our forces. He had been wounded—but our medical men have given him their best attention."

"Indeed that's true," said the American. "I must own, sir, that from first to last, I have been treated by your officers with nothing but respect and politeness . . . As if I had been a brother."

"Why, that's the cruelest part of all," said Brock. "We speak the same language—we share the same heritage . . . Ten times over, during this black day, I have felt as if I were engaged in attacking my own family . . . "

"Was that the noise of our artillery just now, sir," General Ross asked, "continuing the assault on the city?"

"No, sir," interposed the American officer. "What you just heard was the noise from our final stronghold—the American navy yard, only a bare mile from here . . . Rather than let that prize fall into British hands, my men have blown it sky-high."

393

"Well, sir—I hope we may meet again one day, under happier circumstances," said Brock. "In the meantime, you must be held as our prisoner tonight, and as soon as we find suitable accommodation—"

"Permit me, sir," said a voice, and a thick-set man in civilian dress emerged from the shadows under the portico. "I was within doors, and I could not help overhearing your conversation. I think I may be able to assist you."

"How is that?" asked Brock. "Who are you? Might I know your name?"

"The commodore here will vouch for me," said the newcomer, "for he knows me well enough—we have met at many a staff conference, under Mr. Madison's leadership."

"Yes, sir—allow me to introduce you—Major-General Savage, this is Mr. Harry Vanderburg, the president's personal and confidential secretary."

"So, Mr. Vanderburg," said Brock, as they shook hands, "you too are placing yourself in our hands, as Commodore Barney has done?"

"Not exactly, sir—as a civilian, I have the right of a private citizen to be left unmolested. But it seems we must all bow to the inevitable—and I shall be happy to offer you, and the commodore—and anyone of your immediate entourage—shelter under my roof tonight. This war is monstrous—but we may at least try to behave in a civilized fashion toward one another—don't you agree?"

And so it happened that Garnet accompanied Brock, together with the prisoner and escort, as their host opened his front door wide, and they entered the Vanderburg residence.

They passed through the entrance hall. Garnet noted that the house was small but elegant, decorated with all the marks of feminine taste and discrimination.

As they walked into the parlor, Brock said to Mr. Vanderburg: "You have a very fine residence, sir, if I may say so."

"Thank you, sir—I certainly appreciate your compliment, but I can't take too much of the credit, for I leave that side of things entirely to my wife . . . Mrs. Vanderburg is upstairs at the moment, but I know she will be down to greet you directly."

Brock and Garnet exchanged glances, with slight surprise.

"Your wife is still at home, Mr. Vanderburg? Even at this hour of crisis? I imagined your house had been temporarily vacated—it never occurred to me that we would be imposing upon your domestic situation—"

"Don't give it another thought," said Harry Vanderburg, smiling like a cat that had just polished off a saucer of cream. "Mrs. Vanderburg will be delighted to make your acquaintance, gentlemen . . . She's the most hospitable soul on God's earth, I do assure you—"

He broke off as Esther Vanderburg, looking slightly pink and flustered, but with an unwavering smile fixed in place, came down the staircase and into the reception-room.

Introductions and explanations were effected, and then Harry continued: "I was just telling our friends, my dear —how very hospitable you are; why, only half an hour ago, she was actually entertaining another unexpected visitor—and a visitor from the British Isles, too!"

Esther shot her husband one stricken glance—but her smile never faltered.

"A British visitor?" Garnet repeated. "Why—how was that?"

"An unhappy lady—a Mrs. Kean—married to a British officer, and separated from her husband in the recent onslaught . . . We could not persuade the poor creature to stay any longer, despite all our entreaties—in fact, she left us quite suddenly, did she not, Esther?"

Harry turned back to Garnet and added carelessly: "What a pity you didn't arrive a little earlier . . . You only just missed her . . . "

6

Nightmare

The Vanderburgs were most hospitable people, Garnet thought—or at least, they seemed to be—and they had done all they could to make their British visitors comfortable for the night. Although Mrs. Vanderburg was certainly rather tremulous and distracted, her husband watched her with a strange, ironic grin that appeared almost cruel at times as she fluttered about the house . . .

Garnet was given a small bedroom on the top floor, too far from Brock's bedchamber for her to risk going in search of him. But the mattress was soft and the sheets were an unaccustomed luxury. Was it just because she longed for Brock's embrace that she could not get to sleep?

The last few days had been a very severe strain upon her, and Garnet's body felt as if it were on fire . . . She thought of Brock's strong limbs, and his tender embrace, and could find no solace in the smooth sheets and the cool pillows . . . She wanted to blot out the memory of recent horrors clasped tightly in Brock's arms . . .

When at last she fell into a restless doze, her dreams took on the quality of nightmare. She was running away —but from what, she could not tell. And somehow, at the same time, she was running toward something or someone—and she must reach her goal before it was too late.

It was Brock she was running to find, of course—it could be nobody else. But the night was dark, and on all sides faces came at her from the gloom—enemy faces, intent on stopping her, preventing her from finding her love.

An army sergeant, who put amorous hands upon her breasts . . . She shook him off and hurried on; then a ghastly leprous face rose up, with a crumbling jaw, and blood-red holes where the nose should have been . . . She screamed in terror—a silent scream, for no sound emerged from her lips. She wanted to cry for help, but no one could hear her. A series of violent thunder claps deafened her, and lightning bolts exploded before her eyes—then a huge rushing wind—and with the wind, a storm of snow . . . Millions of snowflakes, that quickly piled up around her in deep drifts, so that she could run no longer—her legs caught and dragged down by the weight of snow . . . Soon it would cover her completely, and she would suffocate.

Suddenly she saw Brock, far ahead—she heard the sound of a shot, and his horse reared up, to fall lifeless . . . Brock disappeared into the snowdrifts, and she could not reach him . . . She would never see him again—!

She awoke in terror to find the light of dawn at the bedroom window; she had kicked off all the covers, and lay sweating—for Washington in August was sultry indeed . . . How stupid to dream of snow, when the weather was so warm and oppressive.

Her head ached, and her heart ached as well; and the soft hair between her thighs was moist with desire . . . She wanted Brock so desperately . . .

Somewhere below, within the house, she heard sounds of movement, and forced herself to get up and begin the day.

At noon, she rode out at Brock's side; by now he had requisitioned a new mount—a dappled stallion that took a great interest in Garnet's chestnut mare. As they rode up Capitol Hill, the stallion made repeated attempts to nudge closer to the little horse, and when Brock controlled him sharply, the animal reared and curvetted, eager to display his sexual prowess.

Brock swore under his breath, then apologized to Garnet.

"The confounded brute's in a frisky mood . . . You'd better keep your young miss at a respectable distance, or she'll be in for a surprise."

"I think perhaps she is as eager as he," replied Garnet, and glanced at Brock with a clear message of love in her eyes.

He took a deep breath, and looked across at her—every line of his body expressing his tightly-controlled emotion.

"My dear . . . " he said very quietly. "We must be patient—just a little longer . . . There is so much work I have to do . . . "

As they rode, he talked of the problems which the unconsidered assault upon Washington had created.

"The men are uneasy—they're becoming superstitious, and saying that fate itself is against us . . . There have been too many deaths—unnecessary losses, for what should have been a bloodless victory. And most of them so damnably stupid. Do you know, a whole platoon of riflemen got drunk last night on rotgut American whiskey, and finished their orgy by jumping from a rooftop, swearing that they could fly? Eight were killed outright, and of the remainder four will never walk again, I'm told. Then an accursed tornado sprang up from nowhere, in the small hours, and whipped the tiles off several buildings. Some men were killed by flying debris, and others were crushed in their beds when a chimney stack fell, bringing the roof down on top of them . . . "

They turned into the wide sweep of Pennsylvania Avenue and the full force of the wind hit them, head on.

"I dreamed of a tornado last night—a mighty wind that roared in with thunder and lightning—and snowstorms—" Garnet began.

"I don't know about snowstorms, but the wind was no dream . . . It's blowing up with hurricane force . . . Bless my soul—look there—"

Brock reined in the impatient stallion, and pointed.

For a moment, Garnet thought her nightmare had come true, and that there was actually a blizzard in August . . . Then she saw what it really was: millions of tiny scraps of white paper whirled through the air, like an artificial snowstorm.

"When the government took to their heels, they were determined not to leave behind any documents that might assist us. Some painstaking clerks must have destroyed every official paper they could lay hands on . . . And look what our men have done to the president's mansion— dear God, what a mess . . . "

The great building stood, doorless and windowless, burned out and blackened by fire and smoke.

"It will need rebuilding, or repainting, at the very least . . . What destruction we have brought to this great city . . . "

Brock sighed, trying to imagine Washington as it had been—as, he trusted, it would be once again, when the invading army had departed.

"For we are not going to stop here another day," he told Garnet. "I think General Ross is already regretting his impetuosity; he has informed me that we are to pack up and march off tonight."

"March—tonight?" Garnet repeated, bewildered.

"Yes . . . It sounds equally rash, does it not? A night march imposed upon troops already weakened by sickness and exhaustion . . . But the man has determined that we must retreat, as soon as possible, and I could not talk him out of it. The quartermasters are going round the city at this moment, commandeering food supplies—meat, bread, flour—anything they can carry off. And we shall be on the move by nightfall. Ross calls it a strategic withdrawal. I call it one blunder compounded by another— but for God's sake, don't repeat that to anyone!"

He shared a swift, private smile with her, and leaned closer as the two horses sidled together. Instinctively, their hands met, and at his touch Garnet's whole body shuddered with a spasm of desire, as if she had been pierced by a sword. Brock's fingers closed around hers for an instant, and she knew from his face that he was suffering the same torture of frustrated longing.

Then a shout interrupted them; Mr. Vanderburg was riding up the avenue, and they moved apart . . . The spell was broken.

"Well, sir, I hear that you're to depart from Washington very shortly?" asked Harry Vanderburg, falling in beside them.

The three horses proceeded at an ambling jogtrot, as Brock replied.

"Yes, sir, that is correct. We have too much to do to sit back and rest upon our laurels. We must press on as fast as possible."

"Press on? Why—where are you making for? Or perhaps it's indiscreet of me to ask such questions?"

Brock tapped the side of his nose with one finger, and looked inscrutable, then said, "It's confidential, of course, but I know I can trust you not to let this go any further . . . We understand that there are troops based at Baltimore and Annapolis, and though I can't give away state secrets, I think I may say that we intend to pay one or two surprise visits, Mr. Vanderburg . . . "

Later, when they were alone for a moment during the afternoon's activity, Garnet asked Brock: "Do you really think you should have trusted Mr. Vanderburg? I know he's been very courteous and helpful, but he *is* the president's secretary, after all—"

"I wouldn't trust the man one single inch," said Brock cheerfully. "He's a two-faced rogue."

"But you told him of the plan to march on those other cities—"

"As a precaution—nothing more. For if Mr. Vanderburg should happen to pass on the news, I trust that the enemy forces will be so busy defending Annapolis and Baltimore, they will not cause us any trouble while we go back the way we came . . . To Benedict, where we first set foot on American soil!"

Brock smiled at Garnet's surprise, and added: "It doesn't do to take chances, you see . . . The whole city is thick with American informers—go-betweens . . . spies . . ."

Less than a mile away, Sergeant Chalky White was at his post, supervising the systematic looting of a warehouse, and badgering a sweating file of soldiers who were engaged in loading a wagon with provisions.

"Come on, come on—jump to it, lads—the sooner you get that lot packed up, the sooner we can be on our way, and out of this damned 'ole. Barker—look alive—stow them barrels of flour alongside the potatoes . . ."

He was standing on guard, at the entrance to the yard behind the warehouse, keeping an eagle eye on the lines of men who went to and fro, gradually filling the wagon with supplies.

Suddenly he was aware that he had been joined by a newcomer: a slight figure in a silk dress of dove-grey, with a voluminous mantle wrapped round her shoulders, and a matching bonnet pulled well down, shading her face.

"Good afternoon, ma'am . . . And what can I do for you?" he asked, springing to attention automatically.

Gerard took a deep breath, and plunged in.

He had decided that he must continue the ludicrous masquerade that had been forced upon him—at least until he had got through the lower ranks of the British troops. To try to explain his humiliating situation to the non-commissioned officers would be to risk disbelief—or even worse, downright suspicion. Some of these simple fellows, he had been told, were inclined to shoot first and ask questions afterward. With this in mind, he determined to request an interview with someone in authority, and then make a completely frank statement of his circumstances.

But first he had to persuade this infantry sergeant to pass him along to the commanding officer.

"Good day, sir," he said, using a nervous, light tone that he hoped would pass as female. "I need your help . . . For I am in a desperate predicament."

And that's true enough, in every respect, he added mentally. He had never felt so foolish—or so vulnerable—in his life. It did not make matters any easier that he was totally naked under his few flimsy garments—for Mr. Vanderburg had not bothered to furnish "Mrs. Kean" with underclothes when he hustled Gerard into the costume.

"Why, whatever's wrong?" asked Sergeant White, immediately sympathetic and protective at the sight of a damsel in distress. " 'Ere—you don't sound like no Yankee to me—where d'you come from, ma'am?"

"I—originally—well, from England . . . " stammered Gerard. Acting—speaking someone else's lines—was one thing; but having to extemporize his role was another matter altogether.

"I thought as much . . . So might I ask—'ow do you come to be 'ere—on foreign territory?"

Gerard remembered what Mr. Vanderburg had suggested, and clutched at the story for want of any better explanation.

"My name is Kean . . . I am a married woman," he rattled off the lies at top speed. "And my husband—Captain Kean—is serving with his regiment. I sailed out to America in the troopship, to be with him—"

"Newly-wed, I'll be bound? Couldn't bear to be parted from one another?" Chalky White sighed sentimentally. "I appreciate your feelings, ma'am—very right and proper, I'm sure."

"Only—in the confusion last night—during the attack on this city—we somehow became separated, and I lost Captain Kean . . . Will you please take me to your commander, so that I may tell him of my awful plight—for I am all alone, and very much afraid . . . "

Careful now, Gerard told himself. You're overplaying this part—don't get carried away . . .

But susceptible Sergeant White was completely convinced by the performance. His kind heart warmed to the unknown lady, and he responded at once, taking her hand in his own.

"Don't you fret yourself, my dear," he said in a fatherly manner. "You can 'ave confidence in me—Chalky White won't let you down."

"You're very kind, sir—" Gerard tried to withdraw his hand, without being too obvious about it, but found it wasn't as easy as he expected.

"Not at all, my love," Chalky continued, "for I'm always ready to do anything I can to oblige a pretty woman. Come inside the ware'ouse, my dear, and we'll discuss the problem . . . "

He drew Gerard gently but firmly in through the gateway, and then led the way into the main building, where more troops were at work, emptying the shelves.

"Step into the office, Mrs. Kean, and let's see what's best to be done to 'elp you . . . "

He shut the door as he spoke, and Gerard realized with dismay that he had escaped from the frying-pan only to fall into the fire . . . For Sergeant White's intentions were by now becoming all too apparent.

"Sorry we've only got one chair in 'ere," Chalky continued, pulling it out from the desk as he spoke. "But I dare say if we squeeze up a bit, we can both make ourselves pretty cozy—eh?"

And he put his arm round Gerard's waist and drew him down beside him on the chair.

"Please—Sergeant—I must ask you to behave yourself—" Gerard began to protest, but Chalky brushed these objections aside.

"Never fear, ma'am—you're as safe as 'ouses with me—for I'm a 'appily married man with a family of me own—an' if there's one thing I'm strong about, it's the sanctity of marriage . . . "

Even as he said this, his right hand was exploring Gerard's waist, his ribs, his flat, masculine chest—

" 'Ullo—!" Chalky frowned. "What's this 'ere—?"

"Let me go—" Gerard began to struggle, but it was too late. The sergeant's left hand was also in action by now—pulling up Gerard's long silk skirt—investigating beneath it—encountering a firm, hairy thigh—and despite all Gerard's attempts to stop him, prying further and higher still.

"Bloody 'ell—!" exploded the sergeant, outraged. "You're no perishing lady—!"

He let go of Gerard as if he had suddenly become red-hot, and snatched the bonnet from his head, revealing closely cropped hair and plainly masculine features.

"Let me tell you the whole story—" Gerard babbled, frantically trying to adjust his clothing. "I'm an actor—with the Irish players—I happened to become involved with—"

"You're a flaming Irish spy!" shouted Chalky White, scrambling to his feet. "Put your 'ands above your 'ead, you bloody traitor . . . You'll bloody swing for this!"

The retreat from Washington was another nightmare for Garnet. The officers rode at the head of the column of infantry as they marched out of the city under cover of darkness. Brock was somewhere in the lead, with General Ross, and Garnet herself was forced to take a position several hundred yards behind—unable to communicate with him, or even, at first, to see him in the gloom.

Then when they reached Bladensburg, and the battle-field that they had left only a short time ago, the moon came out from behind some clouds . . . And that only made matters worse. For by moonlight, the scene was illuminated in an unearthly blue-white glow that picked out every detail . . . The bodies of the dead men had been left behind to rot. Now stripped by the rapacious inhabitants of the little town, the corpses seemed to shine with a luminous radiance, their limbs contorted hideously, and their faces twisted into bloated masks.

Garnet closed her eyes and rode on blindly, trying to shut out the spectacle she had witnessed.

"How are you?" asked a low voice, and she gasped with relief, to find Brock beside her, on the dapple grey.

He had guessed at her feelings of horror, and made some excuse to ride back and rejoin her, even if only for a moment.

"Bear up . . . " he whispered. "The worst is over now."

But in one sense he was wrong; the worst was yet to come—for after this point in the journey the road petered out, and they had to make their way through thick forests, trying to follow a half-overgrown trail through dense undergrowth.

It was hard going, even for the officers on horseback, but for the foot soldiers it was a hundred times more difficult. Time and again the men lost their way in the darkness, stumbling from the path and finding themselves in a tangle of bramble or creepers—or worst of all, up to their knees in muddy swamps . . .

"Sir—" Garnet hesitated to make the suggestion, but she realized that she knew the route better than anyone else on the march, since by now she had followed it so many times. "If you'll permit me—I could lead the way, I believe . . . Will you ride with me, to blaze the trail?"

"In this murky darkness, the troops will still find it hard to pick up our tracks," Brock pointed out. "We can't leave signposts for them to follow . . . "

"Perhaps we could," Garnet said. "I seem to remember

—when I was young—a fairy story that my governess told me . . . Something about two children lost in a forest, and how they scattered a trail of breadcrumbs . . . ”

“What?” Brock frowned, half amused, half impatient. “We have no breadcrumbs—”

“We have barrels of flour in the wagon,” Garnet reminded him. “If we ride on ahead and leave handfuls of flour to mark the way we have taken, that might serve as well as any signpost.”

So it was that the British army retreated from Washington, along the line of the Patuxent River, following the white patches of flour that showed the pathway among the trees.

The long march continued throughout the night, and it was late the following day when at last they arrived at Benedict and the flotilla of British ships that were anchored offshore.

The sailors on board, seeing the advance party, set up a cheer of greeting. Garnet thought of Jem, and felt a chill of apprehension. If he were waiting for her, on board the *Tonnant*—if he tried to make any further trouble—she would have to carry out her threat, and denounce him to the authorities . . . Even if such a course led—as it inevitably must—to her own humiliation and exposure . . .

When she followed Brock up the gangplank, she kept a sharp look out for Jem—but could not see him anywhere. And yet—was it just her imagination?—she had the uneasy feeling that she was being watched; that Jem was under cover, close at hand, with his eyes fixed upon her . . . She could picture the expression on his face—steadfast determination to revenge himself upon her yet again; blind, stubborn desire—and she shivered, feeling the skin crawl at the back of her neck.

General Ross strode into Admiral Cochrane’s cabin, with Brock at his side; Garnet stood by the door, awaiting instructions.

The admiral thumped his fist upon the table.

“I am informed that you had the temerity to make an

attack on the city of Washington—despite my clear and detailed orders! Is this true, gentlemen? You disregarded the dispatch I sent you?"

"I received no dispatch from you, sir," replied General Ross. "And I decided I could wait no longer—I had to snatch the opportunity when it was presented to me."

"You—boy—Mallory, or whatever your name is . . ." The admiral turned a baleful glare upon Garnet. "Stand forth, lad—and tell me the truth. Did you or did you not deliver the letter I entrusted to you?"

Brock replied smoothly, on Garnet's behalf: "He arrived at Bladensburg when the battle was already at its height, and the enemy on the run . . . I took it upon myself to inform the boy that the message had come too late . . . The decision had already been taken and acted upon."

"Here is the letter, sir . . . Still as you gave it to me," said Garnet, producing the document, with its seal unbroken, very creased and grubby, from the recesses of her tunic pocket.

"I see . . . I should require your officers to punish you for having failed to deliver my message—" the admiral began, but General Ross interposed.

"Under the circumstances, sir—do you not think the omission might be justifiably overlooked? For we took Washington: the attack was victorious, and the Yankees are still licking their wounds."

"Well . . . You may be right . . . Though, indeed I think you were more fortunate than prudent, General . . ." The admiral recollected Garnet's presence and added hastily: "Very well, Ensign—you are dismissed. You may return to your duties."

"What would my duties be, sir?" Garnet asked uncertainly, looking to Brock for enlightenment.

"Go to my cabin, on the deck below, Mallory," Brock said crisply. "I will deal with you later . . . Wait there till I come to you."

Garnet saluted, and left them to confer together, thankful to have got off so lightly. As she ran down the companionway, she sensed the same eerie feeling that she was being watched—and whirled round, defensively—but there was no one in sight.

She went into Brock's cabin, and sat there waiting . . . willing him to finish his business and come to find her very soon. In fact, it was no more than ten minutes before the door opened and he came in, starting to strip off his uniform even before he was inside the cabin.

The moment the door shut, she was in his arms.

"Oh, Brock—at last . . . I've waited for this moment so long—" she whispered, giving herself up to the rapture of his arms about her . . .

But he pushed her gently from him, saying: "My dearest girl—there is no time, even now. Ross and I have only returned to our cabins to wash and change into fresh uniforms. We have a long evening ahead of us—a staff conference, a plan of campaign to map out over dinner, and a hundred and one routine duties that must be attended to."

"And what about me? What am I to do, while you are so busy?" she asked, trying to cling to him.

"You must go back to your quarters, on board the *Enterprise,* where you were before this confounded upheaval—"

He broke off as a knock at the door heralded the arrival of a sailor with a can of hot water for Brock's ablutions.

When they were alone again, Brock continued to undress, saying, "You can help me by pouring some water into the wash-basin—and take care it's not too hot; I don't wish to be scalded . . . Put out soap and a towel, and then wait till I've finished, like the dear good girl that you are."

She obeyed—but mutinously, muttering: "I don't want to be a dear good girl . . . I want *you* . . . I want to be with you all the time—"

She looked at him as he began to wash; he stood half-

409

naked, his broad shoulders tanned and powerful as he stooped over the basin—his strong forearms lathered with soapsuds, his handsome face shining as he rose dripping from the water, groping for the towel.

"Where—?" he began, blindly.

"Here . . . " she said mischievously, placing herself between his outstretched arms. "Here I am!"

He pulled her toward him, and opened his eyes, their faces only an inch apart.

"You'll get wet," he said gruffly.

"Do you think I care about that?" she asked, and put her face up to his.

His mouth closed upon hers, and his tongue thrust fiercely between her parted lips. Their pent-up longing burst from them like a flood that breaks down a dam, and he uttered a strange, choking sound, somewhere between laughter and relief, as he pulled her to his bare chest, still running with droplets of water.

They could not kiss enough, or hold each other close enough; they could not stop feeling one another, caressing and clinging to one another, running their hands over one another as if they would never be parted again. Abandoning herself to this delirium of passion, Garnet felt him tearing at her clothes, and could not wait for the moment when she was naked with him—lying upon his bed, beneath him, above him, giving herself to him in every way . . . Her own fingers urged him on, plucking at the waistband of his breeches, unbuttoning, unfastening . . .

A knock at the door shocked them both into awareness.

"Savage—? Are you fit and ready?" asked General Ross from the passageway outside.

"In—in a moment . . . " Brock's voice was breathless and unsteady.

"Very well—I'm going up to join the old man—I'll see you there," said Ross, and they heard his footsteps retreating.

"Oh, Brock—don't go—now—*now*—!" she begged him.

He kissed her once more, with a hunger that matched

410

her own, then said huskily, "This is madness . . . I must go . . . "

"Don't send me back to the *Enterprise*—let me stay here tonight, for God's sake—with you—" she gasped.

"Of course . . . you shall not be away from me for one moment more than I can help . . . Wait here: I will be as quickly as I can."

He contrived to put on his clean uniform at top speed, then ran his fingers through his hair, and asked, "How do I look? Not too disreputable?"

"You look like a king among men," she replied with complete sincerity.

He put his finger under her chin, lifted her mouth for one last kiss, and was gone.

She wiped a trace of soapsuds from her cheek—and suddenly decided that she, too, needed to freshen her appearance. She had no change of uniform here, but at least she could be clean and sweet for Brock when he returned. The water in the basin was still warm. Swiftly, she began to peel off her clothes.

On the main deck, Brock followed Ross into the principal Stateroom, where they were to dine with the other senior officers.

Admiral Cochrane looked up as he entered, and smiled.

"Come here, sir—and sit by me . . . For I have some special instructions to give you, which I think may be pleasing to you."

"Sir?" Brock took his place beside the old admiral. "More sealed orders? I hope that you do not intend to follow up our success in Washington by making a sortie against Baltimore?" he added, semi-seriously, and glanced at General Ross who sat at the other side of the admiral.

"No, no—I think we are content to let sleeping dogs lie, eh, Ross?" asked Admiral Cochrane, smiling.

"Yes, indeed—I wouldn't be so foolhardy as to attempt a second assault of that kind . . . Certainly not so soon, at any rate," replied the general.

"I'm glad to hear it . . . For I do most earnestly beg you not to entertain such a notion," said Brock. "Another victory like Washington might well destroy us!"

Ross frowned slightly, and looked away, unwilling to be drawn into this discussion, even on so friendly a level.

"Rest assured, Savage, you may go back and report to Lord Bathurst that we have no intention of capturing Baltimore," Admiral Cochrane continued. "Tell him that, with my compliments."

"Lord Bathurst—the secretary for war?" Brock stared at him. "But surely—Bathurst is in London—?"

"Quite so, my dear chap . . . And that is where I require you to go, also. Someone has to report back with the news of our victory in Washington; and General Ross and I have both agreed that you shall be the bearer of these tidings. The fast frigate *Iphigenia* arrived today from Portsmouth, and I intend that when she returns to England, she will take you with her—together with our official dispatches."

Brock was speechless; this news had taken him completely by surprise. He turned to Ross for further confirmation, and the general said rather irritably, "Yes, yes—it's all arranged, my dear chap . . . You're the best man to go—much as I regret losing your invaluable advice and assistance and all that—we'll have to manage without you, somehow."

The thought flashed through Brock's mind: He's glad to get rid of me . . . I spoke my mind once too often, and he doesn't like having his errors pointed out . . . Damme, I half believe he *does* plan to go for Baltimore, after all—!

But General Ross was changing the subject.

"Now, sir—before we get down to any detailed discussion, there are some matters of business to be cleared away . . . The daily orders must be dealt with—oh, and there's a little question of espionage that has to be tackled."

"Espionage?" Brock repeated. "It's the first that I've heard of it."

"I was only informed myself a short while ago. It seems that one of your sergeants apprehended an Irish spy, trying to infiltrate our ranks . . . A young mercenary by the name of Kean—in the pay of the Yankees, obviously . . . He had the gall to dress up in women's clothing and try to pass himself off as the wife of an English officer!"

"Very regrettable," said Brock, solemnly.

"It's no laughing matter, if that's what you mean . . . At any rate, your Sergeant White picked the fellow up and brought him along on the march from Washington, under close arrest. He's here now, in one of the punishment cells below decks, awaiting trial. I propose that you should deal with the man as he deserves . . . It's a mere formality, after all."

In Brock's cabin, Garnet had just completed her toilet, and was drying herself with the towel. The scented soap smelled like perfume upon her skin, and she imagined for a moment the pleasure of being able to step into a petticoat . . . stockings . . . a silk dress . . .

She looked at her image in the little mirror as she enfolded herself in the towel—dreaming that the rough white cotton was a shimmering veil of lace. It was strange to realize that Brock had never seen her in feminine attire . . . She cupped one hand beneath the curve of her breasts, and considered her reflection . . . Would she be pretty enough to please him, as a woman?

She stopped short, listening, at the sound of a faint tapping . . . Someone was knocking at the door.

Quickly, she covered herself with the towel, and asked: "Who is it? Who's there?"

Silence . . . And then, a moment later, another quiet tattoo upon the door.

"Who are you? What do you want?"

413

A longer silence, and further tapping—very gently, so that no one else should be disturbed. Whoever it was, he did not wish to draw attention to himself.

She stood uncertainly for a moment. Could it be Brock, back from his meeting already, announcing himself in this playful style? She made up her mind, and crossed to the door, opening it just an inch.

Immediately, the door was pushed out of her grasp, and flung wide open—and Jem Bolt walked straight into the cabin.

"*You!*" she gasped. "How dare you—how dare you spy on me—and follow me—"

He shut the door, and gazed at her; looking her up and down with exactly the same expression of determination that she had anticipated.

"I got to talk to you—urgent-like—" he began.

"You must be insane . . . " She retorted. "I gave you fair warning—I told you what would happen if you ever dared to come near me again—get out of my way, for I'm going to fetch help—"

He grabbed her arms. The towel slipped and fell, uncovering her breasts. She felt a stab of anger, knowing that her hard, erect nipples betrayed her physical excitement—and knowing that he must be aware of it too.

His eyes flickered over her bosom, and he licked his lips—but he still continued with what he had to say.

"Don't be a fool, Garnet—do you listen to me, for 'tis a matter of life and death . . . It's about your brother . . . He's here."

"*Gerard?*" She stared at him. For a moment, she really believed that he *was* insane—stark, raving mad. "What do you mean—he's here? That's impossible—you're lying—let go of me—"

Doggedly, Jem managed to give her the bad news that had to be told.

"I seen Master Gerard only half an hour since—in the cells . . . He's been arrested like—as a spy and a traitor . . . They say as how he's to be tried by court martial . . . And tomorrow at first light, he'll be took ashore and strung up to the branch of a tree, and hanged by the neck, until he be dead . . . "

7

Daylight and Champagne

Quite suddenly, Garnet knew without any shadow of doubt that Jem was not mad, nor was he lying to her . . . Incredible as it seemed, he spoke the truth, and Gerard was on board this ship, awaiting trial—and execution . . .

"How do you know this? When did it happen?" she asked, trying to marshal her thoughts.

"I seen him brought on board, between two soldiers, with a sergeant walking behind. His hands were tied, and —I don't know for why—he was dressed in women's clothes . . . "

She stared at him, trying to make sense of this amazing news.

"Gerard—dressed as a woman? But why?"

"I couldn't tell you . . . All I do know is, they do say he's an Irish spy . . . He were caught last night, and brought here for trial, seemingly."

Garnet made up her mind.

"I must go to him—can you take me where he is?"

"Aye, that's why I did come to find you . . . I'd have stayed out of your way else—after—you know . . . "

He reddened, and turned his head away, scratching the rough blond whiskers on his chin.

Garnet had already begun to get dressed as quickly as possible, putting aside any feelings of modesty or shame in this moment of crisis. But now one thought gave her pause. As she pulled on her shirt and started to button it, she asked curiously:

"You knew that I would keep my word and have you punished if you came to me again . . . And yet you decided to risk it nonetheless—why was that?"

He would not look at her, but stared at the wall, his ruddy face darkened still further as he muttered: " 'Cos I do love you, Miss Garnet . . . And Master Gerard's your brother. . . . And I couldn't stand by and do nothing, could I?"

She finished dressing, straightened her tunic, glanced at herself once more in the mirror, and said, "Very well— I'm ready . . . Take me to him . . . And—Jem—"

He had his hand on the door, about to lead the way.

"Yes, miss—?"

"Thank you." And she kissed him once—swiftly and sweetly—before they set out together.

The cabin cell was in the bowels of the ship, opening off the hold; the place smelled of sweat and urine and filth, and Garnet felt her gorge rise as Jem gave instructions to the soldier who stood guard at the door.

"This here's the young officer what's come to question the prisoner—you're to let him in," Jem explained.

The soldier accepted this without curiosity, and selected a heavy key from the ring which hung from his waist, then unlocked the door.

Garnet walked in, and as the door slammed shut behind her, and she heard the key turn in the lock again, she wondered how she would ever escape from this death trap.

As her eyes became accustomed to the dim light from the candle-end that sputtered in a pool of melted wax, she recognized Gerard, and her heart turned over.

Attired in a woman's gown, with a crushed bonnet lying beside him, he sat on the single wooden stool, without hope, without even—it seemed—enough interest to look up at his unknown visitor. He should have presented a clown-like figure in his ridiculous costume—tattered and smeared with mud and dust as it was—but his head hung in an attitude of complete despair, and Garnet felt an overwhelming sense of pity and sympathy.

She took a pace toward him, saying softly: "Gerard . . . Don't you know me?"

He raised his head slowly, as if in a dream—and stared —and stared again, unable to believe his eyes.

"Garnet—it *is* you—isn't it?" he asked, in a flat voice that was drained of all emotion.

She nodded, and put her hands upon his shoulders.

"It seems we have both put ourselves into bizarre situations, my dear," she said, and tried to smile, though she felt close to tears.

"Dear God—what are you doing here? And in that uniform—?"

"Your uniform, Gerard . . . For I took over your place in the army when you went off to join Bella . . . I have served as Ensign G. Mallory all this while—and I have the documents to testify to it . . . "

"You—serving as a soldier—?" he repeated, blankly. "I don't understand—"

"And I don't know how you come to be here in your disguise—but there is no time to explain that either. We must act fast, my dear, if we are to save you."

"What do you mean?"

"They claim that you are an Irish spy, but we know that's not true. You are Ensign Gerard Mallory—and we can prove it!" She began to unbutton her tunic. "Quickly now—get out of that dress, and exchange clothes with me, for there is no time to be lost."

He did not understand all she said, but the general meaning was clear enough, and as he saw Garnet turn away from him and begin to pull off her uniform, he followed her example.

They talked quickly as they undressed, back to back, throwing words over their shoulders, and tossing their clothes in a little pile beside them, a garment at a time.

"Bella left me long ago," Gerard explained. "I joined an Irish theatrical troupe—I have been an actor ever since—and then we came on a tour of America . . . New York—then Washington—"

"You—an actor? Perhaps the talent must run in the family, after all—for I suppose I have been acting a part ever since I ran away from home . . . " said Garnet.

Totally naked, she stooped to deposit her shirt on the pile of clothes, and Gerard bent to do likewise, at the very same moment. Their nude hips touched, and they both straightened up involuntarily, turning to look at one another.

For a long moment, neither moved nor spoke. They had not seen one another undressed since that day—so very long ago now—when they both went swimming in the fishpond . . . And they had both grown up since then.

"You're a man, Gerard . . . " she breathed at last.

"Garnet—you're a woman—" he said. "A lovely woman . . . "

Slowly he raised his hand—tentatively he took a step closer to her, and touched her smooth, full breasts . . . And as if drawn by some blind instinct beyond their control, they moved together, brother and sister, in an embrace that held a strange joy which, neither of them had ever known before.

For a few seconds they clung together and kissed—almost as though they were two halves of one soul, reunited at last . . . Then they broke apart, and smiled.

That was all that happened between them, but it was an instant of deep, indescribable love which they would both remember for the rest of their lives.

"We must make haste," said Garnet finally. "Put on the uniform—and I must do the best I can with this old dress of yours . . . For shame, Gerard—don't you wear any undergarments at all?"

"I had no choice," he apologized. "I was forced into the costume at gun-point—by an irate husband!"

She bit her lip, and tried to appear shocked, as she slipped into the dress, and began to fasten it up.

They had only just completed their exchange when there was the sound of a key in the lock, and Garnet caught her breath.

"Now keep your wits about you," she said quickly. "And pray—!"

The door swung open, and Brock Savage stepped into the narrow cabin.

He took one long, comprehensive look at the two figures that confronted him—then turned to the soldier who stood jailer outside, and said, "Very well—you may leave me to deal with this . . . Shut the door."

The door thudded behind him, and he continued in the same even tone: "My dear Garnet—would you be kind enough to tell me what the devil is going on here?"

"Yes, Brock . . . " She lifted her chin bravely, and began. "Allow me to present my brother—Ensign Gerard Mallory, of the Third Dragoons . . . Gerard—you may show Major-General Savage your papers—they are in the left-hand pocket of your tunic."

Between them, they somehow managed to pour out the whole explanation, and when they had finished Brock sat on the wooden stool, trying to digest what he had just been told.

"A woman—who is a man . . . And a boy—who is really a girl . . . I don't know what to say to you—it's like something from a play—"

"It's like the end of an old comedy—" Gerard suggested, and quoted: *"Daylight and champain discovers not more . . . !"*

"There speaks the actor," Garnet smiled at her brother.

"You always had a good grounding in Shakespeare."

"Shakespeare be damned—what am I to do with the pair of you?" Brock demanded. "I'm supposed to be presiding over a court-martial in half an hour, Gerard Mallory—to charge you in your alias of 'Mr. Kean' with espionage and treachery—"

"That won't be necessary now," Garnet interrupted. "For you see that there is no such person as 'Mr. Kean'—there is only Ensign Mallory, who has served you faithfully for many a long day, and you may certainly vouch for his loyalty."

"I see . . . " Brock began to relax a little. "And what of you—'Mrs. Kean,' or whoever you are—in your bedraggled finery?"

"There is no 'Mrs. Kean' either . . . There is only Garnet—newly-come from England—to join the man she loves . . . "

Garnet put her hands in Brock's, and concluded: "The man she hopes some day to marry—if he will have her . . . "

For answer, Brock rose to his feet and embraced her.

"What should I do without you?" he asked, adding to Gerard: "You will forgive this moment of informality, I trust, my dear sir—since we are soon to be members of the same family?"

"You have my sincere congratulations, sir," said Gerard, and for the first time in his life he clicked his heels to attention and sketched a salute.

"How do you think you will take to a soldier's life, Gerard?" Garnet asked, smiling.

"I have played a great many other parts in my time—the role of a military man shouldn't be altogether beyond my powers," he replied. "One thing's certain—it beats playing a death scene any day!"

So matters were speedily arranged. Brock called for the jailer outside to open the door and release the "prisoner"; in the dim light, the soldier did not even notice any change—a woman and an ensign had gone into the cell, and a woman and an ensign came out of it, escorted by the major-general, who took full responsibility for them both.

Two dinghies were launched—one to take Gerard across to the *Enterprise,* where he had temporary quarters all ready and waiting for him—and if anyone aboard should query this, he had the documents to prove his identity, and a safe-conduct pass from Major-General Savage to back them up—and the second boat was to row Miss Garnet Mallory, the major-general's fiancée, out to the fast frigate *Iphigenia* which rode at anchor in deep water, some half-mile farther down the estuary, awaiting her return voyage to England.

When Garnet set foot on board the frigate—impatient with the long dress that clung round her ankles and made it difficult for her to clamber up the rope ladder over the ship's side—she made herself known to the captain, explaining that Major-General Savage would be joining her before long.

The captain had his wife with him on the vessel, and this good lady made a great fuss of Garnet, as soon as she set eyes on the condition she was in.

"My dear—your dress—your bonnet—your shoes are quite ruined—what ever has happened to you?"

Garnet improvised rapidly. "I met with a slight mishap on shore, madam; I landed in America under very trying circumstances, and all my luggage has gone astray . . . You must forgive my appearance, I beg of you—I had a long, difficult journey from Washington, during the military retreat . . . "

"You actually traveled all that way—in the company of a regiment of soldiers? Oh, you poor soul—what a truly fearful ordeal for you—how ever did you survive it?"

Garnet could find no satisfactory answer to this question, but luckily no answer was necessary, for the captain's wife was running on sympathetically.

"Come with me, Miss Mallory—I will take you to my cabin, and you shall borrow any clothes you require . . .

They may not be quite in your size, but at least they will give you something clean and fresh to wear during the voyage home . . . Please take anything that you've a mind to, my dear—you are very welcome."

Garnet picked out a simple day dress of green watered silk—and remembered the ball-gown she had worn to the ball in Guildford, a lifetime ago . . . Bella had said that green was an unlucky color, and it was true that she had had her share of misfortunes since then—but had she really been unlucky? She thought of Brock—and she knew that she had had all the luck in the world.

When Brock came into her cabin aboard the *Iphigenia* the following morning, he found Garnet looking as he had never seen her before; her short curling hair trimmed with a ribbon, and the simple green dress showing off her soft, feminine outline to advantage.

"Well, sir—?" she asked, her eyes dancing. "How do I look? . . . Not too disreputable?"

He recognized that she was teasing him, and capped her quotation.

"You look like a queen among women . . . No—a goddess," he replied, and took her in his arms.

"I like to look well—for you," she said, pressing herself to him. "Now that I know you enjoy seeing me in pretty clothes, I will always try to wear them."

"Not always," he corrected her, and squeezed her gently. "Sometimes I enjoy seeing you *without* your pretty clothes even more . . . "

"Then we must do something to remedy that," she said, and made a move as if to unfasten her bodice, but he stopped her.

"All in good time, my dearest," he said. "First—I have news for you."

"More news? What has happened now?"

"Don't be alarmed—nothing untoward . . . Except that —after what you told me about your erstwhile stable-lad —what was his name again?"

"Bolt—Jem Bolt . . . What about him?"

"I made inquiries before I left the *Tonnant*—I felt that I should at least speak to the young man, and perhaps reward him for his part in rescuing your brother last night . . . But I had no luck."

"I don't understand—couldn't you find him?"

"I was informed that some time yesterday evening, Master Jem must have taken himself off and gone ashore without permission . . . He's jumped ship, for some reason; perhaps fearful that he would get into trouble, for his part in these events . . . Whatever the reason, it seems that your Jem Bolt has bolted indeed!"

"Not for the first time . . ." Garnet remembered. "But what will become of him—alone in a foreign land?"

"I dare say he's able to fend for himself. Though it's strange he should have taken to his heels, for it appears to me that he had shown you nothing but kindness—he has done you good service, has he not, Garnet?"

Garnet bit her lip, then replied slowly: "Yes . . . Yes—I think perhaps that is true . . . God be with him, wherever he is . . ."

"And may God go with Gerard as well. I saw him briefly before I left this morning—we exchanged good wishes and I commended him highly to General Ross—for of course he will be serving with the general from now on . . . Let us hope he proves to be as good a soldier as his sister—eh?"

Garnet tried to smile.

"Poor Gerard . . . I pray that all will go well with him . . ."

"Take heart—he will survive, I'm sure—he has a whole new life of adventure ahead. I feel confident that we shall hear great things of young Gerard Mallory, before very long. And lastly—but by no means least—"

As he spoke, Brock produced a package, carefully wrapped and sealed with many seals.

"This parcel has followed you halfway round the world. It was addressed to Ensign G. Mallory, and arrived yesterday with the mails, aboard this very ship. However, when it was passed on to Gerard this morning, he opened the accompanying letter, and he told me that he feels sure it was never intended for him . . . Almost a love letter, he declares—from an old friend . . . "

Brock handed the letter to Garnet; she scanned it rapidly and found her eyes suddenly brimming with tears.

"It's from Edmund—" she explained. "Captain Challoner—he must have written it as soon as he returned to England; this letter has chased me all the way to Bermuda—and now here . . . How very strange . . . He wishes us both well in our new life—"

"He realized about me, then? You never told me that."

"I never told him either—but he had seen us together —and he watched me ride off to join you, that last afternoon at St. Jean-de-Luz . . . I suppose it wasn't hard to guess . . . He says he will always remember me with love and gratitude, and—he says that in my hasty departure I left something behind—something that I may have need of, in the future . . . "

Impatiently, she tore at the package, ripping off the paper and string—and drew out the white lace veil that Brock had bought for her, before they left Europe.

"Oh, Brock—look—it's as beautiful as ever—and I thought that I had lost it!"

She held it up, laughing for joy, and looked at Brock through the flurry of white lace—as if she were seeing him through a cloud of snowflakes . . . She remembered her dream—Brock, separated from her in a snowstorm— and swiftly threw the veil over her head, pulling him toward her.

"Never let me go . . . Never again—" she breathed.

From somewhere outside the cabin, at water-level, they heard a splash, and the rattle of an iron chain.

"They've weighed anchor—we're sailing," Brock said, holding her tight. "Come, let's go on deck and say our farewells to America."

Outside, it was a gloriously sunny morning; the best weather they had known since they had come to the New

World. Seabirds wheeled and called against the cloudless blue sky, their plumage dazzlingly white in the sunshine. Garnet and Brock stood together at the ship's rail, looking back at the shoreline as it began to fall away behind them.

"Goodbye, Maryland," said Garnet. "I'll always be grateful to you . . . "

"Grateful—for what?"

"For giving me back myself . . . For turning me into a woman again—so I could be here with you, like this . . . "

He put his arm round her waist, and smiled.

"I don't know whether to thank Maryland for that—but I certainly thank God, in all sincerity," he said.

Approaching footsteps across the deck made them turn, and the ship's captain, looking very slightly agitated, came up to join them.

"Major-General Savage, I believe? I'm very glad to have the pleasure of your acquaintance, sir. Miss Mallory informs me that you are sailing back to England with us . . . Very pleased to have you aboard, of course, but . . . " He cleared his throat. "There is one slight—ah—problem . . . "

"What problem might that be, Captain?" asked Brock.

"I understand that you intend to—ah—share a cabin with Miss Mallory—which presents certain difficulties, you see, since the young lady is after all only your fiancée."

His voice trailed off into an embarrassed silence.

"That need be no problem at all, sir," Brock assured him genially. "For I believe that you will be able to regularize the situation as soon as we are out at sea . . . As captain of this vessel, you are authorized to perform a marriage ceremony, are you not? And as you see—my fiancée is already wearing her wedding-veil."

When night fell, the deep blue canopy of the sky was embroidered with a million jeweled stars, and the *Iphigenia* rode serenely across the ocean, making her way home.

Garnet and Brock retired to their cabin early and shut

the door behind them. On the table stood a bottle of champagne, with two glasses beside it, and a handwritten note. Brock read the message.

"From the captain and his good lady—with their best wishes for our happiness."

"They've been wonderfully kind . . . I still can't believe it's all happened so easily . . . I really am your wife, Brock."

"You really are . . . It's happened—and it will go on happening, for as long as we live."

He struggled with the cork for a moment, and then —pop!—it shot out with a triumphant explosion, as the wine frothed over the neck of the bottle. Brock filled the two glasses, and handed one to his bride.

"Here you are . . . Mrs. Brock Savage," he said, raising his own glass in a toast. "Here's to us—to this moment— and to our lifetime together."

They both sipped the dry, heady wine, and then he added, very softly: "It's time for bed . . . "

Slowly and carefully, they put the wine glasses aside. Slowly and carefully he helped her to undress, removing her clothes without any haste, watching her all the time with adoration in his eyes . . . Eyes that were ice-blue no longer, but blue as the flames from a frosty log when it is consumed by fire—a deep, intense blue, burning with love.

She stood naked before him at last and held out her arms, offering herself to him.

He looked at her for a moment, then in one easy movement he picked her up and carried her onto the bed that awaited them. It was the first link in the chain of love that was to bind them together—not only through this night of passion, but for all the days and nights that were to come.

As their bodies touched, and took fire—as they clung together, needing one another, and satisfying one another —as he embraced her again and again, raising them both to new heights of ecstasy—she gave a little sigh.

At once, he paused, alert for any sign that she might give, by any move she made, or any sound she uttered.

"What is it?" he asked swiftly. "What's the matter?"

"Nothing's the matter. I'm happy—so very happy, my darling . . . Except . . . "

She hesitated, and he pursued: "What? Tell me . . ."

"Except—I can't help wishing—just a little—that this was the first time . . . "

He smiled at her then, and held her close to his heart.

"Dearest Garnet . . . With you it will always be the first time."

THE BEST OF THE BESTSELLERS
FROM WARNER BOOKS!

STOLEN RAPTURE by Lydia Lancaster   (81-777, $2.50)
Everything about Linnet was a charade. Even the man in the Virginia colonies for whom she had crossed an ocean to marry did not know her true identity. What he wanted was the spoiled, dissolute heiress he expected, whom he would degrade and savagely cast away after he had taken his pleasure. . .

THE FRENCH ATLANTIC AFFAIR   (81-562, $2.50)
by Ernest Lehman
In mid-ocean, the S.S. Marseille is taken over! The conspirators—174 of them—are unidentifiable among the other passengers. Unless a ransom of 35 million dollars in gold is paid within 48 hours, the ship and everyone on it will be blown skyhigh!

DARE TO LOVE by Jennifer Wilde   (81-826, $2.50)
Who dared to love Elena Lopez? Who was willing to risk reputation and wealth to win the Spanish dancer who was the scandal of Europe? Kings, princes, great composers and writers . . . the famous and wealthy men of the 19th century vied for her affection, fought duels for her.

DRESS FOR SUCCESS by John T. Molloy   (81-923, $2.50)
Clothing consultant John T. Molloy gives information on exactly which clothes to wear for success in business. 8 pages of color photos and 72 diagrams.

SUGAR BLUES by William Dufty   (81-924, $2.50)
Like opium, morphine and heroin, sugar is an addictive, destructive drug, yet Americans consume it daily in everything from cigarettes to bread. SUGAR BLUES is a hard-hitting, eye-opening report on the nationwide abuse of this sweetest of killers.

GLENDRACO by Laura Black   (81-528, $2.50)
She was ravishingly beautiful, fiercely independent, funny, warm, passionate and intriguing. Why is there a rumor that the girl has bad blood? Why is she driven to the slums of Glasgow at the hands of white slavers? Why does the man whose face she sees while in the arms of others fall in love with her but refuse to marry her?

W A Warner Communications Company

THE BEST OF THE BESTSELLERS
FROM WARNER BOOKS!

THE OTHER SIDE OF THE MOUNTAIN   (82-935, $2.25)
by E. G. Valens
Olympic hopeful Jill Kinmont faced the last qualifying race before the 1956 Games—and skied down the mountain to disaster, never to walk again. Now she had another kind of mountain to climb—to become another kind of champion.

THE OTHER SIDE OF THE MOUNTAIN:
PART 2 by E. G. Valens   (82-463, $2.25)
Part 2 of the inspirational story of a young Olympic contender's courageous climb from paralysis and total helplessness to a useful life and meaningful marriage. An NBC-TV movie and serialized in **Family Circle** magazine.

SYBIL by Flora Rheta Schreiber   (82-492, $2.25)
Over 5 million copies in print! A television movie starring Joanne Woodward, Sally Field and Martine Bartlett! A true story more gripping than any novel of a woman possessed by sixteen separate personalities. Her eventual integration into one whole person makes this a "fascinating book."—*Chicago Tribune*

A STRANGER IN THE MIRROR   (81-940, $2.50)
by Sidney Sheldon
This is the story of Toby Temple, superstar and super bastard, adored by his vast TV and movie public, but isolated from real human contact by his own suspicion and distrust. It is also the story of Jill Castle, who came to Hollywood to be a star and discovered she had to buy her way with her body. When these two married, their love was so strong it was—terrifying!

Ⓦ A Warner Communications Company

Please send me the books I have selected.

Enclose check or money order only, no cash please. Plus 50¢ per copy to cover postage and handling. N.Y. State residents add applicable sales tax.

Please allow 2 weeks for delivery.
WARNER BOOKS

P.O. Box 690
New York, N.Y. 10019
Name ....
Address ....
City .... State .... Zip ....
_____Please send me your free mail order catalog